LOST
PLACES

Black Shuck Books
www.blackshuckbooks.co.uk

First published in 2010 by
Ash-Tree Press
British Columbia, Canada

Set in Caslon
Cover art and interior design © WHITEspace, 2022
www.white-space.uk

978-1-913038-82-3

Lost
Places

by

Simon Kurt
Unsworth

BLACK
SHUCK
BOOKS

For Ben, just because I love him.

| Contents |

≁

|Foreword|

When it came time to rerelease *Lost Places*, one of the things I had to think about was whether to update the stories because, although they aren't particularly time and place sensitive, there are a couple of contemporary references that might date them. I could, I thought, bring them right up to date, putting in references to recent events and people so that new readers would think I was a with it and cool dude… and then I thought, *Nah, fuck it.* These stories are a reflection of the man I was at the time I wrote them and of the things that concerned me back then. Updating them would feel like a betrayal of that man – a man who in some ways I don't recognise, and I'm not sure I like that much, but who still deserves his work to remain unaltered. I'm not sure I was a particularly nice or good person back then, or that I treated the people close to me well, and my only defence is that I was still learning to be an adult and I didn't know what the fuck I was doing most of the time. It's not much of an excuse, I know, but we are what we are and what I produced in that period was, for better or worse, directly influenced by how I was feeling and how I thought I fitted into my world. These are a product of their time, written by a young man who was often lonely and working far from home, and reading them now makes me proud but a little sad – I can't imagine being that far away from home again, nor that lonely, and for that I'm more than grateful. My life has changed massively since this collection's initial release in 2010, thankfully for the better, and I'm happier, more confident in myself and I think I'm a better person, and if I wrote these stories today I suspect they'd be very different.

Ultimately, it's interesting (to me at least) how much what I was writing back then can be seen, with the benefit of hindsight (always the most perfect of visions), as a series of screamed warnings to myself about what was happening in the darkest and most secret places in my head. However much I thought I realised it at the time of writing my first Endword, *Lost Places* was clearly a far greater warning to me than I understood even then, and I have only myself to blame that I didn't recognise and react to the warnings sooner, quicker and more effectively. My life was, I now realise, becoming increasingly chaotic and difficult, and all the difficult and destructive things that eventually bubbled out and came to be of critical importance to me were already there lurking under the surface, and even if I wasn't conscious of them I knew they existed and was scrabbling to face them as best as I could. Of course, that I did so by writing horror stories rather than recognising them outright and facing them directly probably says something worrying about me and is almost certainly not the recommended way to proceed. Still, to each their own, I suppose. I've been created and recreated since then, and the new shape I occupy is one I'm much happier with, and the fact that these tales (thankfully) seem to still stand on their own merits despite the emotional place in which many of them were written is both gratifying and surprising. I remain enormously proud of them individually and as a collection, and I'm glad it's come out again to hopefully upset and disturb a new set of readers. These stories are the people in my wardrobe, not yours, but hopefully you'll enjoy them nonetheless.

Simon Kurt Unsworth
2022

|A Different Morecambe|

Huw's hangover was pulsing.

It had been a late night; another long talk with Ro about their future, another discussion about fault and no-fault, blame and responsibility. Another too-large quantity of wine gone and another hangover sweating itself out through his pores. But, illness or not, Huw had promised Lennie a morning trip to Morecambe and Lennie would not be denied and so to Morecambe they were going.

Every bump in the road sent queasy ripples around Huw's stomach and made the blood slither in his ears. Even with the car window open the cold autumn air, just picking up the first scents of the sea and tightening his scalp, refused to help his head to clear. When Lennie spoke he missed it at first.

"Pardon?" he asked, not liking the way his voice wavered as it emerged and wondering if Lennie could tell how rough both he and Ro had felt that morning when he burst into their bedroom with a three year old's wild, joyful abandon. Or, worse, whether he could tell how rough Huw still felt.

"I don't want to go to this Morecambe. I want to go to a different Morecambe."

Momentarily, Huw was stumped. His brain, still coasting on the sour after-effects of alcohol and a miserable, late night, refused to process what his son was saying to him. "A different Morecambe?" he repeated, looking at Lennie in the rearview mirror. The car jolted again and Huw swallowed down an acidic, burning throat of dead wine. Just visible at edge of the reflection in the mirror, his son stared solemnly at him and said again, "I want to go to a different Morecambe."

"Well," said Huw, "there's only this Morecambe to go to, Lennie. You like Morecambe, don't you?"

"Yes. I just want to go to a different one today."

Huw didn't respond immediately. Lennie, named after his paternal grandfather, shared more with the old man than just his name; they were both given to flights of fancy and, rather more annoyingly, tantrums when they didn't get their way. This bore the hallmarks of a tantrum's beginning, and Huw wasn't sure he could cope with a full-on Lennie rage now.

"Well, why don't we see what it's like when we get there?" he asked, placatingly. "I could park somewhere different and we could try and go to some new places if you like?"

"No," with the start of childish anger in the voice. "Not this Morecambe. A different one."

"Lennie, there isn't a different Morecambe, just the one we always go to. This is the only one, I promise."

"It isn't!" and with that, Lennie was shouting and thrashing in his seat, the straps preventing him from doing much more than writhing slightly from side to side. Huw risked turning away from the road for a moment, trying to catch Lennie's eye. Lennie shrieked in a helpless toddler's fury, his voice spiking and sending a jolt of pain into Huw's head that dropped, becoming a wave of nausea as it fell through him. "Lennie," he managed to say and then he had to turn back to the road, pull across the lane which was thankfully free of traffic, let the car mount the kerb and open his door in one clumsy movement and in one spasming rush he was vomiting. The sound of it swilled around his ears, his own retching and gagging merging with the sound of Lennie's shrieking before collapsing in on itself like a dying star.

It only took a moment; there wasn't much to come out except bile and jagged memories. Perhaps Ro and he needed to split up, he thought. Huw couldn't keep going through this cycle of argument-friends-argument, with all of its attendant emotional and physical ups and downs. He sat back in the seat, took a deep and torn breath and turned again. Lennie was watching him with cool eyes, and Huw managed to think, *So that's how we distract him from his tantrums – just puke!*

"I'm sorry, Lennie. Daddy's not feeling very well," he said.

"Why aren't you feeling well?" Quiet and calm; the storm settled and gone.

Because your mum and I don't seem to be able to go a week without arguing about something, and the arguments are getting worse and I'm not sure either of us can cope with much more. "I don't know, son. Maybe I have a tummy bug, but it's gone now. I feel better." This was true; puking seemed to have cleared some of the bitterness from his stomach, and although the taste of vomit was harsh and unpleasant, it faded as he swilled saliva around and spat it onto the pavement.

"Thank you for bringing me to this different Morecambe, Daddy," said Lennie from behind him.

Huw turned back to face his son. Lennie was placid now, sitting motionless in his seat. In his neat little dungarees and red jacket, with his legs stuck straight out in front of him, he looked curiously doll-like at that moment and Huw felt a wave of helpless, stifling love. How could he and Ro make such a beautiful thing, such a perfect little *person*, hold his future in their hands, make decisions for and about him, decisions affecting his entire life, and then not sort out their own differences? It made no sense. Huw smiled at Lennie. Lennie did not smile back.

"It's all the same Morecambe, Lennie," said Huw. "Look, it's just like it is every time we visit."

"No, it's the different one," said Lennie and there was a finality in his voice that Huw really didn't have the strength to argue with. He twisted back, intending drive on, but something brought him up short.

At first he couldn't work out what it was. Through the windscreen, he saw the road and the side of the library and the carparks and the small train station platform and in the distance a grey sliver of the sea framed between the large supermarket and cinema. Morecambe, as ever.

Only, quieter.

There were no cars on the road or moving along the seafront, no people going to or from their vehicles in the carparks, nothing. Certainly, Huw wouldn't have expected much activity this early on a Saturday morning, but even out of season, Morecambe tended to have visitors at most hours of the day.

"This is much better, Daddy," said Lennie, his voice the self-satisfied sound of a child that had got its own way. Huw ignored him for a minute, instead looking more carefully around him at the town he had come to know so well over the past few years. It seemed the same at first glance, but the closer he looked the more he saw little things that jarred. The library's square-edged shape was blurred with what looked like moss or hanging vines clinging tightly to the brickwork. The surface of the almost empty carpark was rippled as though the concrete had settled in some of the bays, and was being pushed up from beneath in others. What cars there were appeared abandoned, covered in leaves and litter and streaks of dark, oily dirt. At least one sat on deflated tyres whose rubber puddled around metal rims that were dark with rust. Further away, the superstore and the cinema both looked overgrown, dark with the same kind of hanging or climbing plant that was smothering the library. Huw wondered if this was some new kind of hangover, an effect of alcohol poisoning that made him see things that were not there, or maybe just magnifying what was there to absurd levels. Morecambe was run down, but this looked more than that: it looked lost and abandoned.

Decaying.

Huw went to pull the door shut, seeing as he did so his pool of vomit on the ground. It had already dried and formed a skin over itself, had darkened so that it looked weeks-old rather than minutes. He stared at it carefully. No smell reached his nose from the pool. Beyond it, his saliva had also dried, leaving just a stain on the dusty pavement. He wondered briefly whether it was a result of dehydration, then dismissed the thought as ridiculous. Dehydration caused his headache, it wouldn't make his puke or spit dry any faster. *This is stupid,* he thought angrily. *I'm spooking myself because I've got a self-inflicted injury, nothing more. I should learn to control my drinking when I'm arguing with Ro, and if I can't then I should at least learn to take the consequences like a man!* He put the car into gear and pulled out into the road, driving carefully and looking straight ahead until he had passed the carparks with their deserted cars and uneven surfaces and fat white questing roots gathering in the sunken bays and slithering out from gaps in the concrete.

Roots? No. He had seen nothing of the sort. It was just rubbish blowing across the concrete apron, or some odd effect of the sun making shadows or shapes that moved as he passed, made worse by his misfiring senses. *I'm not safe to drive, probably,* he thought. *We need to stop and get out of the car before I crash. A walk will definitely do me some good.*

Huw pulled into the carpark he and Lennie used on their trips out. It was past the library, nearer to the sea than the shops, but like the earlier ones, it too was almost empty. There were a couple of cars huddled on its far side, close to the back of the Winter Gardens, but he ignored them. There were no roots coming out of cracks in the concrete, and although its surface was uneven, it was no worse than normal.

Normal. Huw liked normal.

"Can we get out, Daddy?" said Lennie, startling Huw.

"Certainly can," replied Huw with a cheerfulness he did not feel. He still could see no movement, no people walking about, no birds in the sky. Even the clouds that hung above their heads, dirty grey clusters that looked like sodden kapok, were still. When he got out of the car, his feet sent dull sounds across the open expanse of ground that returned from the theatre's rear wall in flat, empty plosives. The noises of him opening the boot and getting out Lennie's buggy, taking Lennie from the car and installing him in the buggy and finally locking the car settled into the air around them, reflected in toneless whispers by buildings that were themselves a flat monochrome not far removed from the colour of the sky above them.

"Do you want to put the money in the ticket machine?"

"No, thank you."

Huw crouched by Lennie, peering at him. Usually, Lennie loved to put the money in the slot, laughing as each coin fell into the machine's guts and then pressing the large green button that produced their ticket. Today, however, he simply sat in his pushchair and stared about him, a faint smile on his face.

"Hey," said Huw gently, "are you okay? Does Daddy get a kiss? Are you sure you don't want to help me get a ticket?"

"No," replied Lennie, emphatic, peering over Huw's shoulder. "I'm looking."

It wouldn't have mattered anyway; the ticket machine's slot was rusted closed, the black strip clustered with an orange bloom that resembled ferrous moss. The digital display was dark and the pricing information sign next to the machine streaked with oil or some other heavy, dried liquid. Huw gave up trying to push his money into the slot, deciding that if the council expected him to pay his parking fees they ought to at least ensure that the machines were working. Besides, he didn't like the way the coins were coming away from the slot streaked with rust, and he liked even less the way the rust transferred itself to his fingers and wouldn't rub off, instead leaving pale orange patches on his skin that felt slimy and unpleasant. Walking away from the machine, pushing Lennie, Huw tried again to come up with some rational explanation for what he was seeing and experiencing. Perhaps there was some event happening that he had not heard about, and everyone was attending? No, not everyone would go. Besides, the superstore that he and Lennie were just passing as they moved towards the seafront would still be open, and it was not. Its illuminated sign was dark, the great revolving doors shut and still. One had a cracked star across its glazed face, brittle fragments of glass hanging from the damaged section and littering the ground in front of it.

The cinema was no better. Its doors were shut and filthy with mud and dust that obscured the foyer beyond and reduced the large advertising stands to formless shapes that lurked just at the edge of Huw's perception. When he leaned closer to the paneled door, trying to peer through the dirt and make some sense of what he could see, he glimpsed the food counters and ticket desks. The desks were hazy with dust, and the trays behind the clear counter of the food stall were black with some kind of fungus that spilled out around the Perspex and crawled down the counter and onto the carpet below. Had the cinema and the store closed and Huw missed the news about it? Morecambe was definitely moving, developing and growing, but things shutting, being abandoned? Had he and Ro really been so mixed up with each other that they had missed such major changes happening on their doorstep? Surely not.

"This is fun, Daddy," said Lennie, unexpectedly. "I like this Morecambe more than the other one for now. I'm glad we came."

Lennie's voice sounded odd. Normally (*ah, God, for something normal!* thought Huw miserably), he was an excitable child, serious about things although never less than joyful, but the voice coming from the buggy in front of him was somehow flat and withdrawn. Emotionless. Huw leaned forward over the top of the buggy so that he was looking down on Lennie. Upside down, his son's face stared back at him, his eyes pale against skin the colour of old parchment.

"I don't think I like it," replied Huw. "It's very quiet, isn't it? Perhaps we should go home and play a game?"

"No, Daddy," said Lennie patiently, and Huw had the oddest feeling that their roles had been reversed, that he was the younger person there and Lennie the older one, "we'll find people soon, or they'll find us. You'll see, this is a much better place than usual!" As he spoke, Lennie's face grew animated for a moment, a great smile stretching his lips to reveal a mouthful of small, white teeth. Huw nodded carefully, aware of the pulsing, sick waves of the hangover still beating in his skull.

"Okay. We'll go up around the corner and we'll see what's happening, but if things don't change, we're going home. Deal?"

"Deal!" said Lennie, but the excitement in his voice never seemed to reach his upside down, unblinking eyes.

Rounding the corner they were on the seafront, Lennie silent and observant in his pushchair while Huw pushed. As they walked, he became more and more uneasy. Even here, where usually there were throngs of people, the roads and pavements were empty. The seafront kiosks and stores were closed, their windows covered by grills in whose slotted faces leaves and paper stuck, and against whose bases more rubbish gathered. The beach beyond the sea wall was empty too, the sand unmarked by footprints. It was a strange colour, as though it had faded in bright sunlight or been too long in the water and had some of its vibrancy leached away. The sea itself was a dank grey, its surface untroubled by waves and lying smooth and glassy. Huw had never seen the ocean in Morecambe like that before; it looked unnatural, painted and artificial rather than the moving, energizing thing it usually was. The whole place looked false, somehow, as though they had stumbled into a film set made to scale but with all of its angles subtly wrong. Things at the corner of Huw's eye looked just out of kilter, resting against each other in ways that they should not, as if the construction had been made by someone who had seen pictures of Morecambe, studied it but never been there and never seen how its buildings and streets and walls connected. Huw looked around, an impotent anger filling him. What the *fuck* was going on here?

They were coming to the Midland Hotel now. The grand white structure was encrusted with scaffolding, the metal struts crawling over its surface. At least that was normal, thought Huw. The work to refit the old hotel had been going on for months now, and was one of the town's talking points; boards around the perimeter showed pictures of how the hotel would look when it was finished, but the actual work was hidden from view apart from the top few floors. It was *supposed* to look half-formed, yet even here, things seemed wrong. In recent weeks, the old hotel had been repainted or resurfaced, and the newly-white walls had gleamed behind the scaffolding cover like a tooth behind a brace. Now it was darker again, streaked with grey and green patches that looked unhealthily damp. The surrounding boards had warped and one or two had come loose from their neighbours, revealing at the front of the hotel an expanse of cracked concrete and flowerbeds choked with brambles and dead, twisted plants. He did not know why, but Huw also had the distinct impression that the scaffolding had become brittle, would collapse if the least weight were placed upon it.

They left the Midland behind them without speaking, which was itself an oddity; when they had walked past the Midland on earlier trips, Lennie liked to tell Huw what he thought was behind the wooden barriers, coming up with wilder and wilder ideas that made Huw laugh. Today he passed it in silence. Huw, looking down surreptitiously at his child, saw that Lennie's eyes were fixed firmly on the sea, ignoring everything that they walked past. There was a grin playing at his lips, but it was one Huw did not like; it looked hungry and hard and anticipatory. Lennie's tongue poked out from between his lips, and in the dull light it looked too dark, black where it should at worst have been a deep fleshy red. Then, as though becoming aware of Huw's attention, Lennie looked up and smiled more broadly.

"I think we'll see people soon," he said.

"Do you? Who? What people?" asked Huw.

"People," Lennie repeated as though that explained everything. "You said you wanted to see people. You will soon."

"How do you know?"

"Can't you hear them? They're not far away now."

Abruptly, Huw wheeled about, turning them back the way they had come. He began to walk fast, not letting himself run but coming close to it. This whole place was wrong; the look of it, the feel of it and the *smell* of it were all wrong. There was no sea scent, no salt or water odours, just a smell of rottenness and decay that had been building as they walked. They passed the Midland at a controlled dash, and Huw ignored that fact that the 'after' pictures on the hoardings showed a place that was corrupted and blighted and not the normal artist's impressions of the intended gleaming edifice. Lennie began to giggle as his buggy bounced up and down, but it was not the giggle of a happy toddler. This sounded as though it came from some other place, from some other person, someone taut and humourless. "Son," Huw gasped as he rushed, "please tell me what's wrong. Please!"

"Nothing Daddy," replied Lennie, only his voice was harsh and sharper than it should have been. "We came to the different Morecambe, just like I asked. Thank you Daddy!"

Huw tried to ignore the changing timbre of his son's voice, just as he had ignored the things he had seen and was trying to ignore other sounds he could hear. Try as he might, however, he could not help but hear them. There was a distant rustling and hissing, the sound of feet shuffling and stepping along, the murmur of voices. After his experiences of the previous minutes, Huw would have expected to be glad to hear the sound of other people, but he was not. The rhythms of the noises were wrong, as though there were too many legs trying to walk and not enough space for them to walk in. The murmur of voices rose and fell, but in it were rumbles and cries that sounded like no recognisable words. Huw wanted to be gone from this Morecambe, back to the banal miseries of his life with Ro where their arguments were about money and sex and domestic chores, where Lennie was a cheerful child whose voice wasn't rasping and raw and where Morecambe was a seaside resort finally beginning to win the battle to reinvent itself for a new kind of tourist. Huw fled, heading for his car and for the life that he knew, even if he didn't like it.

"There are people coming Daddy," said Lennie, his voice harder than it had any right to be. Huw let out a cry when he heard it, keeping his eye on his car and his mind on the thought of escape. If he could drive back, back to the place where this had started, he could get home, get Lennie back, get away. Something had happened when he puked, he had brought them somewhere, so reversing their trip would surely allow them back. Wouldn't it?

Wouldn't it?

He fumbled his keys as he approached the car, dropping them in his haste to point them at the vehicle. Bending to pick them up, his face came level with Lennie's. Huw let out a tiny, torn cry when he saw his son close to; his face was desperately pale and veins like worms rippled across his forehead. Like everything else around them, he was *wrong*, Lennie but not-Lennie, his son but not his son. He looked distorted, pushed out of shape from within, sweating and sickly but with eyes that glittered with a horrid, terrible alertness.

"Where's my son?" said Huw, still scrabbling for the keys.

"I'm here, Daddy. Don't you recognize me?" replied Lennie in his proper Lennie voice, childish and high. "Why don't we wait here for the people?"

"What people?" and the keys were in his hands and Huw was pressing the button to release the door locks and opening the door.

"The different Morecambe people, silly. They're almost here."

Huw did not respond. Hurriedly, he unbuckled the unprotesting Lennie and moved him to his car seat. Even if, God forbid, it was not his son, he could not leave him behind. Huw could take them back, Lennie could be his son again. He could. Lennie, watching with a detached expression on his shifting, changing face, said, "What's wrong, Daddy?"

"Shut up."

Lennie started to cry, fat tears rolling from his eyes down towards his jutting bottom lip, a gift from Ro's side of the family. The sobbing sounds were good, almost real, but not real enough. Huw knew his son well, knew the noises he made in almost every circumstance, and what was coming from his mouth now was simply not good enough. Another fake, another falsehood, mimicry that had technique but no emotion in it, and then Lennie was in and Huw was running around the car to the driver's side and getting in.

The car started with a twist of the key. With the door shut, the distant sounds were muted but still audible. They rose and fell, with the rasping shuffle sometimes in the ascendant before being drowned by the grumbling and roaring like muffled voices. Under it was another sound – or rather, other sounds. There was a grinding, like metal being dragged against metal, coming from the direction of the train platform.

From further away, Huw could hear the ocean heaving even though, when he looked, the strip of grey sea visible between the far buildings was motionless. He pressed his foot onto the accelerator, letting the engine roar its response to the encroaching sounds, and then drove. The car jolted and bucked as it bumped across the carpark and Huw could not help but turn, say "Are you okay?" to Lennie, concerned that the bouncing may have hurt him.

"I'm fine, Daddy. You look poorly," replied Lennie, the not-Lennie voice trickling from his mouth and his not-Lennie eyes gleaming.

"I'm fine too," said Huw. "We're both fine. That's good." Just mindless chatter to distract him from the sights around him, from the fat white roots that he could see sprouting at the edge of the carpark and which hadn't been there before, from the air that hung too low above them like old sacking, and then they were out of the carpark and into the street.

The metallic grinding sound was louder here. The road ran parallel to the train track, separated from it by a width of pavement and a heavy line of trees and fencing. Behind the trees, something dark moved unhurriedly along, a black mass of shadow that slowed as it pulled up to the platform. Huw caught the shriek behind his teeth, trapped it there to prevent it escaping, and accelerated back along the road. Whatever it was behind the trees was long; a train, Huw thought, catching sight of dirty glass and rusting metal between the tree trunks as he drove. Behind the glass, he had the impression of movement, of figures pressing against the grimy glass and smearing dampness across its inner surface.

They were approaching the place where Huw had vomited. He pressed his foot harder on the accelerator pedal, hoping to coax more speed from the vehicle. Lennie laughed from behind him, an empty sound against the throated growl of the engine. Huw did not look around. The car sped up, rolling past the darkened pile of puke on the pavement. Huw clenched himself, tightening his grip on the wheel and praying with his whole body that he could get back, go *home*. For a moment, just the briefest of moments, there was a flicker in the air and Huw saw Morecambe, his Morecambe. It flashed with colour, loud with energy and movement. The buildings were solid, unadorned with plant growth, the roads smooth and uncracked. No train moved behind the trees, and no white roots rippled their way across the car park. There were people. Huw shouted, a cry of triumph, and then Lennie hissed and the image fell in upon itself, crumpling away to a grey nothing. The different Morecambe rushed in to fill the space it left, its bleak walls gathering in around Huw as he brought the car to a shuddering halt. He craned around, staring out through the rear window hoping to still see the remnants of the brighter place, but it was gone. Lennie giggled again, bucking in his seat as mirth shook his tiny body.

"We can't leave yet, Daddy," he said brightly, "we haven't met the people!"

By the train station, indistinct shapes moved. They milled out from the entrance, spreading like oil to fill the street. Huw had the impression of squatness and width, of arms that were just too long and bent in the wrong places, of legs that writhed and of features that were moist and eager. He looked again at Lennie, the not-Lennie that had taken his son's place, and saw that he had managed to undo the straps of the safety seat.

"We came to a different Morecambe, Daddy, just like I wanted to. Don't you like it?"

"No," said Huw.

"I do. Thank you for bringing me here, Daddy. It's nice that you brought me when I wanted to come so much."

Huw opened his door and climbed out of the car, backing away on legs that felt like brittle, fracturing twigs. "Why did you want to come here?" he asked, watching as the tiny figure clambered between the car's front seats and jumped delicately to the floor.

"Because we've been here so long," said the not-Lennie, no longer making any effort to sound or act like the Lennie that Huw had helped create, that he loved with all his being. Its voice was hoarse and the poor, beautiful flesh of Huw's son was already distorting into a new shape. "We made a different Morecambe and we try to use it just like you use your one, but it's not the same. No one comes here so it's empty apart from us, and it's not as good as your Morecambe. It feels different and it smells different because we can't make it like you do. We can't make it work. We can't make proper colour. We can't make it real."

"Where's Lennie?"

"I'm Lennie, Daddy!" said the thing in front of him in a tone of mock indignation. It grinned again, its lips stretching far, too far, back from teeth that were still small and white but were now too numerous. "Don't you recognize me?"

"You're not my son." Saying it made it hurt worse than a hangover, worse than every pain he had ever felt. "Give him back. Please!"

"But he wanted so much to come somewhere different, and you were so ill and were almost here anyway because of how you felt, so we just pulled you through to where you both wanted to go. You're the first ones we've managed! Do you like our different Morecambe?"

"No."

"Don't be nasty. It might not be as good as your Morecambe, but we did our best even though we're not made for creation, only other things. We watched for so long, kept seeing the other Morecambe but couldn't get there no matter how hard we tried, and then you and little Lennie came along and look! You helped us make a door so now we can go through and finally visit yours. Isn't that nice?"

The crowd gathered.

|Haunting Marley|

Marley once said that if he died, he'd haunt me, just like his literary namesake. Typical of him to get something like that wrong, and all the more satisfying that when I died I was able to put it right; haunting Marley has been the great pleasure of my death.

Marley and I had met as children, become friends as adolescents and business partners as adults. For a time, we had an excellent relationship, I doing the accounts and the stock inventory and tending to the administration of our small business, and Marley attending to the customers, their orders and the hunting out of stock. It was an arrangement that played to both our strengths; my love of order and his gregarious need to impress people. Our profits were up, our reputation gaining solidity and our friendship untroubled. And then, there came Adele.

For forty years, Marley and I argued over who had the strongest claim on Adele. Marley announced this victory as his own, stating that he had seen her in the company of Piers Chanter at the theatre at the beginning of March. He knew, he said, because it was at a revival of one of Wilde's plays that he had treated himself to as a birthday present, and his birthday was March 2nd, ergo, he had seen her first. I claimed that Adele was mine because I had spoken to her at Mark Haig's party; Haig's party was mid-April, later than March, agreed, but speaking to her meant more than merely seeing her. As in everything after Adele, Marley and I couldn't agree, and in the end, the truth of it was unimportant. Only the arguments mattered.

Adele was beautiful, pleasingly full-chested and dark haired, and she betrayed me by ignoring my advances and taking up and making plans for the future with the oaf Marley. How could I have been a friend to this man, who ignored my entreaties to him to step aside and leave Adele for me? He was ignorant and selfish, and their relationship could not last. She was not for him, that much was clear; quiet and reserved where he was outgoing and loud, pretty and agile where he was flat-faced and flatter-footed, she was better suited to me, but Marley saw none of this. Or rather, I suspect, he saw it but refused to accept it. She was with him, he would say with maddening patience, I had to accept it and find another. But how could I? The too few times I had spent with Adele had opened up to me a world of new experiences, of conversations with someone my intellectual equal as well as my emotional counter-part. I could not let her waste herself on Marley.

Rumours are such simple things to start, yet so complex, impossible to stop. One or two indiscreet comments in ears whose mouths could not help but flap, and it was done. Nothing about the business, of course, as this might affect me, but about Marley's private life. His staying in a suite of rooms above the shop was because of his having been thrown out of his last home; his apparent bachelorhood prior to Adele a careful front to disguise immoral and possibly obscene activities. Docks were mentioned, and cheap ale houses with sawdust floors and poor hygiene. And I, his long-suffering business partner and friend had helped him to cover his shame, find his way out of the messes he so frequently found himself in. It was wondrous to watch these little untruths grow, to see them take a life of their own. Details made their way back to me that I had never considered, had not uttered. People made new claims, insisted on the truth of their statements, and all the time I watched, delighted, and waited for Adele to hear and rush to my arms.

She did not do this; on hearing the dreadful stories of her beloved Marley, she came to the shop, gathered herself up, told him she was leaving and, as an afterthought, slapped my face. Marley was bad, she said, but could no more control his urges than a rat could live a decent life, but I? I had colluded, and that made me worse than him. Ignoring both mine and Marley's protestations of innocence, she turned and left and I do not believe either of us saw her again. And that was the start.

Marley blamed me for the loss of his beloved; I blamed him for taking her from me when she was rightfully mine. I told him that I had assumed that there was honour among friends, and that he would see that she was better for me than him, but no. Marley had showed himself to be boorish, insensitive and a betrayer of friendships, and I could no longer count him as being amongst my friends. I could not remain in business with him, of course. Accordingly, I made him a generous offer for his half of our small business so that we could untangle ourselves from each other and go our separate ways.

Marley would not sell. Instead, he made a counter-offer for *my* half of the business and became angry when I refused to sell to him. He called me a back-stabber, a spineless traitor and other, worse things. For my part, I told him that selling and buying was the easy part of the business, but that he would have been declared bankrupt long before were it not for my careful fiscal management and organisation. I told him that I would not see a business I had worked so hard to build be put in the control of such a man as he so that he could run it into the ground. He replied that the business was his by moral right; he had bought all the stock, dealt with dealers and customers and any profit we showed was because of his hard work and that *he* wasn't prepared to see *his* business destroyed by selling it to such a "boring, spiteful idiot". Impasse. Neither of us prepared to move, and thus we remained.

We barely spoke for forty years, except to discuss specific business matters. When it came to new ideas, Marley accepted mine without undue resistance, and I was magnanimous in allowing him to try out schemes, some of which I admit were not unsuccessful. The silence between us suited me, as I could find nothing of interest in my once-friend's conversations, and became amazed at myself for ever having considered him to be more than an acquaintance. I stayed in my little office, keeping our expanding business on track with careful management of the income and expenditure, whilst Marley did little other than talk to the customers and operate the till. But, if we were silent with each other, *about* each other we were positively verbose. Rumours and slurs reached me on a almost weekly basis, about my miserliness, my social ineptitude, my lack of humour, all spread by Marley to discredit me and blacken my name with these foul slurs. I, for my part, missed no opportunity to tell people the truth of what Marley's carefully cultivated mask of bonhomie covered. I hoped that he might be shamed into leaving if he knew that people understood the truth of him, but his thick skin and lack of concern for the social graces kept him well insulated, and he remained an unpleasant presence in my life until my death.

My heart attack was quick. I remember nothing of it save for a brilliant wave of white pain that grew from my chest to suck at my whole body, and then I was gone. In the shock of that time, I paid little attention to Marley when he found me, or to the medical men bustling around me as I lay on the floor, head pointed towards the door, drool collected unflatteringly beneath my open mouth and staining the dust black. I remember thinking that I looked old and crumpled, as though I had been partially deflated, and wishing someone would clean away the spittle from my chin. It was unseemly; ugly.

I have discovered many things since I died. For example, I know now that death is neither frightening nor particularly spiritual. In the period after my demise, whilst I was buried and arrangements presumably made for my estate, I investigated my new state. Alone in my shop and unencumbered by flesh, I would drift along aisles, letting myself brush against the stock or the shelves. I could feel them, sense their solidity, their *reality*, but seemed unable to have any effect on them. I could not move them, pick them up, carry them, yet I did not miss my body at all. I did not need sleep, found time an irrelevance and needed no food or water. I saw no angels and did not hear the voice of God calling to me to join Him. There was simply me, and what I chose to do. Experimenting, I found that I had the ability to slip through the narrowest of spaces and could lose myself in the tiniest of objects, marvelling in their complexity and solidity. I could not leave the building, discovered that its boundaries acted upon me like tar, dragging at me and eventually pulling me to a halt, hemming me in with its familiar walls, but this too did not bother me. This place had been my life; now it was my death. I was oddly happy in this period, enjoying the experience of this placid haunting.

And then, Marley came back.

I had not noticed his absence. It was only when he burst into the shop in a riot of laughter and scent that I realised I had not seen him since my death. I had taken little notice of a sign, neatly placed in the shop doorway. It read, *Closed Due To Bereavement* and it was typical Marley. The writing was florid, overblown and unnecessarily capitalised. Extravagant and showy, like everything he did. I had been enjoying myself, and now he was back to spoil it. He wandered the

Marley and I had, even in our worst moments, agreed on how it should be. Books, we said, should be loved and in company. Shelves should be piled high, order at a minimum. There should be trails to follow through the shop, lost corridors leading to dead ends, anterooms and open spaces sprouting unexpectedly from between shelves and cases, and it was to these that I went. Marley had stocked these places, to be sure, but it was my financial expertise that had allowed for it, had *created* them. God only knew what mess Marley would make now that I was gone. I drifted, becoming in those hours and days the ghost that I am now. Walking was not required; I have no weight for legs and feet to bear. I am only thought, and must float as I see fit.

And in floating, I have discovered that the place I haunt is greater than I could ever have imagined.

My first comprehension of this came when I found myself in a corridor that I did not recognise. Shelves stretched about me, and I found that I could not see their end. Where had they come from, these new shelves, and what things were upon them? Peering closely at the books, I found that I could read no titles on their dusty spines and pull none of them from the shelf. In my misery, I panicked, hurling myself down the grey length, but could find no end. I wanted to scream, did so, to no avail. Where was I? More corridors beckoned from either side and tiny rooms appeared, like eddies at the edge of a stream. Stopping in one, I tried to catch the breath that I no longer needed. Terror overcame me, lost in these grey places, and I threw myself back into the small space. I backed as far as I could go before I bumped into the shelves. A cloud of dry, sweet-smelling dust rose around my shoulders. Flailing around, my fear becoming a helpless, shrivelling anger. I knocked books from the shelves, kicking at them as they lay on the floor, trampling their pages and bending their covers. In that moment, I hated them, hated myself, hated this haunting death that trapped me in the building of my employment, and most of all, I hated Marley, and every page I tore and leaf I mutilated was him.

I was touching things.

The damaged books around me were testament to my force, to my touch, and yet these were the first things I had been able to touch for many days. Reaching down, I tried to pick up one of the torn pages, but my fingers passed through it. Irritated, I flapped at it and watched, surprised, as it snapped away from me. Tentatively, I reached out again, only to have my fingers drift through the paper once more. Slumping down, I kicked out, and again my touch had weight, connected with the detritus on the floor, surrounding me with drifting pages. Was it my anger and frustration that gave me the ability to touch, to have an influence on the world? It certainly seemed so; thinking back, I remembered that it was only when I shouted at Marley in anger that he appeared to notice, however barely, my presence. Perhaps anger gave me solidity, even if it was just for a moment? And if so, a moment was all I would need.

This time, the featureless corridor held no fear for me. I hurled myself along it, knowing instinctively how to return to the more reassuring surroundings of the shop. Through the jumbled aisles, past the offices and upwards, moving into the suite of rooms above which Marley slept and where I would take my revenge.

I could not do it. Oh, I do not mean I was taken at the last minute by regret or some moral barrier. No, I tried to attack as he slept, but my hands had lost their weight and no matter how angry I became, they obstinately refused to have an impact upon his bloated, puffy flesh.

I had not realised how much living humans smell! The stink was awful in those rooms, of meat and sweat and perfumes which covered but could not remove the odour. Had I smelled like this in life as well, unaware of the rich, sour scent that I was producing? My God, I hoped not, but I knew that I had. Marley himself produced a smell unlike anything I had ever come across before, so thick that I could almost see the pores of his sleeping skin open to let it out like sweat. I hated, *hated* him, but still my fists had no effect. How angry did I have to be, I wondered. How furious, how deep should my hate run? How could I have my revenge?

The answer lay in those seemingly endless grey corridors. Leaving Marley that night, I was frustrated and angry, still unable to touch anything. Books remained on the shelves, inviolate despite my best efforts to tear them down and cast them to the floor. Like Marley's flesh, they resisted my touch. As I threw myself up and down the aisles of the shop, I found that they were once again stretching, opening out and becoming a place new to me. Rank after rank of high shelves appeared, filled with identical books. Dust coated them, and here my anger could have effect. I could take the books from the shelves, open them, hold them. Rip them and pull them to pieces. But why these and no other? There seemed no answer, no reason to it. I drifted along becoming more and more despondent, passing more and more of those curious rooms at the side. These rooms were ever unfurnished and apparently without function, simply blisters off the corridors filled with more books. Sometimes I entered these rooms, but mostly I ignored them; they held little interest for me. Until, that is, I found the cavernous room where the walls fell away to nothing.

I have realised something about death; not everyone's perhaps, but my own certainly, and the realisation came in the entrance to that great room. The dead have two simple choices. Either they can accept that they are one of the ended and give themselves to the nothingness, or they can open themselves to the darkness and let it enter them.

The cavern was massive and black, its entrance at the rear of one of the small rooms. The walls, lined with shelf after shelf of books, fell away from the entrance and were lost in the blackness. I could not see the far side of the cavern nor the ceiling above me or floor below. Its blackness was the blackness of an absolute vacuum and I clutched at the sides of the entrance, terrified that I would be sucked into it and lost forever. My fear was massive, an overwhelming thing, and I felt my fingers dig into the wooden doorway, gouging out great chunks in my desperation to stay. It beckoned, the cavern; the darkness inviting me to join it, to lose myself in it, and I did not want to. I had to find a way of taking my revenge on Marley. After all, that was the reason why I had come to haunt the building, and I was not about to relinquish my chance without a fight.

The darkness was not absolute. As I hung in the entrance, fighting to stop myself drifting out into it, I perceived prickles of lights above me. They were like tiny stars, lost somewhere in the firmament and glittering miserably. *Come*, the limitless space seemed to whisper, *you simply need to accept that this is the end and you can be with them. No more worry or anger or disappointment. No more fear. Simply accept and let yourself truly cease to exist*, and I was tempted despite myself. To stop thinking, to worry no more, to not be angry sounded relaxing. Pleasant. Dull. I screamed my resistance to it, and in that moment my choice was made.

Instantly, the urge to let myself become lost in that great cavern was gone, replaced by a desire that was as close to animal lust as I have ever felt; I let go of the entrance and opened my arms to the darkness and the lights above and instead of going into it, I let it into me. It filled me, soaking into the corners of my being and swelling my anger like a deluge taken into a bone-dry sponge. In it, there was the comfort of fury and the knowledge of great spaces and the cold, interstellar reaches of fear. It is not power that it gives, exactly, but something else, something sharp and focussed. It gives the dead a choice, this afterlife, and I have chosen to remain. At that moment, I understood; *I am a ghost, and I am the darkness becoming.*

Marley never stood a chance. My mistake before had been to attack him, to try to physically abuse him. By concentrating, I might make my presence felt, but I would never be able to bruise him. Flesh is simply too brutish to respond to the delicate entreaties of the spirit. Instead, the spirit must be subtle. Returning from the cavern, I was languid in my travels, drifting down aisles and letting my fingers trail across books that I could not feel. How could I? I was dead and they were of the living, things for flesh to hold and love. It was night, but not late, and Marley was still awake. He was in the office, once more reading through the paperwork I had left so meticulously, once more drinking my single malt in great swallows that worked his Adam's apple under an unshaven neck. I watched him for a few minutes, peering at his great, bloated body as I imagine a collector might stare at a particularly rare butterfly as it twitched in the killing jar. So ugly, so corpulent! To think that I had once considered him my friend.

There were changes in the office already, new furniture nestling up against the carefully chosen pieces of my tenure, clashing and garish in their modernity. Typical, thoughtless additions that made me tremble with anger. It was time. I let Marley feel my presence, calling his name softly. Volume was no longer needed, only intensity. He looked around nervously, reaching out for the fine crystal tumbler filled to its brim with my whiskey. His previous arrogance was gone; even now, he could feel the difference in me.

"Are you here again?" he asked, his voice shaking. "I told you the last time you were here; this place is mine now. Go to Hell, you old devil!"

Such obscenity! Such ignorance, such shallow intellectual rigour. He sat at my desk, drinking my whiskey, benefiting from the financial skill I had brought to the company, and this is how he talked to me? Well, no more. I shall not go to Hell; no, I bring hell to him! I moved in to the light, and let myself be seen.

I am dead; the vast, chill hold of the afterlife holds no fear for me. Unfettered by the sacking of flesh, my mind is able to embrace the infinite distances of the places beyond life. When I made my choice, when I took that smooth blackness into me, I became it and it me. In exposing myself to Marley, I allowed him to see what awaited him when his sad, abused flesh gave out. Spreading my arms, I imagined the shadows billowing around me like the approach of some terrible storm, glowing and roiling and unsympathetic. Joyously, I saw that Marley saw it, *felt* it. He screamed, just once, and backed away from the desk. The tumbler dropped from his hand and I had a momentary flash of regret that the precious liquid in it was wasted, soaking into the desktop blotter and dripping to the floor, and then I turned my attention back to Marley.

He had fallen to the floor, clutching at his chest. His flesh, the stuff of life, could no more cope with exposure to what comes after than a fly could cope with exposure to a furnace flame. Silently, he writhed, spittle flecking his lips, eyes bulging. I leaned in to him, still allowing the darkness to flow from me, and whispered, "Do you see? This is what awaits you." I have no idea if that was true, but that last spark of fear that I saw in those bugged eyes made the lie worthwhile. And then, with no more sound, Marley died.

Another realisation; I believed that I was haunting the building, the place where Marley and I had spent our years in constant battle, but I was wrong. I was haunting Marley himself, and with his death came not a release but an expansion. My revenge is still a burning thing, is still aflame with my anger. Marley touched so many people during his excessive life, and a piece of him is with them still. He lives on whilst there are memories of him, even ones that are buried and long forgotten, and I cannot have that. I *cannot*. All of you who met him, this larger than life fellow, are keeping him alive, and so my haunting is not over. You may not remember him, or have only the most fragmentary recall of a man whose boisterousness overrode your initial impressions of him, or of a shop full of piled stock and nooks and crannies and the proprietor serving you with a cheery wink and a joke, but it does not matter. He is in you, and by being in you, he opens you to me.

I am coming, and I bring my darkness with me.

|The Derwentwater Shark|

~

It started as a joke.

"Then, of course, there's the shark," said Tom. He waited, gauging the reaction of the American in the seat next to him.

"Shark?" the American said. Not outright dismissal, then. Tom felt his throat relax, felt the lubricant of story slick his tongue and teeth and then he was speaking.

"The Derwentwater Shark, haven't you heard of it? It was quite famous in the sixties and seventies, although it's not been seen recently, which is good."

"Why? Is it dangerous?" Still disbelief in the tourist's voice, though his eyes had turned limpid, like pools of still water waiting for the thrown rocks. Waiting for the ripples.

"No. Well, not really. There was a child who vanished. She could have been kidnapped, but it was quiet the day she disappeared and no one saw anything funny. She could have drowned, but it's a lake and bodies float after a bit, don't they? People said the shark got her."

"Sharks can't live in fresh water!" exclaimed the American suddenly, anger spiking his voice and tensing the flab of his jowly face.

"Some can," said Tom, defensive but not *too* defensive, just a little hurt creeping into his tone. "Anyway, the Derwentwater Shark is only name, it doesn't mean it actually is a shark. It could be a big catfish or a pike or anything. No one's ever photographed it or even really seen it clearly, they've just seen a big pale shape moving in the water. The year after the girl vanished, a couple capsized one of the rowing boats when they were out in the middle of the lake. The man drowned, but the woman survived and she swore that something had hit the boat from underneath and forced them over. Of course no one believed her, not really. Not until they found his body."

The sun made Derwentwater's surface a rippled sheet of burnished copper. The American leaned forward in the bench seat of the launch and dropped his voice, conspiratorial. Tom had a sudden image of him as a great fish, a different sort of Derwentwater Shark, wriggling and hooked. Being reeled in.

"Was he eaten?"

"No. Well, they *said* no. Back then, there weren't half the rules about boats on the water that there are now, so what happened to him, to his face and body, could have been caused by a propeller. If it was going fast, that is. My dad told me that all that summer, people were talking about how few ducks and geese and swans there were on the water, and how pets were going missing, drowning in the lake, or at least, going swimming and not coming back. Eventually, some people from the Natural History Museum came up and did some tests, looked around, but they said that nothing was wrong. It was one of them that gave whatever it was the name Derwentwater Shark, actually. He was being interviewed in the local papers and said it as a joke, that maybe Derwentwater had its own shark, and the paper used it as a headline and that was that."

"Really?"

"Really. Nothing serious has happened since, but every time someone goes missing around here and they've been seen on or around or even in the lake, or if something happens to one of the rowboats, people say it's the shark. Every now again there's some sightings and a TV crew comes and does one of those humourous end-of-show segments, but no one ever proves anything." The pier was approaching; Tom had to wrap this up fast. "People don't like years like this year, though."

"Why?" Total trust, total belief. Later, maybe, the American would question, but not now. Now, he was Tom's.

"Look around," said Tom. "There's not many birds."

So indeed; it was a blustery day early in the hatching season, and the birds would most likely be in the less populated areas on the islands in the lake's centre, still mistrustful of people, but to the American? "There are no birds because they're being eaten. It means the shark's around."

It wasn't that Tom disliked tourists; in fact, he quite enjoyed their company. Living in the Lake District was far from the romantic ideal that people imagined; it was claustrophobic with people and noise in high season and cold, wet and depressed off-season, and Tom hated it. Tom's father had come here as a child and loved it, returning to live with his family when Tom was young. When he talked about Keswick and Lodore and the other surrounding towns and villages, it was with quiet pride in his voice, with awe and love and belonging, and tourists had the same tone in their voice. With their garish clothes and bulging bags and too-loud voices, they gave Tom's world colour and shape, stretched its edges to new horizons.

If he had been able to articulate it, Tom might have said he was returning a favour by telling stories, making the tourist's world a little more interesting by giving them a mystery to savour and enjoy. Tom's stories populated his home, a place whose economy was based on transient visitors, low wages and minimal opportunity, with the kind of things he wanted to be there, smothering the mundane reality. So, for him, a simple question about the lake ("What fish are in there son, do you know?") was a springboard to a more exciting world. His idiot fish, the Derwentwater Shark, would give the American something to ponder, speculate about, and would ensure he remembered Derwentwater for the rest of his holiday, if not the rest of his life.

Tom's shift in the bar didn't finish until late, and he was exhausted by the time it was over. The launch didn't run at night, so he took the bus around the lake to his home near Hawes End, its lolling rhythm sending him into a half sleep. Rattling along the dark roads, his head resting against the dirty pane that let out onto the shadowed stone walls and sloped earth of the countryside beyond, Tom let himself drift. The mild susurrus of conversation surrounded him like a delicate massage. As ever, the other passengers were mainly residents of the area returning to their homes after working in Keswick, with a smattering of tourists thrown in. Their conversations reassured Tom, a varying constant of moans about wages and workloads, discussions about the love-lives of colleagues, planning future trips or meals and ongoing commentaries about how *dark* it was with no street- or houselights, how *bright* the stars were and how *many* of them there were in the sky, about how *wonderful* it all was.

About sharks.

Tom's head jerked upright, processing the just-heard conversations until he pinned down the right one. Unobtrusively, he turned towards its source; two women opposite him, both tourists. Carefully, he let his ears join in the talk.

"…and he said there was a shark, something big, in Derwentwater."

"No!"

"Yes! It attacked some people a few years ago but hasn't been since, so it's likely died or maybe found a passage to the sea or to another lake. But if there's been one, it stands to reason that there could more, doesn't it?"

The passage to the sea or another lake was new, Tom thought, smiling. His shark was growing!

Tom was busy for days after that; his dad needed more help than usual around the house, and one of the other bar staff left suddenly. Between the extra shifts and doing more at home, Tom had little time to eat, and certainly none to speak to friends or spin tall tales. His daily trip across the lake to Keswick on the launch was a time to rest and he kept himself to himself, avoiding conversation, so when he opened the *Keswick Reminder* the following week and saw the headline LOCAL FISHERMAN SEES WHOPPER GET AWAY, it was the first he'd heard of the story.

Reading on, Tom was startled to discover that "…local man Kerrie Armstrong was fishing off Low Brandelow when he saw a 'large grey fish' break the water about sixty yards from shore." The article, written in the slightly tongue-in-cheek tone of a reporter who doesn't really believe what he's writing about, went on to say that Armstrong, who lived out at Rosthwaite, and who Tom knew by sight but not to talk to, was definite that the thing in the lake was not a log. "It was," he said, "something that moved, and was bigger than anything he'd seen in Derwentwater before in 'fifty years of fishing'". Tom grinned as he read the article; Armstrong had been drinking, seen a big plank or tree trunk and assumed it was his "whopper" fish. Tom wondered if the American had seen the article, if he taken it as further proof of the shark's existence. His shark was swimming by itself now!

A couple of days after Armstrong's sighting, Tom arrived at work to find his colleagues talking about the thing that had been seen in the lake. Apparently, a full launch of seventy people, on a journey between High and Low Brandelow, had watched for five minutes as something large had kept pace with them, fifty feet or so off the starboard bow.

Mostly seen by the wake it made, it broke the surface several times, briefly revealing a grey flank and the impression of fins. The wake made by the thing was large, and most people on the launch were agreed that the thing was metres in length rather than feet. Finally, as the launch came into High Brandelow, it disappeared with a splash. All of the photographs taken showed little more than swirls on the water's surface or a grainy shape, indistinct, under the ripples.

Opinion differed as to what the thing was; Kelly, the youngest member of staff, was convinced it was a lake monster because, she said seriously, all lakes had monsters, didn't they? And besides, all lakes were linked by subterranean passages, so even if Derwentwater *didn't* have its own monster, one could have swum in, couldn't it? Ollie, older and wiser and desperate to bed Kelly, agreed but said it might be a sturgeon, which were huge and were often *mistaken* for monsters, and said he'd heard about the subterranean passages as well. Mary dismissed the idea out of hand, saying it was an uprooted tree moving in the launch's wake, or currents swirling as the boat passed and giving the impression of something alive, and Jenny said it was most likely a collective hallucination. No one mentioned the *Reminder's* article about Armstrong, and Tom didn't raise it. No one mentioned sharks.

At the end of his shift, Tom just wanted to be home, but his bus wouldn't arrive for half an hour so kill the time, he walked down to the lakeside and sat on the dock. The sound of the water lapping at the jetty's pilings and licking its way along the shore was comforting, helping to wash away his tiredness. At this time of night, the sound of the town and its lifeblood tourists was a background hum rather than a primary shout, and the air felt clean and fresh, renewed by the darkness. He liked the way the water lapped against the side of the boats and it was at times like this, when the world was quiet, that he came closest to understanding his dad's feelings; the landscape itself was a drama that both calmed you and raised you up, redolent with permanence and solidity and strength. It was calm, quiet, gentle.

Too quiet. There were no bird noises.

All the way home, as the bus jolted its way along the country roads, Tom tried to dismiss it as a coincidence. There was nothing in the lake, nothing large, and certainly no sharks. Nothing had eaten the birds or scared them away, they were simply asleep in their roosts or nests. What had started as a story was still a story, and everything else was happenstance, unrelated things he was looking at wrong. It was nonsense.

Nonsense.

By the time he made it home, Tom had mostly persuaded himself, and anyway he had to help his father, who hadn't gone to bed but had fallen asleep in the chair. Missing birds or not, life went on, and everything was okay until the dog got eaten.

Actually, there was no evidence that the dog was eaten, but the *Reminder* strongly implied it. It was in a story about a local man, Amos Heart, whose dog ("poor Nipper") had been swimming in Derwentwater when "something large and grey" had risen up from the water behind him and come down on the unfortunate dog with a large splash. Poor Nipper had let out "a yelp that were cut off half way through" and disappeared under the water with the large shape, never to return. Although the word 'shark' was not used in the article at all, there was a comment about a "large carnivorous fish" somehow having been introduced into the lake. Other explanations for the incident were suggested – that Nipper had suffered some sort of fit and made the large splash himself as he cramped and went below the surface, or that he had had somehow wrapped himself up in a submerged tangle of plants or branches, and that it was this that Heart had seen as Nipper thrashed and tried to free himself – but neither of these explanations was treated seriously. Heart was said to be "devastated" by his loss, and called via the *Reminder's* pages for "something to be done". What the something was, he did not say.

Whatever the *Reminder* said, Tom was sure that no one would give the story (or at least, the explanation offered for it) credence, but he had forgotten how much people liked his tall tales, how much they apparently *wanted* to believe. Both his colleagues and the customers at the bar were full of the story, and every one of them seemed to have some additional detail not reported in the paper. There was the fisherman who had had his pole yanked from his hand and seen the wake of something large swimming away with it trailing in the water behind it, and the other dog that now refused to go in the water despite previously swimming regularly, and the hotel manager on his way to work early one morning who had seen something pale moving through the water about twenty feet from the shore, something that moved fast before disappearing with a flick of something that looked disturbingly like a triangular fin. Tom had the uncomfortable sensation that the world was tilting and yawing around him as he listened to these anecdotes; everyone had something to add, some extra little detail that made the thing in the lake more real, stories of sightings and near-misses and things a friend had definitely seen, and all around Tom the shark swam and he could only watch in belly-clenched wonder.

It was Maggie that said the most disturbing thing, though; sensible, humourless Maggie who co-owned the bar and treated life as though it were a set of entries in a register rather than a thing to be lived and enjoyed.

"Of course, it's happened before, back when I was a girl," she stated one day. "They did investigations."

Tom thought he'd misheard. In the week following Nipper's suspected demise (although his corpse had not been recovered yet), the story had circled and swooped around the district, and every version Tom heard was different, larger or broader or deeper than the previous ones, but this? Cautiously, not wanting the answer, he asked, "What investigations?"

"Back in the sixties or seventies, I don't remember exactly. No, wait, it must have been the late sixties as I hadn't started school and I started that particular joy in seventy one. There some sightings of the shark then, and someone died so some scientists came from London to investigate. Of course, they didn't find anything, but they never do, do they? I mean, the death was probably an accident, but still. You don't know, do you?"

"Are you sure?"

"Yes, of course I am!" snapped Maggie, suddenly back into the now from her memories of then. "Work, Tom, not gossip. That's what I pay you for."

That night, Tom's dad was asleep in the chair again when he got in from his shift, but instead of helping him up to bed, Tom woke him up and started to talk to him. Tom's dad, who seemed to have collapsed in on himself since the death of his wife three years earlier, listened with rheumy-eyed concentration.

"Dad, did you ever tell me about something in the lake, something big? Or about people coming from London to investigate it?" It was the only solution, as far as Tom could see: that the Derwentwater Shark was real, was something that Tom had heard from his dad who loved to tell Tom about the history and myths of the place they had moved to, and then Tom had all but forgotten it, only for it to spout forth as a story on that stupid day weeks ago.

"Something in the lake? You mean like a fish, or the Loch Ness monster?" Dad was smiling; Tom didn't smile back.

"Yes. No. I don't know. Just something in the lake, something that bothered people? Bothered them enough to call people in to investigate, I mean?"

Tom's dad thought for a while and then said, "No. There was never anything like that. Derwentwater's a fairly dull lake for monsters, I'm afraid."

The next day, during his lunch break, Tom went to the library and asked to see the old issues of the *Keswick Reminder*. He flicked through the huge bound collections, not bothering to read the articles, just the headlines. In a town where little ever happened, the arrival of investigators looking for a creature in the lake would have been headline news, but it did not appear at any point in the issues from the sixties or seventies. It hadn't happened, and yet everyone was saying it had. His shark, it seemed, was gaining weight.

In the first film, the man is smiling. He sits in the back of one of the rowing boats that tourists hire by the hour, and the sunlight glints across the lenses of his spectacles as he laughs at whoever is filming. Over his shoulder, the flat expanse of Derwentwater sparkles in the early summer light; the man has his arms crossed over his knees and the oars pulled into the boat, lying loosely by his ankles.

"So, Tamsin" asks the man, "how are you enjoying being rowed around the lake?"

The unseen camera operator replies, her voice thick with laughter. "It's very pleasant thank you, Steve, but don't stop yet. We appear to have stopped in the middle. Onwards, lazy husband!"

The man, Steve, grins even more widely and goes to pick up the oars. As he bends forward, however, the boat jerks violently, jolting up.

For a brief moment, the picture shakes wildly, showing first sky and then grey water. Someone screams, although whether male or female it is impossible to tell. There is the sound of splashing water and then Tamsin lets the camera go. In the brief, spiralling view the water can be seen, and in it the impression of someone thrashing alongside a large moving shape. There is another scream as the camera finishes its fall in the bottom of the boat, ending up staring blindly into the sky as the scream cuts off sharply. The clip ends with a moment of stillness before Tamsin's voice sounds, crying "Steve!" in an endless, desperate wail.

The clip, taken on Tamsin's mobile phone, was the headline item on the main news shows. It rolled in constant repetition on the news channels, with banner headlines scrolling across the bottom of the screen: *Man disappears in Derwentwater* and *Barrister Steve Marsh, 37, feared drowned*. It was the most shown piece of film for perhaps 8 hours, until the second clip was released.

This one is taken from one of the search boats. It starts as a mass of black and white, blurred flashes, resolving as the focus tightens into the surface of water at night. The tips of the agitated waves catch light from somewhere but lose it in the heavy troughs and eddies. People are shouting, hoarse voices, although the only word that escapes the melee is *"Jesus!"*. Whoever is holding the camera or phone is shaking and moving, running along the side of the boat which, it becomes clear, is moving; their left hand comes into view for a brief moment, reaching forward to grasp the rail and stop them stumbling. Finally, they come to a standstill and train the camera at the water again. At first, there is nothing except reflections and glittering, broken light, and then something pale comes into view.

At first, it stays several feet below the surface, a large grey torpedo-shaped thing keeping pace with the moving boat but without detail because of the intervening water and darkness. There are more shouts and, at one point, the camera swings about to show people in uniforms lined along the boat's rail. One of them gestures furiously down at the water and the camera swings back to the lake; the thing has risen and is now just below the surface.

It is a shark.

Its breed is hard to determine, and later experts will argue about *morphology* and *genus*, but it is clearly a shark. Pale and long, its fins scythe out from its flanks and back, its tail flicks lazily and the black slashes of its gill slits are clear behind the bullet head. The camera wobbles again, and then a light appears, a circle of bright and constant illumination that plays across the surface of the water. It darts back and forth, and someone's voice can clearly be heard shouting "Keep it fucking still!" and then the light takes hold of the shark and grips tight. Whoever is holding the torch or spotlight dances the light up the great, undulating body until it finds the head and for perhaps three or four seconds, the creature is in sharp focus. It turns as it swims, tilting over slightly as though attempting to get a better look at the boat and the people on it. Its black, depthless eye stares at the camera and its mouth opens, a dark triangle against the pale grey of its head. There is a flash of teeth, vast and numberless, and then the fish wheels away from the boat and dives, dropping out of view as the gloomy water swallows it.

In the days following the two clips being made public, things moved very quickly. Tom watched as, around him, Keswick and the surrounding towns changed. Police prevented anyone except officials from going out onto the water, and suddenly there were lots of official men and women with badges and cameras and boats in the streets and on the television. The atmosphere changed as well; new tourists arrived, and brought with them a sense of expectancy and danger. Most crowded along the shores of Derwentwater and stared out across it, filming every ripple and splash and shouting with exaggerated whoops and cries when they believed they saw something. Tom, working double shifts at the suddenly busy bar, heard the kinds of conversations he had only ever dreamed about. Clustered around the tables, the officials talked increasingly desperately about *water vectors* and *relative temperatures* and *food chain imbalances* and, once, *primary predator intrusion* but what no one did was to explain how the shark had got into Derwentwater, or how it was surviving.

On the third day, just as the film of the shark was being shown less, replaced by the latest terrorist atrocities abroad, the shark was seen again. This time, it was caught as a sonar trace, cruising through the water at the north end of the lake. Printouts of the sonar appeared on the news, along with interviews with the machine's operator, telling in breathless excitement how he had tracked the thing for minutes before he lost it. Tom watched in disbelief. *How had this happened,* he thought to himself, not for the first time? He had made the damned thing up! It wasn't real, it was a story he had invented for a gullible American and yet, all about him, evidence of its existence was growing.

There was more film, taken from the shore, showing a triangular fin slicing through the water forty yards offshore, jumbled eyewitness reports from observers on the boats, three still photographs taken with an underwater camera showing a mouth like a gasp turned upside down, heavy with jutting teeth. Tom watched as the shark gained in solidity until even he could not deny its existence. However it had happened, the Derwentwater Shark (and, Heaven help him, they were even using that name in the newspapers now!) had become flesh and blood, was prowling the waters of the lake, and he could not help but feel that it was in some way his fault.

Tom finally told someone about how he felt the night the boy got eaten.

The boy was part of a group of teenagers, the news reports and eyewitnesses said, and they had been drinking all day. At some point in the afternoon, the boys in the group started daring each other to wade out into the water as far as they could, clearly enjoying the shock they were causing in the watching tourists. The first of them got to knee-depth, several more got to mid thigh and one, wading with a lurching, drunken gait, got out to a point where the water lapped at his waist.

No one filmed what happened next, which was maybe for the best.

The boy, Neil Something (Tom never caught his last name) turned to the shore and raised his hands above his head in a victory stance, calling, "How's that?". He began to dance, jumping clumsily up and down in the water and sending ripples out from him in expanding rings. People on the shore called for him to wade back in, but he ignored them, continuing to dance and shake his fists about. Several of the bystanders called the police, and out on the lake, the timbre of the boat engines changed as they turned and began to head towards the bay in which Neil cavorted. Those watching from the shore saw the distant boats heading for them and began to relax; everything would be okay, they reported later, because the authorities were coming.

It was another change in the pitch of the engine tones that was the first sign that something was wrong. Suddenly, the boats were powering across the water and even from a distance those on the shore could *hear* the urgency in the sound. They heard the shouts from the crews and then the first of them saw the wake approaching the boy. A vast triangle, it was several hundred yards away from Neil but arrowing at him at massive speed. The teenager stopped dancing and started to wade in towards his friends as everyone on the shore began to scream and shout, but he never stood a chance. The shark, its mouth open, rose up from behind him and bit down, its mouth crunching onto the boy's torso with a sound like the breaking of thick twigs before it disappeared in a red, wet thrashing. Neil didn't get as far as opening his mouth to scream.

The shark twisted, its great flank rolling out of the water as the watchers onshore screamed, and then it dived, passing beneath the first of the arriving boats and out into the depths of the lake.

At first, Tom tried to tell people that the shark wasn't real. He started at work, talking to Mary and Jenny, but both of them looked at him as though he was mad, and Jenny said that it was in poor taste to make jokes about the shark seeing as it had killed two people. When Tom tried to explain, Jenny got annoyed with him and told him he was being horrible, so he stopped. He got the same reaction from everyone else, or at least, variations of the same reaction. His friends thought it was a bad joke and the one official he told, who was sitting in the bar nursing a pint of locally brewed ale, simply stared at Tom until he backed away, apologising. No one believed him, but it was true; the shark was a *joke*, a fucking *story*, and it couldn't be swimming around Derwentwater.

Couldn't be, but was.

Finally, he went back to the library; he would *prove* that this was nonsense. He took the *Keswick Reminder* collections down from the shelves again, hoping to show someone that there was nothing there, but even as he carried them to the table, one fell open and a headline, in stark black and white, glared up at him: KESWICK SHARK – NO EVIDENCE SAY EXPERTS.

The article was old; it was bound into the collection in the same way as the others were, the pages were yellowing and brittle with age, the printing was the same hazy print of the others. It was real, Tom knew as he read through it. It just hadn't been there the other day when he looked. It was a new article, but old. It was new history. He had no idea what it meant, or how it had happened, but it meant the shark was real – not just now, but then as well.

"My shark is eating people," Tom whispered to himself on the bus home later and, very quietly, he began to cry.

It was Tom's dad that told him what to do in the end. When Tom got back from work, the tears still pressing the backs of his eyes and creating salt streaks across his cheeks and down the back of his throat, the older man said, "What's wrong, son?"

"Oh, dad," said Tom, "I've done something awful. I made something up and now people think it's real. It *is* real, it's become real and there's nothing I can do. People are being hurt, and it's all my fault." Relief ballooned in Tom as he spoke; his dad sat nodding, his eyes sympathetic. He had become wizened and mostly helpless in recent years, crumbling away and leaning more and more heavily on Tom for help with even the most simple of tasks, but in that moment, he was neither old nor helpless, he was just Tom's dad, and Tom could be a child again and need help.

"It's easy to say things you don't mean," said Tom's dad when Tom had finished, "but not to unsay them. Things have a way of escaping from you, don't they? And sometimes, if you can't stop what you've said getting away from you, you have to go to the heart of what you said and face it, stop it that way. It might hurt, but our pride is a small price to pay, I'd say, if it stops others being hurt. Wouldn't you agree?"

"Yes," said Tom quietly, and helped his already drifting father to his bed.

The water tapped quietly at the side of the boat, chuckling against the wood. The boat pitched and rolled as Tom rowed, keeping his movements slow and careful as he aimed the small craft out into the centre of Derwentwater. He had to be quiet, as the curfew imposed after the first confirmed sighting was still in place, and only official boats (mostly larger yachts or the launches commandeered for the purpose) were allowed on the water. In the midnight darkness, Tom's craft was a small blot of moving shadow against the softly breathing water, or so he hoped, and now he was away from the dock and the lights from the town, almost invisible.

What his dad had said wouldn't leave him alone, had been in his belly all day, clumped into a ball like mud gathered around a stone, even though he was not sure his dad had really understood the situation that Tom found himself in. He found that he liked the idea that his dad had been giving him advice thinking that he had hurt some girl's feelings, or offended one of his friends, rather than about how he might undo a giant shark's reality; it made things manageable, and it made him happy that he had protected his dad from the world beyond their home's walls. *Let him stay happy*, thought Tom, *and not know what I've done.* And if Tom couldn't tell people (or rather, he could but they didn't believe him, despite his best efforts), then he would have to do something else. Question was, *what*?

It helped that his shift finished late, and that even the tourists were mostly in bed by the time he made it out of the bar. The scientists were also gone from the streets and the lake, and he knew from overheard conversations that they did little at night except guard the lake and maintain the curfew. So far, several people had been arrested for trying to get onto the water with the intention of catching or killing the shark, but they had all tried to do so using big, noticeable boats. Tom's plan was simpler and smaller; he was going to steal a rowboat.

The rental agencies had suffered because of the shark, with their rowboats left dry on the shore by the main dock. Although they were chained, it didn't take Tom long to cut one free with the bolt cutters he had brought from home. The noise was loud in the night, but not loud enough to attract anyone's attention; no one came and stopped him as he pulled the boat into the water, or used the oars as a punt to push him away from the shore, and no one stopped him when he reached the middle of the lake and began to throw meat into the water.

The chum was from the bar restaurant, another small theft that Tom would have to pay back later. He hated stealing, hated what he had become, but he could see no other option. He had to face the shark, stare it down and make it unreal again, make it a story and not a thing of cartilage and blood. It was almost unreal anyway, he thought; no shark should have been able to survive in the cold, fresh water of Derwentwater, and certainly not one as large as this was. There wasn't enough food for it, for a start, and the water would poison it. Surely, he thought, it wouldn't take much to tip it back from *mostly* unreal to *completely* unreal. Just a little pressure, just a small push, and it would be gone, back to wherever it came from. He just needed to call it, to see it and to let it see him, and then apply the pressure. The meat was his calling card and soon the scent of it, rich and dank, filled the air around him and covered his hands as he threw more and more in the water and watched it sink in slow, lazy swirls.

It was surprisingly noisy out on the lake. The air in the small boat seemed to vibrate like the skin of a drum, magnifying the sounds around Tom. Water struck against the boat's wooden flanks, distant birds called, car engines caught and slipped as vehicles made their way around the lake on roads that dipped and rose, their headlights slithering across the surface of the water. A breeze snagged in the trees, whispering around him as he baited the water, and the oars shifted and settled in the rowlocks in metallic counterpoint. Tom could see the lights of Keswick, a razor's slash of pearls along the line of the horizon that separated the cold stars above from the glitter of the water around him.

Tom had almost run out of meat when something bumped against the boat.

It wasn't a hard bump, just enough to make the small craft rock slightly, tilting it one way then back the other and sending Tom into a wobble that slid him off the seat. He fell into the base of the boat, landing in amongst empty bags that were smeared with blood and stinking of meat. One of the oars shuddered, its voice a quiet shriek in the night and then Tom was up and peering over at the water as the boat rocked and splashed and the water licked up and then down its wooden sides.

He could see very little. The water's surface caught the light and broke it, sending shards of yellow and white this way and that and hiding the blackness below. Tom tried to remain still so that the boat would stop rocking, but it did not help. A wave shifted, a moving hump of water that set the tiny craft back onto its heels and then dragged it into the trough it left behind. *A bow wave*, thought Tom distractedly and then he was looking further out trying to see where the wave had originated. There? No, that was just more ripples and fractured light.

There?

No.

There?

No. *Yes*, Jesus yes, and Tom saw the shark.

It was huge, far bigger than the boat, and it was moving slowly along just below the surface of the water. He could see its pallid flanks and, as it rose up, an emerging fin creating a smaller wave which haunted the larger one. It moved glacially along the side of the boat as Tom watched, its great snout just below the water, fragmented and broken by the dancing lights but still *there*, still *real*, its black and hopeless eye glimmering and its mouth a serrated blackness darker and deeper than the water could ever hope to be. Tom could not move as he watched it, its tail flicking lazily and circling the boat as though sizing it up. Tom had the awful feeling that the thing was staring out past the water and directly at him, challenging him in some way. Perhaps it was growing; it certainly seemed larger than in the film taken from the search boat. Maybe it was his own fear giving it flesh, magnifying it to terrible proportions. How big could it grow, he wondered? How big could it get before its impossibility was too strong to ignore? Thirty feet? Forty? A hundred?

No. That was preposterous. This was *all* preposterous, and Tom had to finish it now.

"You aren't real," Tom said quietly, gazing into the shark's featureless eye as it continued to move around him. The circles were getting tighter and tighter, Tom realised, the distance between the fish and the boat lessening until finally it bumped against the boat again.

"You are not real," Tom repeated. The shark continued to bump against the boat, pushing against it with its nose. The book shook, sending Tom to his hands and knees again, gripping an oar for stability and feeling the cold lakewater as it splashed over the side and sprayed against him. Unsteady in the darkness, he saw that the shark had moved away, was turning and starting towards him. It was gaining speed, its tail thrashing the water to white foam behind it and its mouth stretching wide. *This cannot be happening*, Tom shrieked to himself as his mouth released a wordless scream, *this is not real it is not real it is not it is not it is not it is not it's not not not not* and then the shark was rising up against the side of the boat and it mouth was crunching down on the wood and shaking the boat like a terrier with a ragged toy and Tom was swinging the oar and shouting, "You are a story I made up! You are *not real!*"

The oar passed through nothing but air.

The boat jounced violently as it settled, dropping back to find its own balance only slowly. The shark had vanished, leaving Tom staring at a patch of black, reflecting water. He looked around the boat, staring out over the lake for the telltale V-shaped wake of the fish or its great pale shape moving under the water, but the patterns of ripples were uniform all about him. Was that it? Had it finally gone? Was this just the lake again, Derwentwater, a place Tom now realised he loved as much as his dad did? Had he done it?

Tom ran his fingers over the side of the boat, but the wood where the shark had bitten was unmarked. Tom allowed himself a small smile, and though *Perhaps this is what God feels like when he creates and destroys things*, and then the boat was rising through the air and tilting, pitching Tom out and the water was rushing to meet him and then he was submerged.

It was cold; beyond cold. Freezing. Tom started to shiver almost instantly, and for a terrible moment was so disorientated that he could not work out which was up or down, where the surface was, which direction to kick for. He saw his bubbles rise, felt how he was floating and chased them, breaking the surface gasping. He tore air into his stunned lungs, feeling the bitter water cling and drag at him. He stared about, kicking his legs in an effort to stay afloat, whipping his head around but seeing nothing besides the waves he himself had made and, beyond them, the capsized boat floating, turtle-like, back towards the shore. Thrusting his face into the water, he peered through the gloom, trying to spin and see all the directions at once. There! *There!* In the distance, something pale moved against the darker curtain of water.

The shark was coming.

How can it still be here? thought Tom as he watched the shape come slowly towards him, no hurry or urgency in its movement. He could make out its mouth now, opening and closing as it came for him, its teeth stark against the black maw. How could it still be in the lake? *I faced it. I won!*

Lack of breath forced Tom to raise his face from the water, and he saw the lights from the town ahead of him and suddenly he knew. He might have faced it, asserted the shark's unreality, but they had not. All of those people believing; all terrified, maybe, all horrified, but wanting mysteries, wanting to believe in a fish that should not be there. All of them, giving it life.

Tom screamed as, below, a vast pale shape rose towards him.

|When the World Goes Quiet|

Johnny Cash and I were in the nursery when I saw my first. It staggered up the centre of the road in the loose dusk and I shrank down from its sight as it passed. The Man in Black carried on, low and weary and mournful.

The first reports had been half-formed, disjointed items about a new virus sweeping its way across Asia in a ragged wave. The film accompanying these reports was amateur, handheld and shaky and showing people driven apparently mad by their illness and staggering and flailing. Attacking people. Eating them. The tone of the reports had quickly become hysterical, and Carmel and I watched them in the evenings after I had returned from work and wondered, how serious was this really? After all, bird flu and before it SARS had been equally deadly according to the news reports, and yet neither threat felt real or serious in England. When I look back, and knowing now what ultimately happened, I'm horrified by the way Carmel and I were. I, blithely massaging the swelling, tautening skin across her pregnancy and telling her about my day at work, Carmel updating me about this pre-natal class or that lunch, while the reports played in the background. How could we have been so unconcerned? How could we have been so terribly blasé about the end of our world?

I think it was because no one else we knew seemed bothered. If people mentioned it at all, it was to dismiss its imminence or to brush it off with a wave of the hand and a secure belief in England's island status as our great protector. I'm sure that, behind the scenes, the various authorities were making plans and preparations but to those of us commuting, working, shopping and living, nothing changed. At weekends, Carmel and I carried on decorating the nursery and in the evenings we took it in turns to cook, Carmel's meals being healthier, mine more filling. At work, the paper and emails kept on slipping into my 'to do' pile, then slipping out again as I filed and updated and delegated. Idiocy, when we should have been stockpiling, learning and building.

And then the first was found in England.

It was a Tuesday night and I had cooked. Carmel and I sat in front of the television and watched as the reports of an 'isolated case on the south coast' were delivered and dissected and analysed and predictions made and even then, we carried on as though it were the outbreak of some mild flu bug being reported. We were safe, we told ourselves and each other, safe in our village and safe in our life. It would not spread, would not creep up northwards, would be stopped and turned back and all would be well. The next morning I went to work as normal, but for the first time, things were different. The train was quieter, its passengers talking less. There were empty seats at the end of the line when normally it was busy enough that some passengers had to stand for their entire journey. I hope that those people missing from the train on that morning and the mornings that followed are safe, that they used the time wisely and survive still; somehow, though, I doubt it.

I have come to think of that time as a time of falsehood, where we pretended that everything was well. We were like the characters in the Carry On film that eat their meal without apparently noticing that artillery shells are destroying the building around them. It was a time of brittle, false calm that I foolishly helped to sustain, and it did not last long.

Early the following week, the trains stopped running and 'non-essential' workers were advised to stay at home. The news reports, previously rushed and wild accounts of the creep of the demarcation line between safe and unsafe areas, suddenly stopped; now all we got were written statements printed in the papers or read out on the television and radio in toneless voices advising caution, little or no movement from place to place, and the immediate notification of anything suspicious.

Suspicious, like the dead walking.

In our little home in our little village, Carmel and I stockpiled what we could and settled down to wait it out. We watched as our neighbours got in their cars and left, although where they were headed

I never knew. Carmel and I talked about leaving once, but quickly dismissed it; where would we go? We could not think of anywhere and besides, Carmel has never coped well with change or the things that happen outside the walls of her home. She is, perhaps, the most fragile person I have known, beautiful and single-minded about what she wants and quite unable to handle it when what she wants does not happen, or when her plans are changed by anyone other than her. Her way of coping has always been to bury herself inside the security of the walls around her and her relationships like a hermit crab and wait for the change to settle, to revert, to unmake itself. And I, if I am honest, enjoyed that about her. We could close our doors, just be with each other with no distractions and nothing to take our attention from ourselves, intense and private and personal. And, if I am even more honest, I think that, despite all the evidence from the other countries that had been affected before Britain, we still expected the army to appear, clearing the land as they went and making it safe for us. Handing out mugs of hot tea and biscuits, no doubt, to bolster our flagging spirits, talking in cheerful cockney accents with the natural wit of the happy working class. Restoring our social order. Restoring *normality*. Nonsense, of course; a nice fantasy that finally fell apart when we heard the last new broadcast made before the television went off the air. To a black screen, a man's voice intoned, "They are everywhere. Help is not coming. Defend yourselves in any way you can from the dead. Do not let yourselves be bitten or scratched as the infection will kill you and you will rise again. Destroy the dead before they rise. May your God protect you." This repeated, looping for two days before it, too, stopped and silence reigned.

Left to itself, the world is *quiet*. When the cars and lorries stop running, when the television and radio fall to noiselessness, when the pubs and restaurants and stores fail to open for customers, when the looting and chaos and panic has died, the world becomes vastly, coldly, quiet. Sometimes the sounds of the ocean, three miles distant, would reach us in our home, the first time it had ever done so. Other times, we could hear the lowing of the cows on the nearby farms or the birds whistling in the trees and hedgerows, but mostly we were surrounded by the implacable sound of a world turned mute. Even the screams that had formed part of the background to our world for the weeks following the end of the broadcast finally stopped. Occasionally, we would see greasy columns of smoke on the horizon, and more rarely we would see the glitter of movement on the tracery of roads just visible from our upper storey windows, but mostly the world closed itself off around us.

If the earlier weeks were the ones of false calm then that period was, I suppose, the peaceful time. We had food, we were safe in our home and we had each other. It lasted just less than three weeks, and during them we did little but talk to each other and plan for our child's arrival. The electricity and gas stopped not long after the broadcasts did, but we had a log-burning stove for cooking and heating and the taps still gave water. Carmel and I have always preferred each other's company and been happiest when there is no-one else around, and as awful as it may sound, I think we actually enjoyed that time. There were fears, to be sure, but we felt little threat. We live in a tiny village off the main road and rail routes, surrounded by farmland and rising at our rear into brutal hills and wide, scattered lakes; some three hundred houses and a few stores and an adult education college. Its solitude was why Carmel and I moved here, to a stone-built cottage that was half the size and three times the price of the home we left in the city. Looking back at those weeks I wonder if we knew, unconsciously, what was coming and were simply taking what time we could together before it was withdrawn from us. I honestly don't know, but I'm glad I had those scant few days alone with the woman I love and our growing, unborn child, although even if it were a lifetime of them I don't think it would be enough. How could it be? How could there ever be time enough?

The water stopped flowing just before the food supplies ran low. We had a water butt in the garden containing perhaps ten gallons of collected rainwater, and some cans of soup and vegetables left, but the reality of our situation was that things were suddenly tight. Should I have seen the situation coming? Of course, but I had ignored it in the hopeless idea that something, some *solution*, would present itself. I can look back and curse myself for that, but I believe that things would not ultimately have turned out any different no matter how I acted. Perhaps I might have had more of that peaceful, private time with Carmel, perhaps not. It wasn't just the food and the water that made me realise that things had changed, were constantly changing, however; it was the sight of my first that told me that our safe haven was safe no more.

Carmel tended to fall asleep not long after it got dark, exhausted by the pregnancy, but I would stay awake. With no television or radio, I found that I read more than I had in years, sitting on the floor below the nursery window and using the moon's light to see the pages. I had a battered personal stereo and a store of batteries that fitted nothing else I owned, so I played my old CDs as I read, plunging myself back into a life that no longer existed. Some nights I played rock, others classical, yet others soul or country. That Johnny Cash was playing as the dead walked for the first time along the street outside my home seems now to be appropriate, for in Cash's stricken and wind-blasted voice I found a sudden reflection of the emptiness of the world outside my window. Maybe I'm reading too much backwards into the incident, but it felt like one of those rare times when life gave me a soundtrack that fitted absolutely.

The dead man, for it was male, was no one I recognised. It staggered like a lost drunk up the slight incline of our road, one arm hanging loosely by its side, the other reaching out in front of it as though to grasp something I could not see. It was dressed in jeans and a t-shirt but was barefoot, and it left dark smears when it dragged its feet into each step like one of those foot placement charts that you have to follow when learning a new dance. The t-shirt was mottled, white with dark and glistening patches and seemed to be sticking to the body underneath. I didn't see its face, but the back of its head was covered in greasy, straggling hair. It looked somehow pathetic and lethal at the same time. The new reality was encroaching, and I could no longer ignore it. Seeing it decided me, and the next morning I spoke to Carmel.

"I don't want you to go."

"I don't want to go," I said to her, "but I have to. We have no food."

The discussion had been going for most of the morning, ever since I told Carmel of my plan to go out foraging. We had been through the upset, angry and quasi-reasonable stages of the disagreement and were now in some place where we could at least talk honestly.

"I'm scared," she said, not for the first time.

"Me too," I said. "I'm terrified, but I don't want to starve. Do you?"

"No," Carmel said quietly, "but I don't want you to go either." There was nothing I could say to this. We simply sat in the aching silence and hugged, feeling each other's warmth and loving each other and letting the hours pass.

I went early the next day. I dressed in my running gear; although it was months since I had been out for a run, it felt the best way to dress. I had considered wearing my leather jacket but decided that, despite the protection it might offer, its weight might slow me down. In the end I put on my thin waterproof, hoping that its slick surface might cause problems for anyone trying to grab me. For any *thing* that tried to grab me. I carried two light kit bags when I went, and before leaving I hugged Carmel as tight as I had ever hugged her. She was crying when I let her go. So was I.

"Lock the door after me and don't let me back in until you hear me speak," I told her. "If I won't speak to you, then I'm not me. Understand?"

She nodded, weeping hard.

"I love you. I'll be back." And I went.

The walking dead did not seem to be clever, according to the news reports, but clearly had some rudimentary intelligence and hunting skills. They were like predatory animals, able to execute only the simplest of actions and planning, so rather than leave the house by the front door and letting any lurking things see me and alerting them to our presence, I left by jumping over the fence at the rear of the house. This led into the garden of the home that backed on to ours and from there I slipped as quickly and quietly as I could along the side of the building and out onto the street. Let them see me come out from some other house entrance, I decided. Let them think there were people in that house and not mine, I thought, and hated myself for thinking that way.

Out on the street, I had intended to go as fast as I could to the village store but instead, I stopped. The sheer *difference* in the place that had been my home for more than three years brought me up cold. I should have been looking at a tree-lined street, the houses set back from the pavement behind narrow gardens and driveways, each home possessed of at least one car, sometimes more, with most parked on the street and everywhere busy with life. Instead, the street looked forlorn and broken. Early autumn leaves drifted across the road and pavements and gathered in heaps against the shut gates. There were no cars on the street and none that I could see on the driveways, although the street's surface was marked with the tattoos of tyre-marks, black arcs that swung and crossed in front of me. A fan of shattered glass was strewn away to my side and the tree nearest to it showed the new scar of impact. Bark and chewed wood hung from its damaged trunk and more glass was embedded in the ripped flesh of the wound. Across from me, the tyre tracks mounted the pavement. There was a suitcase on the ground, its leather battered and scuffed. Its locks had held, although whoever had packed it had done so sloppily and a white shirt arm trailed from it, now dirty and wet. All the houses I could see looked empty; two had open doors and one had broken windows. Had everyone left, run? Were Carmel and I the *only* ones who had stayed? Surely not. And yet, nothing moved and I saw no signs that anyone remained. Everything looked tired, as though it had tried and tried for years and suddenly the effort had caught up with it, and seeing it like that frightened me. Did I look like that? Carmel? Our home? Were we wearing the mantle of exhaustion already?

I finally began to move because it was either that or turn and return home. I walked slowly to the top of the street, stepping away from the pavement and into the roadway as I went. It felt odd to be out in the open after so long indoors, both exhilarating and threatening at the same time. The air smelled of old smoke and rain and, faintly, farmland at silage time. I walked as fast as I comfortably could, moving away from the garden walls and trees and leaving as much space around me as I could. As I walked, I looked around for signs of life, but saw none. It reminded me of when life was normal and I used to run early on a Sunday morning, before the village awoke. I had enjoyed those runs, when everything was still and serene. What day was it now? I could not remember. At some point in the previous weeks I had lost track.

I had already dismissed the idea of breaking into the houses around me. For all their appearance of abandonment, I had no idea if people still remained in them and did not want to be attacked as a looter by someone defending their home or family. Besides, I still harboured the idea that these were *homes,* not simply buildings, and the idea of breaking into a home bothered me in ways that I still cannot easily explain. My hope was that the village store would be a better proposition, and if by some miracle life ever returned to normal, I could make sure I paid the owners back for anything I took. Even as I approached the store, however, I saw that I was too late. The heavy security shutters had been pulled away from the windows and glass lay beneath them, broken and sharp across the ground. Ripped and torn food cartons were mixed amongst the glass, and rotting food lay in smears and trodden mounds by the cartons. There were more tyre tracks around the store and a slather of something that looked horribly like darkened and dried blood stretched up from the floor by the store's entrance to a twisted point perhaps three feet high. More of the dark stain curled away from the store and around into the dark loading alley at its side, lying across the floor with its edges creeping up the base of the wall. In the alley's shadowed depths I could see something twisted, hunched against the far wall. It was motionless. A gentle breeze picked up and it brought with it the smell of corruption and age from the store, of things rotting and broken, and I knew that I did not want to go closer than I already was, and that I did not want to see past those dark stains and into the interior of the place where I had bought milk and bread and wine and newspapers and had met friends and acquaintances and had lived a small part of my life for the past years.

Instead, I turned away and wondered just what to do next. My plan had been to raid the store, and I had not thought past that. In a life that had flowed smooth and easy, I was not used to things not working out, not simply falling into place, and I did not know what to do. I started to walk, following the curve of the road away from the store and to the outskirts of the village, still moving away from my home and from Carmel. I could not return, I told myself, without food but I was still terribly aware of the danger of leading the dead too close to Carmel.

The road ribboned out, passing more houses and then touching on the farmland. I saw no signs of life in the houses. Some were closed down, introspective in their posture, and others were open, windows or doors swinging in the gathering wind. In one garden a handmade sign had been thrust into the lawn. It read TO THE HIGHLANDS GATHER THERE. As I wondered if the author had made it, I suddenly started crying again. Standing there in the centre of the carriageway, I wept for everything that had gone. The people who I had known were gone, scurrying for shelter and safety, and I had no idea where they were or if they would be back. The Morgans, with whom we'd had a boundary dispute; Mary and Mollie Harper, the twins who played on the village streets in summer and whose blond hair was always tightly plaited; Eddie, whose second name I did not know but whose dog always crapped in the gutter and who played guitar in his garden in the summer; Lynda and Andy who had been so friendly when we first moved in and so excited when they found out that Carmel was pregnant; all those others who we had known and liked and disliked and not known but seen around; all of them, gone. The weight of it was terrible, too much to bear, and for a moment I felt it as an almost physical thing upon my shoulders driving me to my knees and crushing me. How easy to simply lie there in the road and wait for the end, however it came. How easy, and how relaxing, to let my responsibilities and my fears go and have them float free of me. How easy to simply give up.

And I could not. Those responsibilities were tied into me not for duty's sake but for love's; I had chosen them, not had them forced upon me, had made my promises to Carmel in front of my friends and family and God and in front of Carmel herself and I intended to keep them as far as I was able. I would provide what I could and do what I felt best for her, no matter how hard that might be. I could not shrug the terrible desolate weigh off; I would have to carry it.

Out past the homes, farmland began to creep to the edge of the road. The fields had an unkempt look to them, and in the first I came to were dead cows. They were bloated and smooth, their stench reaching me on the wind in little bursts as though their corpses were breathing. In the distance I could see a tractor, still and abandoned. Dark shapes littered the ground around it but I could not tell what they were and I did not want to go closer to identify them. I still had no plan, no clue as to what I should do. Breaking into the homes of my neighbours was beginning to appear to be the only way I might obtain food, but I still did not want to. It was only partly my old values, although the idea of trespassing into the private spaces of the people I had known was not a comfortable one. I was also aware that the houses in the village were small, would give me little room to manoeuvre if something happened whilst I was inside. There was the added problem of not knowing which house to go to; some might have people still in, or people who moved but were people no longer. And how did I know which house would have food left there? I could make noise breaking in somewhere, draw attention to myself, all for nothing. I had an inkling, then, of just how far we have civilised ourselves, how far this has led us from being able to act quickly, react to the unexpected. I had locked myself so firmly into routines and expectations that I could not cope with this, and I was useless and out of my depth.

The Lecture Hall.

It came to me in a flash, an almost literal burst of light in my brain that stopped me as I walked and made me laugh out loud in surprise and delight. The Lecture Hall would have food!

Although based in the adult college, The Lecture Hall has always been a well-kept local secret. It's a small restaurant business run by the catering students; it's not even a restaurant really, just a converted teaching room with about eight tables, connected to a small kitchen. The menu changed daily, advertised only by word of mouth, it served no alcohol and all the staff were students. Carmel and I discovered it not long after we moved to the village, and going there was always an adventure. The service and food could be excellent or terrible, the menu traditional or highly experimental, but the prices were always low and it was always fun, an experience to savour and to be shared. More importantly, it was not well known, and it might still have food in its cupboards and kitchens.

The college, and The Lecture Hall, were just out of the village. If I followed the road, it would take me perhaps half an hour to walk as the route curved widely and moved out to the coast before falling back in to the college grounds. On the other hand, I could take Cooper's Lane and reduce the time it took by half or more. Cooper's Lane is little more than an alleyway, overgrown at the sides with grasses and bushes and overhung by tree branches that form a canopy that lets only stained green light through. It runs all the way from the village to the coast and passes along the rear of the college, and in summer it is often used by the students as a place to drink or smoke and occasionally have sex. It is wide enough for bikes and prams but not cars, something which Carmel and I had thought would make it a nice place to take our new child.

It took only a minute or two to get to Cooper's Lane, but on peering down its entrance I halted. Its muted green and brown length was claustrophobic, with the trees at the side bunched in close and tight. I listened carefully, but could hear nothing. The longer route was safer, but it would take me so much more time. Cooper's Lane would be quicker but less safe, less certain. I deliberated for a moment, unsure and scared and then I thought about Carmel, alone and crying, and that decided me. I stepped into the lane and started along it. I shook as I jogged and saw shapes lurking in every patch of shadow between the trees about me. The dead man I had seen only a couple of nights ago had been heading in this general direction and I expected to see him lurch from out of the tall grass, one arm outstretched toward me, his feet still leaving dark smears across the mud and leaf mould that carpeted the ground. He did not appear, for which I am still grateful; I am truly not sure what I would have done. Turned and run, perhaps. Screamed, certainly, and tried to escape, but could I have fought him? I do not know. Bites and scratches from the dead were infectious, this I knew, and would kill and then make the infected person rise again. I had no weapons, no idea of how to fight something that was already dead and which could condemn me to something worse than death with even the slightest injury. And if I were injured but still escaped? Could I return to Carmel, knowing that I would soon die and become a danger to her? How could I, and yet how could I not? I would need to say my goodbyes, to tell her how much I loved her, and then I would need to leave before I became something else that would do her harm. My head throbbed with this as I moved swiftly along the lane, my arms and legs trembling with tension and my readiness to flee.

I smelled it before I saw it, drawing in the scent of something burned that was neither meat or wood but sharp and chemical. The lane kicked left and the air was heavy with the scent as I cautiously went around the corner and found the scooter. It was on its side and had been on fire sometime in the past few days. Scorch marks crawled over its fuel tank and handlebars, and the tyres had melted and puddled under the blackened wheel rims. It was lying on its side, blocking the path, and more black patches under it showed how the fire had tried to stalk away from it and failed because of the mud and damp. Long scars across the earth showed where it had skidded before coming to a stop. There was no sign of the rider.

No sign? That was not true. The bushes at the side of the scooter were broken and twisted and the ground around them churned and furrowed. Much as I did not want to, I could imagine the story of this place. Something, someone, had been dragged from the vehicle and into the undergrowth, and I had to step past the place where they had been dragged if I wanted to carry on. The dark opening into the bushes gaped at me like a shark's mouth and staring into its terrible throat, I was more afraid than I have ever been. The air was noiseless and still as I walked closer, balancing on the balls of my feet in my readiness to flee. I stepped over the scooter, stretching precariously to avoid using the surrounding branches for support and keeping myself high enough for the charred handlebar end not to poke into my groin, and it was as I was at my most unbalanced that the bushes shifted and I heard the groan.

I know I shrieked and fell, launching forward to land in a heap on the far side of the scooter, and I have the vaguest of memories of looking back over my shoulder as I fell in time to see the branches shift and buck. The noise came again, a groan that rode on a wave of fetid air that I could smell even above the burned fuel and metal, and then I was running down Cooper's Lane. It seemed to stretch for ever, shifting about me as I ran, an endless corridor of shadows and light, and from behind me there were more groans, fading, and just under them a ripping sound like old cloth being split by hand. I think I shrieked again as I ran; I do not clearly remember.

Cooper's Lane opens out into a wide, flat expanse of grass behind the college, a communal green that narrows and becomes a lane again at its far side. I tripped as I came to it and fell onto the ground, sky and earth flashing before my eyes as I rolled. I could hear nothing but my harsh breath and the pound of the blood in my ears, tasting the burn of vomit and bile that clutched at my throat. I dragged myself on, away from the lane's exit, twisting around onto my back and going crabwise so that I could see my pursuer. Eventually, I bumped into the college fence and could go no further. With my shoulders hunched against the unforgiving chainlink barrier and my feet scrabbling in the dirt, I stared back along the lane awaiting the dead.

They did not come. Perhaps it had been my imagination. More likely, I had disturbed something at its meal and it had chosen not to abandon the food it already had. I could not help but remember that awful ripping sound and wonder, what does old flesh sound like as it comes away from bone and muscle? What sound might the dead make as they ate, and when they warned others away from their food? What would it smell like? And I knew that I knew the answers to those questions, and wished I did not. I had torn my jacket and lost one of my bags in my flight, but it seemed hardly to matter. As I lay in the dirt with my back to the college and my face to the sky, I felt weak and helpless. I had run, exhausted myself with fear, and from what? Noise and shaking bushes? A dead person? My own wild imagination? This trip was becoming disastrous, and dropped bags and torn clothes seemed the least of my worries.

Eventually I got up. What else could I do? I had a wife, an unborn child who needed me even as the world crumbled further and further away from me.

Climbing the fence was easy; walking across the open playing fields to the college entrance was not. I felt open, naked and exposed to an attack that never came. The silence hugged me and the memory of Cooper's Lane already felt muffled as I forced open one of the college's windows. I was lucky in finding one that was already partly open, although it stuck as I pushed it and squealed fiercely as wood grated against wood. When I had it open far enough, I pulled myself in, realising as I did so how out of shape I had become and how hard my arms had to work just to lift my own weight through the open window. My legs waved in the air behind me and I did not stop feeling horribly exposed until I was in and lying on a classroom floor.

The walls were covered in posters and advertisements about courses and events and concerts that would now never take place. Desks had been pushed against the far wall and chairs stacked neatly beside them, and the dusty floor was unmarked by feet. I walked quickly and quietly out of the room and into the corridor, stopping to listen and hearing nothing. This new world is a place of quietitude, of vast and heavy noiselessness, and I have realised that I do not like it. The lack of sound feels tomb-like. Perhaps it is, and the entire world is one enormous tomb and we have simply not realised that we are dead and move through habit. I do not know; I only know that the college echoed to the sounds of my movement and to no other noise and I saw no signs of life as I passed through its dim corridors. Here and there were signs that people had passed before me, however. Papers were scattered in front of the administration offices, their surfaces dark with footmarks, and some of the doors were open and swinging, revealing empty rooms behind. Once, I found the remains of a fire and empty tins of food, their bases burned black and charred. I hoped that those who had come before me had not known about or found the Lecture Hall. It was selfish, but I was starting to understand that selfishness was the only way we might survive.

The Lecture Hall is on the second floor of the college, in an annexe above the main cafeteria. Like the rest of the college, it was deserted, but a solitary set of tracks across the floor showed me that someone else had been here in the past few weeks. One of the tables had been overturned and there was a grimy handprint in the centre of the frosted glass window set into the door. I wished I had a weapon as I went in, and just as quickly realised that I would have no idea how to use one. Inside, I looked sadly at the decor and the board on the wall, blank except for the word *Menu*. Carmel and I had talked about children here; I had learned of our child's existence in this room.

Entrance into the kitchen is through a double set of swinging doors, which were closed. They have porthole windows at head height, and peering through the windows showed me a deserted space, the shining surfaces empty. I entered cautiously. Here, there were no signs of disorder at all. Pans swung from hooks above the surfaces, knives stood sentinel in their blocks, cupboard doors and drawers were closed. Faint scuff marks across the floor showed where someone had crossed to the walk-in cupboard, but the scuffs themselves were already dusting over. Whoever had been here, it had been a while ago.

The food store had a solid door, with a handle that operated a latching mechanism and that I had to pull hard to get open. I pushed at the door, letting it swing silently in, and choked on the smell that came out; a rank, rotting odour that coated my teeth and slipped into my throat. Holding the door open, I leaned back and choked on the smell, which felt like a physical thing in my mouth. I spat and wafted the door, hoping to shift some of the old air from inside the room. Something had gone off in there, rotting quietly to itself and filling the air with its stink. Even as I wafted the door, however, I could see through the stench to the room beyond.

It was bigger than it appeared to be from the outside, probably two or three rooms knocked into one, and it was full of high shelf units in rows running away from the door to the far wall. And they gleamed with food! Cans, bottles, jars, packets, even the few shelves I could see were full. Forgetting the smell, I stepped inside, unslinging the remaining bag from my shoulder as I went. I think I may have wept just a little, and I know I salivated. I wandered down a dark aisle, trying to decide what to take. It was overwhelming, as if there was almost too much choice. Carmel liked vegetables, and they were healthy, so I put several large cans of peas and sweetcorn into the bag, along with packets of dried sauces that simply needed water adding to them. Cans of meatballs followed, and vacuum packs of scallops that I found on a low shelf. Bottled water followed and the bag started to feel heavy. Crouching to see what else was there, I realised that I could see through the shelves to the next aisle, and was trying to work out what food the farther shelves held when something moved and I heard a sound like air wheezing from old pipes.

I lurched back from the shelf, dropping the bag with a clatter. The sound immediately changed in pitch, became more urgent, and the shadows in the far aisle bent again, moved in a shuffle. I bit, clenching, onto a scream and backed away, bumping into the shelf behind me. Cans tumbled, scattering across the floor and under the nearby shelves. Some banged up against the moving shadows, and the sound changed again. There was a bang as something thudded into a shelf and more things fell, a rain of food that broke and spattered around what I could now see were dirty shoes, laces trailing, and streaked jeans. There was another wheezing groan and the shelves shook again. More cans and jars came down and then the feet were moving, heading back to the end of the aisle and to the door.

I ran.

All I could think was to get out before the dead person got between me and the exit. I tripped as I ran, staggering over a can or bottle of something and having to use the wall as a support, and I caught a glimpse of something as I burst out from the aisle and made for the door. It had swung shut whilst I had been inside and I hit it hard, yanking it towards me and scrabbling at it to open quick, open *faster*. When there was enough gap, I jumped through into the kitchen, glancing over my shoulder as I did so; something hunched and clawing and was close to me, its ragged dewlap fingers waving inches from my face and beyond that, its brown face slipping away from its skull like melting cheese. The smell was almost unbearable, a rolling and clinging thing that came ahead of it and clutched at me, wrapping itself around my head like a muslin cloth. The thing groaned as I looked at it and brown flecks leapt from its mouth like burned-out fireflies. I shrieked and dodged its grasp, pulling the door shut behind me as I went and falling to the floor of the kitchen and crying.

It must have only taken me seconds to get out from the food store but in my memory it has stretched out to last for minutes, a great swathe of fractured and uneven time, of falling cans and wobbling shelves and my own harsh breath and the weary, furied exhalations of the thing in the other aisle. I wonder how much I aged in those seconds; years perhaps. Months, certainly.

The thing in the cupboard was desperate, and the sounds of ferocious yowling came from the other side of the door, making the wood shake in the frame as it crashed against it. Looking around, I could see nothing to use to secure the door. It crashed again and again, howls coming with the crashes. It was like nothing I had heard before, not even animal in its desperation but more basic and primal. Another crash and the sound of scratching, of fingers dragging against the smooth wood of the door's surface. The handle began to rattle back and forth, jerking and banging, the latch opening and closing. It would only take the thing to pull the handle and hit the door at the same time for it to open, I realised. I stepped toward the door, half considering holding it shut but then saw how stupid that would be. At some point I would have to let go, and the thing on the other side would not quit. Instead, I turned and ran.

I had left the bag behind but by then it was too late. I was running and could not stop. Suddenly, this world was too threatening and I wanted to be home, to be with Carmel and my growing child, to hold her in my arms and be held, and to be told that everything was going to be alright even if it was not. I took the long route back, staying in the centre of the deserted road and jogging as fast as I could manage. I passed more farmland, with its dead cows and unkempt crops, and then houses as hollow and dead as any wandering corpse. As I ran, I thought about Carmel, about me, about what we would have to do to survive. I imagined long winters scraping though the dirt trying to grow food, or searching cold and dark houses, ever wary of attack. I tried to imagine helping Carmel to give birth without help, about what would happen if anything went wrong. I knew nothing about healthcare, nothing about cultivating crops or making things; I had spent my life buying what I needed and discarding it when its use to me was over, always trusting that somebody else could produce and I need only consume and I knew no other way to be. I was worse than a child, who might at least have the imagination to choose another course of action or who might overcome their fear to actually achieve something, but I was an adult with the wrong sort of learning and not enough bravery. I was out of ideas and out of courage.

I stopped in the shelter of the trees at the bottom of the garden before I went into my home, simply looking. I saw how the house looked, how it already seemed to be sagging and boneless, and I did not even have the energy to cry. My legs and arms trembled from running and from the sour tang of old fear and I thought about what this place had meant; safety, warmth, a refuge. I thought about the promises I had made, when the world had been a different place and when I had been a different person, and I wondered, how could I hope to keep them now? I wondered how I was supposed to love and protect Carmel when even obtaining food, previously such a simple thing, was now so fraught with danger and had proved ultimately impossible. Would it always be like this? Each step I took was a step further away from the simplicity of the life I had known, had understood, and into a life I could not make fit together nor fit myself or Carmel into. It was not simply a question of loss, of readjustment; I felt a terrible sense of dislocation and of random, untethered movement over which I had lost all control and had no hope of ever regaining any.

Carmel and I both cried when I returned home, and held each other for a long time. I lied about my trip, told her it had been okay although I think she could tell that I wasn't telling the truth. When she asked what we were to do, I reassured her that things would be fine, that I would return to the college and get food when I was more prepared. She looked at me when I said that, and the trust in her eyes was almost too much to bear. How could I tell her the reality? Later, we ate what little food we had left and I got water from the butt in the garden and drank it as though it were wine, clinking our glasses together and toasting each other and our love. I encouraged her to eat all her food, telling her she needed to stay healthy for her and the baby. In amongst the canned food, she could not taste the powdered sleeping pills and swallowed them down without knowing; she is sleeping now. Her face is peaceful, resting and relaxed and secure in the knowledge that I will keep my promise and look after her, and I will. This silent, stalking world is not a place to live: it will not hurt the woman that I love, and it will not get the opportunity to hurt the child that I never had a chance to know but that I loved anyway. This last thing I can do for my wife and child; I can ensure that they do not wake. I can ensure that neither comes back in any form.

|Old Man's Pantry|

Cally had read near all of it; all the books and paragraphs and monographs about running. Written by runners, ex-runners, coaches, journalists, by those who knew about running and those who did not, and none of them had ever got it quite right. None of them had ever found the words to describe the beauty, the simplicity of the act of running and what it felt like. Cally sympathised, because he felt it and could not find the right words either; how, when you find the right *rhythm* and *pace*, it felt as though the mind actually separated from the body, leaving the body to act and react on its own. In running, the mind had total, unencumbered freedom. All of the problems in Cally's adult life had been solved when running, his mind free to tease and poke and prod and yank at them until they got moulded and reshaped into a solution. When Cally ran, his problems fell behind him like exhausted dogs.

People thought that Old Man's Pantry was the great cave that opened out onto the lower slopes of the West Fell, and that it got its name from the Burney family who, from the 1780s until the 1960s, had owned Neb Farm and who had used the cave for storing meat. As usual, Cally had found, most people were wrong. Old Man's Pantry was not just the cave, but also the network of paths and tracks that led into and out of the cave, and its name came not from the Burneys but from a time before Neb Farm had even existed and when the Burneys were still labourers in bondage to the other farmers scattered across the Lake District. Old Man's Pantry was named for Timid Dill, and Cally passed Timid Dill's places every time he ran.

It had been a bad day at work. Cally had felt trapped in the office and his clothes had chafed at his skin. It was a relief to return to his tiny cottage, its walls clustered with books, where he gratefully stripped and pulled on his loose, comfortable jogging pants and jacket. He left his work clothes on the floor; Ingrid had hated it when he did that, so now it was one of life's little pleasures. Ingrid was gone, and Cally did not miss her.

Once out of the cottage, Cally could feel the miseries of the day lift from him. He started to run, his long legs sweeping the landscape up easily and scattering it behind him. From his home on the outskirts of the village, he approached the gentle slopes at West Fell's base and loped past the cave entrance, where Timid Dill had stored the carcasses of his kills; sheep, deer, rabbits and people. His breathing was easy, finding a relaxed rhythm that could take him miles. His muscles unknotted, limbering and warming, and increased his stride length, speeding up as he did so. Here it came, the unthreading of his mind from his body, the freeing of his thoughts. He considered work for a moment and then left it behind, dropping it at the start of the gentle valley made by Ripple Beck, whose waters Timid Dill had used to wash his food.

Paths and tracks drifted off from the valley, leading across open ground or through copses. Cally sometimes ran these paths, enjoying the springy feel of the soft earth beneath his feet. They were gentle routes, with few challenges, that crossed soft slopes. The copses meant that running the tracks alternated between light and shade, warmth and coolness, a massage to his body as he ran. In one of these copses were the ruins of a hut; Timid Dill's home, so the legend had it. Cally liked the hut, liked the way it crouched in amongst the trees and made no effort to smile at him as he passed. Just a hut, its roof collapsed and three of its walls long gone, the fourth crumbled and grey with age. Timid Dill had lived there, an unassuming, solitary man who avoided company.

Cally stayed with the path alongside Ripple Beck. It was harder going, steeper than the others and more uneven. He ran it when he needed exertion, needed to sweat the tension out from his muscles like a toxin. Above him, West Fell stood, unassailable and remote. Not the district's highest hill, nor its most arduous to climb, its sides were marked by the traceries of distant paths and tracks, but even these petered out as its grey and green sides became too steep for all but the most seasoned walker. Cally, who did not like to walk, had never been to its summit. He stayed, instead, in the maze of paths below, and the highest place he marked as his own was Dill's Chop.

Dill's Chop was a slice cut into one of West Fell's middle flanks. Years of erosion had worn down the earth the same way they had worn down Timid Dill's stories, changing its shape into something new. A gorge, perhaps thirty feet deep, had formed, a stream spreading across its floor and its overhanging walls covered in scree and foliage. Cally liked running it, the mile or so from end to end testing his balance and stretching the muscles in his calves as he loped over the uneven floor and the slithering, sodden mud. There was little light in the Chop; the walls loomed over the path, casting ever-dancing shadows and reflections across the surface of the stream and reducing the sun to a strip above him, as though he were being swallowed by some great mouth and was looking out between lips that smacked above him. Dill's Chop, so the stories had it, was where Timid Dill had waited, motionless at its higher entrance, for passing travellers.

Cally ran the Chop, enjoying its solitude. Water dripped on him from the trees and shrubs above him, their roots clinging to the thin soil and steep walls. The air smelled of earth and grass and was filled with the sound of water. He muscles responded to the uneven ground, his lungs drawing in the damp air and his pores weeping sweat. He felt free. If Timid Dill *had* haunted the Chop, watching lonely travellers walk and selecting his victims from their number, then Cally thought he had picked a good place to do it; it was peaceful here, calming and relaxing. In the spring and summer months, the air drifted with petals and pollen and the smell of regeneration. In the autumn, leaves fell and in the winter the air cracked with cold. Cally preferred the autumn and winter to spring or summer; in the warmer seasons, the Chop could fill with walkers, families on day trips spoiling his solitude with noise and litter. In the damp of autumn and the chill of winter, no one came here, which was just how Cally liked it.

Someone was waiting for Cally at the top of the Chop.

At its height, the Chop's walls opened out. To Cally's right, they fell away, smoothing and becoming the gentle flank of West Fell's most popular slope, a grassy and gentle walk with fine views. On Cally's left, however, the wall became a series of jutting, saw-toothed plateaux, a series of ledges perhaps six or seven feet apart. The ledges were ragged things, covered in sparse foliage and debris. Stones littered their surfaces, along with litter and leaves and loose earth. They looked like giant footholds, cut carelessly into the side of the Fell that surrounded the natural clearing into which the Chop opened. There was a figure sat in one of the footholds.

Whoever it was, the sight of them made Cally start, and in starting he lost his rhythm and stumbled, falling to one knee with a jolt. The figure made no move to help as Cally stood, brushing the dirt from his leg and inspecting the graze that now lay across his kneecap. Blood flowed from it, thick strings amongst the sweat and hair. He looked up at the figure; they still had not moved.

"Hello," said Cally, loudly. The figure did not reply. Cally moved closer as he waited for a response, but none came. Close to, he saw that the figure was dressed in an odd assortment of clothes. Old trousers that were too short clad its legs, revealing pink shins and bare feet. Its shirt was rumpled, an old check thing that looked faded and worn. Despite the weather, it wore no coat. Cally was kept warm by his running, but the person on the ledge must be freezing; the wind and rain had been hard all day and had only recently relaxed their grip. It was perched on a scree slope, and its seat looked precarious. Shadows draped themselves around its shoulders and pooled around its feet. There was a gust of wind and the figure leaned forwards, and in that moment, Cally knew fear and shrieked at the figure's hideousness. Even at this distance, Cally saw that it had terrible deformities; its face was marked and ridged and discoloured.

Capering on the heels of Cally's shriek came understanding. It was a dummy, a joke, placed on the ledge to scare the unwary like himself. As it had become wet, leaves and dirt had stuck to its smooth face, making the ripples and lined flesh that Cally had first seen. He laughed, even as his heart raced from the fright. It was a good joke, really; a model of Timid Dill, staring out of his kingdom, on the lookout to stock his pantry. This had been his place, after all. This was where Timid Dill sat, in silent contemplation of the paths that lay on the slopes below. Actually, the joke became more accurate the more Cally thought of it. Timid Dill had been, according to the stories, terribly ugly and wore ragged garments stolen from his victims. He had stalked barefoot, the skin on his feet hardened by years of walking and running the paths of Old Man's Pantry. Cally grinned, and waved at the dummy, calling, "Goodbye, Timid, my man. I must be off now" like a gentleman taking leave of his friends. Cally was nothing if not polite. Turning, he fell back to his run.

Cally's normal route after running the Chop was to follow the curve of the hillside around before letting himself drop away into the tangle of paths that were wrapped around the lower slopes, picking at random the forks to take to take him home, and today was no different. With beautiful views to his side and the Chop to his back, he could relax, let his body greet this gentler run and thread his way down through the paths of Old Man's Pantry and to home. He jogged loosely for a minute, trying to find his rhythm again, letting his body regain the smooth interlock of legs and arms and balance and breath that had been interrupted by the sight of the figure, but it would not come. Something about the figure had disturbed him, and he stopped. Turning, he peered back up the slope to the Chop. He could just see the figure, still in the same position on the high ledge.

Of course it was in the same position. Why wouldn't it be?

In the falling dusk, details were dissolving into each other. Shadows crept around the clearing, seeping down into the Chop and swelling like bloating paper to absorb the ledges. As Cally watched, the figure suddenly lurched, rolled and dropped off the ledge, disappearing into the darkness of the ledge below. Another gust of wind, he thought, had caught it and dragged it from its seat. He stared hard at the place where the figure had fallen to, but could see little. Was that another movement in the shadow? Another wind, shifting the figure's arms or legs or head, flapping its ridiculous clothes? It had to be, of course. What else could it be? Only, if it was wind, why hadn't Cally felt it as well? He was only a couple of hundred yards away. Maybe it wasn't wind, maybe the figure had been balanced precariously, and Cally's appearance had been enough to upset its delicate balance. Whatever, he needed to run on. Darkness was coming, and running at night here was a shortcut to broken bones or twisted limbs. He turned again, set his face to the paths (already shaded grey by the growing dusk, picked out against the darker grass that waved gently at their sides) and his back to the figure, and started to run.

Cally was not imaginative, not at all, yet he could not help feel the figure stealthily uncoiling, stretching, dropping to the floor and creeping on silent feet after him. What was happening to him, to be spooked by such a silly thing? Yes, it had looked unpleasant, but he had seen unpleasant things before and had not reacted to them this way. He could not help it. Something about the figure bothered him; he felt exposed here on the path with it at his back. He had no cover, no protection. The day, rapidly turning to night, felt like a great breathing thing around him, its flanks wide and fluttering at its edges with things whose attention he did not want to attract.

In his breathing, he started to hear the almost silent whisper of another's inhalations, soft and measured. The sound of it was distant, somewhere behind him, and carried on the zephyrs that swept down the slope and twisted around his ankles and up his body like warming cats. It became louder, still quiet but clearer, a distinct *other* somewhere to his rear. Then, a beat to underpin the breath, he heard footsteps. They fell almost in time with his own. Grinning to himself, Cally relaxed; another runner, someone else striding the contours of West Fell, enjoying its solitude and beauty. And yet, there was something not quite right about the footsteps. They seemed too soft to be a runner, too light. His own feet made a solid connection with the earth, but these sounded as though they were only skimming its surface. Cally lengthened his stride, suddenly nervous, and the other's steps kept pace with him. Experimentally, he slowed. The person behind him slowed as well, but Cally had the impression that their stride had stayed longer. That they were gaining on him.

This is ridiculous! Cally told himself sharply. *It's another runner.* He stopped, pulling himself up into an unsteady halt, and turned. He expected to see another runner behind him, someone in shorts and garish shoes, perhaps, the advertising logos that cost so much blazoned across their feet or their vest, their hair weighed down by sweat. They would nod at Cally, the wordless greeting of those linked by a common interest, and pass in a swirl of moist air and active body odour.

There was no one there.

The Chop was lost in a clot of darkness now, and the hillside below it painted in shades of liminal browns and dying yellows through which the path stretched like cord. The pale dusk, stretched and softened by the dropping sun, crept across the earth with apologetic grace. The sound of the breathing and footsteps had stopped and apart from the suck of his own breath and crunch of his heartbeat in his ears, Cally could hear nothing. The only movement was the sparse grass, waving in a breeze that was rapidly chilling the sweat on Cally's skin. He grinned at his own anxieties, amused at himself for being spooked by a dummy on a ledge. So much for hard-headed rationality, he told himself, and turned again to his run.

Within steps, the sounds of the other runner were back. This time, they were no longer behind him but to his side, as though whoever it was had used the short pause in Cally's run to move up alongside him. Darting glances left and right, he tried to see his companion. Still, he saw no one. The steps had taken on a stealthier tone, their sound so light now as to be almost non-existent, the rapid caress of feet that knew the ground, knew where to land for minimum impact and maximum speed. The breathing remained light, untroubled by the exertion. Cally's own lungs sounded clumsy in comparison, great sucking wounds in the tranquillity of the hillside. He desperately tried to ignore the other, whoever it might be, tried to concentrate on his own pace and step, but his normal ability to companionably ignore other runners had vanished. His attention repeatedly shifted back to the unseen runner, to the sound of steps and breath that was light and hard to pinpoint. Something about the sounds made him feel more than uncomfortable, made him feel… what? What was it about them? And then, like a twisting lens bringing something into focus, he realised what was.

Cally felt hunted.

He had an image of something stealthy, speedy, appearing at his side, its claws and teeth and eyes ghostly white in the thickening half-light, and him falling beneath it. Without intending to, he sped up, moving from a loose jog to a more controlled run. Now, the run was no longer a way of relaxing, it had a purpose. Here on the hillside he felt exposed, but perhaps half a mile ahead the path descended, splitting, into valleys and gulleys that had overhanging bushes, steep sides and offered more protection. Up here, Cally felt naked; down there, he might be safer.

As he ran, Cally could not help but see the feet in his mind. The way they hit the earth, the sound they made, was so different from anything else he'd heard that he knew that they were bare. No running shoes clad them, no rubber soles sat between them and the ground; he saw skin that was thickened yet flexible, cleaving itself to the roughened path.

Toes that were crusted with dirt ended the feet, with hair clinging to their tops and great, cracked nails like claws that clicked against the loose pebbles and sliced into the dust. Predator's feet. Predator's feet, and he was their prey. But above the feet, who? What person, lost in the gloom around him, was loping at his side? First one side and then the other, the sound of those footfalls circled him as he ran, his body straining and his legs pushing against his flesh's inertia

The open hillside was giving way now, flattening slightly and allowing taller plants to grow. Trees dotted the sides of the path, and between them clusters of bushes and rocks grew. The path began to thread its way past the outcrops, nudging the trees so that the open night sky above Cally was broken into sections by branches and leaves. He had hoped the appearance of the trees would provide him with cover, make him feel safer, but it did not; now, as he ran, he could *see* something darting from tree to tree, always at the periphery of his vision, always just concealed by whatever lay to his side. Something dark, but that gave itself away with rapid, fluid movements and the yellowed ebony glint of eyes and teeth and nails, and whose clothes flapped around it like the wings of some terrible bird of prey. Cally ran, and something ran with him.

On the lower slopes of West Fell, the path became more twisted, splitting and writhing down through wooded areas, slipping along the base of gullies and across the ridges and dips that made up the land above his home. Home. Cally's stride shortened as he reached the edge of the network of paths and trails. The ground here was more uneven, the earth rippled and split by tree roots and water trails and rocks. Still moving fast, Cally forced his ankles to loosen, *made* his feet land more softly. To trip here would be dangerous; the ground alone could cause him injury, and whoever was tracking him was still there, and God only knew what they wanted or would do if they caught him. Cally could hear their breath, still easy and loose, but now it was accompanied by something else. A smell drifted in the air, something dank and ripe with the odours of old, spoiled meat and flesh that had grown filthy with neglect. It was only a hint of a smell, waxing and waning as he ran, but it was at the same time stronger than the surrounding scents of the earth and the trees. It made Cally gag and he spat as he ran, hoping to clear the taste from his mouth and nose.

As the path dropped into a gully, the sides steep and wooded, the sound of footsteps and breathing retreated and Cally thought for a wonderful moment that whoever it was had given up, but they had not. He caught a glimpse of them, silhouetted against the sky. They were running along one of the gully's uppermost edges, perhaps eight feet or less above but still parallel to him. Christ, they must be confident, thought Cally. The ground up there was uneven, buckled and complicated. Trees, both living and fallen, blocked the way. And yet, whoever it was ran it with apparent ease, keeping pace with Cally. They must know the area, understand the ground, he thought, and ran faster.

There was a heavy crash behind him and something came down the slope of the gully wall. For a moment, Cally knew absolute fear; his lungs locked and his legs tensed, making him stumble. The smell grew stronger, flowing over his shoulders and draping his skin like rain. There was the rustle of cloth, so close he could touch it, and then something touched *him*, something that caressed the skin on the back of his neck and felt hard and moist and repugnant. He screamed then, forcing his struggling legs to increase their pace, and bent his head forward to get it out of the reach of whoever was behind him. Gradually, the smell receded and the touch was not repeated. He risked flicking a look over his shoulder, and saw only a flap of darkness bounding up the side of the gully. His pursuer had come down to the gully floor behind him, touched him and had now gone up the opposite side of the path, was again above him and running with him. They were playing with him. Cally understood it clearly. Whoever it was had no trouble keeping up with him, could catch him at any time.

As the paths branched and joined around him, Cally tried to think ahead. There had to be a place where he could gain some ground, put some distance between him and the person on the ridge. Ahead, the ground around the paths grew even more rocky and denser with trees and bushes. He ran, letting his feet find the safest route, taking this fork and then that one, always aiming down so that home came closer and closer. The branches overhead were interlocked, forming a cathedral arch above him that reflected and refracted the noise of his pursuer into something that surrounded him, darting in from all sides at once. As he ran, lower limbs from the trees and bushes whipped at his arms and legs. Sweat rolled down his skin, gathering in the small of his back and dripping from his brows into his eyes. His breath gasped and his lungs strained on every in- and exhalation. His pursuer's breathing seemed as relaxed as ever, but possibly fainter. Was he increasing the distance between them, Cally wondered? Was whoever it was finally struggling with the uneven terrain and constant dodging of the trees and bushes? Was he finally outrunning his unseen pursuer?

The sounds from around him grew fainter, overtaken by the ragged whistle of his own breathing. He had pushed himself, was still pushing himself, far harder than on a normal run, but on normal runs he had never before been chased. Waves of tension pain rode up his body from his legs; his knees jolted when his feet met the ground. His lungs felt as though bands had been wrapped around them, stopping enough air getting in, but he could not stop now. The sounds of his pursuer had grown fainter still, dropping back into the general susurrus of the night. Cally dared not slow down, but he did allow himself a smile as he ran. Home was only a couple of miles away now, and he began to hope that he would arrive there without more incident.

The path's irregular route, with its kinks and uneven ripples of earth, began to smooth. Connector paths joined and were absorbed from either side of Cally, and he looked along each tributary nervously, but saw and heard nothing. The path itself grew wider as it took in the other tracks, and he stayed in its centre so that an attacker, if they came, would not be able to reach him from fringe but would need to come out into the open. He risked slowing a little, taking deeper breaths to stave off muscle cramps and exhaustion. He did not relax; there would be time for that later, at home. Time for a soak in the bath, time for rest, time to laugh about this whole ridiculous incident. Now, however, it was still time to run.

By the time he reached the clearing and Timid Dill's hut, Cally's confidence was higher yet. He had heard no sounds of pursuit for minutes now, no breathing or footfalls, no (oh, thank the Lord!) touches on the back of his neck that slipped across his sweating skin like old meat. The clearing marked the beginning of what he thought of as the 'home straight': a clear run down past the entrance to the cave system and, beyond that, to his house and its secure, thick walls. The clearing itself was large, hemmed in by trees and ringed with picnic benches and more paths. It acted as the start of the various walking routes across West Fell's flanks, and the tourists loved it because of the hut. Cally looked at the remains as he ran past, and looking caused the breath to seize in him, knocked his rhythm and made him clench his fists reflexively.

Someone was leaning nonchalantly against the hut's only wall.

The figure was wreathed in shadow. Cally had a glimpse of someone short and squat, their entire body wrapped in dark clothes, and then the figure was moving. Something flapped around it and Cally had a momentary glimpse of a face, something distorted and terrible. Its arms came up, the hands twisted and ending in nails that were crusted with dark scurf that Cally did not want to identify. There was a smell, rank and old, that leapt across the gap between the two of them, and then the figure itself was so much closer to him, seeming not to move yet moving so awfully fast and then Cally was running again, a headlong dash of terror.

By design and inclination, Cally was not a sprinter. Long and lean, his flesh preferred a more constant exertion, an accumulated energy loss that allowed him time to settle his stresses and impose order on his thoughts. Sprinting was simply another way of creating pressure, of forcing his musculature and mind into newly stressful situations. It was a skill, he knew; it was simply one he had never had the urge to learn. Only now, he wished he had taken the time, because sprinting felt as though it was the only thing that could save his life. He knew that it was not far behind him, whatever *it* was. He could hear the flap of its loose clothes, the dry whisper of hard-soled feet against the earth, smell the warm musk of a body that was not truly exerting itself yet. Waves of nausea flooded through Cally, as sweat that felt both hot and cold rolled across his skin. His skin prickled as he felt, imagined, *felt* that touch again, the moist slither of something old and rotten over his neck and up into his hair. The nausea seemed to stretch down into his legs, into the very muscles and bones that drove him on, Spittle flew from his lips, clinging to his chin and spattering down the front of his running vest where it was lost in the soaked patches of sweat that gathered there. His feet, normally so sure, found every crevasse and jutting root, threatened with every step to loose their grip on the fragile skin of the earth, let him tumble and leave him prone and helpless to attack, but each time they somehow held on, carried on going.

His pursuer was playing with him. He ran alongside Cally for a moment or two, so that Cally could see him in his peripheral vision. The brief image was of something swift, wrapped in flailing ends and twisted rags but with, at its centre, a savage, solid vitality. Then it dropped back, crossing the path behind Cally and appearing on his other side, this time further from him. Cally dared a fleeting look; the grotesque face, its rippled and mottled skin like damp sacking, was turned towards him, and it was smiling. Yellowing teeth set in a mouth that twisted into a leer filled his vision. Cally tried not to scream, afraid that he would start and be unable to stop, that the scream itself would unbalance him. His own mouth buckled under the pressure of keeping his terror in and he leered back at the thing, man or beast, that even then was dropping away, easing back behind him again. With it gone from his vision, Cally found himself even more scared and he ran, ran, and ran.

Stumbled.

Fell, his arms pinwheeling and his mind yowling its terror as he went, a wordless shriek that might have been in his mind or might have been out loud. Cally sprawled hard into the rocky path, and had chance to think, *But it'll catch me!* before a bolt, a spastic clench, of pain leapt from his ankle to envelop his entire body. It was so strong that it took his breath away, and even the fear was swallowed by it. He felt rather than heard a wrenching crack, somewhere in the pain, felt something give in his leg. His hands slapped hard against the earth and dirt sprayed up into his mouth and cracked against his teeth. He spat in misery, fear returning as the thought *It'll catch me!* occurred again. He tried to get up, but his leg screamed at him once more and he collapsed, his body tensing in preparation for the attack.

It did not come. Weeping in pain, Cally rolled over onto his back and looked around. To his side, the last slope of Eel Beck rolled away from and past his feet, the last fringe of trees waved at him gently. He had an awful feeling that they were waving him goodbye, and in their languid gesture he saw mourning and misery. There was no sign of his pursuer. Cally gritted his teeth in anger and agony, unsure as to whether his pursuer's absence was worse that its presence. This game it was playing was a torture in some ways worse that the pain that emanated from his ankle in waves of cold sweat. Where *was* he, this pursuer who had chased him, caused him to run and fall? Where?

There was a crack from in the trees, the sound of someone treading on a branch or fallen twig. Cally had the horrible feeling it was a deliberate act, an announcement and a message and a thing to cause fear all in one. Here I am, it said. I haven't gone away and you are still at risk. Cally gasped and tried to sit up, to see better. There was another crack, from a different place among the trees. It was moving, edging around him in a wide circle. Another crack, from the edge of the trees at the slope, and then from somewhere lower than Cally could see, the deliberate press of steps across the earth. Cally twisted, listening as the footsteps carried on past him and circled the clearing, until he was looking away from the trees and behind him. Looking at the cave.

As soon as he saw it, Cally saw somewhere he could hide. The cave, incorrectly called Old Man's Pantry by the tourists that flocked here in the good weather, was large and, out of season, dark inside. He started to crawl towards it, aware of how exposed his back was, of how helpless he was. If he could only get inside, he could huddle into a corner and wait. Someone would come; it was no longer tourist season, but the cave and the beauty of Eel Beck still attracted visitors. Even the locals came here. Dogwalkers, other runners, someone would come. His leg bumped and jolted as he crawled and he had to clench his mouth to trap the screams inside. He listened for the other person on the hillside with him, but they had fallen silent. The only sounds were the dragging noises as he pulled himself to the cave and the ragged whoop of his breathing. Stones and grit drove under his nails and scored across his naked legs, pushing past the tops of his running shoes and scratching his knees and ankles. Whatever else happened, he was going to look a mess when he got home, he thought ruefully, and then realised how incongruously normal that thought was. *When* he got home. *When.*

When.

The opening to the cave was relatively small compared to its size, and Cally had to drag himself up a low lip to get inside. The steps down to the cave's floor, new and brightly painted wood, dug into his ribs as he slipped down them and he risked pulling himself upright using the wooden handrest at their side. Fresh pain flared from his leg, and he had to stop for a minute, staring miserably over his shoulder. The final weep of daylight was a pale circle behind him, its edges rough from the cave's entrance. He expected to see something silhouetted there, but nothing was; instead, there was a noise, a crunch of gravel and loose stone. Someone was just outside the cave's entrance. Cally half fell, half hopped down the remaining steps, lurching unsteadily into the dark below. Immediately at the bottom of the stairs, he hobbled off the wide, duckboard pathway and into the forest of stalactites and stalagmites that grew in the shadows.

The space between the spires and tendrils of rock was thin and painful, sharp with edges and points. Cally tried to remain silent as he was poked and gouged, moving through the maze to find somewhere he could hide. He knew that he was making noises, shuffling and gasping, but could not help himself. There was little light here, and his fear and pain made him clumsy and desperate. Turning, he tried to back into the space available so that he could keep watching the entrance. The patch of light, now a dim oval hanging in the air, was growing harder and harder to see. He wondered if was going to have to hide all night, and knew that he was. There! A dark shape, indistinct, had flitted across the opening. Had it come in? Cally held his breath, listening carefully. A sound came to him, the light pad of feet on the wooden steps, the sound made echoey and hollow by the space beneath the risers. With this noise was something new; the chitinous clicks of nail or bone on the ground, its sound hard and threatening. The walker was breathing slowly, as though smelling the air. Cally supposed he must stink, of fresh sweat and blood, and he pushed himself further back through the narrowing spaces and crouched into a ball.

The cave was wrong. It came to him suddenly, a realisation that this place was not as it should be. It was a tourist attraction, cleaned regularly and yet now it smelled bad. It was not simply his own odour, either; the smell was rank and heavy, like stagnant water and meat gone to spoil. It was similar to the odour he had smelled before from his pursuer, but much worse. In the cave, it was sour and trapped. Cally tried to breathe through his mouth but it even had a taste, like bad milk or the sweet, sickening cling of long-turned meat. He tried to block it out, but it clung to his skin and dripped into his sweat.

There was another sound, of feet treading off the wooden boards of the path. One of the metal chains that hung as a barrier to inquisitive tourists rattled and clinked, and Cally thought it had been moved deliberately to make the noise. He huddled smaller, not caring now that the rough edge of the rock around him was rasping at his skin and licking at the blood that it drew forth.

There was another clinking sound, this one above him.

Cally looked up, peering into the shadows that swept around the cave's roof and walls, and at first could see nothing. Then, on the walls behind him, he began to make out uneven shapes. Some glinted in the almost-dark, some spun lazily, disturbed by an unfelt breeze. There were hooks attached to the walls, and hanging from the ceiling by short chains, and what hung from the hooks Cally recognised but refused to accept. How could he? It was impossible, an echo of a myth that had been real three centuries ago but was no more than a campfire story now. What hung on those hooks, the hooks themselves, was not, *could not*, be real. Only, he could see them, see the impossible and smell its reality.

There was a subtle sound, of someone slipping through the outer edge of the stalactite and stalagmite forest. Cally braced himself; Timid Dill was coming.

|Scucca|

Although I was only young when my uncle David discovered taxidermy, I had known him long enough to think that it would be the same as many of his other hobbies; he would enthuse about it for perhaps three months, buy the best equipment possible and then, gradually, lose interest and find something else to replace it with. This habit was well established and I loved him for it, as his house was always crammed with odd items, and visiting him was like entering a magical kingdom, full of mysterious treasures. I assumed that the taxidermy material (the coils of metal, the drawers of eyes, pins, pipes and tubes) would soon join them. I was wrong.

Uncle David became excellent at taxidermy, and his initial passion for it did not abate. For several Christmases and birthdays afterwards, members of the family were given exquisitely stuffed and mounted creatures. I was presented with a grass snake coiled around a rock, my mother and father a pair of lovebirds, and my sister a rabbit whose glassy-eyed stare of terror caused her to have nightmares for weeks. After this, my father had a quiet word with his younger brother and the gifts stopped. I know that my uncle was a little hurt that we did not share his enthusiasm, but he accepted my father's request with good grace and thereafter, taxidermy became an essentially private concern.

I visited Uncle David at least once a month, and I remember those times with joy. My father would deliver me to his home, huddled against the flat expanse of the fens near the village of Hexhall, after school on a Friday and pick me up again on Sunday afternoon. These weekends were a delight; I would sit and listen as Uncle David talked about subjects as varied and as exotic as I could imagine. Often, I would perch on a high stool in the corner of the workshop as Uncle David pored over his latest creature, his eyes made huge by magnifying lenses and his fingers deftly pinning and stitching and posing. It was during these times that I came to understand his other great passion; storytelling. Uncle David was a born teller of tales, and under his tongue even the driest of anecdotes came alive.

Sometimes, Uncle David would look at me over the width of his workbench with the smell of kapok and leather and chemicals in the air and with his eyes seeming to bulge behind the goggles, and he would tell me about things that made my skin tingle and my imagination fire. About the De Montaignes, mentioned in the Domesday book, who owned the land around Hexhall from the middle ages until the late eighteenth century; about Isaiah Swales, an outsider who won the land from the last of the De Montaignes in a disputed game of chance; about the local church, built from Lake District stone, and about the village itself, of the people who had lived there, and their descendants who lived there still.

I came to realise that what my uncle loved more than any other aspect of the history he collected was the merging of fact and myth, how actual events became mythologized and how myths took on the currency of reality. Over my years of visiting, he told me about Isaiah Swales' leaving of the Lake District, to escape gambling debts, and arrival in the fens; about how the Swales eventually lost the land he had won, this time to the distaff side of the De Montaignes, the Tillers, who were in league with the Devil; how old mother Lamey was tried as a witch but acquitted because she put a curse on the presiding judge, and how the same Mother Lamey taught the Tillers the trick of turning themselves into great black hounds after death so that they could remain on earth to protect their family and its properties, and how the Tillers died out finally, leaving a legacy of muttered stories and little else. These were great times for me, when I could lose myself in the tales that Uncle David spun, sheltering from the reality of my life outside, from its mundanity and tedium.

My visits to David remained a regular occurrence as I grew older. He always welcomed me in his fussy, warm way, and then regaled me with his latest finds, describing stuffing a lamb born with six legs or recounting the latest historical tale he had found (how the first vicar in Hexhall's church had liked a secret drink, or how Joshua Swales had been forced to sell the land to the Tillers after he was driven into the sea by a great black dog that would not let him come ashore until he shouted his promise to sell so loud that his throat was sore for days afterwards). His taxidermy grew infrequent, not through disinterest but through lack of new creatures to work on. He had practiced on and perfected most of the creatures indigenous to the area, and quite a few not; deformed creatures bought from the local farmers; snakes, brought in by contacts in the shipping industry; monkeys and, once, a wolf brought down specially from Scotland. It was while he worked on the wolf that he talked to me about his ambitions.

"Ah, Terence," he said, "There are so many creatures that I'll never get to work upon. Elephants! Now there would be a challenge! Think of how much wire and stuffing you'd need, how much time it would take! Or a crocodile, perhaps, its jaws open wide and ready to eat you!" His eyes gleamed as he spoke, a smile playing across his plump face. "Or one of the Fens' hounds," he said, and then seeing my expression of disbelief, hurried on, "oh, I don't mean those evil spirits, the Tillers given flesh and form, no, I mean the real things."

"What 'real things'," I asked, wondering if this was another of David's near-fictions.

"The Fens' hounds," he said in a put-on, schoolmarmish voice, "are a pack of huge black dogs that roam the land around here. They've been here for generations. And before you say it, oh doubting Terence, they aren't simply a folk tale. I've found references to them in the local papers a hundred years ago. They're just big, wild dogs, but in a landscape this empty, the unexpected tends to be made bigger than it actually is. Generally, they stay away from man, although they sometimes scare some poor shepherd in the middle of the night or put the wind up some lonely traveller on one of the paths between the villages. Sometimes, in particularly bad winters, they can come in close to the inhabited areas and may eat livestock, but most of the time, they keep themselves to themselves. They're almost certainly the descendents of escaped hunting dogs, and it's probably where the Tiller's Black Dog legends started. It would be exciting to see one, don't you think?" I did not reply.

And so life went, a predictable waltz that was neither overly exciting nor taxing, until one bitterly cold February. I visited David as arranged, having not seen him since the dawn of the New Year when we had spent a pleasurable week together. When I had left him last, he had been as he ever was; cheerful, running to fat and going grey. When he met me at his door that day, however, he had changed. He had lost weight, his clothes hung from his frame like sacking and his skin, previously so colourful and ruddy, was now pale. Darkened flesh that spoke of little sleep accreted below his eyes. His hair was greyer still and unwashed, lying in drab waves across his scalp. He looked ill and exhausted, but ignored my expressions of concern, waving his hand in the air as though brushing them away.

"Come in, come in," he said, ushering me into the lounge where a large fire burned in the hearth. "Don't worry about me, I'm fine. I've been working on my latest piece and it's taken me longer than I anticipated it would. There have been some unexpected delays, but it's almost finished. I'll show it you after supper, if you like?"

Supper was an odd affair. We ate, as ever, sat on either side of the lounge hearth. The food was pie in rich gravy and whilst I enjoyed it, David clearly did not. He seemed nervous and continually looked at the large windows; or rather, he looked through them, for he had not drawn the curtains, to the snow-crusted Fens beyond. When a knot popped on the fire, he started visibly. He ate little, toying with the food and pushing it around his plate instead. Finally, when I had finished my food, he practically dragged me through the house to his workshop.

Arriving at the workshop, Uncle David opened the door by throwing it wide, a surprisingly dramatic gesture for him. Peering into the gloom beyond him, I could make little out. Then, I saw a gleam of terrible white teeth and the glinting eye of some great creature and I shrieked without thinking.

"Now, now, Terence," said David, moving into the room and lighting a lantern. "It's only Sweet William."

"Sweet William?" I asked in astonishment. Now David had let light into the room, I could see that the teeth and eyes belonged to a huge dog, dead and mounted onto a large wooden plinth. Walking closer to it, I saw a card attached to the plinth. In my uncle's neat hand, it read, 'Fens' Hound: Shot on the railway track between Hexhall and Whinney'. Looking again at the huge creature, I was struck by the art with which my uncle had mounted it. Its coat was slick and gleamed darkly in the light. Its lips were pulled back from its ivory teeth in a snarl and even though it was lifeless, looking at the pointed fangs made me shudder. Its paws were the size of plates and wicked, hooked claws protruded from them like bent penny nails. It was so lifelike, so well posed that I expected it to breathe, to see muscles flex under its fur. I did not like it.

"Well?" asked David, "What do you think?"

"It's very well done," I replied, non-committal. "Very noble."

"Nonsense!" he said proudly. "It's terrifying, which is as it should be. One of the farmers brought it me the other week, and it's been a hard job to get it right. I thought it deserved something spectacular, something befitting its size, don't you agree? I was going to mount it with a slaughtered lamb, but decided against it on the grounds of taste. The right decision, if I do say so myself. Sometimes, the look of it frightens me, hence my calling it Sweet William. After all, how can we be frightened of something called 'Sweet William'?" I could only nod in agreement. The hound simply stared, its gaze never leaving me as I moved around it.

"The funny thing is, the farmer knew how much I'd been looking forward to trying out my skill on one of these beasts, but he would not accept any money for it. He practically threw it at me and then left. Perhaps he thinks that the spirit of some long-dead Tiller is still attached to this flesh, and is only waiting for its chance to reclaim it?" David was laughing as he spoke, but something in his tone made me look more closely at him. His eyes darted to the windows as he spoke, and his laughter climbed no higher than his upper lip. "I might almost believe it myself," he added, almost inaudibly, "if I were a gullible idiot." When I asked him what he meant by this, he would not answer me, but simply started telling me about the practicalities of preparing such a huge beast.

I went to bed late that night. David and I talked until the moon was high and bright, illuminating the cold snowscapes that lay around the house. We drank Uncle David's fine single malt as we talked, the amber liquid warming us against the falling temperature. David appeared to want to talk all night, and even when I made my excuses and said that I must go to bed, he urged me to stay with him for one more drink, which I refused. I wonder now if my decision was the correct one; perhaps if I had stayed with him, things might have turned out differently.

I had not been in bed long, tucked down beneath the blankets, when I heard the most dreadful sound from outside the house. It was a long, mournful howling, which seemed to spiral up and around the eaves before falling down to the cold earth again. Startled, I sat up and looked at my watch; it was far past midnight. The air was as cold as I had ever known it, a cold that even the embers of the fire could not keep at bay. The noise came again, this time layered and rising, both miserable and furious at the same time. I went to the window and looked out over the garden and fields beyond. Nothing moved out in the night, and were it not for the noise that I could still hear, I might have believed that I had dreamt the whole thing. But still the noise came, and then shadows were moving around the house. They were distant at first, tiny black shapes that rushed across the fields in wide circles. Gradually, they came closer, the small shapes growing larger, although they remained indistinct. One moment, they looked like great dogs, the next robed people. Limbs seemed finished with black claws and then with gloved fingers, and they threw up great clods of earth as they ran, breaking through the frozen ice and snow in a frenzy. Steam rose from them in the cold air, trailing behind them spectrally. And they raced, these figures, circling the house in a pattern that grew tighter and tighter.

I heard Uncle David come from his room across the hallway. He was shouting something unintelligible, and I thought he was calling for me. I turned to the door, only to hear it lock from the outside. David had locked me in! I called to him, but his only response was another guttural cry in which words were lost. He sounded fearful and angry, and then he cried the only clear words I heard from him all night: "No more!". I heard him go downstairs, heard him open the lounge door (directly beneath my room), heard him go to the large windows. Heard the windows open.

By pressing myself close to the glass in my own window, I could just make out the edge of the opened frames below. I saw my uncle's hands momentarily, waving at something, and then heard him shout again. One of the shapes beyond the edge of the garden broke free from the pack and leapt the hedge. I had the impression of something of great size, that cleared the hedge without disturbing the snow on its top, and of white teeth glittering in the dark. I could not tell whether it was a man, a dog, a small horse or something else. There was something indefinable about it. As it leapt, it seemed more man than beast, the shadows around it fluttering as if a robe were flailing around a jumper's ankles, but as it landed, its head looked angular and savage.

I heard my uncle cry out again, a wordless howl of terror, and the other howling, that coated the house from all sides, grew louder still until it hurt my ears to hear it. There was a crash from below me and the sound of a door opening with a bang and then another crash further away, from the back of the house. There were more howls, although whether from my uncle or the creature, I know not. Finally, there was the sound of claws clicking rapidly across wooden floors and a miserable, low choking. For the briefest of moments, the shadows across my ceiling reflected a shapeless form rushing back across the snow and then all was quiet. I moved away from the window and, like a child, climbed back into my bed and pulled the blankets around myself. I did not go to the door or try to leave the room, and for this cowardice I will never forgive myself. Instead, I huddled down and hoped that nothing came upstairs to look for me.

I was rescued from my temporary prison the next morning by the housekeeper. She was in tears, and when I followed her downstairs, my worst fears were confirmed. My beloved uncle was sat in his favourite chair, dead. The lounge windows were open and a coating of frost had formed over him during the early hours of the morning, accentuating the lines that crawled across his face, which was twisted into the most awful expression. Although the coroner later said he died of a heart attack, I know that the expression was one of abject terror, his eyes squeezed shut to block the sight of a horror so great that the very sight of it killed him. Apart from some overturned furniture (done by my uncle in the throes of his fatal seizure, according to the coroner), the house showed no signs of intruders. The only thing amiss was in the workshop, where a wooden plinth had fallen to the floor and broken. In the official report, this was described as a coincidence and not remarked on further. No mention was made of any creature being attached to the broken wood, which at least agrees with what I saw.

The plinth was empty, and of the great hound, I could find no trace.

|Flappy the Bat|

~

Jake's first tantrum, his first *proper* tantrum, was on a Tuesday. Faced with a plate of vegetables he had to eat before he could have a yoghurt, he drew in a deep breath and began to scream. Brought by the noise, Andrew stood in the doorway and watched as Danielle calmly ignored the bawling three year old, wondering how she could pretend that the noise wasn't happening; the tantrum was painfully loud.

It was also startling in its violence. Jake was normally such a calm child, and yet as Andrew watched, his son wound himself further and further up. He took great breaths of air and spat them out, his face reddening and clenching. Spittle danced around his lips and his balled fists beat a tattoo on the table. Danielle slid his plate out of the way without comment and sat, waiting. Jake was speaking, or trying to, Andrew realised, long strings of demands and requests that merged with each other, the words running or getting lost together as he asked for yoghurts and biscuits and chocolate and he wasn't going to eat his vegetables, he *wasn't*, and with that he became almost incoherent. Danielle, ever a model of patience, remained next to Jake and made eye contact with him as best she could, speaking calmly, telling him to eat one mouthful, just *one*, and then he could have his yoghurt.

It didn't work.

Jake turned his face away, pursing his lips and actually spitting when Danielle tried to touch the vegetables to his chin in an attempt to get him to eat. It carried on for minutes, far longer than any previous disobedience, his feet kicking back and forth against his chair legs, his fists shaking in the air until eventually even Danielle cracked.

"You can't have something just because you want it, Jake!" she said angrily.

"I can! Flappy says I can! I can!" replied Jake and carried on screaming. "I can! I can!"

It took Jake almost an hour to calm, his screams trailing off first into exhausted sobs and finally into hitching, bitter breaths. Danielle and Andrew ignored him as he calmed, finally praising him when he was back to his normal, quiet self. Even then, however, Jake was sulky and reticent, refusing cuddles and making a childish show of not looking at his parents as they tucked him into his bed.

"You shouldn't do that," said Andrew to Jake as he pulled the duvet up around his chin. "It's not nice."

"Do what, Daddy?"

"Shout and scream like that and be so naughty."

"But Flappy does it, Daddy. Flappy says it's okay."

"Who's Flappy?" asked Andrew, wondering briefly if they were seeing the start of an imaginary friend.

"Oh, Daddy!" said Jake. "Flappy's just Flappy!" and, with the childish logic of a discussion finished, Jake rolled over and closed his eyes. Andrew left him to sleep, no more enlightened than he had been before the tantrum.

It happened again a couple of days later. This time, Jake threw a fit in the local supermarket, screaming and thrashing when he wasn't allowed to buy a high-sugar breakfast cereal whose box was plastered with characters from a television show that Andrew didn't recognise. Andrew watched, alarmed, as his son became a dervish child, banging himself back and forth in the supermarket's trolley seat, screeching and bouncing. Andrew wanted to hold him, stop him injuring himself, even though knew that he should ignore the behaviour. Besides, Jake looked *aggressive*, his arms beating the air and his teeth clicking fiercely between shrieks. "I can have them!" he cried, "I can! I can! I want them!"

That night, Andrew and Danielle talked about the tantrums. They recognised a certain irony in their conversation, held wearily over wine; previously, they had held similar ones about their friends' children, which always ended with the two of them saying how lucky they were that Jake didn't behave that way, that he had never really had a 'terrible twos' phase. And yet now, as their friends' children calmed, Jake had started. That day, the tantrum had lasted all the way home from the supermarket, through a meal he refused to eat and a teeth cleaning session that became a battle. It finally trailed off at bedtime and even then, Andrew had the impression its dissipation was only because Jake was exhausted.

"I don't understand it," Danielle said. "He's always been so good. Why's he started this?"

"I don't know," said Andrew. "I'm sure it's just a phase. He'll stop soon, we just need to be firm and not give in to him." Fine words, he knew, but the sheer embarrassment of the incident in the supermarket had pushed him to the edge of breaking, of buying the cereal for Jake just to shut him up and stop the other people in the store *staring* at him. Their gazes, an uneasy mix of sympathy and judgement, seemed to say *Quieten your child, or are you such a poor, ineffectual parent that you don't have any control over a three and a half year old boy?* And Andrew, somewhere in his head, had to admit that no, at that moment, he had not.

There were more tantrums over the next weeks, each huge, startling, upsetting. They were getting worse, even though all the child psychology texts Andrew and Danielle read said that if they were consistent in their approach (which they were) and kept their tempers (which they tried to do) they should soon lessen as Jake realised that he was unable to get his own way. There was no sign of the tantrums reducing, however. Instead, they became more frequent, starting over the slightest things. Jake could shift from a happy, loving little boy to an uncontrollable, shrieking thing in the space of seconds. If he was told 'no', if he was told he had to do something, if things didn't go his way; everything was fuel to his quick-sparking fire. And through it all, he talked (or, more accurately, shouted) about Flappy the Bat.

They finally realised that Flappy was a character in a programme that Jake watched on one of the children's TV channels. *The Flappy Show* was on one of the more obscure channels, sandwiched between cheap-looking American cartoons that Andrew had never heard of and repeated British children's shows from years earlier, and it was only on once a week. Jake loved it, howling with laughter as he watched, so loud that Andrew initially thought another tantrum was brewing and was relieved to find that it was a glimpse of the old Jake instead. Intrigued, Andrew watched the episode with Jake, and what he saw horrified him.

The show was about a family of bats, two parents and their child Flappy, living in an old house. Flappy was played by a middle-aged, chubby man wearing a black, clinging body suit and a hooded cape that clung tightly to his temples and jawline. It framed his face and fitted tightly to his head before flowing down and out over his shoulders and arms to make his bat wings. The man's face was painted white, with only the hollows around his eyes darkened so that his pupils glittered and his whites shone starkly against the surrounding pooled shadow. Flappy spoke in a ululating voice, peppered with popping sounds and squeaks that approximated the noises Andrew (and, presumably, most other people) associated with bats. His behaviour was manic, constantly moving and flapping his arms, jumping on the spot and doing weird little jigging dance steps. Flappy's parents looked like him in that they wore the same outfits, but they were played by younger actors. They appeared in the show only briefly at the beginning and again at the end, but they weren't really the problem. No, the problem was Flappy himself.

In truth, the first half of the show was actually quite good, despite its obviously low budget. In it (in what Andrew assumed was a regular story device), Flappy was sent to his room as a punishment. The first thing he did was tick his bad behaviour off against a list on the wall; in the show that Andrew watched with Jake, it was 'Not tidying my toys away'. As the camera panned along the list, Andrew also glimpsed 'Being cheeky', 'Not going to bed' and, oddly, 'Not being right'. Flappy's day was then revealed in a series of flashbacks as Flappy told the story of what he had done, identifying the things that had led him to being sent to his room, and Andrew found it quite good. It made it clear that Flappy was being punished for disobedience, and had a filmed insert (shown to Flappy on a little TV labelled 'Flappy's Information Box') about how toys were made and then packaged for sale in factories. It was standard children's TV, educational whilst entertaining, and Andrew couldn't quite understand why Jake was entranced with it. Certainly its mix of slapstick and kinetic volume was amusing, and the man playing Flappy was energetic and surprisingly skilled, at one point crawling across ceiling using a series of small dangling hooks whilst continuing to speak in that bizarre, high-pitched voice. The jokes were a blend of the visual (Flappy trying to juggle lots of toys before dropping them with an over-exaggerated crash; Flappy dangling upside down from the hooks and trying to drink a glass of water, succeeding only in pouring water over himself, all the while mugging furiously to the camera) and the verbal ("I won't eat vegetables unless Mum asks me nice and says peas and thank you!"), but it was nothing special. Andrew had seen lots of things like it before.

And then Flappy decided he wanted to come out of his room.

He achieved it by having a tantrum. His manic behaviour escalated and he began to shriek, banging on the door and demanding to be let out. When his mother opened the door and told him that he could not come out until he was prepared to be a "good boy", he screamed "I can! I can come out! I don't have to be a good boy! I can do what I want!", all the while throwing himself around the room. He crashed into walls, pulling the TV off the table and onto the floor and throwing his bedclothes around the room in multicoloured swirls that floated in the air above him and draped the chaos at his feet. At one point, he scampered up one of the walls, skittering across the ceiling and screaming and screaming and screaming. His parents, standing in the doorway, watched him with expressions that Andrew recognised even through their pancake makeup: tired, hopeless inability, the expression of parents at the end of their tether. And then they buckled.

"Of course you can come out, Flappy darling," said Flappy's mother, holding her arms out, "if only you'll stop that terrible noise." Flappy immediately stopped screaming and calmed down, going to his mother for a hug.

"And I don't have to put my toys away, do I?"

"No, son, not if you don't want to," said his father, and the two parents smiled broadly. Relaxation showed on their faces.

"Oh, good," said Flappy and then he turned and came towards the camera, reaching around the screen so that his wings (*cape*, Andrew said to himself, *it's a cape*) obscured the background, leaving only Flappy's pale, grinning face visible. "You see," he said, his voice dropping to a conspiratorial whisper of whistles and clicks, "you can get what you want. You just have to want it enough. You have to want it lots and lots, just like I do. You can get what you like!" The screen was filled with the whiteness of Flappy's face and the dark scars of his eyes and cavernous open mouth. Deep in its recesses something fat and darkly red moved as he spoke, like a worm wriggling in clinging, bitter mud.

"And if your mum and dad or anyone else says you can't, you just tell them you can. Tell them Flappy said so." And then, with a final shriek of joy, Flappy darted out of his room and the credits began to roll.

Andrew was appalled, and uncomfortable with being appalled. Since becoming a parent, he had noticed that his attitudes, previously liberal, had begun to change and he wondered if he was becoming reactionary. If he thought about it, he still believed in personal freedoms and a 'live and let live' approach to life, yet his *initial* reactions, the thoughtless ones that bloomed before his consciousness stepped in, were often negative. He reacted badly to swearing, to smoking, to rudeness, to thoughtlessness, and he did so because he did not want Jake exposed to those things when he and Danielle were trying hard to bring him up to be thoughtful and polite and to actually care about the people and environment around him. Even when Jake wasn't there, he found himself finding fault with how other people acted and spoke, worrying about the messages their behaviour sent or, at least, the messages he found himself reading into that behaviour. Sometimes, he thought he was becoming an old man before his time, was losing his youth and tolerance in a welter of responsibilities and pressures.

But then, just when he was becoming convinced of the irrationality of his own growing illiberality, he saw something like Flappy and knew that it wasn't just him. Much as he hated to admit it, Jake's behaviour these past few weeks had been noticeably worse and what he was watching on television was a direct cause; Flappy the Bat was teaching his son that bad behaviour was a way to achieve things, that tantrums and aggression and rudeness were a method of getting your own way. It was *wrong*. Andrew wasn't sure what, but he knew he had to do something. Jake had a lifetime for the real world to teach him that some people behaved badly and got away with it without being taught it by the programmes that were supposed to give him more positive messages.

The first thing he did was to tell Danielle about the programme, which led them to argue. Andrew wanted to stop Jake from watching it, whereas Danielle thought that banning it would make it more attractive, a sort of forbidden fruit. Better, she said, to use being able to watch the programme as a reward for good behaviour, and to spend some time explaining to Jake that Flappy's behaviour was wrong. Jake was intelligent, she said, and would understand. Besides, it was only on once a week, so they didn't have to deal with it straight away, they had time before it was on again. In the meantime, Andrew should see if there were rules about what children's television could and couldn't show, and complain officially if Flappy had broken those rules. Andrew was not, she said, to tell Jake he couldn't watch Flappy at all; it was only a phase after all and he might not want to by next week, and besides, she didn't have the energy to deal with the tantrum it would obviously cause. Andrew agreed in the end because he, too, had little energy left to argue. Besides, she was right; it was only a phase, wasn't it?

It wasn't.

Jake had more and more tantrums during the following week, each one seemingly worse than the one before. It was exhausting, trying to cope with it, trying to maintain a calm exterior and not give in to Jake's demands. Danielle cried miserably one night and Andrew could do little other than hug her and reassure her that they were doing the right thing and tackling this the right way.

"It would have been so easy just to let him have some chocolate," she said. "It'd make everyone's life so much nicer, if only he'd just do one thing that was good so I could reward him with what he wanted, but he won't even listen to me. It's like he's obsessed with getting his own way. And he keeps saying about Flappy, *Flappy* this and *Flappy* that. It's not right, is it?" Andrew shook his head, and hugged her tighter.

Andrew found an online community of parents that had similar concerns. Across a range of discussion forums and groups, he found people asking questions about Flappy, about whether other parents had children whose tantrums had got worse, and the number of positive replies was startling. For a programme on a fairly small channel, Flappy appeared to have a lot of children enthralled and copying his behaviour. There were so many of them, so many topic headings, all related to Flappy ('Hour long tantrums after Flappy: advice?'; 'Copying Flappy – how to deal?'; 'Not coping with Flappy tantrums and need help'; 'Anyone else hate Flappy?' and more), a hundred little cries for help from people just like him. The problem was, no one seemed to be doing anything about it. He finally posted a message about it ('Why Don't

We Complain re Flappy?'), and received lots of replies. Most were disparaging; the regulations weren't clear, he was told, and besides, what he would he suggest? Why should the broadcaster or programme makers listen to parents whose children had started having tantrums? Wouldn't they simply say it was one of those things, and that there was no proof that Flappy was a cause or even a contributor to the problem. *They'll call it bad parenting, or an example of blame culture!* wrote one parent with the username StressDad. *How are we ever likely to get them to pay attention to us?*

"Simple," replied Andrew. "Threaten their income."

In the end, a large number of parents put their names to a letter that Andrew wrote to the television production company that made Flappy, *Flapped Bat Pictures.* The letter set out the parents' concerns and asked the company to explain how they thought the programme they made was in any way helpful to the parents of children who were still learning, still impressionable. It demanded action to make sure that Flappy's behaviour improved, or at least that he wasn't rewarded for his bad behaviour by getting his own way. It concluded by saying that if things did not improve "we will have little choice but to take the matter further, to the press or an appropriate authority to bring formal proceedings". A direct threat, couched very politely, to try to get the company to do something.

"I don't expect it to do much, really," Andrew said to Danielle, "but at least I'll know I tried." That evening, Jake had had his longest tantrum yet, one that was so violent it was almost scary. He was so agitated that cleaning his teeth or bathing him proved impossible, and it carried on long after they had him in his pyjamas and in bed. Jake thrashed and kicked under the duvet, screaming and furious and near-incoherent. The awful thing was that Andrew had no idea what it was that had sparked this incident off, or what Jake wanted. It just seemed as though he was angry for the sake of being angry, as though he was enjoying the destructive, wearing effect he was having on his parents. Even with his bedroom door shut and the television on in the lounge, Andrew and Danielle could still hear him. At one point it sounded like he was hitting the walls or stamping on the floor, and then throwing his toys around. Andrew rose to go to him but Danielle pulled him back to the sofa.

"No," she said. "If he breaks things then he'll have to deal the consequences. We'll know if he hurts himself, we'll tell from the screaming. Until then, leave him to it. God, I hope this letter does something." And then, very quietly, she began to cry and Andrew, missing the son he had known for the past years and hating the fact he was beginning to hate this new incarnation of him even as he loved him, found himself crying with her.

Flapped Bat Pictures replied promptly, to Andrew's surprise, with a long and detailed letter that was both conciliatory and positive, and which ended with an offer for Andrew and another couple of parents to meet with the producer, writer and stars of *Flappy the Bat*. "We value the input of our audience (or our audience's parents!) and look forward to meeting you soon," the letter finished, and Andrew would have enjoyed its implications of success if Jake hadn't been in the middle of yet another furious explosion of temper when he read it. Besides, the situation didn't feel like one he could win any more, it was simply felt like damage limitation. Jake's behaviour felt like it had pushed them all over some strange boundary and into a place where there were no positives, only shades of negative.

The meeting was set for a couple of weeks after the letter arrived. As well as Andrew, two other parents attended, StressDad (who, it turned out, was called Reggie and who was the parent of Reggie Jnr,) and the woman who had posted the first query about Flappy, Natasha ("Mine's called Bobby," she said when she met Andrew and Reggie outside the *Flapped Bat Pictures* office, "and he was a lovely little kid until he watched this *crap*"). It took place at the company's offices, which were in the middle of an industrial estate in a town that Andrew had never visited before. The three were escorted to a small boardroom and given fresh coffee by a smiling receptionist. After a few minutes of strained small talk, they were interrupted by the arrival of a small, dapper man.

"Greetings," he said. "My name's Michael Hall, but you can call me Mikey, and I'm the producer of *The Flappy* Show . It's my job to oversee what we make to ensure it's as good as it can be. I should say at this point that Flappy is the most popular show on the channel, and its continued success is important to us, and we're only going to achieve this continued success if we make sure that the people watching enjoy the show. So, can I firstly apologise that *The Flappy Show* has caused you this upset, and assure that we're going to do everything we can to address your concerns. We've reviewed the shows with the stars and the writer, and we agree that the message it sends it out might not be the most appropriate one for younger children to hear or see. In future episodes of Flappy, we hope to give out stronger signals regarding the importance of good behaviour. However, perhaps I should let the person who conceived, stars in and still writes the show explain how we're going to do that. Edward?"

Mikey gestured to the back of the room; Andrew, turning, realised that three people had entered whilst they had been listening. A striking brunette woman and an athletic looking young man stood either side of an older, nondescript blond man. Andrew wondered who he was, and then realised with a start that he was Flappy. Shorn of the black suit and cape and the pancake makeup, he looked entirely different. The couple flanking him were Flappy's parents, Andrew guessed, and they also looked entirely different. Younger, certainly, and more attractive but also less distinct, as though their appearance on the television screen was in some way more real than their appearance in the boardroom. It was a strange thing to think, Andrew realised; why should they be more real on the screen?

"This is Adrian Robeson and Maria West, who you might recognise as Flappy's parents in the show," said Mikey, "and the gentleman in the middle is the creative force behind Flappy, Edward Carnegie. Edward, perhaps you'd like to explain how The Flappy Show is going to evolve in future episodes?"

Edward, Adrian and Maria sat down on the opposite side of the table from Andrew, Reggie and Natasha. Edward, speaking in a low and cultured tone entirely unlike his Flappy voice, began to talk about *The Flappy Show*, about how it would become a more "responsible" and "positive behaviour-directing" programme. At his side, Andrew could see Reggie and Natasha nodding and smiling at what they heard, whilst either side of Edward, Adrian and Maria also nodded and smiled. Mikey, standing at the end of the table, smiled as well, his head making little bird-like bobs as he heard what Edward had to say. It *was* reassuring, Andrew thought, very upbeat and contrite and just exactly what they wanted to hear.

So why wasn't he reassured?

It was something about the way Edward kept looking at him as he spoke, his eyes never leaving Andrew's face and smiling delicately as though he and Andrew were sharing some secret, private joke. It was something about the way Maria and Adrian's wide smiles never wavered, about the fact he kept talking about the future, the fact that what he was saying felt like a rehearsed thing, a script he was reciting by rote but that meant nothing. Besides, it didn't help Andrew with Jake's behaviour *now*. What use was a change in the *future* programmes, programmes that wouldn't be shown for months yet? Andrew looked at Reggie and Natasha, hoping to see some sign of the same disquiet on their faces, but they looked enraptured, caught by Edward's smooth voice and the way his face seemed full of apology and friendliness and *mea culpa* contrition without its expression ever once altering. Looking back at him, Andrew realised that although he suspected Edward was a well-preserved mid-forties, his face itself was almost unlined, youthful. And *still* Edward stared at Andrew as he spoke, his dark eyes holding Andrew's gaze as his mouth formed words that Andrew no longer heard.

Eventually, Reggie and Natasha rose and walked over to Mikey. Andrew, thinking he had missed something, went to rise as well but Edward inclined his head slightly, still smiling. *Stay,* his gesture said, *stay.*

"It won't matter what changes we make, of course," Edward said quietly and Andrew realised that he was talking not with Edward's voice but with Flappy's, sharp with whistles and pops. Andrew looked around to see if Reggie or Natasha had heard, but they were facing away from him, engrossed in something Mikey was showing them on a flipchart.

"I have them all," Flappy said. *Not Flappy, it's* Edward, *not Flappy* thought Andrew briefly and then Edward leaned across the table. His fingers suddenly seemed longer, terribly long, stretching out from his hands almost to the edge of the table in front of Andrew, even though that would make them impossibly elongated. They scratched at the table's surface with a noise like branches against night-time windows. Flappy's face was paler and his eyes were suddenly lost in shadows so that Andrew could see only the dark slashes of eyesocket and mouth against white skin. Flappy smiled an open-mouthed, lazy smile, letting a glimpse escape of a rich, red something darting in his mouth's glittering depths. Andrew glanced at Maria, looking for an explanation of what he was seeing but saw instead that her smile had twisted, wrenched into a silent shriek and that tears were falling from her eyes. *Help us* she mouthed, and Andrew saw that Adrian wore the same expression as Maria and that he, too, was mouthing *Help*. Andrew looked back at Flappy, incontrovertibly Flappy now, sitting opposite him and grinning and showing needle teeth. His long fingers, so long, flexed and Andrew saw the tips ended in twisting, ragged claws and somehow he knew that Flappy's feet under the table were clawed as well, flexing and prehensile and lethal.

"What?" Andrew managed to whisper.

"I have them all," Flappy repeated and then he leaned back and he was simply Edward again.

Andrew opened his mouth and started to speak. Edward smiled almost imperceptibly and Maria shook her head and Adrian widened his eyes in with a look of something like terrible fear capering across his face, and Andrew fell silent. Edward nodded, a tiny movement of approval, and then he rose and the meeting was over.

Andrew didn't mention what had happened to Reggie or Natasha after they left the building; what could he say? That Edward had suddenly become Flappy, but not the Flappy they saw on the television screen? That he had become, instead, the *real* Flappy, the *real* bat-thing that lived within Edward's skin? No, they would think him mad, lying or stupid or something worse and anyway, had he actually seen it? Actually?

Yes. He had no doubts, he had seen it and no matter how hard he tried to persuade himself otherwise on the journey home, his belief did not change. He had seen Edward Carnegie become Flappy the Bat and his claws had been long and his teeth like slivers of glass and Andrew had been terrified even though he had not realised it at the time.

When he arrived home, Jake was in the lounge, but before he could go in to see him, Danielle called him from the kitchen. Going to her, he saw that she had already poured herself a glass of red wine despite it only being early evening.

"How was it?" she asked tonelessly.

"Fine," Andrew replied. "Very positive. They'll change *The Flappy Show* from now." He didn't mention Edward or Maria or Adrian or the real Flappy; what was the point? He would never be able to adequately describe what he had seen.

"He's been a nightmare, screaming every minute since you went out, so I've given up arguing with him," said Danielle, gesturing vaguely towards the lounge and Jake. "I've said he can watch the damned show if he wants to. He can do whatever he wants, I can't cope with another tantrum. If you want to stop him, be my guest."

"No," said Andrew, suddenly exhausted. "I'll go and say hello, though."

Jake was sitting on the floor in front of the television. The lounge light was off so that the only illumination came from the screen, which Andrew couldn't see from where he stood in the doorway. He could hear the theme tune to *The Flappy Show*, though, and saw the smile on his son's face. In the half light, Jake features were almost indistinguishable, his face pale with shadows pooling around his eyes and mouth in depthless swathes. He laughed at something he saw on the screen, his laugh ending with a curious nasal whistle and a sound like the popping, enamel click of teeth. Just for a moment, it seemed to Andrew that the darkness at the corners of the room gathered itself into vast black wings and reached out from the television to embrace the child he had lost.

|A Meeting of Gemmologists|

~

It was not a convention or a conference. There were no arranged talks, no groups discussing the latest technologies or marketing developments, no seminars or agendas; just six men, acknowledged as the best of their rarefied profession, meeting and talking.

It was Harris, most wolf-like of the six, who broke the news. "Did you hear? Berry died" he asked over the meal on the first night.

"Died? Jesus, he was only young. How?" This from Deacon, youngest and least sure of them.

"Heart attack. Found him in his bed, just as dead as can be. Cold and stiff, I'm told."

"When?"

"A couple of weeks ago. His family are keeping it quiet while they work out the details of the estate."

There was a ruminative silence. Eventually, Stephens spoke. "What are they going to do with it?" There was a further silence as the six contemplated Berry's business, his stock and property, his order book. His customer list.

"Apparently, it's in a bit of a state," Harris said eventually. "Berry never did keep brilliant records, and there's all kinds of orders outstanding and debts to be sorted, but I heard that they've got a buyer."

"Who?"

"They're not saying."

"Someone's moved fast," said Pearl, who was always several steps behind the rest of the group but seemed to keep up somehow.

"It's probably Tolley!" laughed Benoit, French by descent but northern by inclination. "He buys businesses as easily as he drinks his single malts!"

Tolley said nothing but smiled and rose to go to the bar.

It came up again at breakfast. Deacon, the worrier, said, "Berry was only a couple of years older than me. How could he have had a heart attack?"

"He was fat," said Harris. "Fat and stupid and careless. He made deals he couldn't afford. He took risks and then worried about the risks he took. He was impulsive. He was not *sensible*." This was a terrible insult to men who made their living dealing in the earth's unchanging solidity, making sense of the comparative worth of rock and crystal and metal, and the group was still for a second as they assessed whether they agreed. Their silence indicated they did.

"Besides," continued Harris when the moment had passed. "He was greedy. He made ill-advised purchases. I heard rumours that he bought the Wisher Ruby."

There was another silence, this one borne of surprise.

"The Wisher?" said Pearl eventually. "I didn't know it was on the market."

"It wasn't; not the open market at least. It was a private deal, the last one he did before he died."

"He was an idiot to buy the Wisher," said Benoit.

"You don't believe that rubbish about it being cursed, do you?" asked Stephens. "It was all nonsense invented by the damned Victorians to bump the price up, wasn't it?"

"No," said Tolley, "it wasn't."

After dinner, seated on their private balcony so that Benoit and Stephens could smoke, Tolley finally agreed to speak. He had spent the day letting enigmatic smiles play across his lips when the subjects of Berry or the Wisher Ruby were raised, refusing to answer anything until they had had a "civilised meal". The other five allowed him his theatrics; in a group without a leader, Tolley was their unspoken head by virtue of his brilliance and by his simple longevity. Hawklike and sharp, even a stay in hospital a month earlier had not dulled him.

"You shouldn't dismiss curses," Tolley said once they were settled. "Even the most preposterous of tales can be true, or at least, have some truth at its heart. You can believe that the stories about the Wisher Ruby are inflated or false if you want, but I'd advise against it. It's a beautiful stone, but it's not worth owning."

"How do you know it's beautiful? It's not been seen for years. There aren't even decent photographs of it," said Harris.

"I know, my dear boy, because I have *owned* it."

Even in a group accustomed to companionable silences, the emptiness that followed this statement was profound. The Wisher Ruby was a gemmologist's legend, a semi-mythic stone that had tumbled through history for the past hundred and fifty years without ever coming to land and without ever losing its glittering tail of stories and whispers and warnings. None of them, so they thought, had ever seen the ruby, and its whereabouts were unknown, lost in a private collection for over three decades. All of them had secretly hunted for it and all of them, so they thought, had failed. Except, it now seemed, Tolley.

"My God, man, when was this? It must have been years ago, surely, before we met?" blurted Stephens. "Why on earth would you buy that stone, with the reputation it has?"

"Ah, but what do you know of its reputation? Of its history? *Really* know?"

Pearl, as though a light had gone on behind his eyes, chimed in. "Well, people have died, haven't they? Its owners, I mean. Right from Wisher himself, the people that have bought it have all died, haven't they?"

"Of course not," replied Tolley. "How could they all have died? It always belongs to someone, and the fact that it's been out of sight for so long must mean that someone has it safely, don't you think?"

"It could have been passed to a museum or some other institution," said Pearl.

"Without us knowing?" said Tolley. "Impossible. Tell me you haven't looked for the Wisher, haven't checked all of the places that could own it, and it wasn't there, was it? All of you have looked. I certainly did. It was a stone that was not to be found because someone had it and wanted it kept."

The group looked at Tolley. The older man lit one of his rare cigars and soon blue smoke curled around their heads in feline twists.

"When the Wisher was offered to me, it was by a man who had inherited it from his aunt. She had died months earlier and left him everything. The Wisher was buried at the back of a safe with a sheaf of papers and documents proving it was legally hers, and giving some of its history. His uncle, he told me, had bought it just before his unexpected death years earlier and she had kept it because she felt that it was disrespectful to his memory to sell it. The nephew was, as he told it, going to keep the Wisher but soon changed his mind."

"Why?" from impatient Deacon.

"All in good time. The nephew came to me in my shop. He was terribly nervous, so much so that when he first came in I believed he was going to try to rob me and I was very wary. He was sweating, looking continually over his shoulder and starting at the slightest sound. He looked exhausted; not just tired, but physically sick with tiredness. He practically begged me to buy the stone, and the price he offered it at was simply ridiculous. I told him that I needed time to check out some details and that I would contact him soon. 'Within the day,' he said, 'I don't have much time left'. I remember that clearly, but thought he meant he had debts he had to settle. He left me his aunt's papers and went, and I spent the day studying them. The aunt had spent the years following her husband's death researching the Wisher, tracking it back through history, and what she had found made for interesting reading.

"When Wisher stole the stone, it already had a history. A reputation."

"Wisher stole it?" asked Deacon.

"Of course. He was an imperialist, one of Victoria's great explorers, reaching out into uncharted lands and claiming them for queen, country and pocket. He was a trader, a good one by all accounts, who pushed into Burma in the middle of the nineteenth century and forged alliances there. He set up trading concerns, made connections with the area's richer merchants and set up lines of commerce that still, in some form or other, exist to this day."

The group settled around Tolley. Chairs creaked and ties loosened as they relaxed and waited.

"I'm sure you know the stone's history; how Wisher bought it on one of his trips for a ridiculously low price, intending it as the centrepiece of his private collection in England, but sold it soon after putting it on display in his home. From there, it passed from owner to owner, with high numbers of them either dying unexpectedly or selling it on fast. The people who owned it the longest were Lady

Martens, who inherited it on the death of her son, and the widow of a gem trader from Birmingham called Harry Bellas. She owned it for thirty years, apparently without incident, before the Wisher vanished after her death, lost in the splitting up of her estate.

"All of this information, or at least the important parts of it, were in the papers my client left with me to look over. He told me before he left that it was his uncle who had purchased the Wisher from Bellas' widow, and that he remembered the stone from his childhood. His uncle kept it in his study for three weeks after taking possession of it, three weeks during which time he changed, becoming short-tempered and nervous. He began staying awake for hours, wandering through the house in the night, began shouting at things that no one could see and jumping at the slightest sound. Eventually, he refused to go to bed or into his bedroom. The three weeks ended when his uncle killed himself by leaping from his office window.

"His story appeared true, at least as far as I could research it. The aunt's husband could well have bought the stone, and the paperwork that the nephew provided me with was certainly genuine-looking. Days, dates, times, costs all looked real. But still, I wasn't happy. The price being asked was so small for what the Wisher was, and I determined to push the nephew as to why. I demanded that he meet me with the stone, so that I could inspect it. I had some idea that he might try to sell me a fake, or an inferior ruby instead of the Wisher, hoping that its reputation might blind me to the switch. I was wrong.

"He came to my shop that night, as requested, carrying the ruby in his pocket as though it were a packet of cigarettes. He dropped it on my desk and actually backed away from me as I inspected it. I noticed he was more nervous than before, if that were possible, sweating and trembling and looking at me with such pleading in his eyes. He looked even more tired and I wondered if he were addicted to something, if that was behind his need to sell the stone quickly. I knew instinctively that something here was wrong, but for the life of me I could not identify what, and eventually my greed overcame my reservations, and I agreed to its purchase."

"Greedy, you? Surely not!" said Benoit.

"Of course I am. We all are. I want to make money, just as you do. Normally, I keep my greed in check. After all, a deal that looks too good to be true is most often just that: too good to be true. When faced with the Wisher, however, I forgot it all.

"I paid for the Wisher in cash. The nephew did not count the money I gave him but simply thrust it in his pocket and left, almost crying his thanks on me. Then, in the solitude of my room, I inspected my purchase more thoroughly.

"It is, without doubt, the most beautiful ruby you can imagine. It is a genuine pigeon's blood stone, and has a depth, a fire, that I have never seen matched. It has been cut exquisitely so that each facet allows you to look into its heart and see reflections of every other angle and plane. That it is an untreated stone is clear, as it has the most glorious rutile inclusions, tiny dark threads around its heart, forming a perfect star pattern that seems to shimmer and shift as the stone itself is moved. It is as perfect a thing as I have ever seen and held, an egg of such solid glory that I spent over an hour simply inspecting it. Holding it. *Loving* it."

These were such strong words for the usually reserved Tolley that no one knew how to respond. Love for a stone? Desire for its ownership, yes; a need to possess and sell it, yes, but love? No. "It must be wonderful," said Harris eventually.

"Wonderful? No," replied Tolley. "Glorious, yes, and spectacular certainly, but it is not wonderful. It is too brutal to be wonderful, and it carries at that perfect heart a terrible darkness. It is a savage thing, wearing a cloak of beauty that fools the weak and vain and greedy. That fooled me. I went to bed that night, God help me, thinking of the profit I would make when I put it on the market."

Tolley stopped talking. For the first time that any of them could remember, he looked perturbed, his forehead creasing slightly and his lips pursing. He sipped his whiskey slowly and then said, "That first night was quiet.

"The next day, I started to make very discreet enquiries. It was already clear to me that the Wisher was worth far more than I had paid for it, even without the added value of its history, and I aimed to make as much money from it as possible. Most of my regular customers couldn't afford the prices I intended to charge, but one or two could, and it was to them I went, along with other individuals who I thought might be interested and who were rich enough to afford the chase. No details of course, simply a question: would they be interested in owning a very impressive stone with an equally impressive history? Receiving several positive responses, I started to make my plans. A private auction, perhaps, or a series of private viewings that would allow me to play one customer off against the other. By lunchtime, I was feeling very satisfied with myself, and took the ruby from my safe to look upon it once more.

"It was beautiful, beyond any stone I had seen, deep and rich and vibrant. It contained colours, shades of red that I have no name for, all of swirling and dancing as though for my private amusement. The Wisher was only ever an investment for me, but I knew that I would find it hard to sell after the viewings three weeks from then.

"I did not sleep well that night."

"I'm not surprised," said Harris. "I'd be awake most of the night as well if I'd got something that valuable under my roof. My God, the profit you must have been looking at!"

"You misunderstand," said Tolley. "It wasn't the profit that kept me from sleep, it was the noises. All through the night, my apartment was filled with sounds; rustling like silk, tapping sounds like tiptoe footsteps across the wooden floor, once the sound of gentle breathing. There were smells as well; the scent of perfume or something similar, and something underneath that. Something burning.

"The next day did not get off to a good start. I had the oddest feeling when I first woke that there was someone in the bed with me, that if I were to open my eyes I would see a person lying beside me who had not been with me when I finally fell asleep the previous evening. Of course, when I did eventually open my eyes, there was no one there, and I dismissed it as another side effect of having had such a poor night's rest. I soon discovered that it was not.

"The first thing I noticed that morning was that I no longer felt alone in my apartment. I am a bachelor by inclination; I am happy in my rooms, and have them set the way I wish them. I clean them, organise them, arrange them how I wish and take few visitors there. My space is *important* to me, and yet I began to feel that someone had, unbidden, taken up residence there with me. It was as though, when I walked into a room, someone else had just left, that the order of it had been subtly altered. Chairs seemed in slightly different places, were the wrong temperature when I sat in them; books felt as though someone else had leafed through them or were left in places I was sure I had not put them. There were smells, of perfume and flowers, that I could not account for, drafts as though doors had opened when they were clearly shut, the odours of food that I had not eaten and drinks I had not taken. Even my bed felt invaded, the sheets pulled into rumpled patterns when I was not in the room and containing the *feel* of someone else. I can explain it no better than this: over those first days, I felt I was sharing my space with a person I could not see, hear or feel but who was nonetheless real and, from my perspective, entirely unwanted.

"That was not all. As the week progressed, this feeling of invasion grew and its signs became stronger and more obvious. I went into my bathroom one morning to find it filled with steam and with water still trickling down the inside surfaces of the bath. Another time, I found the door to my study swinging shut as I came out of my bedroom. I called out and dashed into the study hoping, I think, to find some person there who could explain all that had been happening to me. Even a burglar might have been better than what was there."

"Why, what did you find?" asked Benoit.

"*Nothing!* The room was empty!" Tolley looked at the men around him. "I think I may even have been able to cope with that, persuaded myself that it was tiredness or overwork, were it not for what started to happen during the nights.

"Lying in bed on the fourth night after purchasing the Wisher, trying to sleep, I felt a pair of arms go around me in an embrace that could not be, and I screamed out loud. The feeling went as quickly as it came. When I looked around, the sheets were again rumpled by someone who was not there and the pillow indented by a head that was not mine.

"I hardly slept that night, lying in my bed listening to the sounds of breathing and movement, and waiting for another touch. It did not come. What was happening to me? Was I going mad?

"The next day, I tried to carry on as normal, as though nothing had happened. After all, what *had* happened? Really? Some sounds and an imagined touch? It was nothing, or at least, nothing I could understand, so I chose to ignore it. I continued to make arrangements for the Wisher viewings, moving around my offices and pretending that things were fine, when they were not. All day, I could have sworn that someone was following me, was ever just behind me and watching me with sharp eyes. It wasn't a pleasurable attention either; I felt as though the person watching me *hated* me, was seething with silent, wild rage at something I had done."

"And you never saw anyone?" Deacon; anxious but trying not to show the effect the story was having on him.

"Saw? No. They were only feelings; I had nothing to point at and say, 'That's the problem', no person I could blame or cry 'Foul!' to. So I simply busied myself with work, with the impending sale, and tried to ignore things, to pretend normality. And besides, I had the Wisher.

"I spent hours staring into its depths. Breaking the habit of my professional life, I kept it in the safe in my rooms and took it out each night to hold it. To *covet* it. I think that the only reason I did not cancel the viewings and sale was that, desire the stone as I might, cancelling would have looked bad. Despite its beauty, the stone was still worth more to me as an item for sale that would contribute to my reputation, rather than as an item of beauty for me to possess."

The group nodded as one; if you gave customers reason to think your judgement or professionalism was wavering in any way, they started to haggle over every sale, and haggling was for market traders and privateers, not respected gemmologists.

"On the sixth morning after I bought the Wisher, I woke up to find someone holding me."

"Holding you? You mean there were arms around you again?" asked Stephens.

"No," said Tolley, "I mean I awoke to find a hand that was not my own gripping my cock."

Benoit spluttered, managing somehow to blow twin streams of smoke from his nostrils whilst coughing; Deacon gasped out loud and Stephens laughed too loudly. Tolley merely grimaced and relit his cigar.

"It's a shock," he said, "particularly when you know you went to bed alone. I wondered for a second if I was having a startlingly vivid dream, but no. I was awake. The hand was warm, small, and wrapped around me tightly. It felt feminine.

"Before I could do anything, the hand started to move. To rub me."

Pearl opened his mouth to speak but stopped before any sound emerged. Tolley looked at him, but Pearl shook his head slightly; he had coloured to a flushed red.

"It was a skilled hand. Without moving a great deal, it seemed to touch the whole of me, made me feel on fire with pleasure. I did not try to stop it; it was simply too good a feeling. It was the most wonderful friction, wonderful and continuous and impossible. Only as I arrived at the point where I could not stop my coming did things change. The hand grew rough, gripped me too tightly and twisted as I came so that I gasped not in pleasure but in pain.

"Of course, when I opened my eyes, there no one in the bed with me. As well as being in pain, I now had disgust to overcome; was I a teenager, to have ridiculous fantasies? I am by no means celibate, but sex is never something that I have been overly concerned with and yet here I was, having sordid, strange wet dreams. What else could they be? Angry with myself, I got up and washed and got on with my day. The Wisher sales were shaping up nicely, and I had lots of interest in the stone without ever having mentioned to my prospective customers that it was the Wisher. I wanted this sale to be a secret one, to keep it quiet at the very least until it was done, and I didn't want to be bothered with the calls and visits that would inevitably occur if news of the stone got out. After all, I had a business to run.

"The next night, I was woken by the feeling that someone had taken me in their mouth."

"My God," said Harris.

"Someone once told me that men are closest to God when they are in the act of sex," said Tolley. "That may be so, but let me tell you that this mouth felt very far from God. Certainly, it was warm and the tongue moved wonderfully around me, but I had not asked for its attention and did not want it. I felt vulnerable; I could feel teeth, sharp and hard, brushing against me and I remembered the savage twist the hand had given me the previous night. I sat up swiftly, hoping to dislodge the mouth yet it moved with me. I felt arms pulling at my thighs, digging in and dragging me back to the mattress as I tried to get away from them. In the darkness of my bedroom, I could see little, and in leaning over to switch on the lamp I fell from the bed, tangled in the arms and a mouth that still sucked and licked but that was starting to bite, and hit the floor hard. Even as I fell, I thought that I heard someone laughing, a dreadful cold giggle that found amusement in my tumble and the pain I felt. From the floor, I saw the shadows over my bed twist, flow together and reach down. I felt tiny and powerless and I'll admit that I cried out as something that felt like hands were placed about me."

There was silence, broken eventually by Benoit, who said, "Jesus, man, what did you do?"

"Nothing. I was too scared. The grip was tight, painful, but even as it took hold, I could feel it fall away like wet paper. I had an image of dark shreds collapsing, flowing out to the corners of the room as the thing disappeared. Only when it had entirely gone could I breathe again.

"That wasn't the worst of it, of course," continued the elder man. He stubbed his cigar in the ashtray and swallowed another whisky. Although his hands were steady as they lit his third cigar of the evening, this was the most any of them could remember him smoking in one evening. His voice, like his hands, remained steady. "Not by a long way. The worst of it was yet to come.

"I began to feel followed wherever I went. At my office, I felt as though someone were permanently hovering just behind me, looking over my shoulder and judging what I did. Sometimes, I would feel a hand trail over my neck and once, in the middle of a conversation with a gem buyer from Amsterdam, a hand that I could not see brushed across the front of my trousers before taking hold of me tightly and *squeezing*. I got no respite from this sense of unwanted companionship, from the feeling that the very contours of my life were being invaded. And it got worse when I returned to my home; there were scents, oh god, smells of burning and roasting meat, of shit and perfume and things corrupted and gone sour. I live alone, and yet there was someone with me permanently. Some*thing*. It danced behind me, darting from shadow to shadow at the corner of my eye, wrapped in long robes or something else that hung and flapped as it ran. It touched me, sometime softly but more often with hard jabs, scratches that somehow raked across my flesh under my clothes and left red streaks across my skin.

"If I tried to read, the book would be yanked from my hands; if I tried to write my pen would be snatched from me and flung across the room. Looking back, I don't really know how I got through it, because the most awful thing of all was not the violence, not the smells or sounds, it was the *feelings*.

"Something in my home *hated* me. It was everywhere I went, a directed hatred that followed me like some snapping dog, never giving me peace or rest. The best I can explain is to say that it turned the air in on itself, made things that should have been warm, cold, should have been light, dark. It was poisonous, soaking into the walls. I almost imagined I could see it staining the floors and ceilings yellow with its bile.

"Why didn't you go to a hotel? Or stay with a friend?" asked Harris.

"And what would that have done for my reputation?" asked Tolley. "Besides, I spent many years getting my rooms as I wanted them. They are my home and I will not be driven out of them. Even by something that acted the way it did, something that affected me so strongly. I will not be beaten in that way. So I did my best, and I coped. When I slept, it was because I fell asleep through exhaustion, and I was never allowed to sleep for long. I tried to act as normally as I could at first, retiring to my bedroom at night and going to bed like any civilised man; I soon realised, however, that civilisation had nothing to do with what was happening to me.

"One night, I woke to find someone on top of me. She, and it was emphatically female, had her legs clamped around my thighs and her arms about my head and she was riding me, pushing herself down upon me and grunting with each push, little animal grunts of effort and pressure and anger. I tried to throw whoever it was off, but she remained upon me, invisible and strong and resistant and the most awful thing was that in some way, I was enjoying it. It was the most erotic experience I had ever had. The smell of the woman was incredible, rich and hot and sexual, and the feel of her? My God, the temptation to simply let myself go and be ridden was powerful. I wanted to let her carry on, make no mistake, to let that moist warmth caress me until I came.

"And then the blows started. With every thrust down on me, I felt a punch or slap, across my face and chest and shoulders. They were gentle at first, but became more fierce until they were so painful that they drowned everything else. I know I screamed, but as I did so something was thrust into my mouth and stifled my cries. A tongue. *Her* tongue, and then she was biting at my bottom lips and I could hear her, grunting and crying and hissing and I threw myself from the bed.

"I wish I could say this was an isolated incident, but it was not. Every time I fell asleep, it would happen. Sometimes she would be on top of me, sometime it would be her hand around me, sometimes her mouth over me, all the time starting sensual and then changing, more and more quickly, to violence. Once, I woke to find a breast against my mouth, the nipple between my lips, and in my sleep I was licking at it. Another time, I fell asleep in my chair and woke only minutes later to find myself pinned beneath such a slight weight that I thought I could easily move, but no. Although I was fully clothed, I was nonetheless erect and inside her. I could feel her bare breasts against the skin of my chest, even though I still had my jacket and shirt on. I could feel her move back and forth, up and down, on me and as invaded and violated as I felt, as terrified as I was by what was coming, I could not help but delight in the sensation of her, of being inside her and being as hard as I had ever been in my life. And then, of course, the violence started. Nails digging into me, fists punching at my stomach and face, teeth biting into my cheek. My cheek, for Christ's sake! I fought back, but over the days I felt less and less able to defend myself. I was getting no sleep, no rest, no respite. I was bruised, beaten, scratched. I had teeth marks on my cheek, a swollen lip, so that I did not want to be seen in public for fear that the rumours would start. And it was all the Wisher's fault.

"All those stories, all the silly tales of curses, came back to me. I had heard them, we all have, yet had ignored them. I was a fool, that much was clear. It should have been obvious; the man who sold it to me was evidence enough. If I had taken his shirt off, I wondered, would I have found him battered, bruises in the shape of small fists on his skin, discovered scratches, bite marks? I suspected so. I *knew* so. He had sold me the ruby to free himself from it, and I had bought it because I was a stupid man who had not listened to his instincts. My first thought was to the sales, still two weeks hence, but I knew

I could not survive that long. The violence was escalating, growing more severe and more frequent, and it would kill me or worse before then. Should I simply destroy the stone, or give it away, get rid of it so that I too could be free of it? No. Never. I have spent all my adult life controlling the price, the flow and the ownership of gems, and to have one control me? No."

"Quite right!" said Harris and gestured to the waiter for another round of drinks. There was a gentle sound as the patio heater ignited and soon the men were caressed by fresh warmth against the chilling night.

"My next thought was to see if anything in the stone's history might give me some clue as to what was happening, point me towards a solution. I knew that I needed to go further back than Wisher, of course. It arrived on these shores with a bad reputation, and I needed to know why. Wisher's records are still available, thankfully, and I had the aunt's paperwork to refer to. I spent several days sleeping as little as possible, chasing documents, begging and calling in favours, making calls. What I found was a patchwork of rumours, half-guessed ideas, some truths and some things that were probably lies, but out of them all I pieced together a story, one that starts when the wisher was originally found some time in the sixteen hundreds.

"It was mined and fashioned in Mogok and then bought by a rich merchant as a gift to his wife on their wedding day; she was a much younger woman, forced to marry him to make a strategic link between himself and another strong merchant family. By all accounts, he treated her terribly, keeping her from her family and forcing her to act as his whore and all the time telling her that she had to obey him because he had bought her using the ruby. She had taken it from him on their wedding day, and that tied her to him in a bargain of flesh and crystal and obedience. She was forbidden to leave his rooms, made to wait upon him and always be ready to receive him no matter what the time and no matter what he wanted. If she tried to refuse him, he raped her or beat her or both. She withstood it for only a month before committing suicide by setting herself alight. She burned to death in the courtyard of her marital home.

"Apparently, the merchant was unconcerned. The marriage had given him the business links he needed, the wife herself had only been peripheral to the deal. He acted as though nothing had happened, except for one thing: two weeks after his wife's death, he sold the ruby to his brother. The brother died three weeks after, probably drowned by his own hand. The stone returned to the merchant.

"The man went mad shortly after. He had never been popular anyway, and treated everyone in his life badly, but now his behaviour became extreme. He demanded that priests bless his house daily, and tried to burn the ruby. He was only stopped from throwing it back into one of the mine pits by the intervention of his servants, none of whom would stay in his home by this time. Not long after, the merchant was found dead. He was said to have died with foam upon his lips and with his eyes open. The likelihood is he had a heart attack.

"From there, the stone passed to the merchant's father and then moved on quickly, passing from rich trader to rich trader with startling speed. Apart from a period when a trader gave it to his wife as a wedding gift, the stone kept moving. No-one owned it for long before selling it on, and it's probably about this time that it picked up the reputation of having a curse. They were all male traders, of course, all buying the stone and then for some reason selling it on within weeks. By the time Wisher turns up, there's almost nobody left to sell the stone to in the region, and he got it for a low price. Packaged and sent back, the stone was in storage until perhaps two months after Wisher returned. He put it on display in his home and then, within weeks, sold it on. The pattern starts again.

"It's men."

Pearl was already nodding as Tolley finished speaking, for once ahead of the others. "Yes," he said. "All of the people who died or owned the stone after Wisher, they were all men."

"No they weren't," snapped Tolley. "Women have owned it as well; Lady Martens and Harry Bellas' wife both owned the stone, and neither reported anything amiss about it. It's men that activate the curse, or whatever it is that the stone contains. I have no idea whether the story I heard about its first owner and the way he treated his wife is true or not, or whether it's a convenient fiction to explain what happened to the men that owned the Wisher, but I know that it made sense. Whatever the Wisher contains, it reacts to men. It reacted to *me*. The question is, what was I going to do about it?"

After a moment, Benoit said, "What did you do? Did you stay in your home?"

"Of course. Where else could I go? Besides, if I had learned one thing from studying the Wisher's history in depth, it was that there seemed no escape from it. Harry Bellas died in Germany, two weeks after buying the stone, yet the stone was in his store in Birmingham when he died, and had been since he bought it. Another owner, Victor Hornby, owned the Wisher for four weeks before he died. He held it once and then placed it into secure storage and went home. Home, gentlemen, was two hundred miles away and yet his story is similar: he grows increasingly disturbed, he becomes exhausted, distracted before finally dying. In his case, he ran out into a road and was hit by a car. The driver said he seemed to be running from someone, although no one else was nearby. There are others like that, men who owned the Wisher and fell to its influence without being anywhere near it at the time of their deaths."

The shade gathered around the men. Tolley, his face a funereal blue from the light of the patio heater, closed his eyes and spoke again. "On the eleventh night, whoever she was, *whatever* she was, she nearly killed me. It started just as before, falling asleep exhausted at my kitchen table. I had hoped to stay awake all night, had brewed strong coffee to help me, but I simply could not. I must have laid my head down on the table for a moment, and the next thing I was waking and she was back. She was under the table, and her mouth was on me again. I was as hard as I have ever been, and the mouth was so warm, seeming to hold all of me and moving with the most wonderful, soft pressure and it was so tempting to just give in to it. And then she bit me.

"I have never known pain or fear like it. I felt teeth clench into me and I threw myself back from the table, overturning it as I went. In the space below it I saw something black that scuttled after me as I fell, slithering up my legs even as I kicked out at it. It had no shape, not really, but I had the distinct sense of eyes, eyes and a mouth and something that might have been arms reaching out for me. I smelled smoke and burning, heard the sound of fat bubbling and felt the most awful heat from it, raging against me and *hating* me. I kicked and kicked, backing away and crying and still feeling those awful teeth around me, searching for purchase, trying to bite together, and the waves of pain were the worst I have ever felt. As I reached the doorway, the shape filled the whole room, a vast grasping blot that seemed to have fingers and claws and hair and features and yet had none of those things. One moment they were there, the next gone, then back again and then I was out of the room and it lunged at me as I stood.

"I think I may have cried out for mercy; I don't remember. I know that it clamped about me, and for one terrible moment I felt as though the whole of me was inside a vast mouth, my hair flattened and my face smothered by a tongue that wrapped itself around me. The heat and smell of smoke was intense, as was the sensation of being dragged towards it, towards the ruby, towards something that would swallow me whole if it got the chance."

He stopped, swallowed. Spoke again."And through all this, I was erect. Excited.

"In the end, it was the ruby that stopped me giving in. Not its beauty, or anger at it, but a simple thought: that ruby was mine, and I intended to sell it for a profit. It may seem strange to you; looking back, it does to me sometimes, but I am self-aware enough to know that the great passion in my life is not the stones themselves, not women, not men. It is money, plain and simple, and no ruby, not this or any other, would come between me and the profit I desired. I pulled and pushed against the thing of darkness around me, fighting my way back to the kitchen doorway and then beyond, to the front door. All the while, it sucked and licked at me, lashed at me, scratched me. Bit me. I still do not know why it could not kill me then. Perhaps the poor thing in the ruby can only drive men to kill themselves, or attack them until their bodies give in."

"'Poor thing'?" said Harris. "What 'poor thing'?"

"The girl in the ruby, assuming that's what it really was. Just imagine being so angry, so betrayed, that she somehow came to exist inside a ruby, to use the only weapon she had against not just the person who had treated her so badly but against every member of the sex that abused her so terribly. Just imagine being so blinded by hate and fear and loathing that all you know to do is to attack, to destroy. Imagine being lost in that red heart with no company but your own self, and the bile and bitterness and pain that you bring with you. It would be awful."

The group looked at Tolley. He was sitting, his head tilted back and his eyes closed, his cigar forgotten in his fingers and a whisky untouched on the table in front of him. Pearl opened his mouth, but Benoit waved his hand at him and he closed it again. Slowly, Stephens said, "But she nearly killed you."

"Yes, she did," replied Tolley without opening his eyes, "and I hated her for it. This was my life, and she was destroying it, but I wonder, did she have any choice? Really?" He opened his eyes and leaned forward, looking at the cold cigar for a second before dropping it into the ashtray. He picked up his drink and swallowed some and then looked around the other five.

"Do not mistake understanding for sympathy. She had hurt me, and she had to be stopped, but I could never truly blame her. That night, I walked the streets to stay awake, scared out of my home, and I thought. What to do? How to solve this before she killed me? It seemed to me that I had to cease to be the owner of the ruby, to pass it on as many had done before me, but who to? Not the clients I had arranged viewings with, that was for sure. They were my key clients, and quite apart from the income for me that they represented, I had no desire to be known as the gemmologist who had killed a major customer by selling them the Wisher."

"Ha! Yes!" said Deacon. "Can you imagine the damage to your reputation just as you were setting out in the business?"

"Stephens said that," said Tolley. "I didn't. This wasn't years back, it was a matter of months ago, and I am not long since recovered from the damage to my health this whole damned situation caused."

"Months?" said Pearl.

"It is seven weeks and two days since I bought the wisher and four weeks and five days since I sold it. I worked quickly after that night, cancelling the viewings with many apologies and offers of beneficial terms on future transactions to make up for any inconvenience caused. I needed to sell the Wisher fast, to someone who trusted me and who would ask no questions. I considered all of you, of course."

"What?" said Benoit. "Us? You'd expose us to that?"

"Of course, and don't tell me you would do any different. In the end, though, I decided against it. You are all far too cautious to be taken in, and besides, I like you well enough. Anyway, if I was going to sell it, I needed to get the best deal I could and you are all far too good businessmen to give me the kind of margin I was looking for. No, it had to be someone else, someone whose death might benefit me ultimately if, say, I could sell them the stone and then purchase their estate from the grieving family at a reasonable price. It had to be someone who would buy fast with few questions or thoughts about *why* I should be so keen to sell so quickly, someone who would not be quick enough to understand what was happening after they bought the Wisher. Someone who would think they could handle it when they could not. Someone foolish. There seemed only one choice, really."

"Who?" from Pearl, sounding as though he had an idea but did not want it confirmed.

"My dear boy, who do you think? I sold the Wisher to Berry, of course."

|Where Cats Go|

There is a road near where I live where cats go to commit suicide. It is nothing much to look at, this road, simply a strip of gently winding black tarmac just wide enough for two cars to pass alongside each other if the drivers slow down and drive cautiously. It is bordered on one side by a row of Victorian terraces, all now converted to flats, and on the other by a wall. This wall is perhaps four feet high and separates the road from a towpath and a canal whose oily waters are rarely troubled by passing barges. Past the houses, heading away from the town, is open countryside. The surface of the road is unmarked by white lines and is old and worn. There are no streetlights.

I was first told about the cats by a girlfriend. She lived in one of the houses and we would sometimes sit in her bedroom at night and share a bottle of wine. One time, sitting at the window with soft music playing in the background, she tilted her wineglass as a pointer and said, "Can you see that?"

"What?" I asked, nuzzling into to her shoulder and peering past her into the darkness. At first, I could make out little of anything. Clouds partially obscured the moon and stars and what little light was available was that which escaped from around the closed curtains in the house windows; it lay in diffuse strips across the road like abandoned ribbons.

"There," she said and pointed again. The wine slopped over the edge of her glass, so emphatic was her gesture. This time, I saw what she meant.

"That cat?" I asked, surprised. She had never previously shown any interest in wildlife.

"It's about to kill itself," she said.

"What?"

"Watch. You'll see."

So there we sat, watching the cat. It was an old cat, bulky, and its tail was curled around its feet as though to warm them, the tip flicking back and forth like a horse's in high summer. In the almost darkness, the cat's colour was hard to discern. Shadows mottled its fur as it perched on the wall and faced the road, looking around in that slightly arrogant way cats have. Soon, there came the distant lights of a car. The cat gathered itself and when the car got close, headlights washing out over the road, it leapt. I think I may have shrieked slightly then; I do not clearly remember.

The poor driver hadn't a chance; the car struck the creature even as he braked and screeched into a skid that lasted perhaps fifteen slewing feet. When the vehicle came to a shuddering rest, the driver got out, leaving the door open so that his interior light remained on. Its weak glow fell back across the road, illuminating it in a shade the dry yellow of old milk. He walked back to the cat and I saw he was trembling violently, his shadow palsied and elongated behind him. Next to me, my girlfriend leaned forward to get a better view, raising her glass and tilting it in an ironic toast. My own wineglass shook as I raised it to my lips.

The cat was dead but still twitching. The wheel of the car had crushed its chest and dragged its hips around into an impossible angle, bursting its stomach and releasing grey loops of its intestine. They were strewn across the tarmac in curls and twists that looked like writing in a language that I could not read. Blood had spattered from the cat's mouth in a ragged arc and was draining from its ears to gather below its head; in the sallow light, the expanding pool looked black. One of the cat's front legs clawed at something only it could see and I wondered what it was trying to catch; its departing soul, maybe, or a last mouse.

The driver looked around helplessly, clearly unsure of what to do. Eventually, he returned to his car and drove away. I was horrified and made to go out to the cat, although I was not sure what I intended to do when I got there. Bury the poor thing, maybe.

"Leave it," said my girlfriend. "It'll be gone in the morning." I wanted to reply, to say something, but she had already put her wine glass down and was unbuttoning her top, swaying in time to the music. I stayed silent.

In the early hours of the morning I awoke thinking about the cat. Cautiously, so as not to wake my sleeping companion, I rose and looked out of the window. The cat had gone; all that remained of it were the ghosts of bloodstains across the tarmac. I wondered if a nocturnal predator had chanced upon it and taken advantage of the free meal. Urban foxes prowled this vicinity, I knew, and I thought that they had taken the corpse to feed on at their leisure. Returning to bed, I slept in warm comfort with the skin of my chest pressing against my lover's back.

We saw many cats kill themselves over the next few months. Small and large, young and old, tortoiseshell and tabby, they all came to sit on the wall before tensing and leaping into the path of cars. I saw broken bones and smears of fur and gristle and steam rising from the damaged bodies, I saw cats stagger away apparently unhurt before falling into stunned death and cats that were torn in half by the ferocity of the impacts. I also saw escapes; cats that leapt too late or too early, ones that did not go far enough and one lucky creature who landed and then cowered as the high-axled van thundered over its head, leaving it untouched. Some drivers, like that of the first night, stopped, others sped on. One or two skidded violently or yanked their car from side to side in savage, helpless waves, others never changed their unbending line. I did not question why the cats chose to kill themselves, I simply watched as they did. And after every suicide, there was a carcass left in the road, and every time the carcass had vanished by the following morning.

I began to wonder where all that dead flesh went. I watched from the window, hoping to see something feed upon the cat, take its corpse for food. My belief in opportunist predators weakened, for as long and as often as I watched, the cat's bodies remained untouched, unclaimed. Only once did I see something approach that sundered flesh, an owl that descended and stood by a freshly killed cat, but it started moments after landing, looking around sharply before lifting into the air and disappearing. I waited, expecting to see a dog or other creature approach, but nothing came.

Over time, I came to think that the cats belonged to something else, something that owned them and had marked them in ways I could not understand. I imagined a great creature stalking the midnight streets, vast and black and feline. In my thoughts, it padded the earth searching for the bodies and souls of the fallen, its terrible paws making no sound as they fell, and its inhalations and exhalations containing air that was not of this earth. Rather, it breathed the cold and frigid atmosphere of some other place and when it came across the bodies of dead cats, it gently scooped them into its mouth and took their souls into its lungs. Muscles writhed like snakes under its skin as it walked, in ripples that shimmered across its fur. Like smoke, this creature drifted in and out of focus, its form existing at once in this world and on some different, less tangible, earth.

From suicide place to suicide place it went, shepherding the cats into itself as people slept around it. Some nights, I sat for hours at the window after a suicide, waiting for the dark shape to come, to turn its baleful eyes towards me as it passed. And its gaze would mark me, I came to think, so that I might never be truly free from it. It would always know me and would always know where I was, what I was doing. It would make its plans for me. Once seen, I wondered, would it always be there, stepping delicately along with me? My hands clenching and unclenching in my lap, I peered helplessly into the darkness and prayed both that it came and that it did not. To see its shape outlined against the road, to watch as it tenderly licked the remains of some poor cat from the ground, might be impossible to bear. And yet, I could not stop watching.

"Do you care about those dead animals more than you do about me?" my lover asked me one night, her nipples hard points against my back as she pressed against me and tried to pull me back from the window. I did not answer. The words of denial rose up in me but caught, flies in amber, at my throat for the truth was, I did.

The cats' destruction of their own flesh was a mystery, an ever-opening doorway into a world that was wider than I could grasp but so dark I could make out little detail. The flesh of my lover, however, was bright and exposed. When I contemplated it or peered into its depths I saw every nuance, every smooth surface, every dip or rise, saw repeated patterns of days and nights shrinking down until nothing remained. She tasted as sweet and as soulless as plastic.

We argued. Harsh words were spoken. Things were said that, once free, refused to be chained or forgotten and she asked me to leave. I went and did not see her again.

I discovered that I did not truly miss my lover in the days that followed. Where before I had been distraught at the end of relationships, this one felt as distant to me as a dream or as a story I had been told as I child. I found it hard to remember her face although I could, for some reason, remember with absolute clarity the smell of her. When I closed my eyes and thought of her, conjuring her into my mind, I smelled her, but what I saw were the cats. Soon, I began to associate her scent with those broken and cooling bodies and I stopped thinking of her at all.

When I saw cats on the street, I wondered where they were going, if this were to be their last journey on the earth. I had no urge to stop them; their decisions were their own, it seemed to me, but I felt a dull pressure to understand. I tried to follow one or two of these cats, but they were agile and quick and escaped me easily.

Once, I went to the road in the evening, watching its scarred surface as darkness fell around me. Whilst the canal cooled and the houselights vanished one by one, I stayed, observing. From my vantage point on the towpath I waited for something, *anything*, to happen, but nothing did. No cats came that night. Sometime during the morning's darkest moments, I paced around the road's surface, placing my feet over tired and old bloodstains as though they might give me some insight or understanding, but they did not. Eventually I went home, walking as slowly as I could to prolong my vigil. As I walked, I wondered where the great cat had gone that night, what broken bodies it was gathering to itself. I wondered if it would come to me on the street as I walked and I trembled at the thought of it.

Cats became everything; I sliced away the other pieces of my life, increasingly focussing myself on them alone. Why did they offer themselves in this way, and in that way? Why that place, and where else? And although these questions came to obsess me, I found no answers, gained no understanding. The world became a giant, feline eye, staring at me as I went about my days and nights, never flinching and giving away nothing.

I think I may have splintered under the weight of it in the end. I know that I spent time in awful places, places where my life was exposed and derided, where everything about me was leached of colour and stripped back and poked and prodded. I remember other details, a smell of cold cleanliness and wheels that squealed and gentle touches upon my brow that became flashes of light that danced in my vision like lighting.

I remember, for the first time in months, an absence of cats.

Gradually, cats came to obsess me less. That terrible, capering light dulled the feline eye's glare, and I ceased to wonder about them when I saw them on the street. They became as they had once been, a part of the panoramic skin that the small and shrivelled world formed about me, neither more nor less important than many other things. I found a new girlfriend who lived in a busy, well lit part of the city and accepted my past without question, and soon moved in with her. Her skin is like silk and tastes rich and deep upon my tongue and she smells like flowers and heat and never of blood and broken, twisted flesh. We married and had children and our lives have become fat and comfortable. The memory of the suicidal cats became a distant story that I told myself with a curious detachment, as though it was not truly real. I could not recognise the young man that I had been or really understand that young man's actions. I still cannot understand how I came to be so fixated upon those poor creatures.

He is not completely gone, though, that lost refraction of me. Even now, if I have to drive along that strip of road at night, I find myself slowing, peering to see if there are cats around. I cannot help but glance at the wall in case I see the shadowed, still shape of a creature that has decided to kill itself using me as their tool. My foot automatically hovers over the brake, ready to stop if I see one of those seated, world-weary forms, its eyes wide and its body tense. And I cannot help but wonder, is the great black cat somewhere down the road, padding inexorably towards me?

|The Baking of Cakes|

There is an assumption that the baking of cakes must be either an art or a science. It is not; the baking of cakes is something between and beyond these two things. It takes the best elements of science (the careful weighing and measuring of the ingredients; the exact use of heat and air and time) and art (the use of colour and texture; the manipulation of size and shape) and blends them into something new. In truth, it is a form of alchemy, where the science and art are shaped by the will and desire both of those who bake and those who consume. It is a true partnership between creator and client. Cakes created by this alchemical process are more than simply pleasant confectionaries; they can represent anything. They can be a symbol of love or friendship or joy or sorrow or even hate. Cakes are a way to communicate at a level where language has lost its meaning.

I have been a baker of cakes since I was a child. My father taught me the principles, my mother taught me to use my creativity and I taught myself to give my creations meaning. I am a master baker of occasions; I make celebration cakes and from the very beginning I have made cakes that are more than simply food. Every element of the cake means something, and every meaning is relevant to the eaters and to me. The eggs I use are from healthy well-kept birds, so that their life and freedom and vitality may pass into the cake; the flour I use is milled by hand and so carries with it a sense of care and attention and craftsmanship. The tools I continue to use to this day were my father's, and in their grip and heft is a sense of history and pleasurable duty and the continuance of the past into the future.

The shape of the cakes I bake is decided by my customers; the ingredients are mine to pick. I have made sponge cakes in the form of dancing girls containing a hint of thyme (for activity) for sprightly octogenarians, and I have made sombre squares containing persimmon (for burial among nature's beauty) for the relatives of the recently deceased. I have decorated cakes with honeysuckle (for devoted love) to give on anniversaries and with hollyhock (for fecundity) to celebrate the announcement of pregnancy. I have made cakes in the shape of cars and people and animals; I create to mark events.

Even the type of cake has meaning; fruitcakes are for fertility and can be kept, held as close to the heart as a child is. Sponges are gone in an instant and are for those transient moments, for the marking of days that quickly pass. My customers include children, the old, men, women, those who are single and those who are surrounded by family. I make cakes to celebrate or to mourn or to announce, and I make them well. I am a master baker, and must be this more than ever now, for tomorrow I bake the hardest cake imaginable for the most demanding customer there is.

I shall not rise early; my kitchen is prepared and I have purchased my ingredients in advance. Instead, I shall rise when the sun is high and sit in my garden where I shall gaze at the sky and calm myself for the task ahead. Once this moment has passed, I shall go to my kitchen (the only room in my home that I consider to be entirely my own) and I shall start.

This cake is to be a sponge; truly, it should be a fruitcake for the bitter irony that would entail, but they can be months in the preparation, time to prepare that I do not have, and so a sponge it will be. This makes my task harder, but meaningful creations are often also challenges and in challenge there is learning, and we must always learn.

First, I shall mix the basic ingredients carefully. The flour shall be my normal hand-milled variety, delicately sifted and shaken, but the eggs I shall use are different. They will come from a battery farm, and the albumen and the yolk shall hold in them a memory every broken bone and scream, every cramp and blister and brutalised moment that those poor birds felt. Thus, this cake will have at its heart pain and misery and craft and attention, and on this platform I shall build.

The cake shall also contain ground almonds (for giddiness) and dark chocolate for its initial sweetness and shocking, bitter aftertaste. Into the mixture I shall then add the essence and flavours of fruits. Apple (for temptation); strawberry (for perfect excellence), apricot (for doubt), pear (for affection) and cranberry (to cure heartache). The balancing of these flavours is vital. None must overpower the others, yet all must be there, distinct and noticeable. Each has its part to play in this creation.

I shall bake the cake in my oven, where every other cake I have made has left its imprint, and then I shall leave it to cool on a wire rack. When it is cooled, I shall slit it lengthways and add a delicate layer of cream and raspberry (for remorse) that will help to keep the cake moist and soft during the day. Finally, I shall glaze the top with Demerara sugar, caramelised with the use of a tiny, sharp flame (for passion). Finished, the cake will hold inside itself all these meanings and the symbols of all the hopes and fears of my customers. There will be something to represent their joy in what might have been and their despair about what is and the things that they felt in-between these two extremes. It will be, for them, an attempt to gather in one place their contradictory emotions and feelings about their life and the things they face.

The cake is to be served at the end of a meal that will be rich in flavour. Aloe (for sorrow), juniper (for succour) and basil (for the giving of good wishes) shall be present in the food. The table will be decorated with a bouquet of cinquefoil (for a beloved child), chrysanthemum (for hearts left to desolation) and willow (for mourning). At the end of the savouries, I shall carry in my cake, and it will be served with a tea made of fennel (for strength) and cloves (for dignity), for even in the hardest of places there must be an attempt to face the future. The top of the cake will be scattered with dried white roses (for death before the loss of ignorance). I shall take my knife and press it to the top of the cake, where the caramelised sugar will resist the blade's pressure for the shortest of moments before cracking. In this brief show of strength, the cake will symbolise the flaring of life and then painful loss.

I shall sit, then, and my wife and I will eat a slice of this cake each, although it will taste like dust in our mouths and will claw and scratch on its way to our bellies. In this respect, it will act as did its twin a little over a year ago. Every flavour will be there, mingling on our tongues, and every meaning shall be there also; we shall not want to accept that, but accept it we must. We shall cry as we eat.

Together, my wife and I shall eat the cake that marks the death of our second unborn child.

|The Lemon in the Pool|

On the third afternoon, it was a lemon.

The first day, it had been a tomato, half battered and sunk to the bottom of the pool, and the on second a courgette which floated and bobbed merrily on the wavelets by the filter intake, and Helen had laughed. The tomato, she first assumed, had been dropped by a bird; it was small and the damage to it could have been caused by the fall, but the courgette was flawless, its green skin mottled and undamaged. Thinking about it then, she reasoned that it must be an odd sort of joke. Oblique and impenetrable unless you were its perpetrator, certainly, and not something that she understood, it was the kind of joke that children carried out, young children like the ones from the villa up the hill. By the time the lemon appeared, also floating like a reflection of the sun at noon, she was sure of it.

Helen's rented villa was built into the side of a hill. Below her, if she peered over the wall at the end of the garden, she could see the roofs of the shops that lined the road around the base of the hill, and to either side were villas inhabited by retired couples. Neither had grandchildren that visited as far as she knew, which only left the villa behind her, up the slope. Standing by her pool, holding the lemon (still warm from bobbing at the surface of the water in the afternoon's heart), she looked up at it. Her back wall was high, over fifteen feet, and it obscured most of the villa's lower floor, but she could still see the upper storey. No one moved on the balconies or behind the windows, and she could not hear the children playing.

She put the lemon in the kitchen, next to the courgette. It was full and bright, and Helen thought she might cut it into slices for her evening gin and tonic. She hadn't thrown either of them away because it seemed a shame to waste them and, although she didn't find the mysterious appearance of fruit and vegetables particularly funny, she was slightly touched by the effort the children were going to. Every day for three days now, they must have waited until she went in for her siesta and then threw things into her pool. Or, if they weren't throwing them, they were sneaking in and placing them in the water. Either way, it showed a strange commitment that she liked. It was, she thought, nice to be the focus of someone's attention again, however gentle and odd that attention might be.

On the fourth day it was green peppers, large and emerald, the type she had thought were overlarge chillies when she first arrived in Spain. She fished them out and turned to the villa up the hill, waving at it even though she could see no one. She hoped she might hear the laughter of hidden children, and intended for her wave to show that she was enjoying the joke, but she received no response. The villa's white walls and glittering windows reflected the afternoon sunlight back at her, sending glints across the pool's surface and catching the splashes on the tiled poolside. Shielding her eyes helped block the brightness, she kept looking at the villa, tracing around its whitewashed walls and shaded verandas with vision that was bleached by the glare, but still she saw no movement. The building remained blank and stolid.

Helen put the peppers with the courgette and lemon, still untouched in her kitchen. She hadn't wanted to slice the fruit in the end, partly because she felt that cutting it up would be in some way rude or dismissive of the joke that the children were taking such care over, and partly because of the way it felt. Mostly because of the way it felt, actually. When she picked up the lemon the previous evening, it hadn't felt very right, not at all. It was still bright, its yellow skin gleaming and slightly waxy, but it was soft and pulpy when she squeezed it and she wondered if its time in the pool had affected it in some way. It felt mushy, somehow. Rotten inside. In the end, she found another lemon and used that, having a couple of drinks on her veranda and enjoying the cooling day's end as the pool chuckled to itself in the slight breeze.

On the fifth day, the joke started to wear a little thin. Helen came out after her afternoon rest (*Siesta,* she told herself, *it's a siesta and everyone does it*) to find that the pool was covered a floating scum of redcurrants, a myriad little spheres dancing in the splintering gleam of the sun. Like the courgette, lemon and peppers, the redcurrants were undamaged and looked juicily ripe, but there were so *many* of them.

They covered most of the surface, a slick that tinged the pool a deep and lustrous pink as the light glittered off them and down into the water. It took Helen almost half an hour to clear them all, scooping them out with the net she usually used to clear dead insects and leaves from the surface of the water before they were drawn into the filter. By the time she finished, she had filled a large metal bucket with the fruit and it was almost too heavy to lift, so that she had to tug it to make it move and then drag it tilted onto its lower rim, shrieking and leaving a white track behind it. Hauling it across to the kitchen so that she could put the fruit into bags, she looked once more at the villa up the hill, hoping that the children would see her, see that her face no longer showed amusement. Apart from anything, it was a waste of fruit because she couldn't possibly eat all these redcurrants, and she had left her jam making days behind her when she left the grey drear of England and moved to Moraira.

Day six, and the joke collapsed in on itself completely.

Emerging from the cool shade of the villa when the sun had moved around far enough to lose some of its glaring power, Helen found two large fruit floating in the pool. They were the size of melons, but it was impossible to tell what they actually were; they were disintegrating and rotten. Strings of yellowing, slimy flesh trailed from the fruit, whose dark skin was mottled green and brown. The water around the two floating things was hazy and opaque, coloured like stale urine with the fruits' juices. Even as Helen watched, tendrils of pulpy flesh drifted from the two globes, along with things that looked like seeds, performing somnambulant spirals as they sank to the pool's bottom. Once there, they joined more of the yellowing tendrils, like shed snakeskin, all of them drifting in currents that made them dip and rise in a low harmony. It looked like they were dancing.

Helen tried to fish the large pieces of fruit out with the net but they broke apart as she pulled them to the side, the green skin flapping like a torn flag and the insides escaping and floating back towards the centre of the pool, spreading in the eddies created by the net's movement and the breeze that tickled at the water's surface.

"Shit," muttered Helen. There was no way that she could get it all out with the net; it was dissolving as she watched, breaking into tiny fibrous pieces and giving the surrounding water a pale yellow corona as though it were haloed by corruption. It smelled too, a sharp, scraping odour that itched in her nose. The whole of the pool was fouled with it, and she needed to run a full backwash filter cycle before she could use it again.

As Helen went to the pool controls, she looked up at the hillside villa and glared, wondering if the children could see her and tell how angry she was. She only had to run a full filter cycle once every few weeks normally; apart from bugs and a floating layer of sun cream, the pool stayed generally clean and she could freshen it by hand and with a little water turbulence from the jets once a day. Between the net and the pool's own filter, she had little to do to maintain the water and could, instead, just enjoy it. She had only run the full cycle 6 days ago, and now she had to do it again, and it annoyed her. It wasn't funny.

As the jets circulated the water in the pool, pushing the debris towards the filters, Helen fished out the larger pieces as best she could. Most of it had sunk and she had to reach deep with the net to catch it, and it was hard work; the water was heavy against the mesh, pushing the pieces into a swirling dance around the pole and making her arms ache as she dug and chased. She couldn't reach the middle of the pool very easily from the side, but she didn't want to get into the water. It might have made things easier, but the smell of the fruit hovered, viscous and unpleasant, and if that was how it smelled, it would surely feel worse. She didn't like the idea that, unseen, tiny particles of it would be brushing against her, clammy against her skin, worming their way below her costume, tangling themselves in her pubic hair, getting inside her, into her mouth, her throat, her nose. Her stomach. No, whatever this rotten fruit was, she wanted as little contact with it as possible.

The last thing Helen had to do was clean the filters themselves; she had removed all of the larger pieces from the water and had regulated the level of chlorine, testing and adding until the water was back to something approaching normal and safe. In the hours that it had taken her, the water in the pool had been cycled through the filtration system, which meant she now had to remove and clean the meshes themselves. It was never a particularly pleasant job, cleaning away the broken bodies of insects and scraping off the scum of dirt and grease that collected across the fine nylon netting, but today it was awful.

The filters were clogged with torn and pulpy flesh and with a thick, clinging slime that stank. Seeds clustered in the slime, nestling against dead insects whose bodies looked wrong somehow, half-formed and dissolving as though the slime was corrosive. Helen didn't want to touch it.

She found a pair of old rubber gloves in the kitchen, and a wooden spoon that she no longer used, and began to scrape the filters clean. Each time she dragged the spoon through the muck, she uncovered new things, little treasures given up like dinosaur bones from tar pits. A large grasshopper, its wings almost gone and its face weirdly distorted; a clump of leaves, soaked down to a dark blob like melting toffee; a single cranberry, ripe and apparently unmarked but softer than it should have been, shifting between her fingers like jelly as Helen squeezed it; a larger piece of fruit that smelled like fermenting star fruit. She put it all into the bucket along with the pieces she had managed to strain from the pool, where it settled in viscid puddles. The smell from the bucket as it baked in the heat was overpowering, like ammonia or bleach.

By the time Helen finished, the bucket was full and heavy and getting it to the villa was difficult. She didn't want to slop its contents on her as she walked, so she ended up dragging it, stretched out, her back aching and her muscles singing in protest. This wasn't what she had thought she'd be doing when she retired, she reflected, looking again at the villa up the hill. All those years of drudgery in the office, all the meetings and reports and filing, all the late nights in the office completing the work for bosses, and the lonely nights at home, all the insincere greetings and hollow works parties, they were the bedrock on which her villa was built. Somewhere hot and private, where she could rest, read and never, ever be at anyone else's beck and call again, that was the plan. Not this.

"Shit," she muttered again, and carried on dragging the bucket towards the bin.

The next day, it was meat.

One of the pieces looked like a haunch; the other was a ragged mess of redly gleaming flesh and white bone that she couldn't identify. Furious, she swung at them with her net, watching in dismay as both chunks broke into smaller pieces even as she drew them from the pool, watching as the water tinged pink around them and knowing that she would have to run a full filter cycle again. Like the fruit, the meat smelled, a corrupted, sour scent of bile and decay, and as it dried in the heat its surface mottled to a patched and bruised grey. It had looked fresh in the water, certainly, but the way the flesh sloughed off the bone as it lay in her net convinced Helen that it was old, kitchen waste or something scavenged from the bins behind the supermarket. Using the net to keep the meat away from her, she went to the gate, intending to go to the villa up the hill and complain, but she stopped before going out onto the road. She had no proof, only suspicions, and besides, even if she was right, the likelihood was she would be dismissed as a foolish, raving woman, going senile in the heat. *Meat?* they would say. *Our children? No, not our children. You must be mistaken.*

As the filter cycle ran, Helen sat in the shade drinking juice and wondering about her options. The sound of the pumps was calming, like hearing the distant hum of bees. She could go to the villa in person, she thought. Not carrying a net of meat and not in her swimming costume, definitely, but still go, explain politely and rationally that it had been amusing at first but that it wasn't amusing now, that it was a waste of her time having to keep cleaning her pool. The problem was, she knew, she had no proof. She had never seen the children throw anything, never seen them looking at her over their wall or heard them laughing. *And besides,* she thought, *how likely is it that this is the work of young children? The fruit, maybe, but meat?* No. It didn't seem likely.

Then what? Tell the police? Again, no. Moraira was a tourist town, so she wouldn't be dismissed entirely because they relied on tourism and had to make sure they listened when tourists complained, but they wouldn't take her seriously. It wasn't exactly a major crime. "Excuse me, officer," said Helen quietly to herself, "someone appears to have thrown a courgette into my pool, and then a lemon, and then redcurrants and then some meat. No, I don't want it stopped, I just wondered if you could find out who it was and ask them for an onion and rice and some pastry as well. I was hoping to make a risotto and then a fruit pie to follow." She sighed and sipped her drink. It was so stupid.

The filters were clogged with meat, greying and semi-liquid, and Helen wore the gloves again to clean them. There were more pieces of fruit in the mesh as well, tiny fragments of something that looked like it might once have been orange segments and more of the yellowing slimy residue that wrapped itself around her gloved fingers and stank like raw shit. At the bottom edge of one of the filter screens she tugged loose a long, thin piece of meat. It stretched out before snapping free and she had the impression that it was covered in tiny suckers like an octopus' tentacle. It curled around itself in the palm of her hand, disintegrating as she tried to unwrap it so that she could look more closely and releasing an oily, bitter smell. Finally she dropped it in the bucket with the other pieces of flesh and slime; whoever it was was dropping pieces of octopus in her pool now. Fine. Brilliant. Fucking *wonderful*. And Helen, kneeling by her pool in the day's dying sun began, very quietly and calmly, to weep.

The next day, Helen didn't go inside for her usual siesta. Instead, she set herself up at a table in the shade, where she could read and keep an eye on the pool. She brought a huge jug of juice, clinking with ice cubes, several magazines and a book she had been intending to start for a while. Let them, whoever *them* was, try to throw things into her pool now. Perhaps, if she did this for several days and stopped them having their fun, they would grow bored. Helen no longer thought it was the children in the villa; the addition of meat had made it feel nastier, one of the pranks of youth rather than childhood. Expats were, she knew, not always popular and she was particularly vulnerable. Older, female and on her own, she must have seemed like a perfect target.

"Well, fuck you," she said loudly, pouring herself her first glass of juice, using the language she would never have used back home but which she had secretly always loved. "Fuck you all."

Even though she sat and read through the hottest part of the day, the sweat gathering in a thin slather across her skin despite the shade, Helen saw nothing. Several times, she rose and walked to the edge of the pool, peering into its blue waters in case she had missed something falling or being thrown in, but the water remained clear and clean. She managed to read her magazines, but the book proved too dense for her to cope with when she came up against the impenetrable wall of unbroken black text and heat and sun, her mind moving far more slowly than she would have liked it too. Instead, she finished the juice, the ice cubes long since melted into nothing, and was almost dozing when she heard the noise.

It was like a bath emptying, she thought as she jerked her head up from the table. Or, more accurately, it was like the sound air made as it broke the surface as water emptied away, a sort of deep, bass rumble that seemed to have no end and no real beginning. She went to the poolside, not sure what to expect, and found that the surface was choppy and broken. Fat bubbles rose from under the water, emerging in gross mushroom domes that burst and splashed. Watching the agitation, Helen smelled something sulphurous and dank and corpulent that bloomed with every new bubbleburst and then faded as the water calmed, dissipating like the scent of a match after it had been extinguished, until nothing of it remained but a sour memory and the itch of it in her nose.

When the water finally settled, Helen checked the pool carefully. She thought at first that it was empty but then saw, floating near the bottom of the deeper end, something small and black.

"Another piece of fruit?" she asked herself aloud, and then the black thing shifted sluggishly. Helen watched as it unfurled, stretching out until it was a few inches long. It jerked and then moved through the water before slowing and stopping, finally drifting to the bottom like a half-furled parachute. She picked up the net and trawled for it but couldn't reach; the bottom of the net passed over the top of the thing, making it drift towards the centre of the pool in lazy, curling arcs. She tried to use the net to create updrafts in the water to bring the thing within grabbing distance but it remained stubbornly low and out of reach. Not liking the way it hung there like a tiny black shadow intruding into her clean, clear pool, Helen took her sarong off and slipped into the water.

Diving down, Helen remembered with something almost like surprise how much she enjoyed being in the water, and why she had been so insistent about finding a villa with a pool for her retirement. These last days had taken away the joy of it, replacing it with dull irritation and a tension in her chest whenever she thought about the pool, and it was nice to rediscover pleasure once more in the water's cooling embrace. She swam around the pool's floor until her breath gave out, looking for the thing and not finding it but not really minding. Surfacing, she released the stale air from her lungs and drew in a fresh breath. It was sweet and warm, and she liked the taste of it in her mouth. Turning onto her back, she floated for a while without moving, feeling the light against her face and her closed eyes and enjoying its warmth. This was why she had come here; the lightness of the air and the caressing weight of the heat, the way her skin seemed to open when the sun hit it and the smell of olives and oranges and the sea, all of it making a world as delicate and far removed from her lumpen, leaden old home as could be. There were no commuter journeys here, no weekends trapped inside by rain and boredom, no layered clothing to deal with unexpected rain or cold snaps, no dismissive bosses or condescending work colleagues, no pitying looks in shops when she bought only enough food for one, no endless days of drudgery and repetition, only lightness and exhilaration and enjoyment.

And no one was going to spoil it for her.

Turning, she dived again, this time making a more precise search for the small, dark thing. She found it in the corner of the pool, not quite sunk to the bottom. Without her goggles on she couldn't see it clearly, grabbing it and rising to the surface rather than trying to work out what it was whilst underwater. It felt warm and soft, rubbery and smooth. An olive, she wondered? A ball of some sort? Emerging and making her way to the side, she shook water from her eyes and looked at the thing in her hand.

It might have been an octopus or a squid, it was hard to be sure. It had tentacles, certainly, 7 of them and a ragged stump where an eighth might have been and two smaller, almost vestigial nubbins above them. Above these limbs was a bulbous body, looking and feeling like a ripe and boneless fruit in her hand. It was only two inches long and out of the water it was an iridescent black, sparkling with colours that prickled over its surface and faded as she watched. Even as she held it, it deflated somehow, its little bulb body collapsing in on itself. Black liquid like coagulated ink spattered out from between the tentacles and slicked across her fingers. It was warm and sticky and smelled of fish that had been left to rot in the heat and light and closeness. Helen gagged, spat, gagged again and then dropped the thing onto the side of the pool, far enough away so that it wouldn't drip back into the water; she had no desire to clean the pool for a third time. She moved away from it before climbing out, not wanting to be near it, still feeling the bitter swirl of bile in her throat and stomach and unsure whether she was going to vomit or not. The smell of it still clung to her, the tepid clamminess of the liquid on her hand making her want to scream or cry again. She was so angry, and terribly sad at the same time. Whoever was doing this, and however they were doing it, this was *horrible*. The octopus thing, some local fish she assumed, had done nothing wrong except be unable to survive outside of saltwater and had been sacrificed for the sake of what she now thought of as a campaign of harassment. Well, no more.

She washed her hands in the outside shower, went inside and got as far as picking up the phone to call the police before stopping. What, really, could she say to them? Really? The only time she had called them previously, when someone had tried to force a window one afternoon as she slept, had not been a good experience. The young policeman had listened to her concerns and looked at the scratched window lock and asked bored-sounding questions, but seemed more interested in letting his eyes crawl up and down her chest, making her wish she had put on something more covering than a sarong and swimsuit before he had arrived. He had told her, in halting English, that he would file a report and that she should not worry, then left, and she never heard from him again. How would they treat her if she tried to report this? Not well, she thought. They would, she imagined, see her as a silly old woman, come here to escape the casual cruelties of life and to die in peace but unable to stop seeing ghosts in the shadows of every corner. She was too easy to dismiss, neither rich enough nor well known enough to demand attention, another incomer who didn't speak the language and who didn't belong. She replaced the phone in the cradle without dialling. This was supposed to be her safe place, and she did not want to open herself to ridicule within its walls. She went to clean the mess of the dead thing up.

The next day, she had a new idea. At the time she normally went back into the villa to escape the harshest of the afternoon sunlight, she instead slathered herself with sun cream and lowered herself into the pool. If whoever it was threw or dropped something in the pool today, fruit or beast, she would know. She would see it. *See if they dare*, she thought, and out loud said, "See if you dare, you little bastards."

Helen floated. She could swim well, but she enjoyed more letting the water support her, take her where it wanted to go. It was as though a huge hand was holding her from below, cupping her buttocks and back and shoulders with the gentlest touch she had experienced in a long and not always easy life. In the water she wasn't old or young, she was neither spinster nor maid, she wasn't retired or working, she wasn't a collection of aches and pains, she wasn't even female, she was just *Helen*. Helen, who had learned to like her own company but sometimes would have liked to share it, Helen who could cook but rarely did, Helen who read books and wanted to write one but knew she never would. Just Helen, whole and complete and real.

There was something in the water with her.

It was something about the way the water moved, the way it rose and dropped again in a gentle swell, scooping her and then letting her down, that gave it away. Something large had passed below her; impossible, but it had happened. She rolled onto her front, more surprised than anything else, and dipped her face into the water. Her vision blurred, her eyes wanting to shut, treading water and seeing little but the fizzing blue of the water pressed against her pupils. She held it as long as possible, turning around and peering as best she could all around the pool. Nothing. Only, the pool looked deeper, *felt* deeper than it should be, the water chilled suddenly as though she had somehow floated far out into a place where the sun no longer had the strength to reach and reflect back from the tiled floor.

Impossible.

Helen raised her head, convinced she'd spooked herself but not knowing how, and as she shook her face free from her wet hair, a shadow moved in front of her. It was under the water, large and dark and swift, moving around from her front to her rear. Circling her. Instinctively, she stopped swimming; there was something predatory and cold about the shape that made her imagine teeth and black eyes and mouths that stretched wide and gaping. As slowly as she could, Helen turned, letting the currents take her towards the poolside.

It wasn't there.

Or rather, it was, but it wasn't where it should be. The pool was only forty feet long and about twenty wide, but now the side looked as though it were a hundred yards or more away. The water was chilling further, darkening down to a slate grey and beyond, to the roiling near-black of storm clouds in leaden skies. The surface of the water was choppier now, wavelets breaking over her face and sending questing fingers into her nose and mouth, making her choke and cough. She could not see the shadow now, the water opaque and dark, but the moving thing was still there. Helen could sense it, feel the current buffet her as it circled, the play of the water stronger and stronger around her legs and belly as whatever it was got closer. A haze gathered above the water like a heat flicker but denser, distorting the now-distant lip of the poolside, and she wondered for a brief, fractured moment if she had put too much chlorine in the water. But she dismissed the thought – this wasn't a hallucination brought on by too many chemicals, nor too vivid an imagination. This was no longer her pool; it was somewhere she did not recognise, somewhere vast and chill. Then something bumped against her foot.

The bump itself was not hard, but it was rough like sandpaper and it tore at her skin and she screamed and started to swim. All thoughts of motionlessness, of remaining a floating thing and not attracting attention, were gone. The water rose and fell, knocking her, as the dark shape passed underneath her, close enough for her to make out scales and eyes like slick black plates and a fin curved like a sickle and then she was swimming with wild, thrashed strokes. She choked as she swam, water that tasted flat and stagnant filling her mouth and a smell of sour, flat bile burning in her nostrils. She didn't know whether the smell was her own fear or the haze above the water, and didn't care. The only thing that mattered was to reach the side.

It was behind her. She knew it, could feel the water drive her forward as something pushed a bow-wave ahead of itself, the curl of it gathering behind her head and threatening to overwhelm her. She kicked her legs, urging her body on, pulling at the water with hands that felt numb and clumsy, sure she could feel lips kiss at her toes, teeth nip at her ankles. The side was still so far away, shrinking away from her rather than coming closer, the water bucking now, the air leached of colour and metallic-tasting, her hair draggling into her eyes and her body weighted and slow. She choked again, spitting out foul water, and struck out, trying to reach further, pull harder.

Trying to swim faster.

The thing in the water came at her from behind. Something banged into her legs and pushed her up, lifting her out of the water. Helen shrieked, kicking back and feeling her feet strike something rubbery and soft, going into a frenzy as the something clamped heavily around her calves and kicking even harder. Her left foot shifted within a writhing, sucking thing and she shrieked again, still rising from the water as she was pushed from below, water in her mouth and burning her nose. Her other foot scraped against a gelid mass and she kicked as best she could, feeling like her legs were wrapped in a heavy rubber sheet that constricted them and stole their strength. Her toes pushed against something that was warm and pulsed and she pushed, *pushed,* and then she felt it burst and her legs were suddenly enveloped in slimy warmth. The thing that had hold of her bucked, thrashed her further out of the water and she felt something like pulsing plastic ropes grip at her thighs, and then she banged into the side of the pool and was gripping at the smooth tile surface and climbing. The thing gripping her legs pulled and she slammed down into the hard poolside and started to slip back into the water, the ropes around her thighs tightening and the sucking about her legs increasing. She screamed and spat, tensing her arms and pulling and kicking and dragging and then, with a noise like a tooth pulling from a rotten gum, she slithered out of the water, skin scraping against the edge of the wall. She flailed, pulling at the tiled floor and thrashing with her legs so that it could not grab her again and she heaved, heaved with everything she had, and she was out.

Helen collapsed on the floor, gasping and weeping. Sunlight played across her face, warming her skin. She opened her eyes into a bright sky, wincing as the light lanced into them. She squinted and rolled over, rising to her hands and knees and looking out across the pool. It was twenty feet wide, and forty long, the water clear and blue and its surface, apart from the rapidly settling evidence of her own exit from it, was smooth and unbroken. There was nothing in its depths.

Nothing? No. There was a shadow at its centre, a darker smear that dwindled as she watched, shrinking in upon itself until nothing remained except the tiniest patch of shade which broke apart into droplets and dispersed. It was like watching ink escaping from a bottle in reverse and she had the sense of something closing. Those droplets, though, were still there in the water even though she could not see them; it wasn't completely closed, was still open the tiniest invisible fraction somewhere in the pool. Helen spat; the taste of the water was still in her mouth, rich and bitter and foetid. Was she going mad? Unexplained tastes were a symptom of brain tumours, she remembered. Was that it? Was she ill?

No. The stain from the dead thing yesterday was still clear on the poolside; she could see it from where she knelt. Looking down at herself, she saw scratches across her legs, stark against her pale skin. Her thighs were marked with abrasions that curled around in spirals, rising from her knees to just below her crotch. A slick of some darker liquid like grey oil covered her up to her knees and under it, her skin prickled. She stood, unsteady but determined, and went to the outdoor shower. Turning it as hot as she could bear, she let the water flow over her, filling her mouth and swilling it around, spitting to clear the taste. It did not clear the slime on her legs until she rubbed at it and then it fell away in clumps, slithering down the drain like jelly. Helen cried as she scrubbed at her skin, the sick wash of old adrenaline and spent fear making her shake. When she vomited, thin strings of bile spattering from her mouth and disappearing down the drain with the pallid jelly, she hardly noticed.

Later, Helen brought her old photo albums out to the table and leafed through them. Even though they were mostly colour, the appeared black and white to her, fragments of a life that had died the moment she stepped out from the plane in Alicante, collected her luggage and walked to the hire car office. Who were these people, she wondered. People in office clothes, in jeans, in gardens and on beaches, in winter, in summer, smiling and drinking and walking and posing, all of them forgotten by her and who almost certainly didn't remember her. When were they taken, these endless photos of men and women, smiling and blank and unknown? She didn't know. None of the photographs showed her in the villa; she had no friends here to take her photograph, no one to share this place with.

No one to tell about the pool.

She didn't know what was happening in the water, or why, but she knew that it was real. She had seen it, smelled it. Felt it. She looked down at her photographs again and suddenly wished that she was home – not the home she had tried to make here but the dismal home she had left behind. In one of the photographs, she was smiling at the camera and wearing a heavy woollen hat. Had she still got that hat? She couldn't remember but suspected she had thrown it away, thinking she would never need it because she was moving somewhere hot. She was hit by a terrible sadness, wishing that she still had the hat, that things were different, that they were back to normal and dull and boring and grey and cold. Back to *safe*.

The pool glittered in front of her, blue and calm in the Moraira sun.

|Stevie's Duck|

~

"There was a duck in the pond last night. It was really big."

Stevie looked around the breakfast table at his mum and dad, hoping that his news would stir some response from them, but neither moved. William, Stevie's younger brother, merely popped a piece of toast in his mouth and chewed noisily.

"Really, really big," he said again. This time, he got a response.

"Good," from his father and "It's probably the heat," from his mother, who continued, "because our pond must look lovely and attractive from the air. Nice, cool water in a big, quiet garden." She smiled at Stevie, who did not smile back.

"And all the better now that Tanzy the monster cat is gone," said Stevie's father without lowering his paper.

"David!" said Stevie's mother, whose memory of the feral beast that the Mullan family had called a pet for many years was of a soft, cuddly animal that never hurt anything.

"Well, it's true," replied Stevie's father. "That animal frightened away practically all the wildlife from the area, let alone just our garden. It'll be nice to have birds visit now that she's not here to terrorise them."

"Tanzy was a perfectly nice cat, she just didn't like you because you were mean to her," replied Stevie's mum sharply.

It was a familiar discussion, not quite an argument but still edged with tensions that Stevie couldn't exactly name but had felt before. He tried again to talk about the duck. "It was massive, Dad, really big. Bigger than anything I've seen before!"

"Oh, I'm sure it just looked big because it was at night," said Stevie's mum, "and besides, why were you awake? I don't want you staying up late, Stephen, you get grouchy if you don't get enough sleep."

"It was horrible," said Stevie, giving it one last try.

"How can a duck be horrible?" asked his dad. "Be sensible, Stevie. Ducks are perfectly nice creatures." Stevie gave up. How could he tell them what he had seen, what he felt, when he didn't quite understand it himself? There *had* been a duck in the pond at the bottom of the garden last night, he was sure, a huge duck at least as big as he was. He had seen it from his window, its massive body bobbing on the surface of the water and its head raised and looking right at the house, at his bedroom. It had been bigger than it had any right to be and somehow sinister. Most ducks looked friendly or stupid; this one had looked fierce.

By the end of the day, Stevie had convinced himself that his mum and dad were right. He had been hot and tired, his eyes scratchy from lack of sleep and from the scorched, miserable heat, and he had seen a big bird and imagined it bigger. He went to bed early, hoping to fall asleep quickly, but knew he would not. It had been sunny for weeks now, and the ground was as warm as the air most of the time. Even after the sun had gone, you could feel it pumping out waves of heat, keeping the whole world hot right through till morning. It was wearying. Stevie had never thought he would miss the rain and the cold, but he did.

The duck was back that night.

It was clearly a duck. Looking closely, he recognised not just the shape of it but its colours as well. Just a duck, like he sometimes saw on the canal or in the park, except that it was huge and lazing in the pond at the end of his garden. Its head alone was as big as an entire normal duck, and Stevie didn't like the way it was looking at him. Its attention was unwavering, the black and depthless eyes never leaving him. It gave Stevie the shivers; it was as though the duck was smart. It was like being stared at by the school bully, an assessing glare that weighed up his weaknesses and made decisions about where to strike. Stevie stared back, unnerved. Then, as if it had been waiting until it had his full attention, the duck dipped its head quickly into the pond, once, twice, a third time. On the last occasion, Stevie caught a glimpse of something wriggling in the duck's mouth as it slipped down its throat. The fish! Dad's fish! The duck was eating Dad's precious fish! And the worst of it was, Stevie was sure that the duck *knew* how precious all the fish were to his dad and was doing it deliberately.

The duck drifted slowly to the edge of the pond and then clambered out. Its leathery legs looked ashen in the moonlight, its glistening feathers dripping water across the grass. It stretched out wings that cast a shadow across the entire lawn and then was up, seeming to move from land to air in a single graceful thrash of its wings. It circled the house once and then was gone.

"My damned fish!" said Stevie's dad the next morning. He knew how many fish there should be, and he knew how many came to the surface for their morning feed. Three were missing.

"The duck was here again last night, Dad. I told you!" said Stevie. The missing fish were evidence, surely?

"Stevie, it can't have been a duck," snapped his dad. "A heron, maybe. Christ, if we've had a heron it'll be back. I'll have to net the pond or we'll lose all the fish." He turned and went back inside, Stevie following close by.

"But Dad, why can't it be a duck?" asked Stevie.

"For the last time, Stevie, ducks do not get to be 'massive' and they don't eat fish from ponds. They're friendly things, are ducks. Now, I don't want to hear any more about ducks."

"Duck!" shouted William, spitting out pieces of half-chewed toast and banging the table so hard that his glass wobbled and slopped orange across his plate. "Duck!" with more spattered toast and gales of childish, joyous laughter, and Stevie wished he'd never spoken. Stevie's mum motioned him and William to be quiet behind Dad's back; he was sensitive about his fish. The only real argument that Stevie had heard his mum and dad have had been about Tanzy. Or, more specifically, Tanzy and the pond. It was after they moved to Ash Tree Lane and the pond had been dug and stocked that Tanzy had gone wild. She would vanish for days at a time, and refused to let anyone but Stevie's mum pet her. Anyone who tried got slashed with claws as sharp as glass, and she had stopped eating the cat food they put down for her. Even Stevie's mum had to agree she was eating 'elsewhere', although his mum would always mutter that this was because someone else was feeding her rather than the fact that she was eating the things she caught. Stevie didn't like Tanzy at all. It wasn't that she'd clawed him a few times (although she had, and it had hurt), it was the way she walked. She acted like she was a tiger, stalking across the lawn or around the edge of the pond like she owned it. It was as though she was only a tabby cat by accident but was a tiger by inclination and at Ash Tree Lane, her real nature had started to emerge. Birds, mice, frogs, other cats even dogs, all were fair game to her. Tanzy, lord of the garden, Stevie had thought. One day, Tanzy had decided that the fish were also fair game, and Stevie's dad had seen her and had really, *really* lost his temper. The first Stevie knew of it was when he heard his dad shouting.

Stevie's dad had run across the garden and grabbed the startled Tanzy by the scruff of her neck and, before she could twist and slash at him, had plunged her into the water, yanking her out a moment later and then running back across the garden still holding the now-dripping cat. He had disappeared down the side of the house, followed by Stevie's mum, who was adding to the noise with shrieks of her own, and at the front of the house had (as described by Stevie's excitable next-door neighbour, Michael) "thrown the cat over the front gate and shouted 'Sod off!' at it". Stevie's mum and dad didn't talk for three days after that, but Tanzy never went near the fish again.

Stevie's dad had to work, so couldn't net the pond that day. The south of England suffered; in the ever-tightening grip of the heat, the grass in the gardens of Ash Tree Lane yellowed slowly and the earth hardened like concrete. Dogs lay on the pavements, tongues lolling over lips that were black and dry. Stevie stayed indoors, sweating and feeling like a piece of rumpled cloth, unable to get cool, no matter what he did. Even William was quieter than normal, content to push his toy cars around in slow circles on the lounge carpet. Stevie wished that he was young enough to join in. It looked like fun, but he was eleven now, and cars and younger brothers were too childish for him. He tried not to think about the duck, nor about the way it had eaten the fish or how upset his dad had been, but it crept into his mind every few minutes. How could it be real? Perhaps it had been a heron, and it was just that his brain was so baked that he couldn't recognise it?

Stevie was exhausted by bedtime, and managed to drift to sleep not long after he turned his light out. The comforting sounds of the house settled around him like a blanket, holding him as he slept. The television downstairs was a soft background murmur, his parents' occasional voices a counterpoint. The settling of the house's walls came in long, relaxing sighs. Sleep was peace and calm and not long enough.

He was woken by his sweat; it was pooling on his chest and making his skin goose. Even in the darkness of the night's middle, the heat refused to loosen its grip on the house. As Stevie lay, he listened to the after-midnight sounds of the house around him. His dad's slow snores and his mum's restless turns came to him blended with William's sweet mumbles and grunts, all descant to the lower sounds of the house unwinding. He liked these noises, hearing in them the solidity he enjoyed in his life. The Mullan sound; soft, comforting, enjoyable. The noise of water splashing, however, he liked less.

Eventually Stevie had to get up and open his curtains. The splashes and rippling drifting in through his open window became insistent when he tried to ignore them, a deliberate agitation of the water to let Stevie know of their presence. From his window, he looked down the length of the garden and, sure enough, the duck was back in the pond.

When it knew he was looking, the duck bent its head very slowly to the water before darting forward and then back, up, down again, taking two fish in as many seconds. Stevie gasped at its speed and the ferocity of the movements. The duck looked up at him again, its black eyes catching glints of light from the stars and moon above and swallowing them down. Then it glided slowly to the edge of the pond and clambered out. Water showered down from it as it shook itself and started to come across the grass towards the house; it should have been funny, a huge duck waddling in the garden, but Stevie did not laugh. It was terrifying in ways he could not articulate, an alien and *intelligent* presence. Eventually, it came to just below his window, its webbed feet clenching around the edges of the patio flagstones. It tilted its head back, staring at him. He looked down, wishing he could shout or throw something, but he could not move. Then, the duck walked carefully around the corner of the house, sending a last cold stare at him over its shoulder as it went. Stevie slumped, leaning against the window frame and feeling a new sweat on his body, one borne not of heat but of terror, one that crept across his skin with cold, slimed fingers and found its way to his most secret places, buried around his crotch and in the cleft between his buttocks. He let out a lost breath, and then the hammering started.

It was thunderous, like metal striking wood with glass rattling at its edges. Stevie jumped, banging his shoulder against the window frame, and heard his dad's voice from the next room, "Jesus Christ! What's that?" and then his mum's startled cry, "David!" There was a short, frantic silence in which Stevie knew his dad, who slept naked, was putting clothing on, and then his dad dashed past his open door and disappeared down the stairs. Stevie suddenly wanted to cry, *Stop Dad! Don't open the door!* his mind filled with images of the duck carrying on its furious tattoo even after the door was opened, striking his dad in the chest or face with its crescent half moon of beak edge, of his dad reeling back injured or worse. William set up a cry from his room, a frightened wail that Stevie wanted to join but could not, aware of his responsibilities as older brother, and then Stevie's mum ran to William's room and the soft sounds of comfort started. Stevie stayed by the window. From downstairs came the sound of his dad unlocking the back door, calling out as he did so.

"Who's that? Stop that banging!"

As suddenly as it started, the noise stopped. Stevie had the impression of something passing between him and the stars, of it wheeling in tight circles above him, and then it was gone and his dad was coming back up the stairs and saying, "Damned kids. I thought we'd got away from all this when we moved out of the city, but the country seems even worse!"

"We're not in the country," replied Stevie's mum, emerging from William's room, "we're in a suburb. Was no one there?"

"No. Bloody kids."

"Oh, David, you don't know that. It might have been..." and here she tailed off, uncertain. Stevie wanted to go out, meet them on the stairs and say, *The duck! It was the duck!* But he sensed that there was no point. His mum and dad had already proved that they had duck-shaped sealed places in their minds that he could not access. They would never see the giant duck, no matter how hard he tried to persuade them.

The next morning, even before his mum and dad were awake, Stevie let himself out into the back garden. In the faded early light, he saw a series of curved indentations in the wooden door's exterior. Oddly, however, the indentations looked old; the paint covering them wasn't chipped or cracked but whole and unmarked, as though it had been put on afterwards, but how could that be? Stevie remembered his dad painting the door last year, and he was sure that there had been no marks in the wood then. Had there? In the flower bed on the other side of the path was a streaky white mass of bird droppings which he quickly covered with soil, scuffing it over using the side of his foot and trying not to think about how he'd explain to Mum about the dirt on his new slippers. He looked again at the door. The indentations, old or new, were quite deep; the duck had hit it hard. *That duck,* Stevie thought and then, thrillingly, *that* fucking *duck!*

All that day, Stevie thought about the duck. Where had it come from? What did it want? Why *him*? He had no answers, but he did have some ideas. He had heard that, sometimes, the government made genetically modified (whatever that meant) animals, so maybe the duck was one of them, escaped from a laboratory somewhere? Or, maybe, it was the heat. His dad had said lots of times this summer that it "wasn't normal", so perhaps it was the heat had made the duck, swelling a river duck until it got big and angry and mad. The worst thought of all was that it had somehow come from him, from out of his mind, and that this was his fault. Was it his mind that was killing his dad's fish, leaving marks on the door and bird shit on the flowerbeds? That would certainly explain why the duck targeted him and why only he could see it or even wanted to talk about it, but it did not explain what it wanted. Freedom? Revenge for its creation? Stevie could offer it neither, as far as he knew. He was at a loss.

Stevie only pretended to go to bed and sleep that night. He lay on top of his blanket and made his breathing slow when his mum put her head around the door so that she wouldn't suspect anything, and then got up as soon as his door was shut. He stood vigil by the window, waiting for the duck to arrive or appear, but it did neither. Eventually, when his vision was so bleary with sleep that the face of his clock was little but a grey smear, he admitted defeat and went to bed. That it was far past midnight he had no doubt, and he wondered if his staying up so late had in some way beaten the duck, prevented it from coming.

It did not; that night, the duck attacked William.

Well, attacked might be slightly too strong a word, Stevie admitted to himself the next morning when the story emerged fully. It hadn't actually hurt William, just frightened him into hysteria. Stevie had been woken from a heavy and clinging sleep by William's screams. It was still dark outside, and his younger brother's howls had been terribly loud in his night-held room.

"It's coming to get me! Daddy! Mummy!" William had screamed, and his parents' answering calls were no less loud but less coherent. Stevie didn't move as fast as they did and only made it to William's doorway as his parents were already on the small bed with William, both wrapping him into a cuddle and talking to him in the comforting tones Stevie wished they still sometimes used with him. Eventually, Stevie's dad's voice broke free from the cuddle.

"What frightened you, Will? Tell daddy, please."

"It was at the window," replied William, his voice already blurring as he went back to sleep. Stevie's mum picked him up and carried him out of the room, past Stevie, saying, "He can stay with us for the rest of the night."

"Don't let it come in and get me, Mummy. It wanted to. It wanted to hurt me. I could see," said William, almost inaudible now.

"What, Will?" asked his dad again, but William didn't reply. Stevie had a horrible feeling he could have replied on behalf of William, but also had the feeling that his dad still wouldn't believe him. After his parents had left the room, he looked at William's open window. There were marks on the sill, gouges in the wood that were new but also old, painted over like the ones on the door. In his mind, Stevie saw the duck clinging to the sill, its huge feet clenching and its claws tearing into the wood without touching the paint. *That fucking duck*, thought Stevie again, and then *I'll have to get rid of it.*

Stevie had lots of ideas about how to get rid of the duck, but none seemed possible. He considered hiding in the garden and then attacking the duck when it arrived, but it never did seem to come when he was waiting for it. Besides, it was at least as big as he was and probably bigger, and strong; the marks in the door and window sill testified to that, and it was hardly likely to stand still while he attacked it, even if he could find a weapon. Direct attack was out of the question, then. Adult help also seemed unlikely; besides his parents, Stevie mentioned the duck to three grown-ups on the day following the attack on William. His parents snapped at him angrily, and his dad went as far as accusing him of "putting ideas in Will's head and making him have bad dreams". Mr. Perks and his wife Gloria, their neighbours, just laughed and thought he was joking and Michael (who Stevie liked because he had a motorbike) said, "Well, ducks are cute, so why worry?" Stevie was the most frustrated with Michael, who had missed the point completely. Small ducks, *normal* ducks were cute because they weren't a threat, but just ask the smaller fish and insects they ate: is this duck cute? And the answer, Stevie was sure, would be, *No!* Just so with this duck. It was big, and strong, and its size and strength made it dangerous. Its mind may have been the same as a normal duck mind, or it might have been different (more intelligent? insane?), but like normal ducks, it ate and attacked those things that were smaller than it was. Cute, Stevie was beginning to realise, was mostly a matter of size.

Stevie got as far as picking the phone up to ring the zoo before giving up on that idea. What would he say? Please bring a tiger, there's a giant duck threatening me and my family? They'd never do it, and besides, the response he'd got from the other adults he'd told meant they wouldn't believe him anyway. But, but… tigers. There was an idea there. A tiger, or at least, a cat that had come to believe it was a tiger.

The photo of Tanzy was easy to find; his mum took photos by the dozen and then kept them loose in a big basket. She was always saying she'd sort them one day, but never did, which Stevie was grateful for. It only took a minute of rummaging to find a picture of the Mullan family pet. In it, she was crouched on the patio, her tail high and her head low. She looked vicious, terrifying, and Stevie wondered again how his mum could remember Tanzy as an adorable pet rather than the real, savage thing she had become. Adults were so *odd*.

The duck picture was harder to find. Stevie checked all his school books first, but none had a picture of a duck in. One of the nature books on the lounge bookshelf had pictures of *ducks* in, but that wouldn't do. He had enough trouble with one, let alone bringing more into existence. Finally, he got his dad to let him use the computer and found a good duck picture on a website about birds, printing it and telling Dad that it was for a school project. Stevie was thankful that it was so hot, because Dad didn't question him about why he had school projects over the summer holidays. Instead, he just shooed Stevie out of the study and told him to "watch for William". Stevie said he would;

in a way, he was doing. If he could get rid of the duck, William and Dad and Mum would be safe again.

If the duck came from inside Stevie somehow, then other things could come as well. That night, Stevie sat at his window and placed the picture of Tanzy over the picture of the duck, rubbing them together furiously and clenching his eyes shut, praying quietly. He sat that way for a long time, the only sound the rustle of the pieces of paper grinding together and his own frantic repetition, *pleasecomepleasecomepleasecome*. Then, over it all, came the sound of the pond's surface breaking as something settled against it.

Stevie opened his eyes. The baked earth glimmered, the parched grass and hard earthen flesh beneath bleached by the day's sun. The pond was a dark heart in the garden, and at its centre was the duck. It seemed painted in shades of black, the gleam of its feathers reflecting the pale moonlight in a way that hid rather than showed its colours. Its eyes, glinting, were fixed as ever on Stevie. It yawned, a lazy opening of its beak that revealed a maw in which something eel-like moved, wriggling and wet and darting. *Its tongue*, Stevie thought randomly, *it's showing me its tongue*, and then the duck's head went down and another of Dad's fish was gone in a rapid moment. When the duck's head came back up, the curve of its beak lent it a look like it was smiling. Laughing. Stevie rubbed at the paper between his fingers even harder.

The duck moved to the edge of the pond and clambered out. Water spilled from it and was rapidly lost to the gasping earth. Stevie and the duck looked at each other, motionless, and then the duck started across the lawn. Stevie couldn't have said how he knew, but something in the duck's walk told him that whatever the duck wanted, it meant to have it tonight. Whatever it wanted to achieve would be done, its task completed; tonight was the last night and *ohpleaseohpleaseohpleaseTanzyohpleasecome* there was nothing between Stevie and the duck except for doors and windows and walls none of which, he knew, would hold.

The duck came. Stevie rubbed fiercely at the papers in his fingers one last, desperate, time. He was sweating and the coating of moisture across his thumb made the thin, chemical surface of the photograph slippery, slimy with longing and hope. Stevie began to cry, helpless against the approach of the awful bird in the garden whose feet left no mark on the hard-packed ground and who moved in total silence. As it came, it allowed its head to tilt back, keeping eye contact with Stevie. The tongue appeared again like some fat graveyard worm come to view its meal before vanishing into the blackness of the terrible, curving beak. Its wings, flat to its back, trembled as it came, an anticipatory tremor that moved across the creature like a breeze from another world. Further back went the head as the duck came close to the house, its neck stretching like feathered rope and then Tanzy attacked.

Whatever magic Stevie had wrought, it was not perfect. Tanzy was smaller than a tiger and certainly smaller in proportion than the photograph Tanzy, which was the same size as the photograph duck. She was darker than she had been in life, less like a tabby cat and more like the big cats Stevie had seen in documentaries on the television. Even as she leapt at the duck, she was fading in and out of focus, shimmering between almost nothing and then back to solid again as he watched. But, small or not, there or not, she *fought* like a tiger.

Tanzy's jaws clamped around the duck's throat but she wasn't large enough to do any real damage. Her front legs clung to the duck's breasts and her rear feet scrabbled at the bird's belly, ripping out tufts of feathers and scattering them across the patio and back towards the pond. The duck stretched out its wings and beat them down, lifting itself and Tanzy from the ground. Its legs, freed from having to support its body, started to kick out at the thrashing cat. One great paddle foot inserted itself between the duck's stomach and Tanzy and kicked, the reptilian skin crinkling as Tanzy swung away. Stevie, rubbing the pictures so hard that he could hear them rasp together like grasshopper's legs even over the sound of his panting, cried out. The duck beat its wings again, lifting itself and its passenger another few feet from the ground so that it came to the height of Stevie's window. The duck looked in at him, glaring, and kicked at Tanzy again. Tanzy, already loosened from her prey, came away completely and Stevie couldn't even cry out but simply watched in horror as she fell away. His hope fell with her, spiralling down to the hard-packed earth below.

Tanzy twisted in mid-air and somehow grasped the duck's leg, swarming in a frantic instant up and across it and biting into the back of its neck. The cat shook her head fiercely, wrapping her front legs around the duck and digging her claws in. It looked curiously like she was embracing the duck in a tight hug and *now* she was there, all there, not fading and indistinct but real, flesh and wickedly sharp talons and teeth that dug deeper and deeper with every second. For the first time, Stevie heard the duck make a noise, a furious honk, sharp and hoarse and fearful. Stevie saw its eyes roll back to Tanzy as it beat its wings and tried to dislodge the cat, but she was clinging on determinedly. The duck shrieked, bucking in midair as blood bloomed from the wounds in its neck and rolled down its chest, droplets spattering out into the night and glimmering like stars as they arced to the ground. Another shriek, this one all pain and terror and for the briefest moment Stevie felt sorry for it, and then he remembered William's fear and his sorrow was gone and he was glorying in victory.

Tanzy yanked, and the duck's head came around to the oddest angle, looking out over its back as a wet crack sounded. The duck's wings stopped beating and its bowels opened, letting loose a chalky white stream that sprayed down as it fell. In the instant before it hit the floor, Tanzy leapt clear, landing in a ballet dancer's crouch beside the duck and then launching herself at the prostrate creature. Stevie had to stop looking then; the ripping sounds were bad enough, but the glisten of open meat tearing was too awful to see, even while he was glad the duck was dead.

Back on his bed, away from the window, Stevie could still hear the sounds, which carried on for what felt like hours before falling away to nothing. He crept to his window in the silence and was just in time to see the duck being dragged into the darkness on the other side of the pond. His last sight of it was its webbed feet, curled and forlorn as the shadows swallowed them. Then, new sounds came, eating sounds, and Stevie had to bury his head under the pillow on his bed for a long time. In his hands, the two photographs were little more than pulp.

The next morning, there was no sign of the duck. The blood, the feathers, its body, the white streak of poop; all gone. The grass was churned and scuffed in a few places, the only sign that anything had happened the previous night. Stevie was too tired to celebrate, but he was glad that everything was over.

That night, he looked out of his window before going to sleep. The pond was mercifully free of ducks, large or otherwise. The night was silent, the heat smothering the land with its embrace. Stevie was about to go bed when he saw movement at the bottom of the garden. In the far trees, a shape slipped between the trunks. It was hard to make out, but he thought he could see stripes of darkness against paler fur. In the gardens of Ash Tree Lane, a tiger hunted.

|Forest Lodge|

When my dad stopped running, we were in an old hotel perched on a hill above one of the many lakes in the north of England.

The argument had been a bad one, and it had lasted the entire weekend. Closeted in my room, I stayed out of the way and listened with only partial interest. By now, I could chart the flow of my parents' fights, predicting their tidal peaks and troughs with an accuracy that had become boring. My mother's strident shrieks would eventually give way to a sullen, pointed silence; my dad's contained reasonableness would last for a while before cracking like dropped china; there would be insults and bitterness and finally, either a teary reconciliation or my dad would flee. It had been this way for as long as I could remember, and it no longer really bothered me. I sometimes felt as though it *ought* to upset me, but I had long since stopped being worried by the things I heard or saw. My parents' arguments were like other parents' dinner parties; an infrequent inconvenience.

The aftermath of the argument was as predictable as the argument itself; Dad met me as I came out from school on Monday afternoon. "We're going away for a few days, son," he said to me after giving me a long, tight hug.

"Your mum and me, we haven't been getting along so well this weekend. You might have heard," he said with a rueful smile. "So I thought we could give her a little space and we could have some time together, make up for the weekend. What do you say?"

I did not ask where we were going, as I knew that Dad wouldn't know. He never planned, simply went. Previously, we had taken short trips to the zoo and the cinema, and sometimes longer overnight stays with my grandparents or friends. My dad's running was less about escape, I think, than about showing my mother that he could still act without her; the worse the argument, the further he ran and the longer he stayed away, making his point with our absence. It also meant that he avoided further arguments. On our return, my mother would often act as though the fight had never happened, be pleased to see us and shower my dad with kisses. She never tried to contact us while we were away, as far as I know. She just seemed to enjoy her time without us. Once, I heard her say to my father, "Thank you for taking him away, George. Time to be myself does me so much good." For me at least, the flight, and the attendant adventures it provided was always better than returning.

The hotel turned out to be called Forest Lodge, and our room in it was large and paneled in dark wood. A great stone and slate mantle covered the length of one wall, with a fireplace set at its centre. The room smelled faintly of polish and age and woodsmoke. Two beds were set either side of a floor-to-ceiling window and a sofa, bulging with old stuffing, pressed against the far wall. It was a nice room. My Dad had paid a lot for it, I knew, so that we could have some "luxury" on our break. As an added treat, the bathroom had, in addition to the toilet and sink, an old, clawfooted bath that looked big enough to swim in. Its taps were great brass crosses, the white enamel panels in their centre decorated with ornate letters for 'Hot' and 'Cold'. I, and I suspect my dad, had never stayed in a room like it before.

We arrived at Forest Lodge late at night, after a journey that had started on a train, moved on to a local bus service and ended with us walking perhaps two miles along dark country lanes. We had only two bags between us and from the feel of them, neither was full. I wondered about how efficient my dad's packing had been, but was too excited to care. I assumed that my dad would sort us out when we got there; it was what he did. My mother, on the other hand, spent hours packing for even the smallest of trips, checking and rechecking the contents of the bags and planting things in their depths for all sorts of eventualities.

By the time we were shown to the room, I was more tired than I could ever remember being, and despite my excitement, only just managed to strip to my underwear before getting into one of the beds. It was comfortable in a way that my bed at home was not, hugging itself around me with a lightness that drew me into sleep almost instantly. I did not sleep well, however. My dad was restless, and his pacing woke me several times. He walked around the room in the near-darkness, talking very quietly to himself, a rapid whisper in which I could hear no words, only his tone. That he was still upset about the argument was obvious, but I wished that he would keep his misery and anger quieter. My last memory from that night is of being woken by a figure, pale in the gloom, standing at the end of my bed and staring at me. I guessed that it was Dad, stripped for bed, making a final check on me.

I woke early, despite my disturbed night's sleep. The sun was slicing in through the windows and pinning the furniture to the floor with its intensity. Winter sun has always been my favourite, low and bright and powerful, and I enjoyed the sight of it. The shadows it created were magnificent, black and sharp and deep. The crosses formed by the window frames lay across the carpet, quartering the patches of light, and I made a game of jumping from patch to patch on my way to the bathroom. After I had finished, I went to the windows and looked out. In the near distance, the sun glittered on the lake, and its surrounding fringe of trees waved gently in a breeze that I could not feel. In the distance, fields crawled up the sides of the Lake District hills whose green and grey sides stood against a sky as blue as any I have ever seen. Closer, a single road passed the hotel, a quiet black strip that wound its way through green fields and continued, out of sight, up the nearest slope. Everything looked clean and fresh. I found myself thinking that it was a shame that Dad hadn't been able to bring my mother along with us. No one, I felt, would be able to argue in a place like this.

I managed to rouse my dad long enough for him to take me down to breakfast, but he brought me back to the room straight afterwards. He told me to amuse myself and went back to bed, falling asleep quickly, and I knew that he would not rise again for hours. I had seen this before, too; the energy that my parents spent on arguing would exhaust them, and afterwards they would rest for hours or more, doing little other than sleeping or reading. I wondered briefly about making lots of noise in the hope that it would force Dad to wake up, but dismissed the idea. Woken before he wanted to be, he could be short tempered and difficult.

Instead, I spent the morning looking around the room whilst I unpacked our bags, finding things that I had not seen the night before. There were sets of drawers either side of the beds, complete with battered Gideon's bibles, and a wardrobe pushed into a corner. On one wall was a painting of a woman. She was young and pretty and dressed in a white, floating gown that billowed around her. In the background of the painting was a building that I thought might be Forest Lodge itself. Looking more closely, I saw a little plaque attached to the frame that read *Charlotte Rose, 1900 - 1919*. She had been only 6 years older than me when she died. Shaking my head at how someone could possibly have died so young, I carried on with my sorting. I put underwear in drawers (finding in the process that Dad had brought me lots of pants but only two pairs of socks) and hung shirts in the small wardrobe. Doing this was fun, in a strange way. I felt like I was unpeeling secrets, handling things I did not normally get to handle. Dad's shaving kit, a razor, brush and soapstick in a wooden case that had originally belonged to his grandfather, was something I did not often see, but I had the chance to examine it in detail as I was putting it in the bathroom. I marvelled at how Dad's stubble had slightly worn the blade's edge, how the new blades in their waxpaper wrapper shifted when I touched them. I smelled the soap, a rich aroma that made me think of Dad's skin and of cuddles and the times I was closest to him. The velvet lining of the box was worn and stained, yet it felt more precious to me then than anything else I had held.

It was as I was putting Dad's shaving kit and our other toiletries in the bathroom that I decided to have a bath. Not a quick splash with the water up to my hips as I generally had at home but a proper bath, with the water so deep I could float and so hot it would appear to be smoking. I would allow myself some "luxury", as Dad had put it, soaking in the water until I pruned. Delighted with the idea, I started filling the bath straight away. Steam soon filled the room, its dark wood fittings glistening with moisture and the light above disappearing in a swirling mist and leaving only a faded glow showing through the water droplets. The liquid flowing from the taps was clear, and I imagined that it came straight from the lake itself. The noise of it running seemed to swell and fill the room and I was soon surrounded by noise and the dancing reflections that moved, glittering, across the walls. Stripping, I closed the flow off and lowered myself into the water.

Once I got over the shock of how hot it was, I enjoyed the bath hugely. I liked the way I could stretch out and my feet still did not touch the far end of the old tub, and the way in which I could almost float in its depths. Sweat trickled down my forehead and temples as I relaxed and I began to let myself daydream. I have no idea how long I had been there when I heard the person at the bathroom door.

Feet shuffled in the main room. It was a light step, as though the person was trying to move around as silently as possible. I sat up, thinking it might be Dad but his sleeping breathing, just audible, had not changed. The bathroom door was almost shut, with only a couple of inches of light showing in a strip between it and the frame. Through the misted air, I saw someone pass in front of the light. It was definitely not Dad. I wanted to call out, to ask who it was, but did not want to draw attention to myself. The figure had looked female, and I was naked.

There were more delicate steps, and then the creak of the door as it moved slowly. It swung open another couple of inches and a hand appeared in the gap, wrapping around the edge of the door. The fingers were long, slim and pale, and streaked with dirt. One of the nails was bent back to reveal the quick underneath, red and angry-looking. The door opened another inch and now I could see a woman, framed in the gap. Through the mist, I saw that she was dressed in white although, like her fingers, the clothes were streaked with dirt and were ragged. The lower hem of her dress was torn and uneven above her pale calves and bare feet and it was pulled up high and wrapped around her head so that only one eye was visible, and this set back amongst folds of cloth and lost in shadow. I wanted to speak, but could not. My heart beat hard in my chest and my throat felt constricted and dry. She made no sound as she looked at me. Her attention was absolute and I felt pinned by it, unable even to cry.

The woman took a step into the bathroom, moving through the rapidly clearing mist. Where the steam touched her, it whirled and vanished as though it was being sucked into her through her skin. I saw her more clearly as she came closer, her shadowed eye glaring at me. I wanted to flee, but where could I go? I was in a bath, with solid walls behind me. I felt the bathwater chill around me, as though its heat was leaking away, and gooseflesh broke out across my exposed arms and chest. The woman reached her arms out towards me. She took another step and I had time to notice that her legs were encrusted with deposits of black grime that swirled across her skin and nestled down into the cracks between her toes. She was leaving brown streaks across the wet floor as she moved, and then the hands were only inches from me. Her fingers stretched out, revealing palms covered in tiny cuts weeping blood that glistened thickly. Still I could not make a sound.

The woman's legs bumped against the side of the bath and her dress flapped over the water, small sprinkles of dirt falling to the surface of the liquid and dissolving. I saw that the dress was actually a sheet wrapped around her, clinging to her flesh and seemingly stuck there by the dried dirt. I looked up at her, ready to beg, and caught a glimpse of her eye, lost in the shrouding material. It was fixed on my face with a desperate intensity, almost glowing in its darkness. There was no steam left in the air and the bathwater had become incredibly cold as the woman's questing hands came towards me. I yelped involuntarily and jerked away. Slipping, I splashed under the water for a second and resurfaced, coughing and trying to clear my eyes so that I might avoid the woman again. I think I may have cried out then.

The woman was gone. From the next room, I heard my dad call to me, his voice thick. Weeping, I called back to him.

Dad ran into the bathroom a moment later. His hair was corkscrewed about his face by sleep, tufts popping out from behind his ears and across the crown of his head. He stood in the doorway, looking around wildly, and then saw me in the bath. I cried steadily, pulling myself to the side of the tub and holding one arm out to him as though I were drowning and asking for assistance. The light glittered on the drops of water that dotted my arm and then Dad was kneeling next to me and wrapping me in a hug that was warm and safe.

"Simon, what's wrong?" he asked, finally pulling back from me a little. His dark blue pyjama top had got wet and the patches looked black and oozing. I cried fiercely, my chest hitching and wrenching as I tried to ease the fear I had felt. Dad simply pulled me into another hug and held me.

Finally, I managed to control my tears. Dad let go of me and spoke, his voice kind. "What's wrong, son? Why are you crying?" He was looking at me, his face still bearing the scars of the pillow it had been pressed into minutes before. He looked suddenly old and careworn and the tired flesh under his eyes was as dark as I had ever seen it.

"Son? Talk to me. You're freezing. The bathwater's cold. Why are you in a cold bath?" He lifted me out and, pulling a towel off the rail behind him, held it open before him. I stepped into another embrace, this one clouded with cotton and the smell of fresh washing. I shivered, and Dad rubbed at me through the towel. He had not had to dry me for years, not since I had become old enough to feel uncomfortable being nude near him, yet now I let myself be taken care of like a child. Drawn by his comfort, I told him what had happened.

Dad listened without interruption until I had finished, and then turned me around to look at the bathwater. "There's no dirt in it, son," he said softly. "Look at the floor. It's clean, no footprints or mud. I think you got into a hot bath and relaxed and you were more tired than you thought. It's been a long weekend, and you fell asleep and dreamed of the woman in the picture." I wanted to disagree, but couldn't. He was right; the floor was clean and bright, the bathwater clear. Looking at the door's edge, I could see no sign that anyone had touched it.

"You have to be careful in water, son. It's dangerous. You could have drowned. Look at your fingers and toes, they've gone all wrinkled. You must have been in there for ages." I wanted to tell Dad that he was wrong, that I had seen the woman, that she had seemed so real that she could not have been my imagination, but he had already turned away and gone back into the bedroom.

Dad and I spent the afternoon exploring the area around Forest Lodge. Between it and the lake were lots of small roads and tracks, dotted with shops. We ate lunch in a tiny café and then Dad bought us both outdoor clothes from a camping and hiking shop close to the lake. I enjoyed these treats, but both times when he paid, I saw that the look on his face was one of anger and I knew that the argument with my mother had been about money; Dad was spending to get back at her, and the generosity of his gifts was in direct proportion to the ferocity of the preceding fight.

After buying the clothes, we walked along the water's edge, me kicking at pebbles and Dad silent, carrying bags that pulled his shoulders into a stoop. Lagging behind him, I stared at the trees that ringed the lake. They were in constant movement, bending and straightening from the touch of distant winds. As I watched, a pale figure moved amongst the shadowed darkness around their trunks. I felt a tightness around my chest as I thought of the woman in the bathroom but when I looked again, the shape had gone. Shivering, I quickly followed Dad and we walked back to the hotel.

In the Forest Lodge reception, Dad stopped to read some of the leaflets on the desk, leaving me to look around. High on one wall, I saw a painting of an older couple standing in front of the Lodge. The were dressed in formal clothes that made me think of black and white films and pictures I had seen in history books. The little plaque attached to the picture read *Charles and Alicia Rose, 1920.*

"There a grumpy looking pair, aren't they?" said a voice from over my shoulder, making me jump. Turning, I saw the man who had checked us in last night.

"Who are they?" I asked, intrigued. The couple looked so formal and so miserable that I wanted to know more about them.

"They're the people who built Forest Lodge, the Roses. They were here until 1920, when they sold the place to my granddad. Their daughter's picture is in the room you and your dad are in."

"She died when she was quite young, didn't she?" I said, remembering the dates on the plaque.

"She vanished," said the man, "in 1919. The Roses hoped for months that she'd come back. They organised search parties, dragged the lake, did everything they could. Eventually, they found her dress, ripped up, in the forest. The police said that she'd probably been attacked by a soldier, come back from the war, and that he'd buried her somewhere or weighted her down and thrown her in the lake. The Roses left a couple of years after. She's never been found." I thought of the woman in my room and shuddered. The man, seeing my reaction, said, "Don't panic, son. There are no soldiers around here now and even if there were, they're a peaceful lot." He grinned, but I could not smile in return.

That evening was an uncomfortable one. Dad and I ate in the hotel restaurant. We did not talk much as we ate, and when we did, we avoided the subject of home. I wanted to ask when we were going back. This had been the longest we had ever been away and I found that, to my surprise, I missed my mother. I missed the way she organised things so that I did not need to think. With her, things just seemed to happen before I even knew that I wanted them to. Dad was moody and difficult to predict where she was, at least, consistent. With him, I was unsure of what he wanted from me; to be quiet, to talk to him, to be his companion, to be his son? What he expected of me changed often and without warning, and I had grown tired of it and wanted to be home. At least there I knew my place and my role.

After our meal Dad and I went back to the room, where Dad soon fell asleep. He snored gently as he slept, his mouth open. Even as it got dark, I did not turn the light on for fear of disturbing him. Besides, I had nothing to read even if there had been light. Instead, I got into bed and tried to rest. Had I really seen a woman in the bathroom or had I, as Dad thought, simply let my own anxieties twist the picture I had seen of Charlotte Rose into a nightmare? I did not know. She had looked real, to be sure, but what proof was that? And if what I had seen was real, what precisely was it? A madwoman? A burglar? The ghost of Charlotte Rose, come for some terrible, unimaginable revenge? No, I told myself, there were no ghosts here, only a sleeping man and a young boy who was homesick and wanted his mother but did not like to admit it.

Even with my reassurances to myself, I did not find it easy to fall asleep that night. The sounds of the room settling around me changed, became the quiet tread of Charlotte as she came for me, her arms outstretched and her face covered apart from that one, glaring eye. When I tried to blink the image away it persisted, first hiding in the shadows by the door, then stalking towards me, now leaning over the end of my bed. Eventually, I buried my head into my pillow and squeezed my eyes shut and I suppose I must have, at some point, fallen asleep.

Dad was in a better mood the next day, and decided that we were going to go for a walk so that we could both enjoy our new outdoor clothes. He was cheerful and talkative and he kept me amused as we walked by telling me about things that he and my mother had done before they were married.

"We used to laugh all the time," he said, "and go dancing. Your mother, she was light on her feet and I used to feel so clumsy next to her, like I was a great elephant treading all over things." As he talked, we went around the end of the lake, following the shoreline, and then followed a trail away from the shore and into the trees.

Here, the clear air that blew in across the water was softened and thickened by the smell of pine and earth and moss. The sun came to us as a fractured thing, reaching the ground in patches that shifted and stretched as the tree branches moved above us. Fallen leaves and needles crackled and squelched beneath our feet as we walked. The sounds of the wind caressing the trees and of animal life was above us and around us and ever-present. Finally, the trail brought us to a clearing on a hillside with a wooden bench and picnic table settled in its centre, and we sat and ate our lunch looking out over a view that took in the lake and forest below us and the open farmland on the lake's far shore.

As we sat and ate, Dad carried on talking, now about the things he and Mother would do to get on better. I stopped listening as I had heard many of them before, but it did not matter; I think he was talking more to himself anyway. Chewing on my last sandwich, I looked around me. The trail we had come up stretched out from one side of the clearing and continued from the other, sloping down, back towards the lake. I was trying to gauge how far we had come and how far we might have to go when something pale moved in amongst the trees.

At first, I thought it was a dog or possibly a sheep, but it could not be. It was too tall. Besides, there was something stealthy about the way it slipped from behind one tree trunk to behind another, as though it was taking care to be as unobtrusive as possible. I immediately thought of Charlotte Rose, of the woman in the bathroom the night before, and gasped. I stood, peering along the path at where I had seen the movement. I wanted to tell Dad, but my voice froze. I felt him stand next to me and looked at him, so grateful that I felt sick. He had seen, I thought, and was looking, but he was not. Instead, he was picking up our litter and saying, "You're ready to go, are you? Okay then, off we trot". I watched, horrified, as he went towards the path and the pale shape beyond.

"Can't we go back this way," I said desperately, waving my hand behind me.

"No, we can not, lazybones!" he said, laughing and continuing to walk, and then he was on the path and I had no choice but to follow him or be left alone.

In amongst the trees, it was as though night had started to fall. Shadows lay across the ground and drew at my legs as I chased after Dad. I was aware of thick, dark trunks hemming me in on both sides. Despite seeing nothing in that glowering darkness, I did not stop to wonder whether the figure was real; it was, a solid whiteness in the gloom that had slipped from tree to tree as I watched. I wanted to believe that it was gone, but I did not. The air was colder here, a chill that slithered across my flesh. I could feel that we were being watched, stared at, and that whoever was there was keeping pace with us in the trees.

There was a white flash to my side, gone as quickly as it came.

I saw someone, dressed in white, moving between the trees. They were closer now, close enough to see it was the woman from the room, moving alongside us and nearer to us. I saw a flapping pale cloth and then she was gone again.

Another glimpse, and the air grew colder. My breath fogged in front of me.

The woman stepped out from behind a tree only feet away and now I could make out her shape, see the way the cloth had started to unwrap itself from her head and hang down across her shoulder. She was moving quickly without seeming to, her dirt-streaked arms hanging by her sides, and was still barefoot. The sheet caught on trunks and twigs as she passed, swirling out behind her. She was glaring at us and I wanted to run, but did not. I knew that she would catch me, and that the only place of safety was with Dad. I gripped hold of his hand tightly, curling my fingers around his, and practically pulled at him to go faster. He would not speed up and I was forced to walk with him as the woman came closer and closer to us until she was darting from tree to tree along the path's edge at our side. Terrified, I tugged at Dad, but he appeared not to see her. I pulled again, and this time he responded.

He stopped walking and turned to face me.

"What's wrong?" he asked, crouching so that his face was level with mine. I tried to answer but could not. Over his shoulder I saw the woman, her eye a baleful gleam almost lost in the material that hung around her face, move silently onto the path.

I tried to speak, to warn Dad, but no sound came. Just as it had in the bathroom, the temperature dropped and my throat tightened.

I could only watch as the woman walked along the path, her arms reaching out before her. Dad knelt, holding on to my shoulders and shaking me gently.

"Simon, what is it? What's wrong?" he said, his tone exasperated. I felt my jaw clench and my teeth grind together as the woman stopped just behind Dad. Her fingers were clawed and her skin a dank grey. I thought at first that she was reaching for Dad, that she was going to hook her hands around his head and yank him backwards, but she did not. Instead, she stretched past him, her arms either side of his head. Dad did not move, and I could not understand it; surely he could see her? Surely he could see the arms, the pale wrists and splayed hands with their broken nails and ground-in dirt? I was desperate for him to react, to see the woman, to defend me, but he did not. He simply shook me more violently, saying, "Simon! What on earth is wrong with you? For God's sake, son, will you please say something?"

The woman's arms were around Dad's head, curling in front of his face but not touching him. Her hands came at me, tilted so that I could see again the cuts on her palms. They were still moist-looking, their depths dark and sullen. Her flesh looked puffy, as though the skin was swelling and pulling away from her bones. I felt a wave of coldness roll over me. My skin contracted into prickles at the touch of the chill air and I reared back as far as Dad's hold on me would allow. Behind him, the woman's wrapped head bent forward as though she was going to kiss him on the cheek. Everything seemed to have fallen silent; no birds sang in the trees, no wind moved through the forest. Dad had stopped talking. I wanted to look away, but could not. I looked at the woman, wanting to scream but still unable to, and in that moment, her eye seemed to fill the whole of my sight. It was a dull glitter, recessed into the folds of cloth and rimmed by red, cracked flesh. The socket around the eye was grey and soft-looking and when the woman blinked I saw that her eyelid was swollen, stained the colour of old bruises. A tear, thick and gummy and dark, rolled down from her eye as she looked at me. It left a broken streak across her skin before trickling out of sight behind the folds of cloth. For a moment, the swollen outline of her face looked familiar, as though I had seen it somewhere before.

The hands came closer, the woman leaning further over Dad's shoulder. Her fingers flexed as though she was desperate to grasp me. The cold intensified and with it came the smell of old water and something else, something rotten and earthy. I saw the ragged edges of the broken nails as the fingers moved, bent and ripped. With a final thrust, she was upon me.

Her fingers brushed against my cheek, and they were as cold as anything I have ever felt. The flesh moved unpleasantly below the skin of her fingertips as she tried to grip me, shifting as though there was a layer of grease between it and the bone. I took another wild step back, pulling Dad with me as I went. He stumbled and let go of me, falling on all fours on the packed and cold earth of the forest track. I took another couple of stumbled steps and then my foot caught in something and I fell. I saw the sky pinwheeling above me and then I hit the ground hard enough to drive the breath out of my body. I lay, wheezing, and waited for the woman to take hold of me.

It was Dad that I saw next, not the woman. He gripped me by the shoulders, looking frightened as he pulled me to my feet. I thought it was because he had seen the woman, but it quickly became clear that he had not. He ran his hand across my head and arms and asking continually, "Does it hurt?" His near-panic was oddly comforting, giving me the sense that some things in the world were still normal; my dad still loved me and cared about me, even if the woman wished me harm. This sense of safety did not last long, however. Dad, seeing that I was okay, began to lose his temper with me.

"What were you playing at?" he demanded, and when I did not answer immediately, he said angrily, "I thought we were supposed to be having a good time together? Why did you try to run away from me? You could have hurt yourself, and you've scratched your cheek. For God's sake, tell me, what's *wrong*?"

And I could not tell him. I wanted to, of course I did; he was my dad and I wanted to believe he could make everything alright. Only, this time, I did not think he could. He had not believed I had seen the woman the first time, had not seen the woman even when she was leaning over him and her arms were reaching for me from either side of his head, and if he could not see her, how could he protect me from her? How could my parents protect me at all? My mother, the endless worrier, was not even with me. My dad, the great adventurer, could not sense the danger even when it brushed up against him. I was alone.

"What's wrong?" Dad said again, growing angrier. This, too, I had seen before, Dad growing angry when things interrupted his plans, especially things that he considered to be trivial or he could not understand. The part of his personality that made him run from arguments also made him quick-tempered when running was not an option. He could not leave me, so he became angry, and his anger was hot and fast and sharp. I knew from experience that the only way to avoid it was to provide some form of explanation, to mollify him.

"I'm sorry," I said, "I thought I saw something in the forest and it frightened me."

"Saw something? What?"

"I don't know. A sheep, maybe," I said, telling my Dad the first outright lie I had ever told him.

"Then why did it frighten you?" he demanded.

"I don't know. I think it reminded me of what happened in the bathroom and I just got scared."

"Oh, son," Dad said, gathering me into an irritable hug, "you have to learn to relax a little, to take things easy. You'll be just like your mother if you carry on like this, a nervous wreck." I said nothing, savouring his hug and the way his arms wrapped around me like strong bars. The temperature rose again in the centre of the hug and my scared flesh relaxed. Just for a moment, I felt safe.

The journey back to Forest Lodge was not a pleasant one. Dad, his day spoiled, was still angry and he walked fast, one hand clamped around my left wrist and tugging whenever I started to fall behind. He ignored my attempts at conversation, keeping his eyes focused ahead of us on the path and saying nothing. As we went, I thought I saw a white shape flitting between the trees to our side. I did not know if it was the woman, but we were moving so fast that it did not seem to matter, and even if it was her, she came no closer. Finally, the ground fell away on that side, becoming a steep gulley with a thin stream trickling along its bottom, and the white thing vanished. When I stumbled and went close to the edge, Dad yanked me hard away and swore at me, telling me not to go too near the water.

As we walked, I tried to think about what had happened to me over the previous days. Twice, now, the woman had appeared. Who was she? What did she want? Was it Charlotte Rose, come back to take her revenge, and if so, why on me? It made no sense, but I had no other explanation. The pretty girl in the flowing white dress who had died (or, at least, vanished) so young was coming for me, and I had no idea why.

Returning to our room was a comfort. The great fireplace and dark wood of the beds had a solidity that drove away some of my fears. How could ghosts exist here, in a room where everything was so solid and heavy? Even seeing my face in the mirror and realising that the woman's fingers had left their mark, like old blisters, across my cheek did not feel too frightening. Strangely, it was almost reassuring; if she had marked me, then the woman was real and not just in my imagination.

I discovered that I was exhausted after the events of the walk and lay on my bed, hoping that Dad would calm down and talk to me. He did not. He sat on the sofa and gazed into the distance, the clenching and unclenching of his fists his only movement and the crack of his knuckles the only sound. I wanted to fix the situation, to say something to him, to tell him that I was sorry for lying, that it was not a sheep I saw but a woman I thought might be the dead Charlotte Rose. I wanted to ask him to keep a careful watch out for her, but dared not. I did not know what words to use. Wanting to stay awake, I instead found myself asleep within minutes.

Dad woke me later, his face back to cheery normality. "I've had some food sent up for supper," he said, "and crisps and drinks." On the coffee table were plates, heavy with sandwiches, glasses of juice and a bowl of crisps. I found that I was hungry and was soon sat with Dad, eating the food and enjoying the rich, dense flavours of cheese and fresh butter and bread still warm from the oven. Dad talked non-stop as we ate, and I was glad his mood had improved whilst I slept. He made no mention of our walk, concentrating instead of the things we could do in the forthcoming days. I wanted to ask if we could go home, to get away from this place and its shrouded ghost, but did not. Dad was planning, and I knew from experience that I would not be able to divert him from these plans. Besides, his good mood was new and delicate; the slightest disagreement could damage it, make it melt into something darker and less pleasant.

"Would it be okay with you if I went out?" said Dad as soon as he had finished his meal. He stood, clearly anticipating that I would say yes. I was so surprised that I did not speak. Go out? Where?

"I'll only be an hour or two. I just thought I'd go for a drink in bar downstairs, so I won't be far and you can come and get me if there are any problems. You'll be fine, though, won't you? You're not a child now, after all." And then, before I could say anything, he was gone. Perhaps I should have tried harder to stop him, said something, said anything to make him stay, but I did not. I wanted him to be here with me, but I also wanted him to know this without being asked, and his inability to see what I needed from him hurt me in a way that I had not been hurt before. I suddenly saw my Dad as a selfish creature, one who disliked not getting his own way, and I felt hopeless after he had gone. He took my strength with him as he left and for a time afterwards, I simply sat on the sofa and cried.

I stopped crying when it began to hurt my head. Wiping my eyes and my nose on my sleeve, I looked up at the painting of Charlotte Rose. In the creeping shadows of evening, her face was pale, her dress a light patch against the dark background. "What do you want?" I whispered, feeling helpless and angry. "Why can't you leave me alone?" The figure in the painting did not reply. Feeling my tears build again, I looked away.

Swathed in dirty material, the woman was sat on the sofa next to me.

This time, I screamed.

Without thinking and still screaming, I threw myself away from her along the sofa. Its low, outcurled arm caught me in the small of my back and my momentum carried me over in a tumble of flailing limbs. The room whirled around me and then the floor caught me in its hard embrace and I was lying sprawled, my head partially under the sofa. I shuffled out from under it, wriggling furiously and pulling myself along, my hands digging into the thick carpet. As I came out, I saw the woman looking at me from over the arm of the sofa, the grimy sheet untwisting itself from around her face. Dried dirt flaked away from the material and fell on to my face and into my eyes. Blinking and crying, my screams now little more than hoarse exhalations carried on air that was rapidly chilling, I rolled over onto my front and began to crawl. Terrified that the woman would catch me if I stopped moving even for a moment, I bumped into the table as I crawled by, but felt no pain as it jolted into my shoulder. The table wobbled and a cup fell off it and landed on the floor in front of me. Knocking it aside, I crawled on. Although I could hear nothing except my own wailing breath, I imagined her following me, this terrible creature whose purpose I could not understand, and I crawled faster.

Once past the table and the sofa, I was in the open space between the furniture and the door, which stood in mute offer of escape. I felt exposed and vulnerable on my hands and knees and, still moving forwards, pushed myself up into a headlong stagger. I tripped as I came close to the door, falling back to my knees before it. Reaching out, I grasped the doorknob and tried to turn it but my hands, wet with terror, slithered over its brass surface helplessly. I tried again, but was still unable to gain purchase. Weeping, I felt the woman's hand touch my cheek, brushing her cold fingertips against the mark that she had already left upon me. Jerking away, I tightened my grip and twisted. Feeling the embossed pattern pressing into my palms, I managed to open the door and used it to support myself as I got to my feet and ran. I had taken only a couple of strides when a hand gripped my shoulder.

It was not a strong grip and I broke it by thrashing my arm around wildly, but doing so made me stumble once more and I fell heavily against the far wall of the landing and then to the floor. Rolling onto my back, I saw the woman walk though the doorway, the greying sheet swinging around her and her arms outstretched. I think I may have screamed again. I wanted my Dad very badly then, wanted to be wrapped in his arms and protected by him, wanted to have him see the woman and force her to leave me alone, and I got to my feet as quickly as I could and ran for the stairs.

The staircase was wide and, in the subdued lighting of the hotel's evening, gloomy. It bent back on itself halfway down, becoming a mezzanine balcony lined with pictures before turning again and continuing down into the foyer. From the top step, the shadows looked rich and heavy and as I ran down, I felt as if I were sinking into dark water. The wood of the banister was dark, smooth to the touch from the caress of countless hands over the years, and I clung to it as I descended. The thick carpet swallowed the sound of my feet and I could hear my sobbing and the squeak of my hand along the varnished wood. I thought I felt the air freeze about me, puckering my skin with its chill touch. I ran, and it felt as though the woman clutched at me at every step. I imagined hands grasping at my shoulders, fingers twisting themselves through my hair and pinching at the flesh of my cheek, nails digging into the exposed flesh of my neck, and the pain of these assaults was as real as the throbbing in my face where she had touched me and yet, when I reached the mezzanine and turned, the woman was still at the top of the stairs. She stood in the centre of the top step, looking down at me. Her hands hung at her sides, and her head was bowed. Her shoulders were shaking, a movement I took for mirth. She was enjoying this, enjoying the fear she was creating in me, and I hated her then more than I have hated anyone before or since. I ran on.

The people in the pictures looked on, impassive, as I dashed past them. I wondered if these were more pictures of Charlotte Rose's parents, or other family members or friends. Would she stop and look at them as she walked by, or would she would simply ignore them and continue after me? Would their formal, composed faces sadden her? Would it anger her to see them, to be reminded of her lost life? What was it she *wanted* from me?

The foyer was empty except for the leather armchairs lining its walls. I stopped by the reception desk, wondering if I ought to ring the bell, but did not. Even if someone came, would they be able to see the woman? I did not think so. I simply wanted to be with my Dad, to have him gather me to him and make things right. Looking back, I saw the woman walking down the stairs, stepping into the brighter light of the foyer. Her ankles and calves were grey and swollen. Vivid purple marks had crept across her feet and the sheet was unravelling itself from around her body as she came on, so that one arm and shoulder were exposed. There were more purple marks here and other, blacker patches. The sheet dropped further, revealing one darkened, muddy breast and even in my fear, I felt embarrassment at seeing her exposed like that. I could feel waves of fear and hate and desperation coming off her, and the air became cold as she came closer. I wanted to scream at her, to ask her what she wanted, but did not. What she was doing made no sense to me; she had had ample opportunity to hurt me, but had not. Apart from the mark on my cheek, I remained unharmed. Why chase and chase and chase me? Or was it just the chase itself that mattered, the fear she could make me feel by appearing and disappearing and appearing again? Why me? I did not know and felt helpless in the face of my ignorance. Instead, I did the only thing that I could think of; I crossed the foyer and went on. I went to find my Dad.

Forest Lodge's bar was at the end of a short, dark corridor. It was separated from the rest of the hotel by a heavy, glass-panelled door, and as I came closer I could see Dad through the glass. The thick panels had a pattern etched into them which distorted the way Dad looked, stretched him and made him angular and thin. Sat at the bar talking to the barman, he looked like a stranger. The barman said something to Dad and the two men laughed, a harsh sound unlike the way Dad laughed when he was with me, and I paused at the door without opening it. I could see my reflection in the glass and then a pale smear moved behind me and the woman's face, with its sagging sheet wrapping, appeared above my shoulder. Arms wrapped themselves around me and pulled me away from the door. I felt them tighten against my stomach and chest. I felt the soft flesh shift across her bones as her grip tightened and my flesh prickled and contracted.

I tensed, expecting something awful to happen, but it did not. The woman pulled me tight against her and I felt the rough tremble of the cloth as it dangled from her head and lay against the side of my face. Her arms were cold even through my shirt and I could smell her, a sickly odour of mildew and earth and of something spoiled and old. Reflected in the glass, I saw that she was staring straight ahead. She glared forwards and her eye, its surrounding flesh dark and swollen, narrowed. I could sense the fury in her, but I also sensed fear and did not understand. I was frightened, but why should she be? Through the glass, I saw Dad lift his drink, his head tilting back as he swallowed. The woman's arms tightened around me, squeezing my chest. I tried to beg her to stop, but all that came out was a wheeze. I saw her head twitch when she heard it, and then turn towards me. The reflected eye seemed to change and soften as it focussed on me and her arms loosened their grip.

She tilted her head as she turned, so that more of the sheet untwisted itself and drifted loose. I heard the crackle of dried stains shifting and breaking as the sheet moved. The lower half of the woman's face was uncovered now, revealing blackened lips and skin that was grey and puffy. She lowered her face towards mine and I tried to move away but could not; the woman's arms held me firm. Perhaps she means to eat me, I thought, as her face came against mine. However, with lips that were warm and soft and gentle, she kissed my cheek and the painful throb from the mark she had left on me earlier immediately faded. Then, letting her arms fall away from me, she stepped back. As she did so, the sheet came completely away from her head and I saw her face. Before I could speak, she had vanished into the shadows of the corridor and when I turned, she had gone.

I do not clearly remember the next few minutes. I felt oddly detached from what was happening, as though I was watching it happen to someone else. I was not thinking, exactly, but was simply going over and over the events of the previous days in my head, trying to see them differently. I must have walked back down the little corridor and into the foyer, for the next thing I knew, I was sat in one of the comfortable leather chairs watching as cold blue light swept across the floor and up the walls. The light jolted me and made me blink, and I looked around to see two policemen come in through Forest Lodge's front door and go to the reception desk. One was about to ring the bell for attention when the other, older, policeman shook his head and turned the hotel's register towards him. After a few moments checking something, the policemen went up the stairs. I did not wonder where they were going; I think I already knew.

The policemen were only gone a couple of minutes before they reappeared, this time moving with a little more urgency. The older one saw me as they came down the stairs and looked as though he were about to stop and talk to me but the other one ran straight past me and down the corridor to the bar. The older man followed. I heard shouts and a crash and then the two policemen came back out into the foyer, dragging my dad between them. He was handcuffed and crying out, hoarse roars of fury and foul language mixing in a loud mess of words. He struggled and pulled at his captors, but stopped when he saw me.

"Simon, I'm sorry," he said. "I never meant…" and then he was gone from the foyer and I was alone.

The elder of the two policemen returned after a few minutes and came over to sit by me. He looked friendly and he had a comforting smell to him, of aftershave and soap and solidity.

"Son," he said quietly, "I know you just saw us take your dad away and must be wondering why. It shouldn't be me that tells you this, but then, you shouldn't have had to see that at all. I'm afraid I have some bad news for you." He seemed to expect a response from me, so I nodded at him.

"There's no other way to say this, so I'm just going to say it. Your mother's dead," he said. Hearing it said like that, even when I was so sure I already knew what he was going to say, made my stomach ache and my vision blur. Reality, the truth of things, came upon me in a nauseous wave and I only half-heard the policeman as he carried on speaking.

"I know you must feel bad now, but you may as well know it all. It'll be in the papers soon enough, and better you hear it from me than read it or hear it from some reporter shouting questions at you in the street. We think that, on Monday after you went to school, your mum and dad carried on arguing. They'd been arguing a lot that weekend, hadn't they?" I nodded.

"We think that your dad lost his temper with your mum and hit her a lot and that he killed her. Perhaps he didn't mean to kill her, but he did. It looks like he panicked afterwards and wrapped your mum in a sheet from their bed. He went to some woods near your home and threw her into a stream before picking you up from school and bringing you here. We found her body a few hours ago. I'm sorry, son. Maybe it should have been someone else who told you, but there's no one here but me."

Tears came then, and I leant against the solid policeman and hugged him. I had known when I saw the ghost's face, but had not wanted it to be true. I cried and cried, for me and my dad, but mostly for my mum. I wished that I had understood better, that I had not been so frightened. I wished that she had been able to talk to me, to let me know what she wanted and how she felt, that she had not been as scared of my dad. I wished that I had had longer with her.

I wished that I had known that a dark hotel corridor was where I would see my mother for the last time, and that the lips of a ghost on my cheek were her goodbye kiss.

|The Station Waiting Room|

Gaskin hated his job.

It had seemed like such a great opportunity; promotion within the company and responsibility for restructuring the Administrative Records Section, an out-of-town department in Low Hold. Only, 'restructuring' in this case, Gaskin soon discovered, meant 'closing in preparation for the company developing the offices into a new corporate headquarters', and Low Hold was a dismal place somewhere in the hinterland between the coast and the inland farms, nestling miserably in the neck of a valley called Middle Fell Drop.

As much as he hated the job itself, Gaskin found the commute worse. Low Hold had its own train station, the last stop at the end of a decaying branch line, but to get to it Gaskin needed to change trains three times. After each change, the train he went to was smaller, grimier and older than the last, the scenery outside the streaked windows flatter, greyer and more desolate. The third train was little more than a cattle truck, with seats too cramped and exhausted to be comfortable and aisles whose narrowness forced him to move in a kind of crabwise shuffle. Handstraps dangled from the ceiling above the seats, anticipating (or perhaps pining for) a time when the carriage was full, but there was only ever Gaskin and one or two others using the service, and his fellow travellers got off at earlier stops. By the time the train reached the end of the line, Gaskin was alone in a carriage whose seats had been rubbed bare by countless buttocks and whose faded signs were dusty with old sunlight. Travelling into Low Hold felt like falling out of the world.

Evenings were worse. Instead of feeling happiness at going home, Gaskin was normally exhausted and miserable, and he found himself sometimes wondering if it wouldn't be worth getting a flat in Low Hold and staying there. It would be convenient, and would mean he did not have to wait on the near-empty platform at the station for over an hour before the engine and its solitary carriage rattled into view and laboured to a stop. Most of his staff seemed to have done that; all lived within walking distance of the office, yet not one of them appeared to like Low Hold. When they spoke, they professed to hate its smallness, its lack of amenities, the weather, the way it made them feel, and yet they stayed. Gaskin didn't want to spend his money to end up living in a place he hated with people he didn't like, but could it be any worse than boarding that train each night?

It was the waiting as much as anything; uncomfortable, depressing and fiercely tiring. There was no waiting area on the station, just a wooden bench that fitted his body in all the wrong places and a ticket office that was never staffed and had a faded sign in the window that read, *Closed - purchase tickets on the train.* By his feet knots of weeds forced their way out from the grey cracks in the concrete apron of the platform and the painted line at its edge was faded and splintered. Down near the tracks, grasses sprouted around the rails and crept over the rough wooden sleepers in tangled whorls and the great, coiled springs of the buffers rusted disconsolately behind their metal pads. Litter staggered in ragged circles around his feet when the wind gusted.

There was another bench at the far edge of the platform, and most nights, an old man sat on it.

He never got on a train and Gaskin never saw him arrive or leave. He simply sat and looked around, staring at the line or across the tracks and sometimes at Gaskin himself. Gaskin did not attempt to talk to the man, and avoided making eye contact in the hope of sending out a clear message: *I'm not interested. Leave me alone.* Sometimes, the man stood at the edge of the platform, his head cocked as though listening for something or peering intently at some unseen item of interest. One day in summer, despite Gaskin's fiercest body language, he walked over to Gaskin and said, "All this used to be houses."

It was such an unexpected thing to say that Gaskin responded with a polite, "Pardon me?" before he could stop himself. The man sat down on the bench beside Gaskin and said again, "All this used to be houses." As he spoke, he gestured around slowly, his hand sweeping around and taking in the flat scrubland beyond the station and the distant offices. "All of it. Low Hold was a village."

Gaskin did not respond. His initial surprise had hardened into wariness, but it seemed he was too late; the man continued, unbidden.

"It was a farming village, really. Most of the men worked the farms that covered the valley, although there was some industry. Small quarries, local stone, that kind of thing. It was never a very pretty place, and most of the people here had it hard, but they survived."

"Really?" Noncommittal, disinterested, almost rude. Go *away!*

"By the time the second war started, most of the farms were struggling anyway, so the army requisitioned parts of the land and built an overflow camp here. I came in Forty-One to run it."

Gaskin stayed silent.

"Listen!" said the man, his voice a sudden, fierce hiss. He leaned over and gripped Gaskin's wrist hard, squeezing so that Gaskin could not pull away. "Listen!" he hissed again, "I have to tell someone. I have to tell you. Someone has to hear!"

"Get off me!" said Gaskin, pulling back, but the old man held on, his fingers digging into Gaskin's flesh and making him wince.

"Do you feel that grip? Do you feel? It's nothing like the grip that this place has over people. Nothing!" The man finally let go of Gaskin's arm and he yanked it back, rubbing at skin upon which crescent bruises were already flowering an angry red.

"Please," said the old man. "Please, just listen to me. I have to tell someone." His voice cracked as he spoke, and the strength that had given his hiss venom was gone. He sounded lost and ancient, a tremulous thing sagging into his heavy suit and crumpling like old branches back onto the bench. Gaskin said nothing; old and weak the man may be, but he clearly had the capacity for aggression and there was no one here to help if he turned nasty again. Gaskin waited, resigned, for his story.

"Back when this was a village, it was bigger. It had a two-line train track. If you look, you can still see what's left of the other line. There was a waiting room on the other platform as well; it's still there, can you see?"

Although there was only one set of tracks, Gaskin saw that the old man was right: the cutting was wide enough for two sets of rails. There were faint indentations where a second line had been, a sign of Low Hold's more prosperous past. Beyond this second, lost line a disused platform faced Gaskin. It had been seized by nature and now, at summer's height, was thick with bushes and plants. Flowers bloomed, but their scent did not reach him even though he was barely twenty feet away. The blooms looked unhealthy and he wondered if the soil was sick with pollution from the long-gone trains; the petals seemed drab and sickly and the leaves curled downwards around their own discoloured edges. Thick shadows, made solid with the trunks of the growing plants, pooled behind the flowers. Gaskin could hear the wind hissing through the foliage and tiny animals skittering as they dashed back and forth through the roots and branches. When Gaskin looked more closely, he saw that the ground on the second platform was thick with rotting vegetation.

Buried in the shadows of the foliage was a darker, regular shape. Interested despite himself, he leant forward, staring hard. By God, the old man was right! It was a building, squat and stretching most of the platform's length, now buried in the rough ocean of root and branch. He made out the dark maw of a doorway and of windows, choked with twisting plants. Alongside, there was a wall stained dark grey and even, he saw, a clock hanging above the door, wrapped in leaves and vines and dust.

"That's not where it started," said the old man, "not by a long shot, but it's where it started for me, so I suppose I'll start my story there as well. That waiting room was the first thing I saw as the train pulled out of the station after I was posted here in Forty-One, when the war was still relatively young. Back then, the waiting room was in use, but it looked old even then. The paint was peeling around the door and on the window frames, and I remember thinking that it wasn't a very welcoming place.

"Low Hold was surrounded by farmland, and a great chunk of it had been requisitioned by the government to set up what was essentially a sorting station. All the soldiers that hadn't got regiments, or who were delayed and needed to be sent after units that were already overseas, all the sickly ones and the troublemakers that no-one wanted, they all came here to wait while someone decided where they should go. Discipline was a nightmare; it was hard to keep track of the men because they came in by themselves or in small groups, and left in the same way as they got their postings. Most of them were draftees, and none of them wanted to be here. They either wanted to be fighting, or back at home, and no one knew anyone. We had officers, of course, but they'd change as often as the men did, so no one really had any authority. I was sent here as chief officer, but in reality I was a glorified paper pusher, filing this form and copying that one, sending this form on and making sure that one stayed. It was a terrible job."

The old man stopped and looked across the quiet train line; on the other platform, the plants waved gently as though in greeting. He stared, squinting as though trying to focus in on something, although Gaskin had the impression it was something further away that the platform.

"The first job I did was a complete inventory of men and equipment. It took me over a week, sorting out the records of what we should have had, and there were discrepancies. Men that weren't there, equipment missing, men here that we had no record of. Some of it was easily sorted out; there were black market trades going on with the people the surrounding areas, easy enough to stop, and the missing records were almost always in transit from some other base or headquarters, but the missing men were a problem. No one seemed to know where they'd gone. We checked posting records, troop carrier records, even followed through with the various regiments that they were supposed to have gone to, but very few turned up. We had to list them all as AWOL and turn their details over to the military and civilian police. Low Hold camp had the highest AWOL rate among the British military during wartime. It also had the highest rate of soldiers who never turned up anywhere."

"Where were they all?" asked Gaskin.

"The next problem was the villagers," said the old man, ignoring Gaskin's question. "They looked... wrong. The joke in the camp was that family'd been fucking family, and we were seeing the result. The people were stunted and sullen, twisted and bent like wood that's warped because of sun and rain. They had no energy, and never seemed to do anything. The state of the waiting room was my first sign of it, but I soon saw others. Shops were dusty, houses badly maintained, people didn't talk or socialise. Of course, it doesn't mean anything these days, but back then the sense of togetherness was strong in these kind of villages. It was what kept them going through the poverty, the unemployment, the fear; at least they had each other. And you didn't feel that in Low Hold, not at all. And that was another thing! There were no damaged men in the village, and no missing ones."

"What?" asked Gaskin, surreptitiously peering over the man's shoulder to see if the train was in sight. Nothing.

"After the first war, entire generations were gone. You'd see places were there weren't many middle-aged men, because the previous generation had gone off to fight and died in the mud and the shit, and if there were men left after the end of the fighting, they were the cripples and the cowards, but in Low Hold? It was as though the first war had never happened. It was odd; it was almost as though they were ashamed of it but defensive. People here had a way of trudging and dragging their feet when they walked, like their heads were too heavy or their feet were numb, but ask them if they'd ever been anywhere, or what they'd done in the Great War, and they'd get aggressive."

The man slumped back against the bench with a sigh. Gaskin hadn't realised it, but the older man had become tense, hunched over and bent at his waist as he spoke, his shoulders shaking as though the words were being released from him like bile or vomit. And, much as Gaskin would have preferred to be alone, his story *was* interesting. In the old man's descriptions of the Low Hold villagers, Gaskin could see echoes of his colleagues. His *staff*.

"We tried to get some of the villagers to work for us, building other camps and stores up in the valley or in other parts of the area, but none would do it. *None*. They refused, even though we were offering good money, money they needed.

"I remember talking to one of my commanding officers about it and joking that it must have been a miracle that any of the Low Hold villagers volunteered to fight in the Great War, and he told me that they hadn't. Not one.

"And then there were the farms. Most of the valley was farmland, mainly livestock but some crops on the lower slopes and around the village on the flatter areas, but I found that we were bringing food in from other villages and towns. When I asked why, Q took me to a local farm."

"Q?" asked Gaskin, thinking of James Bond and the enigmatic inventions of his science officer.

"Quartermaster," replied the old man. "In charge of stocks and stores. Our Q was a veteran wheeler-dealer called Culley, and I couldn't understand why he wasn't using local produce – it had to be fresher and cheaper. The farm visit explained it all. What came out of the ground around here was awful, practically inedible. Potatoes that were shrivelled and tough, carrots that looked desiccated, plants that wilted and rotted even as they grew and tasted foul when they were harvested. The farmer didn't seem to care, even though most of his crops ended up ploughed back into the ground as compost or used as feed for the animals. And the animals! Sheep that didn't wander but stayed in the same place and starved because there was nothing near for them to eat, cows that produced milk that was bitter and sour, and meat that was tough and tasteless. I asked the Q why, and he said that all the local produce was like that. 'Nothing grows healthy here', he said, 'it's like the soil sucks life out instead of putting it in.'"

Gaskin watched as the man, seemingly unable to remain still, leaned forwards with his elbows on his knees. He looked across at the far platform again. "Like everything was being poisoned or drained," he said quietly. "I asked the farmer why he carried on, why he didn't leave and he just said, 'I can't leave Low Hold'. Simple as that. Of course, at the time, I thought he meant because his family had been here for decades, or that he'd never sell his land, given how poor it was. I remember that as he said it, though, he sagged and just for a minute, he looked as twisted and shrivelled as one of his awful vegetables."

The breeze turned, zephyrs dancing across Gaskin's face and with them he caught the edge of a scent, something hot and unwashed and decaying. The old man's coat flapped open, showing Gaskin a suit that hung in loose folds and that was decorated with old stains and fresh dirt. Above it, the man's wattle neck sprouted from a shirt collar that was too big for him and was the sour yellow of white cotton gone too far from cleanliness to rescue. As though sensing Gaskin's scrutiny, the old man turned his head to Gaskin. He looked tired. With a wintry smile, he turned his eyes back down to the floor, at his shoes with their splitting leather and trousers whose turned-up cuffs trailed loose stitches, and then said, "It wasn't just the farmers.

"When I looked at the village after my trip out to the farm, everything was the same. The women were quieter, sadder, more downtrodden, the children pulling things that looked as weak as old milk. Even the buildings looked on the verge of collapse, and the worst of it was, no one cared. As long as they were here, in Low Hold, they put up with it all. They didn't try to leave, they didn't try to improve things, they just accepted it and sat around like they were all ill or too tired to move. I asked the Q about it, and he said that they'd been like that since the camp was set up. What was worrying was that you'd see it in the men in the camp as well. They'd arrive full of piss and wind, telling jokes or fighting or trying to fuck the local women or moaning about how none of the local women were worth fucking, and within two weeks, they'd have that same expression on their faces, as though they'd not slept for days. I think that, even then, I thought it was just the fear of being sent overseas. Perfectly normal, I thought, a perfectly safe and healthy response to the possibility of being sent to battle and being fucking killed.

"And then I saw what happened in the waiting room.

"We'd received orders to send a group of men on. They were given travel warrants, told which trains to get, and then left to get on with it. I was in the camp that day, and I saw one of the men when he should have been on the train; I know, because I had stamped his warrant and made all the arrangements myself, and yet there the bastard was, slouched against the wall in the exercise yard. I went to speak to him, but he just stared at me as I shouted. Eventually, I called the guards and had him placed under arrest, but it was only as I walked away that I suddenly wondered about the fucking others."

Gaskin noticed that the man's language was coarsening, his voice itself roughening, and in its new timbre, he could hear echoes of the soldier that the man had been. There was command there, and solidity, and something hard to identify; maleness, or masculinity, or authority. Something unflinching, and for a second Gaskin wondered what would happen if this old man was young again and doing Gaskin's job. There would be no delays and no staff ignoring his instructions, he was sure, and the realisation made him feel weak and small.

"I came to the station in time to see the train pull out," the man continued. "I asked the ticket officer if he'd seen the men board the train, but he was a Low Hold villager and he barely replied to me.

He waved in the general direction of the waiting room, though, and I remember becoming not just angry but furious, thinking that the men were still in there. I didn't run, because I was an officer and I was fucked if I was running to find the men, but I walked fast and I was bubbling like a blocked kettle by the time I got there and looked in the window. They were inside.

"There were seven of them, and they were asleep. I swore, shouting at them through the window as I walked to the door, but none of them moved. Seven of them, sleeping like babes in that little waiting room as though they were on a Sunday outing rather than going to fight for their country. I was so angry that I kicked open the door and was in the room before I slowed, and that was when I saw it.

"The men were dissolving.

"Maybe dissolving isn't the right word. I don't know what is, really. They weren't breaking apart or melting or dripping or anything like that. No, they were fading like old photographs. I thought for a second that it was me, that I'd got so angry that I'd given myself a stroke and that this distorted vision was the beginnings of it, but it wasn't. I wish it had been.

"The men were vanishing, fading somehow. The colour was going from them, so that they got paler and paler, past white and into a greyness that was hard to see in all the shadows. Oh, God, the shadows! As I looked, it was as though the shadows around the men were thickening, sucking at them, drinking them, taking their colour, coiling around their necks and arms and legs like those snakes that crush you to death and eat you whole."

The old man stopped again, gasping for breath. His whole body was shaking, trembling like the surface of the sea in a rainstorm. He looked at Gaskin and said, "You don't believe me."

Gaskin did not respond. The anger was back in the old man's eyes and his hands were clenching and unclenching in a way that made Gaskin uneasy. *Please come,* he wanted to pray to the train, *please come and let me escape this old lunatic with his fantasies and hallucinations,* because that would be normal, the sensible thing to think, but he found he was more anxious about the idea of the train arriving, of having to climb aboard and surrender to his journey again. Over the old man's shoulder, the train track remained empty.

"As I watched, the men faded even more. I saw the shadows tighten around them, squeezing, and then the first man just… went. Gone. For a moment, there was a thicker pool of darkness in his shape and then he was gone and the darkness was gone as well. Then the next man went. I saw the bench he was sitting on through his chest and belly, and then he and his equipment faded away. The others went quickly then, vanishing like steam in warm air. Before the last one went, there was a moment when the room was suddenly filled with countless darker patches, hundreds and hundreds it seemed, all of them in the shape of men. I could see the outlines of helmets and packs and hands holding cigarettes and one holding his tea mug, and then they were gone and there was just me. I realised that I was on the floor, sat against the closed door and that all around me the shadows were capering like mad children. Black tentacles of darkness were coming for me, slithering across the floor without making a sound, appearing from under the benches and from the corners of the room, and the worst of it was, I didn't move. I wasn't really frightened, not angry any more, not anything. I wanted to lay back, let the slipping things take hold of me, wrap themselves around me like tongues, and then let myself go. I was tired, so tired, and all I wanted to do was sleep. Just sleep, and I think that was what saved me. I felt sleepy, and even as I wanted to let go and let the shadows hold me, I couldn't help but remember the poor bastards that had been in the waiting room just a few minutes before. Did they see the shadows move before they fell asleep, or were they gone before they knew anything was wrong? They had friends, family, that would never see them again because of what had happened here. Maybe it sounds ridiculous, but I'd rather they'd been blown to pieces in some pointless battle; at least then their life might have looked like it served some purpose. How pointless a way to go, to simply be taken from here"

"Taken?"

"Taken. I saw the truth of it then, realised something about this place. The poor crops, the attitude of the people, the disappearances, everything. There was something under this town, something that sucked at the life above it. Like a good parasite, it didn't normally kill, just drew enough energy to live off, but with the war, there were people in and out all the time. Maybe it got greedy, maybe it felt threatened by the constant change and movement, I don't know, but it started to eat people, sucking at them 'till they were nothing instead of stopping short and leaving them stunted and exhausted but alive, and now it was coming for me. I screamed, and kicked and thrashed trying to wake myself up and make those dark things back away, and it must have worked because the next thing I remember I was running as fast as I could back to the camp and to my office."

In the distance, Gaskin heard the train. The old man heard it too and started to speak quickly.

"There's little more to tell. No one believed me, of course, and no trace of the men was ever found. They were listed as AWOL along with all the other poor sods who must have been taken. I started to see things everywhere in Low Hold. Shadows felt darker and thicker, and seemed to trail people, hanging on them longer than they should do. Every time I looked around, I saw great pools of darkness near me, darkness where there should have been light. I made sure I never stopped moving, was never alone, but even then I knew I wasn't safe. Whatever was under this place knew I knew about it, that I was a danger to it, and it needed to be rid of me. I tried to get myself posted away, but was told that I had done too good a job here, that they needed me to stay. Even the food I ate seemed a threat, as though I could swallow some of the terrible thing by accident and be absorbed from the inside out. I was a nervous wreck, jittery and tired and I couldn't concentrate. I knew I had to do something, but what? And then the Germans came to my rescue.

"There were more and more air raids happening and the skies above London and other cities were alive with fire and noise. Of course, they never bothered with Low Hold, because it was just an insignificant smear of shit on a map, but they did sometimes fly over it to get to Manchester or Leeds or up to Scotland. So, I committed treason."

Gaskin started. "Treason?" he asked, surprised. He had no urge to hear a confession as well as a story, but had no idea how to stop the old fool.

"Treason. I waited until the next air raid was passing over on its way somewhere important, and I set fires. It only took a couple of burning bales of hay, and that was enough; one by one the German pilots started dropping their bombs early, fooled by the flames, and the town was filled by the brightest, most glorious light I have ever seen. The entire valley was on fire, and even the *sound* of the planes and the bombs was hot, as though the air itself was burning, and in the centre of the flames, I saw it. Great black tentacles writhed around, reaching out to the sky and across the hills, grasping things that looked like octopus arms one second and pincers the next, but huge and so many, all desperate to escape the heat but there was nowhere for them to go. The more flames there were, the more bombs fell, and the more bombs that fell, the more flames there were and the more the earth was torn apart and the flames burned at the darkness beneath. I killed it, whatever it was, and I watched it die and thrash out its death in the middle of a firestorm that people died in as well and which was my fault and I was glad. Better that they died in fire than allow the thing under the earth a chance to draw another person down to it."

The old man stood. "I was a traitor, but no-one ever found out. Low Hold was practically destroyed and no one wanted to rebuild it. People had been released and they moved away, vanished, and the town simply rotted where it fell. The army rebuilt some of the camp, but they didn't use it for long before it was decommissioned. I was posted to Africa, where the ground was hard and dry and there was nothing under it to feed on us, and despite the danger and the shells and the tanks, I loved it."

Gaskin stood as well, his chest tight with the thought of the miserable train and the journey ahead.

"I killed it," said the man, "and the town died with it. When the Beeching Axe fell, Low Hold was lucky not to lose both train tracks. It only kept one because there were still quarries near here that used trains to transport the stone. I lived my life knowing that I had betrayed the country that I love, but I was sure that I had done right, that it was worth it." Gaskin saw that the old man was crying, tears rolling down his stubbled face as he walked to the edge of the platform.

"I was wrong. It is not dead. I must have injured it badly, because it lost its hold on the town, but just recently things have started being drawn here, growing here. Companies buying land, setting up offices, and the staff almost always move here to live. It's been pulling at me, wanting me to come over to the waiting room. I think it's weak, because it's more like a whine than an order, but it's stronger every day.

I didn't kill it but I hurt it and it has taken years to recover and now it wants me. It already has you, I can see it in the way you move and the way you sit and the shadows that gather under you.

"I will not go to it."

The man opened his arms wide and, before Gaskin could move, let himself fall back onto the track. The train was still advancing, slow but implacable, and even as the brakes yelped to life the wheels ground across the old man's chest and hips with a cracking, juddering wail that sent blood across the knotted weeds and Gaskin's scream into the high summer air.

Gaskin's two weeks off work did not help. The first few days he spent alternately shivering and then crying, and after that he found himself restless, wanting to return. The old man had been mad, clearly; the police had implied as much after they finished interviewing Gaskin. Gaskin hadn't told the police the story the old man had told him; they hadn't asked, simply took his name, enquired what happened and sent him home. It was his doctor who told him to take time off work, but it was Gaskin who decided to return even though his doctor wanted him to take longer.

The first evening Gaskin sat on the platform, it was warm again. He could hear bees in the distance, and birds fluttering in undergrowth on the platform opposite him. It seemed a far remove from the horror of his last time here. The old man's blood had left rusting stains on the earth around the rails, and although Gaskin was sure it was his imagination, the plants looked thicker where the blood had fallen. Leaning forwards, Gaskin peered under the bench beneath him. Surely the shadows were thicker under him, darker than they should be? He could hardly see the wall of the deserted ticket office, yet it was only a couple of feet away. Maybe the old man was right?

Nonsense.

Only it wasn't, not really. Throughout his time away, he felt an urge to return to Low Hold, a sense of being pulled and called and cajoled and ordered all at the same time that had eventually proved impossible to resist. There were other things as well; Gaskin had spent his first day back looking, really *looking*, at his fellow workers, and had seen, or thought he saw, what the old man was talking about. They walked as though something below them was pulling down, weighing them with a terrible burden. Looking at himself in the mirror at lunchtime, he had seen the same mark on himself, a deepening of the ridges along the side of his mouth and a rounding of his shoulders that made him look as though he were being yoked and crushed.

The buildings were as bad; even the newest of houses appeared to be crooked, falling apart. The office, which was comparatively new, felt old and brittle, with pale yellow stains to the glass in the windows and doors that didn't hang quite true, and electrics that never worked just they way they should. It was as though something was drawing the energy away, leeching it off and causing decay in even the most solid of structures.

Total, total nonsense. *Bullshit.* Wayward dreams and an old man's nightmares and he was a fool for listening, and a bigger fool for giving them credence.

And yet, he could not convince himself not to. As he looked at the opposite platform, long abandoned, he saw the shape of the waiting room through its fur of plants and bushes. It was there that the old fool had believed this thing was concentrated, wasn't it? Where all those men had been taken? *Perhaps,* though Gaskin, *if I look and find nothing, I can put this rubbish behind me.* And as simply as that, it was decided.

He left his bag pushed under the bench and walked down to the end of the platform. Here, under a sign that read *No unauthorised personnel past this point,* the concrete apron sloped away to the weed-entangled earth of the track bed. Looking up at the solitary CCTV camera and seeing the rust that streaked across its lens and the fraying wires that slipped from a crack in its skin, Gaskin decided that no one could see him. No one cared. Very carefully, he walked down the slope.

It was like entering another world. Even though he was only three feet lower, the air felt warmer and more sluggish and the sound of the insects' buzzing was louder. There was another sound, a metallic tension that he took a moment to identify; the rails, humming with pent-up electric intent. Looking to make sure that the train was nowhere in sight, and remembering uncomfortably the terrible grinding of the old man by the wheels, Gaskin took several cautious steps over the rails. He had no idea if one of them was a third rail, or dangerous, but knew that he could be careful and stay safe. One step, two, and his heels felt alive with shocks and trembling and then he was over and the other platform beckoned.

Beyond the rails, the ground became uneven, with sunken ruts where the second set of rails had been and plant roots bucking under the surface of the grass and weeds. There was an increasing smell, of old metal and wet soil and something else, something unhealthy and rich and fizzing with decay. Gaskin pushed on, wincing as the plants left streaks of green and brown moisture across his neat trousers and his shoes started to pick up lumps of dark brown matter that he could only hope was mud. By the time he reached the platform itself, he was sweating with the exertion of forcing his way through the tightly wound plants and he was beginning to wish he had left his jacket with his bag. He debated dropping it on the edge of the platform and leaving it to pick up later, but one look at the grime and liquid glistening there convinced him not to.

The platform was even harder to walk across than the track bed. Bushes had wound around each other and resisted his attempts to separate them, springing back to wrap around him even as he pushed them apart. Birds flew, twittering angrily at the disturbance, and at least once something small skittered over his foot, making him jump. The smell was worse here, the aroma of old meat roiling heavy in his every breath, wet and clinging and slippery. He scratched his hands on tough branches as he pushed his way through, leaving bloody markers behind him on the leaves and stalks. He tried not to imagine them being greedily absorbed as soon as he passed.

The waiting room door had long since rotted away from its frame and was tilted crazily across the entrance, stopped from falling by a thick mat of foliage. Gaskin stepped on it, balancing on its flat surface until it cracked loudly under his weight and shifted loosely. He pulled himself through the doorframe, hating the way his fingers felt as though they were digging into wet mulch as he heaved but needing to get inside now, determined to finish this idiot's quest that he had started. In the distance, he heard the sound of the train and knew that he did not have long, and then he was through and in.

There were fewer plants in here, although the windows on the far wall were thick with some crawling vine that had spread across most of the floor. There was the odour of piss, and the blackened remains of a fire in the far corner of the room. A solitary bench was pushed into the centre of the floor, its varnish peeling to reveal wood that was stained and swollen by years of damp and cold. There was nothing else. No monsters, no ghosts, no terrible sucking, clawing things. He was relieved, but oddly disappointed.

Gaskin turned to go and caught movement from the corner of his eye. He glanced around expecting to see a mouse or rat or even bird, but there was nothing. The sounds of the train were louder now, its rattle an insistent message for Gaskin telling him to move, to go *now*, but he ignored it. In the far corner, what he had taken to be the remains of a fire was opening, tendril arms fluttering apart like some night-blooming flower. At its heart, Gaskin saw a shadow as deep and rich as anything he had known before. Terror came to him on arachnoid legs, yet still he did not move. He could feel it in the palsied skitter of his heart and the clench of his bowels, but it felt as though it was happening to someone else. Or to him, but to a version of him that was somehow unreal, separated away by a sheet of glass or a dense wrap of plastic and untouched by the churning, lapping reality at his feet. *Run* he told himself, *run! The old bastard was right!* But even that knowledge did not start him to movement. The dark thing had left its mark on him, as surely as if it had branded him, marking him as one of its own. Could he run far enough? Fast enough to avoid it? Or would he end up here eventually, no matter what he did, too scared to fall beneath the great steel wheels of the train and find the release that the old man had achieved? And in his heart, he knew.

The shadowed thing parted itself around him. With the sounds of the train in his ears, a tattoo beating to the rhythm of a life he had left the second he stepped away from the other platform, Gaskin fell into its wasting embrace.

|The Animal Game|

The Wednesday Night Group met on the eighth floor of the Psychological Services building in Meeting Room 6, a room made miserable and grey by the fact that its windows were small and grimy and blocked the light coming in, but that was alright because none of the group really cared about the surroundings; most of them were miserable and grey too. Every week they met, and every week they sat around and discussed each other and themselves, and every week they carried out some stupid activity or other. "Think of it as a game," said Kevin, the group leader who made sure that everyone there knew he was senior to Gabrielle even as he told them that there was no hierarchy in the group. "Just think about who you are and who the other people in the group are, and think about what animal best represents you and best represents them."

Eldon grimaced; he hated this stuff. The Wednesday Night Group (that was how it appeared in his referral letter, *The Wednesday Night Group* in self-important capitals, and he had been unable to think of it in a different way since) was, for him, a last attempt to work out the little kinks in his personality after one-to-one sessions and self-help had failed. He had expected an intense experience, welcomed it really, looked forward to digging into his lack of ability to connect emotionally or maintain long-term relationships with other people, wanted to do it with people who dug into their own secrets with equal intensity. In reality, of course, it was nothing like that.

For a start, they were the only people in the building. The group met at seven, and normally the receptionist had her coat on when Eldon arrived, signing him and the others in quickly and sending them up to the eighth floor in a lift that smelled of old oil and sweat. She had to use her security pass to call the lift, rarely meeting Eldon's eyes if they had to wait for it to arrive. He was, after all, one of the outcasts, a sad unfortunate in need of psychological services, unable to cope with the world as it presented itself, or so he assumed the receptionist thought. *Perhaps she's scared of us, of me,* he wondered, and found that he liked the idea, just a little. No ever got in the lift besides members of the group, and it never stopped between the ground and eighth floor.

The eighth floor was a featureless length of corridor punctuated by doors and noticeboards. Between the lift and Meeting Room 6 were eleven doors and five noticeboards, the doors mostly unmarked and the noticeboards buried in drifts of union announcements and flyers for local events and, curiously, a poster for the local STD clinic. The room was unchanged from week to week; square, a fire safety notice its only decoration, containing 10 chairs, one table. Sometimes, the table held a small vase with a plastic flower in it and a box of tissues, other weeks only the vase and flower. This week, there were no tissues.

"So, animals?" Kevin asked, his eyes gleaming and his voice dripping with relaxed assurance.

Eldon might still have enjoyed the group despite the blandness of the surroundings were it not for the other members, seven of the most boring, self-centred, obnoxious people it had ever been his misfortune to meet. Knox, with his serial adultery and refusal to take responsibility for it, the misses Carlton and Lowe who were never seen apart and who clearly struggled with the concept that the world had moved on from their youth back in the 1940s, Kay who talked about himself in the third person and preened as he did it, Abbas who wouldn't argue or defend himself even when attacked, and Burns, who was so dull he almost wasn't there, except when he could talk about his parents. Then, he practically fizzed with anger, hating them so much he stuttered and became red-faced and upset. And then there was Millie.

"So, let's talk about which animal you think best represents you first," said Kevin, "and then I'll ask the group to come to a joint decision about whether they agree, and if not, which animal *they* think represents you. If there are differences, it's important for you to think why those differences might exist and what they could represent, and whether you need to do anything about them. Now, who wants to go first?"

No one spoke. As ever in the group, there was instead a low mumble of foot shuffling and floor-gazing and downcast eyes and little coughs and *mmmm aaaah* noises as people thought and avoided and hoped that someone else would go first. Kevin smiled broadly and encouragingly but leaned forward predatory in his seat, and Gabrielle looked from person to person with a look that said, *It's okay, you're safe here, please break this silence.* Eldon liked to watch Gabrielle squirm at these times; it seemed a nice counterpoint to Kevin, her anxiety for the group and her hope for its success undermining the professional front she tried so hard to present.

"I think I might be a gorilla," said Knox eventually, "one of those silverback ones that leads the family or pack or pride or whatever it is that lots of gorillas is called."

"A troop," said Kevin helpfully. "Why a gorilla?"

"Because I care about my wife and children, I do, and I want the best for them, but I can't help going with those other women. They practically offer themselves to me and I can't say no."

"So these women, they're part of your troop?" asked Eldon, wondering if Knox was being serious or not.

"Of course," replied Knox, warming to his theme. "And I have to keep them happy and see to their needs." He was serious, Eldon saw, completely without humour.

"What do the group think?" asked Kevin.

"Not a gorilla, a chimp," said Kay immediately, "self-deluding and insignificant."

"Fuck off," said Knox. It was an old refrain, boring and dusty with repetition. Knox and Kay hated each other because, Eldon thought, they were the same, coming at identical traits of selfishness and vanity from different angles and both thought they were the most important member of the Wednesday Night Group.

"Kay thinks you're a chimp," said Kay, "jumping up and down and making lots of noise but not actually achieving anything."

"Fuck off," said Knox again, fury in his voice and his clenched, reddening fists.

"Chimp," said Kay again and Knox rose from his seat.

"Mr. Knox, please sit down," said Kevin, also rising from his seat. "Mr. Kay is entitled to express his opinion, as we all are. Mr. Kay, I wonder if you could explain a little more clearly why you think that Mr. Knox is more like a chimp than a gorilla?"

"He doesn't think Knox is a chimp, he's just saying it to wind him up," said Eldon, tiring of the bickering. "And besides, even if he did, he's wrong. Knox is a dog, a big one, dumb but strong with a few dogs that follow him because he fucks them, and a wife and kids he dominates, all of them weak and unable to stand up to him, and they're all just part of his little pack. Aren't they?"

The Misses both giggled and Kay grinned and even Mille nodded, poor silent beautiful Millie who always sat next to Abbas but who never looked at anyone for longer than a couple of seconds. Knox looked at Eldon, more confused than angry, but everyone in the group was nodding and Kevin was speaking, cutting off anything he might have said.

"So, Mr. Knox, there's a difference between how you perceive yourself and presumably how you'd like the rest of us to see you, and how others actually perceive you. Perhaps you might like to think about this over the coming week? Think about what that difference might mean? Now, who's next?"

"I'm a lion," said Kay immediately, no hint of irony in his voice. "I'm strong and determined."

"So determined you need to attend a weekly psychotherapy group to deal with the fact that every relationship you ever had ended up in the shit," said Eldon. "You're a fucking peacock not a lion, all bright feathers and loud fucking squawking," and everyone in the group laughed, even Kevin (although only for a moment, hiding it by turning it into a cough behind one of those long-fingered hands with their curved nails). Kay smiled with them, although the smile barely touched the edge of his lips and didn't crawl any further up his face than his nose. His eyes were frozen, dark chips.

"Miss Carlton?" said Gabrielle, finally speaking. "What animal do you think you might be?" Miss Carlton, reddening, shook her head and looked down. Every week the same, thought Eldon, the two of them sit there like mutes, embarrassed to be taking up space in the room. Miss Lowe sometimes would speak or nod agreement to things but Miss Carlton rarely did even that. They were like every cliché of maiden aunts rolled into two old women, he thought, not animals but plants, some delicate orchids or other bright things that were useless and still.

"Fish," said Abbas suddenly," Miss Carlton and Miss Lowe are like those little fish, the bright ones that swim together in big groups."

"Schools," said Kevin, ever the font of knowledge. "Fish? How do you feel about that, Miss Carlton? Miss Lowe?" Neither replied, but Miss Lowe gave a little bob of her head, somewhere between a nod and a shake.

"He's right," said Mille, unexpectedly. "They're fish, keeping together for security." She fell silent again, her large eyes flickering around the room as if to gauge whether she'd said the right thing or not.

"And Abbas is one of Knox's dogs," said Eldon sharply, not liking the way that Abbas was looking at Mille, or the way she flashed a smile shyly back at him. Just a flash. Just too much.

"And what about you, Mr. Eldon?" said Kevin. "What animal might you be?"

"I might be anything," said Eldon. "I might be an elephant or a cat or a whale. I might be anything, but I'm not, I'm a human, a man, which is why this whole fucking thing is so stupid."

"He's a scorpion," said Abbas in a rare, angry retort, "sharp and mean and full of poison and not caring about anyone." Eldon grinned as he saw the rest of the group nodding and Knox said, "A big ugly one with sharp pincers and a fat tail like grapes strung together."

"Maybe so, but better that than a deluded dog who thinks he's a gorilla, or a bird who thinks he's a lion," Eldon said. "Better full of my own poison than of my own self-importance."

"You think that's better?" asked Gabrielle.

"Don't you? No, you wouldn't, would you? What animal do you think you are, Gabrielle? Kevin?"

"Well, said Kevin with a smile that showed his teeth, "I'm not sure Gabrielle and I, as group leaders, need to necessarily join in the activity, we—"

"'There are no leaders or hierarchy within the group, everyone here is equal'," quoted Eldon. "You're in the group, so you join in. Your rules."

"Not rules," said Kevin, "and not mine, the group's. We all agreed them."

"Did we? Good. Name your animal."

"Well, I suspect I'm something like a goat," said Kevin, the smile never leaving his face. "I eat enough, after all." Eldon was about to reply when Knox got there before him.

"Bullshit, you're the spider at the centre of the web. You set these tasks and ask us questions and then you sit back and watch and you smile as we tear each other to pieces and all the while you're feeding from us because it makes you feel good."

The group almost cheered, Eldon saw, at this attack on Kevin. None of them liked him, probably because he had power over them that the other members, Gabrielle included, did not. Even the Misses were nodding, their bobbing assents accompanied by smiles that hovered around their mouths and darted to their eyes before they were gone. Gabrielle maintained the blank-faced neither-agree-nor-disagree look of a professional in a complicated situation. Eldon, seeing an opportunity, said, "Gabrielle agrees. She's just as caught in your web as we are. She's like Abbas and Burns, a member of the pack and not the leader. Right, Gabrielle?"

Gabrielle said nothing. Kevin raised a silencing hand and said, "Time's nearly up. Does anyone have anything else they want to discuss?"

"We haven't done Millie yet," said Kay, complainingly. "We all know what we are now, but what's Millie?"

"Millie?" asked Gabrielle. She spoke to the women in the group, Eldon saw, but not the men unless she absolutely had no choice but to. She was so far lost in Kevin's shadow she was practically invisible.

"I don't know," Millie muttered. "A mouse, maybe? A cat?"

"Mouse, maybe," Knox repeated. "That could be it. You're frightened of the whole world, aren't you? But no, it doesn't work, not quite. A cat? No. You aren't self-contained or arrogant enough. Perhaps a rabbit. Yes! A rabbit, that's it, cute and quick and easily startled. Well? What does everyone think? A rabbit, yes?"

"Eldon wants her to be a rabbit because he likes her, and we all know what rabbits like to do!" cackled Kay and Eldon, for once, remained silent as Millie reddened like the sunset and the rest of the group dissolved into laughter.

The thing was, the group were right, Millie *was* like a rabbit. She was slim, her eyes were dark and large in a pretty face and her legs long and elegant and yes, Eldon wanted to fuck her, to be with her.

Quite apart from the prettiness of her face, there was something about her that made him want to hold her, to wrap himself around her and protect her from the world. She always seemed so diffident, so timid, as though she were permanently on guard against an expected attack from a something bigger and harsher than she could cope with. Eldon wanted to armour her, provide her with a framework within which she could function, could survive the world outside.

The problem was, he couldn't talk to her.

Every time he had the opportunity, Eldon froze, the words locking in his throat. Sarcasm, he could do. Digs and pokes and unpleasantness, he could do, but when he thought of compliments, of even everyday conversations, he ran out of words. *Hello* seemed so banal, and compliments tasted fake in his mouth. Once, they had been the last to leave Room 6 and she had bent to collect her bag from the floor, her T shirt riding up to reveal an expanse of smooth, brown back and, peeking from the top of her jeans, the top of her panties. He wanted to tell her she had nice skin, or that the froth of material of the waistband (lace and cotton, he thought) was possibly the most erotic thing he had ever seen, but he could not. It would either come out sounding aggressively sexual, he knew, or unreal, false. So, mostly, he remained silent.

The next Wednesday Night Group, however, presented him with the perfect opportunity. Eldon arrived, as ever, a few minutes before the group's half past seven start time to find Millie in the foyer but the receptionist nowhere in sight. Her little office cubby, framed through the dirty glass sliding window, was empty. She was still around, he saw; a coat hung on the back of the chair, a bag lay open on the floor, its purse and phone and diary guts exposed, and a half-drunk cup of coffee was perched on a coaster by the computer keyboard. There was a faint smell of perfume in the air.

"I've been here ten minutes," said Mille as Eldon peered through the hatch. "There's no sign of anyone."

"Perhaps she's been called away to an urgent receptionist's emergency?" said Eldon, trying for a joke and falling short, its humour stillborn.

"Perhaps," said Millie.

"The lift's here, though," said Eldon, nodding the open elevator door. "Maybe she called it before she went because she knew she'd be a while. At least we can go up."

Their ascent passed in silence. Millie looked everywhere in the lift except, it seemed, at Eldon, whilst Eldon for his part could think of nothing to say that wasn't either disparaging of another group member or that risked being interpreted as crude. Instead, he took surreptitious glances at Millie, at the swell of her breast under her blouse and the smooth line of her buttocks and thighs in her jeans, and he thought about how to cross the divide from acquaintance to friend or more but could find no path that seemed safe.

When they arrived at Room 6, they found it empty. It had been set out for the group, the chairs arranged in a loose circle and the table pushed to the side of Kevin's chair. There were tissues this week, Eldon saw, but they had been knocked to the floor and not picked up. The vase with its plastic bloom was also on its side, but had stayed on the tabletop.

"Where is everyone?" said Mille.

"I don't know," admitted Eldon. "We may as well wait for them." Ask her something, he told himself. Something non-judgemental, non-invasive. Be nice. *Ask!* But nothing came.

The two of them sat in a brittle, uncomfortable silence for about ten minutes until finally, Mille said, "Was it cancelled and they didn't tell us?"

"If it was, they didn't tell me," said Eldon, smiling his nicest smile to show he was joking. "We should give up and go and hold our own group in the pub. We'd probably get more done that way, and at least we could get a drink." It was only an aside, a thoughtless throwaway, but Millie surprised him by saying, "Okay. Nothing's happening here anyway," and getting to her feet. Eldon, startled, joined her. As they walked to the door, he started to smile. Not seeing the other group members tonight was turning out to be extremely beneficial.

The Misses were standing at the end of the corridor, by the lift. Eldon called a greeting as he and Millie started down the corridor, but neither responded. They were not standing still, he saw, but were walking to and fro in tiny, weaving rings, Miss Lowe slightly ahead of Miss Carlton. Eldon called again, louder, but still neither woman responded or even acknowledged them with a glance, walking on in those tightly clenched loops.

To and fro. To and fro.

"What's wrong with them?" asked Millie.

"No idea," said Eldon. They were maybe forty feet away from the Misses now, and this close to them he made out other little oddities; their hands fluttered at their sides, sticking out at right angles from their wrists, but their arms were motionless. Both swayed slightly as they walked, and Eldon wondered briefly if they were drunk, but quickly dismissed the idea. This wasn't a drunken sway, it was a controlled one, each of them in time with the other and both describing those little loops, Lowe shadowing Carlton, following her lead.

"Hey," said Eldon as they got closer, "what's going on?" Immediately, Miss Lowe made a weird, darting little jump sideways and started up the corridor, going past Eldon and Millie, pressed against the opposite wall as though trying to stay out of their reach. Miss Carlton was behind her, her movements as Miss Lowe's but just a fraction of a second after, like some bizarre streetmime performance. Eldon reached out and both the Misses flinched, banging against the wall and speeding up. Millie grasped Eldon's arms, the first time she had ever touched him, and said, "Look at their eyes." Eldon looked, and huge black discs looked back at him.

The Misses' eyes were almost entirely black and taking up more space in their faces than they should, most of their cheeks lost to those gelid orbs. As she passed, Miss Lowe gave another of those weird little herky-jerky jumps, twisting as she did so, and for a moment she looked directly at Eldon. Her mouth formed a perfect, tiny circle beneath her eyes and no teeth showed in its moist depths. Her nose seemed smaller, as though her growing eyes were sucking it away and leaving only the tiniest nubbin of smooth flesh between them and her mouth. Her skin glittered, greens and silvers and blues flashing in the reflections of the corridor's neon lighting. Had she got makeup on, he wondered? Miss Carlton was the same, he saw, and he watched as the Misses wheeled away down the eighth floor corridor, never going more than a few feet before changing their direction, crossing and re-crossing the floor, to and fro, to and fro. Wall to wall, looping back on themselves, circling away again, their hands fluttering at their sides, their black eyes depthless when they looked back at him, mouths agape. As the Misses reached the far end of the corridor and disappeared around the corner, they were illuminated oddly. For a brief moment, they seemed surrounded by dapples of light that hung in the air around them, and their hair (Miss Carlton's long and dyed, Miss Lowe's shorter and steel-grey) looked to be floating away from their heads in a gentle, uplifting breeze.

"Did they remind you of anything?" asked Eldon quietly after they'd gone.

"Yes," replied Millie. "They looked like fish."

The lift wouldn't come because neither had an electronic ID card.

Normally, the receptionist let them up to the meeting and Kevin escorted them out, herding them (Gabrielle included) into a cluster by the lift doors like schoolchildren and then waving them into the lift when it arrived with his security badge hanging from his hand. Eldon cursed him under his breath as he stabbed at the button, futile little prods of irritation and anger and confusion, annoyed that he needed the man to do something as simple as leave the building. Millie had fallen to silence by his side.

"We'll have to take the stairs," Eldon said eventually, "this fucking thing's not coming." The security light's LED eye gazed at them unblinking and red. Millie nodded, holding her bag in a clench grip in front of her stomach. Eldon took her hand, thrilling at the touch, and led her down the corridor to the corner. The fire exit and stairs were around it, he knew, because Kevin had lectured them on health and safety and fire drills in the first session of the group. The lights threw their shadows, anaemic and thin, across the cheap carpet as they went. As the approached the door, the Misses appeared again, wheeling and turning in those tiny to and fro curls. The light still lapped around their heads, shimmering in front of eyes that were now flat and expressionless and smooth and which covered almost half their faces. They came along the corridor unhurriedly, passing Millie and Eldon without looking at them. As they went by, Eldon thought he heard Millie sob.

The stairs were darker than the corridor, the lights spaced further apart and paler. Eldon could see perhaps two floors down before the stairwell descended into a murky jumble of barely illuminated shapes and lines. Wordlessly, they started walking down, their steps echoing around them in a knitting needle clatter. Millie's fingers were laced tightly through Eldon's, her palm warm against his and her smell teasing his nostrils, the clean, floral odour of soap and skin and tension. They had reached the turn in the stairs, midway between the seventh and eighth floors, when the noise came.

It wasn't a breathing exactly, more a long series of grunted exhalations that rose to an ululating sound that wasn't a howl and wasn't a shout but was somewhere in-between, and that filled the stairwell. At its end, it dropped away, becoming a hoarse slobbering that clung wetly to the walls like peeling paper. Millie stepped closer to Eldon, her grip on his hand tightening to the point of pain, pressing herself against herself against him so that the swell of her breasts was against his back, warm and soft.

"What is it?"

"I don't know," he replied and realised that they were both whispering. They remained still, peering over the metal and wood railings down the throat of the stairs. Somewhere below them, a door nagged closed, then opened again, and there was another not quite howl and then a skittering, rapid sound.

"Move," said Eldon. "Move now!" and he pulled Millie, taking two steps at a time and dragging her as the noise got louder, his own breath sounding in his ears, Millie's panting lurking at the back of his head. Then they were passing a large '7' painted on the wall and a sign that read *Corporate Support*, and then Eldon pulled at the seventh floor door and they were through and into the corridor.

"What was that?" asked Millie before the door had swung shut behind them.

"I told you, I don't know," said Eldon, irritated with Millie's passivity and trying not to let it show. All of his instincts, seated somewhere below thought or consciousness, had told him to move when he heard that noise; it was feral, and it had made his skin shiver and his mouth run dry in anticipation, although of what he could not say. Millie, however, had frozen and had done nothing but be led, moving only when he pulled her. Already, he was beginning to wonder if she was going to be more trouble than she was worth.

The overhead lights on seven were low, but it was not completely dark; on the opposite side to them, the third door along was partially open and a yellow lozenge of light escaped from behind it to fall across threadbare carpet. Eldon pulled Millie again, leading her across to the doorway, and looked in. It was an office, a space of desks and chairs and filing cabinets and lamps. On a desk in the middle of the room, a computer was on, shedding cold blue light in a wide semicircle around itself. On the desk next to it a desk lamp glowed. Eldon let go of Millie and went in. After a moment, she followed. *We have independent movement*, he thought, and pushed the door shut behind her.

The room was larger than it looked from the outside, three or four smaller spaces knocked into one, with three doors along the corridor wall in addition to the one they had some through. Clusters of desks filled the floor, mostly three or four workspaces pushed together into pods. Eldon left Millie by the door and went towards lighted area, threading his way past desks and chairs, heading for the desk that held the computer and lamp. As he went, he saw pictures and cards and plants on the desks alongside the keyboards and monitors, all of the little mementoes of humanity and individuality that people used to mark out their spaces, and he marvelled at their mundanity. Closing in on the still-on computer, he smelled something rich and sour, and as he came around the desk, he saw the blood.

There were two spots of it on the desk, another on the keyboard, a larger spatter on the arm of an overturned chair and even more on the floor, where a dark puddle stretched from under the chair, crept back and disappeared under the desk. Eldon moved slowly past the chair, expecting to find a body, but there was nothing except a set of scuffed, bloodied footprints. There was something strange about the footprints, something that at first refused to register. He kept looking, studying. Most of the prints were indistinct, although some showed a diamond pattern that reminded him of the prints his own training shoes left. Several were long and stretched, as though whoever had made them had slipped or skidded. Other prints were clearer, different sizes indicating that more than one person had been here.

These last prints had been made by people who were barefoot.

Eldon moved rapidly back to the perimeter of the room and began to work his way around it, trying not to dwell on how compressed the barefoot prints had looked, how misshapen and splayed the toes had been and how they seemed to end in points rather than rounded arcs. It meant nothing. Nothing.

The rest of the office was undisturbed as far as he could tell except for one of the little four-desk pods at the other end, which looked to have been bumped or shoved so that the desks had gone out of kilter with each other and come apart. Another chair had been overturned next to the disarrayed desks. Eldon reached the far end of the office and turned to look at Millie. In the half light, her shape was all curves and shadows and her eyes were large and dark. He walked back towards her, seeing as he went that she had tied her hair into two loose braids that hung down the sides of her head like elongated ears.

By Millie, the air was dank with a smell Eldon thought might have been her fear. If anything, she had frozen up even more, was so still she was almost trembling, and her eyes were rolling in their sockets, massive in the gloom. At first, he thought it was just the next stage of her terror, another little Millie moment, and he was going to say something harsh to her to snap her out of it, but then he saw that it was something more. She was looking at the door they had come through, eyes jumping from his face to the narrow gap between the door and the jamb, a two-inch-wide slice of grey corridor. He stepped closer, silent and listening.

Another smelled drifted in from the corridor, earthy and dark, riding the air currents into the room along with a noise so faint he might not have heard it were he not concentrating. A low breathing, layered and dense with control, whoever it was keeping their inhalations and exhalations carefully quiet. Eldon leaned closer.

Closer, the gap filling his vision, more of the corridor beyond showing. Every sense he possessed flowered, opened, warned him.

Closer.

More corridor and the sound adding to itself now, becoming a pant, the smell darkening to a rotten-wood odour of wet forest and storm-flooded caves and mud left to dry in sunlit valleys and Eldon had time to think, *What the fuck?* before something hit the door with a ferocious crack.

Quick as the door smashed open, Eldon was quicker, catching it and slamming it back, throwing his weight against it so that it bounced hard against whoever was on the other side. They howled, a shrieking roar worse than they had heard in the stairwell, a noise that broke and ground against itself in fury. Whoever was making the noise threw themselves against the door, jerking Eldon back so that his feet slid before he could brace himself and slam the door back again.

More roars, two or three people joining the cacophony now, one higher, taking up the descant and then something scrabbled again at the outside of the door; Eldon heard the wood begin to splinter and crack. At the same time, the door handle rattled and turned, forcing Eldon to grab it and twist it back around. The handle slid through his hands, which felt stiff and clumsy. For a few moments the violent rattling continued, the scrabbling worsened and the howling sharpened as Eldon tried to keep the people in the corridor out.

There were three other doors.

"Millie, go and block the other doors," he shouted, turning his head to look at her. She was still and mute, clutching her bag to her belly like a shield. "Millie, go!" he shouted and then "Millie!" again because she appeared not to have heard him.

"Millie!" one last time and then he risked lashing out with one foot, catching her a glancing blow to her left hip that sent her staggering sideways and woke her up.

"The fucking doors!" he screamed as he braced himself against another vicious, clattering assault. Millie ran, a clumsy hopping stagger that favoured the hip he had not kicked. As she ran, she grabbed a chair, swinging it around in front of her and pushing it towards the first of the doors. *Good girl,* he thought but as she reached the door it crashed open and the people from the corridor exploded into the office.

Eldon couldn't see them properly. In the confusion of moments following their entry, he saw Millie leap back, slithering over one of the desks and away towards the far wall. The people, blurred shapes that spread rapidly across the room, moved fast and low. They howled, victorious and savage. The door behind Eldon stopped its rattling dance and he heard footsteps, disappearing rapidly along the corridor. Warily, he let go of the door and stepped away, giving his arms space to move. To defend himself.

Things slowed, the shadows solidifying into three new people, and then three more entered as he watched. The last of them to enter moved quickly ahead of the others, who had fanned themselves out into a wide semicircle that stretched across the width of the room. "Millie, come here," said Eldon softly, holding his hand out to her. She remained motionless. "Millie," he said again and this time she turned to look at him. "Come here," he repeated. The leader of the group growled and one of the other darted forwards, blocking the path between Eldon and the girl. Growled? No, it hadn't been a growl so much as an *imitation* of a growl. Whoever it was was still making the noise as the group continued slowly forwards, and now the leader was close enough for Eldon to recognise.

It was Knox, only not completely.

His jaw was wrong, for a start, sloping forward and jutting with teeth that gleamed large and pallid and sharp. He walked crouched over; they all did. The others, Eldon saw, were Abbas and Gabrielle and Burns. Between Millie and him stood the receptionist from downstairs and behind her was a young man he didn't recognise dressed in slacks and a shirt and tie; one of his arms hung loose by his side and his shoulder was torn and bloody. Eldon had no doubt that, at some point earlier this evening, the man had been sitting in this office working late when Knox found him. He was equally sure that, if he looked, he would see that Knox was barefoot.

Knox and his pack crept closer, all of them growling now, all of them bending forward with their shoulders hunched and their hands twisting and clenching. Their nails were long, like talons. Gabrielle was panting as she growled and Eldon could almost feel the sexual heat coming off her, this mousy little woman who had found her subservient place next to Abbas and behind Knox, trailing behind and desperate to be wanted and needed. Abbas was the same, his eyes brown and wide, watching Eldon but unable to keep from looking at Knox with something like adoration. Following their leader, Eldon thought. Following the pack dog, scrappy and weak though he might be.

Knox grunted, looking between Eldon and Millie. Eldon looked at Millie as well. The receptionist, cheap blouse torn open and hanging to reveal one flabby breast in a brassiere that was old and grey, had been joined by the young man and they were now both between Millie and Eldon. There was no clear path for her to get to him. He was nearly surrounded now, Knox and the others coming closer, tightening the line around him. He looked again at Millie, at her beautiful skin and her eyes as large as fear could make them and her slim arms and her sweet, delicate breasts, and for a second he thought about what might have been and then he made his decision.

Turning, he leapt for the door. Millie was lost to him anyway and he heard her scream even as he heard the pack break into savage howls. Darting into the corridor, he caught a momentary glimpse of her falling beneath Abbas and the receptionist and Burns and the young man, as Knox and Gabrielle ran at him. He slammed the door shut and this time he did not try to brace it but ran, scuttling, back down the corridor to the stairwell. Glancing back over his shoulder, he saw the two of them loping out of the office, low and feral and now fallen silent. Their eyes glinted, catching what little light there was in red flashes. Eldon ran.

The stairwell door was closed. Eldon pushed at it, its weight making it slow to open, slipping through the widening gap as soon as there was space for him to do so. Instead of going down the stairs, however, he stopped and crouched, low and sharp, in the shadows at the side of the door. The door's return swing was slow and it hadn't quite closed when Knox burst through it. Fully on all fours now, he bayed as he came through the doorway, his mouth stretched back to reveal teeth that were yellow and curved. Saliva slathered his chin and his nails clicked against the floor, and he saw Eldon too late to stop him slashing out.

He sent one hand low, gouging at the back of Knox's legs, and the other higher, slicing across his face. Knox's impetus carried him forwards, past Eldon, the skin across his cheek opened and blood spattering out from his legs to coat Eldon's hand in a warm, saltlick flow. Knox howled, twisting and crashing into the banister railings, and then Eldon was on him. He pincered at Knox's neck, slashing at the skin and tearing it with one hand and gripping at his waist with the other, dragging him forward to the edge of the stairs. Knox thrashed, clawing at him, but the blow glanced off Eldon's hard belly and then with a final thrust, Eldon sent Knox tiltawhirling down the staircase.

Knox roared as he fell, bouncing and rolling down the concrete steps until he hit the turn in the stairs with a crunch that sounded like damp wood snapping. Knox's bowels let go as he hit, loosing shit; Eldon smelled it, along with the blood that chattered out of Knox's mouth, rich and bleak and raw. He made a noise like a punctured bellows and then he shit and bled out again in dark streams. Eldon breathed its scents deep, enjoying the sensation of victory and liking the way Knox's body was twisted around the stairs below him, his head facing around at a sharp, unnatural angle, and then Gabrielle whimpered from behind him.

She had come through the door silently, but did not attack. Instead, she stared down at Knox's weeping corpse with a look in her eyes that Eldon thought was somewhere between loss and fear. Her teeth were pale and large in the miserable light, her mouth twisted and drawn, and the claws at the end of her fingers curved into the shadows at her waist like fish-hooks. Eldon raised his hands, stepping forward ready to defend himself, to attack as a defence if needed. Gabrielle took a compensatory step backwards, her whimper evolving into a mournful howl as she dropped to her hands and knees and turned so that she was facing away from him. She raised her buttock towards him, offering herself and making little sounds inside the howl that said, *Here I am, don't hurt me,* over and over. Eldon could smell her, could near-taste her musk of fear and sexual readiness and exercised flesh, and he knew as he smelled it that he did not want her. He lashed out, spiking one of her haunches so that she toppled into the corridor. Eldon pushed her again, forcing her all the way through the doorway and then let the door swing shut, blocking his view of her as she rolled in pain. Then, turning, he started down the stairs.

Kay was between the third and fourth floors, scattered across the stairwell in a wide, bloody fan. Eldon stepped carefully over the tacky patches of blood, not bothering to check if the man was alive or dead; he did not need to. Poor, sad little Kay, vain and self-centred and always talking himself up and making himself appear glorious, was beyond the touch of anyone but whichever God he believed in. Knox and his pack had torn him into pieces, leaving his entrails and hair and blood cast about him in a display that looked like peacock feathers painted in shades of red. Eldon went on.

The door into the foyer stuck when Eldon pushed at it. He pushed harder, its resistance tautening and then snapping. He was through and into the reception area before he saw the thin grey cords, felt them before he saw them as they draped themselves across his face and head. He tore at them, backing away, but they seemed everywhere, above him and behind him, torn strands that drifted and stuck as he brushed against them. He slashed at them, feeling them cling at him, tear, cling and tear again. He backed further away until he bumped into the now-closed stairwell door, and then he tore the remaining strands away. Most were thin and tore easily but one or two were fatter, stretching away from him towards the ceiling and these resisted his tearing. Looking back along them, he saw that they went back into the high corner of the atrium where they fastened to the wall in fat, grey clumps. Beside them, he saw a dark shape.

As though it could feel his attention, it scuttled down the wall, its movements fast and sharp. Eldon shifted, turning to face it, his brittle skin prickling. The shape, multi-legged and alien but somehow familiar, carried on around the wall until it reached another of the fatter strands and then it stepped delicately out upon it, moving rapidly down it towards Eldon. As it came closer, he saw Kevin's face, his new eyes glinting, his pedipalps distorting the shape of his mouth. He was silent as he came, and his fangs gleamed. Eldon raised his claws and opened his pincers. He grinned, clicking his chelicerae. His tail came up behind him, swaying above his shoulder, anticipating the battle. Poison, dark and corrosive, dripped from his sting.

|An Afternoon with Danny|

Pirate World was deserted apart from Alex and Danny.

Just inside the door to the pirate kingdom stood a large plastic pirate ('Captain Crossbones Grim', according to the sign above his head), his face stern and his arm outstretched to show his hook, and Alex had made Danny laugh by hanging his coat over the hook and saying in a posh voice, "Would you mind awfully looking after my coat, old man?". Captain Crossbones Grim, his severe face peering down at Danny and his chipped-paint eyes glaring balefully, had then had the further indignity of having Danny's coat draped over his head, and Alex had taken his laughing son to the nearest play area.

It was a cold midweek day on the edge of winter, and Alex had brought Danny to Pirate World because, over the previous months, they had been to all the other places he could think of. Maxine had banned them from going to fast food restaurants after Danny had been sick during the course of the sugar high after one of their trips out, the seafront aquarium was now closed and the museum was too boring to retain Danny's three year old magpie attention for more than a few minutes. Maxine wouldn't let Alex take Danny out on the weekends either, after Alex had lost Danny at a busy fair during the summer and the police had to be called, so Alex was stuck with whatever was open and interesting to a lively toddler during the week. Hence, Pirate World.

Alex had read about it in the local paper; a busy activity and play centre during the summer, it was described as "quiet and peaceful" during the off-season, and the food at the adjoining café (open all year round as well) "cheap and filling". Ideal, then, when Alex had charge of Danny but didn't want to stay in his miserable apartment and money was tight. The pirate theme was good as well; Danny's imagination was just beginning to be fired with ideas of other people, other places, other worlds, and pirates, with their bright colours and larger than life personas, were already one of his favourite things. Watching his son now, Alex felt a wave of helpless love for him, this delicate blond child splashing across the ball pool and throwing the balls into the air. Alex perched on its edge, twisting his fingers into the netting that kept the balls in, and simply enjoyed seeing his son play.

There was a soft *flump* from behind them. Alex turned and saw that Danny's coat had fallen from Captain Crossbones Grim's head. His own jacket was also on the floor, and the figure's hook gleamed dully in the light from the café beyond the entrance door. Alex wondered how the coats had fallen, and then Danny was calling him.

"Come and see!" from somewhere deep in the shadows at the rear of the ball pool. Alex leaned in past the netting cautiously, having some idea of what was coming next.

"Where are you?" he called in a singsong voice, the first steps on a familiar path.

"You have to guess!" replied his son.

"Are you… here?" singsonged Alex, suddenly whipping his head to one side.

"No!" came the reply, emerging from an apparently innocent mound of balls at the back corner of the pool.

"Here?" whipping his head the other way.

"No!" this time with giggles, and the balls of the mound began to shiver and shift.

"Well, then, I don't know," said Alex and then Danny burst out from the mound and threw balls at him, calling, "I'm here!" and Alex threw balls back and the two of them collapsed, cuddling, among the balls and laughing at each other.

From the ball pool, Danny dragged Alex to an open area with a padded floor and a series of large, soft blocks scattered across it and they spent time playing an ever-moving game of hide and seek around the blocks, Alex scuttling around on his hands and knees and Danny running and shrieking with laughter. Alex caught sight of the pirate captain at one point; their coats were still on the floor and the pirate captain himself seemed to be giving them an even more disapproving look. Alex stuck his tongue out at him in retaliation.

After hide and seek was the slide, which Danny slithered down again and again, both forwards and backwards. He made Alex laugh even more by waving his legs in the air as he came shooting down, his denim-clad buttocks adding to the shining patina of smooth reflection created by countless other children over the years. Danny's enjoyment of the slide was total, and soon sweat covered his face and his hair was sticking to his forehead and temple in delicate, sodden waves. Alex, remembering with discomfort Maxine's reaction the last time the boy had become so over-excited he had vomited, finally stopped Danny playing on the slide, looking around him to find a calmer amusement. There was a climbing structure over the ball pool, its sides swathed in netting and full of twisting pipes and ladders and walkways, but Alex wasn't keen. Danny wasn't really big enough to climb, and even if he could, the structure was closed to adults, and Alex wanted to be near Danny. He had so little time with him, so few hours to share with his son, that he did not want to spend any of them apart, even if the separation was only a matter of feet. It sometimes felt as though if he stayed close enough to Danny, if he breathed his son's smell enough, if he touched him and hugged him enough, then his senses would be filled and he would last until the next time they could be together.

So, if not the climbing gallery, that left the bouncy castle. It covered the far wall of Pirate World, an elaborate creation of inflated walls and floors in the shape of a galleon whose masts at the uppermost touched the ceiling and whose bow and stern brushed against the walls. Walking the length of Pirate World, Alex held his son's hand and enjoyed his nearness. The feel of his hand, small and slick with dirt and sweat, gave Alex a sense of pride; his son, small and perfect, and apparently happy to spend his time with Alex when so many others weren't. Maxine, who never missed the opportunity to tell him how useless he was; his parents, disappointed that he had let himself be trapped by fatherhood and who never seemed to realise just how special it made him feel; his friends, who considered Danny a distraction from the recreational opportunities provided by drink and drugs. Alex felt that, in Danny, his life had not just purpose but *value*, and he meant to hold on to those feelings for as long as he could. Already, he dreaded the time when Danny would be embarrassed to be with Alex; it would come, he was sure, but let it be later rather than sooner.

Entry into the pirate ship was through a dark opening in its side reached after clambering up an inflated ramp. Danny laughed as they wobbled up the ramp, Alex making his tilting and staggering more pronounced just to hear Danny laugh more and more. At the top of the ramp, Alex put on a terrible pirate accent and called, "I've come to join yer crew, Cap'n Crossbones Grim, 'cos I knows yer need good men. See, I brought along this little shrimp for a cabin boy for yer as my payment to yer for takin' me on! Take him and keep him if you want, throw him over the side if he's no good!" and as Danny laughed even harder, they went into the swaying ship.

Inside, the scene was oddly effective. Through the entrance, Danny and Alex found themselves in a ship's hold, shadowed and claustrophobic and full. The floor was raised and ridged, decorated to look like planking, and the walls hung with netting. Forced perspective pictures of crates and barrels receded into the painted darkness. Unlike most bouncy castles, this one had a roof, a sheet of billowing plastic or rubber perhaps fifteen feet above their heads and painted to look like the underside of the hold, all brown decking and clutches of barnacles. Here and there, chains and ropes had been hung and they swung in rhythm with the sway of the floor. And around them were pirates.

A series of inflated columns had been attached to the floor, each with a pirate painted on; Danny and Alex found themselves surrounded by swaying, leering, hairy men with eyepatches and wide, grinning smiles and hoop earrings that seemed to twinkle in the smeary light. There was the smell of sweat and movement and dirt in the air and the rubberised floor creaked as they moved across it. Alex had never been on a sailboat, but thought that a genuine hold would be like this; shadowed, full of unstable movement and constant, shifting sounds and scents. It was eerie but also wonderful, and Danny's excited reaction was enough for Alex. He watched as his son scuttled off, darting between the pirates and laughing as he wobbled and tilted, calling for Alex to hurry *up*, to *catch* him if he dared. Alex, grinning, began to chase him.

Soon, the game had become a hunting and pouncing one. Danny would hide behind one of the bobbing, grinning pirates and Alex would wait. Danny, trying to keep his giggles quiet, would try to sneak from one place to another and Alex would leap out from his own hiding place and grab Danny, smothering him in a hug and roaring with maniacal laughter. Then, after tickling him or bouncing him on the floor (Maxine be damned, they were having fun and if Danny threw up, well so be it), Alex would let Danny go and they would start again. Alex liked this game. Danny's ability to stay quiet for longer and longer was improving and in it, Alex felt as though he could see signs of Danny's growing maturity and inklings of the adult he would become. Committed, serious and intelligent, Danny could be so much if only he had the right support and opportunity. *Whatever you are, be more than me,* Alex thought, *be more than I ever was or am going to be.*

The noises of the bouncy castle were surprisingly loud when the two of them were hiding. There was a heavy rustle from the floor and walls as they shifted and gave around them, mingling with the distant sound of the generator. Its hum sounded like the far wash of a relaxed ocean to Alex, almost hypnotic in its rhythm and roll. Crouched behind a gap-toothed pirate whose hands clutched a cutlass, Alex let his thoughts loosen and relax. First, food; they could eat in the café next door. Its prices were cheap, well within his budget, and the dishes it served were Danny's favourite. Chips, beans and sausages all washed down with fruit juice. Then, a walk in the nearby park to make sure Danny had fresh air. Perhaps, when his food had gone down, Alex would take Danny to the swings and push him high, so high, *highest* and make him laugh even more. And then, that terrible moment when he had to return Danny to Maxine. She lived with her parents, and they always made a point of meeting him at the doorway in a line as though blocking him entry into their home, their solidity swallowing Danny in a bustle of coat-removal and *Oh, look at the mess your Daddy's let you get into* comments. Maxine would demand a run-down of everything they did, and then let him know all the things he had done wrong. Alex sighed, miserable in the knowledge that he had only a couple of hours left with Danny and that he would be alone then until his next visit.

Danny was silent.

Alex snapped back to the present, listening carefully. Nothing. Danny's normal hiding volume was low but audible, stifled laughter and panting breath, but now the only sound was the shifting of the ship around him. Could Danny have crept past him, hidden somewhere else as he daydreamed about the rest of the day? No, surely not. His own hiding place was close to the exit from the ship and besides, where would Danny go? Ever since he had got lost at the fairground, he had been careful not to hide too well, always wanting Alex to know where he was. Alex stood, wobbling as the deck pitched below him.

"Danny?" he called softly, not wanting to alarm the boy. He was surely just hiding well, had finally managed to control his laughter and breathing, another sign of his growing abilities.

Danny did not respond.

"Danny?" Again, but louder this time, firmer. "Danny, it's time we went for lunch. Are you hungry? I am!" Excited sounding, not angry. *Don't give him a reason to think you're angry*, Alex told himself, *otherwise he won't come to you*. Still no reply.

Alex walked as quickly as he could around the hold, looking behind the four gently bobbing pirates. Danny was nowhere to be seen. Worried now, Alex made his way out of the ship and into the large room beyond. Danny wasn't at the slide, nor was he in the ball pool. Alex thrashed about in the plastic balls for a minute, digging deep to make sure that Danny hadn't buried himself in an effort to hide *really* well. No. Not there.

Christ.

Alex jogged to the door, past Captain Crossbones Grim, who looked at him with emotionless painted eyes but whose expression seemed to be laughing in silent mockery of Alex's growing fear. Through the door and into the café, and still no Danny. The man behind the counter looked questioningly at Alex as he came through the door, and before Alex could speak, said, "Look, I know you and your kid are the only ones in there, but could you keep the noise down?"

"What?" said Alex, momentarily surprised.

"The noise, man. All that screaming and crying a couple of minutes ago. If you're going to tell your kid off, fine, but he was crying fit to burst and the noise was awful."

"What screaming and crying?" asked Alex stupidly. He felt weighted and slow, unable to get the man behind the counter's attention. Oh, Danny, where *are* you?

"It's easy to get carried away playing with your kid, and I know they can be disobedient" said the man, "and I know it's empty apart from the two of you, but you have to keep it down. And stop messing about with the figure."

"Figure?"

"Captain whatever, the big plastic pirate captain just inside the door there. You've been pushing it about, I saw it go past the door.

Alex looked around. The door to Pirate World was panelled at the bottom but its top half was frosted glass with letters stencilled upon it, made to look as though they were cut with cutlass slashes.

PIRATE WORLD!
- Abandon Hope All Ye Landlubbers Who Enter Here -

Alex turned back to the man behind the counter.

"You haven't seen my son come out of there?" he asked, knowing the answer before the man gave it.

"No. Isn't he with you?"

"No," said Alex. "I think he's with someone else". And, turning and walking fast, he went back into Pirate World.

Inside the door, Alex looked around. Danny wasn't up on the climbing frame, wasn't on the area with the padded blocks, wasn't anywhere to be seen. Their coats were still on the floor, crumpled a few feet from Captain Grim's booted feet. Experimentally, Alex pushed at the statue. He managed to move it, but not much. So how had the man behind the counter seen the figure move? *Had* he seen the figure move? Was it further away from the door than before? Alex couldn't tell, but he knew now that something was terribly, awfully wrong here. The floor seemed to swell and shrink under his feet as he stood there, his stomach hollowing with terror. He looked around for something, anything that would tell him were Danny was. There was nothing, except... their coats were surely further from Captain Grim's feet than they should be if they'd simply fallen, weren't they? No. No! It was a plastic or resin figure, not a real pirate, even if his expression looked sterner than before, less amused. *You offered him to us, remember?* he seemed to be saying, *Clear as a bell, you said we could take him. He was your payment to us to take and keep. So we have.* Panicked, Alex ran now, ran to the pirate ship.

Hadn't there been five pirates when they first went in? There were four now. Four, with one gone. Had they taken Danny? Oh God, had he given his son away?

"Take me!" he cried miserably, "Bring him back and take me!" but there was no response, save the sound of the ship rolling and pitching as it weighed anchor and prepared to set sail.

|The Pennine Tower Restaurant|

Introduction

This is not fiction.

I should, perhaps, explain how I came to write this. Before I became self-employed, I worked for a number of years in local government and the voluntary sector. I did not always enjoy the work, and I never really enjoyed being an employee, but there were some nice things about the experience. I met my wife whilst working for a charity in Manchester and my best friend (and subsequent godfather to my son) working for Liverpool City Council. Indeed, this aspect of the work is the one thing I miss now that I am self-employed, and that I enjoyed most at the time, meeting a wide range of people, some of whom I am proud to now call friends.

One department I dealt with was housing, and over a period of months I worked closely with a member of the committee dealing with planning applications; during this time we became, if not friends, then at least friendly acquaintances. We discovered a shared enjoyment of supernatural fiction and cold lager, that we had both spent time in Scotland and that both of us wanted to make a difference to the people's lives by doing our jobs well. This probably sounds like a cliché, I know, but nonetheless it was true of most of the people I met working for the council. No matter how hard or stressful the work or how much pressure people were under (and they were often under a lot) I rarely met anyone who didn't believe in the work that they did. Despite clients who were sometimes hostile, managers who didn't understand what their workers were doing, workloads that were unmanageable and a government obsessed with targets rather than client welfare, my colleagues carried on with little complaint because they believed in what they did and saw its benefit to the public they tried to serve.

My colleague from housing was involved in all sorts of council tasks and projects, and at the time struck me as a man who was working long hours and driving himself hard to do the best job he could. He was unceasingly cheerful, always helpful, and for a few months, we supported each other and enjoyed each other's company. Like many of the relationships made at work, however, I lost contact with this person after I left and thought little about him until he got in touch by email out of the blue at the beginning of the year. The email read:

Hi Simon

Please help me. I know it's been a long time and we don't work together any more but I don't know who else to ask and we were friends enough for you to trust me, I hope. I know you've had some success with your writing, and I have a story that needs telling and you're the only person I know who has a chance of understanding it. Of believing me. I'm not after money for this, nor any recognition. I don't want you to name me at all if possible. I have a family and I'm the only income we have, and I can't afford to lose my job. I've been told that if I spread any more 'rumours', I'll be fired. Rumours! Those stupid idiots won't see what I'm telling them is true. I can't risk my wage, but I can't afford to let this go either. People's lives are at risk.

What I want to tell you is amazing, unbelievable, but it's true. Everything can be checked – all the information is publically available. The Pennine Tower Restaurant is dangerous, and we have to do something. I don't know what. Something. Anything. Stop it opening again, keep it closed. Burn the place down if needs be. I've told the highest people at the council, but they didn't believe me, called me a liar. Most of them won't speak to me now. You're my only hope. Can you help me? Pray God that you can.

Please can we meet?

At the time, I was wary. Although it hasn't happened often, one of the things that I've noticed since getting published is that people seem to want to tell me ghost stories. Sometimes, these are 'real' stories, sometimes fictions, and normally they're prefaced by the phrase *"Here's something you can use…"*. I've never been entirely sure what people expect from me when they do that – to write the story but give them credit, perhaps, or tell them how to write it and then give them the name of a few friendly publishers? It's not a frequent thing, but it is an irritation, and I expected that this would be more of the same. I replied noncommittally and heard nothing for a few weeks. Then, another email appeared then, in short order, another and then more, each more desperate-sounding than the previous ones. Eventually, I agreed to meet, as much to stop the messages as anything. I thought it would be simple, that I would give him a chance to tell his story, and then walk away and forget it.

It was not.

We met in the car park of Forton Services, with the Pennine Tower Restaurant stretching up above us. My ex-colleague parked at the far end of the car park and when I got in the car, I was shocked by the change that had occurred in him. He looked ill, his hair dirty and his skin bad. The car was full of papers and folders and bags, and food wrappers were crumpled around my feet on the passenger side. The inside of the car smelled stale. *He* smelled stale. As he talked, I saw that he would not so much as glance at the restaurant, telling me the whole story sitting in the driver's seat and with the engine running.

At first, I wondered if this was a complex joke, however unlikely that might seem. It struck me as unlikely, though. There was an insistency about what I was told that made me think that, even if it weren't true, my ex-colleague believed it, and I began to wonder about his sanity. He must have realised that I had my doubts, because at one point he said, "It's madness, I know, but it's true." I remember very clearly that this was the only point in the whole of our time together that he looked up at the restaurant, a darting look that lasted only a fraction of a moment. "It's an evil place. If it opens again, people will die," he said.

People will die.

The Pennine Tower isn't much to look at. A tower with a wide, circular top level, it looks shabby now, like a rusting flying saucer that's been abandoned. I'd always known that it was a restaurant, of course; my wife remembers eating there, and her friend ran it for a period in the early 80s. I also knew it had been shut down in the late 80s because of fire regulations or asbestos or something similar. It's a popular local landmark, and the subject of occasional retrospectives and campaigns to have it reopened. It's hardly threatening, and not the sort of place I would have imagined making anyone fearful.

At the end of our meeting, my ex colleague said one last thing to me: "I know you don't believe me, but you can check it all out. Nothing I've told you is secret. I've written it all down. Here, take it. Check it. Please." He gave me a bag full of loose papers, printed sheets and cuttings and photocopies all covered in handwritten notes. On the top of the file was a report which he said he'd distributed as far as he could but which had been ignored.

"They think I'm mad," he said. "Or stupid or lying or drunk. Something. I don't know. I'm tired. Promise me you'll read it. Promise me. Write it up if you can. That building is *wrong* and people need to know. You need to tell them."

And then he was gone. Truthfully, I was glad to see him go. I've worked with mentally ill people in the past, and those with active psychoses frighten me even though I know that they're rarely a danger to anyone but themselves. I felt very sorry for my ex colleague, and sorrier for his family who were going to have to deal with him and the results of his illness, but ultimately I was glad he was gone. I didn't read the papers straight away. Instead, I left them in my car and tried to pretend that they weren't there because reading them felt like it would be giving validity to my ex-colleague's paranoias. A few weeks later, I went to throw the bag away, but found that I couldn't; I remembered the way he had said, "People will die", and I thought that maybe I should at least look at what he'd given me. I hadn't promised, not exactly, but I had come close enough to feel guilty, I thought, if I didn't at least try. So I read them and then, because it seemed so preposterous, I reread them and then I made some checks and I found that everything he'd given me, every fact he'd written or copied or underlined, was true.

What follows is my collation and rewriting of the report and the mess of papers. It includes some of what I was told that overcast afternoon, and some things I found out later through my own research and through interviewing those people who were prepared to talk with me. I was as thorough as I could be and what I present here are the examples that have the most evidence to back them up, are the most provable, but bear in mind: *this is not all.* There are, literally, hundreds of incidents and suspicions, and suppositions that I could have included but haven't for reasons of space or because there was no proof. What I have included here is verifiable; I have checked the information as well as I can, and what I present is as detailed and accurate as I can make it. I have used footnotes to provide references (should specific ones exist) or to add additional information and/or clarification. I started this by hoping to provide you with an interesting story about a place, nothing more, but it has become something much bigger.

What you make of the following is up to you.

Background

A little history first:

The Pennine Tower restaurant is located at the motorway service station (Forton Services) adjacent to Junction 33 of the M6 motorway. It is 7 miles distant from the village of Forton, south of Lancaster and around 7 miles north of Preston. The restaurant is on the northbound carriageway, although the service station has sites on both sides of the road, linked by a covered footbridge.

Construction on the service station and the Pennine Tower restaurant itself started midway through 1964 and was complete by early 1965. Originally owned by the Rank group, it was built because of its position (almost exactly halfway between London and Edinburgh) to capitalise on both the passing trade and also to tap into the large nearby catchment areas of Lancaster, Preston and Blackpool (whose inhabitants, it was anticipated, would want to travel to the new, futurist restaurant to enjoy its cutting-edge design and cosmopolitan menu). Forton was designed by the London-based firm T. P. Bennett, who allocated the work to Architect in Charge Bill Galloway and Job Architect Ray Anderson; both recall a stress-free build, with the exception of the death of one worker in a falling incident[1].

---

[1] Not uncommon in the 1960s, a period when health and safety regulations were less stringent than today.

The design of the restaurant itself is an unusual one and is clearly of its time; a twenty metre tall[2] steel-frame tower with two cantilevered floors, the lower providing an enclosed dining area and the upper an observation platform. Access to the restaurant was via two lifts and the spiral staircase that encircled them, whilst the restaurant itself consisted of 120 seats in a waiter-assisted silver service establishment. Tables were constructed against the outer wall, giving unparalled views of the surrounding area. For those who preferred it, food could also be taken at American diner-style chairs lining counters looking into the kitchens. In its day, the Pennine Tower was a popular establishment, with people travelling from across the northwest just to experience this new dining experience whilst enjoying the excellent views[3].

Ultimately, many factors worked against the success of the Pennine Tower, most obviously the cost of providing a silver service restaurant that could not seat more than 120. In an attempt to keep it operational, it was converted to a truckers' rest-stop and staff room, but even this proved too expensive to run, and in 1989 the restaurant closed. The closure itself was due to the problems associated with evacuating 120 people down a narrow spiral staircase in the event of a fire or other emergency, and the consequent refusal to grant a fire safety certificate. The cost of fixing this (by constructing an external fire escape), along with the fact that asbestos had been used in the original construction (which, although stable, needs removing if members of the public are to be allowed back in) means that the building has not been used as a public venue since its closure.

The building was not completely closed, however. Most of its fixtures and fittings were removed and placed into storage and its space was partitioned, enabling its use as administrative offices. In 2001 it was refitted as a staff training venue, a capacity in which it continued to serve until early 2008, when the training function was relocated and

---

[2] Original plans had the height of the tower at 33 metres, but this was reduced by 13 metres by the planning committee of the local council. The tower is constructed to allow the addition of a third floor, should permission ever be given.

[3] It is well known that, early in their career, the Beatles often travelled to the Pennine Tower, as it was one of the only places in the North West that offered the cosmopolitan experience of speed, travel and cappuccinos.

the Pennine Tower was, essentially, mothballed. It is currently used for storage only.

Whilst there are no current plans to reopen the Pennine Tower restaurant, this may one day change; many people believe it should be listed as a national heritage site due to its uniqueness, and should this happen the owners may be forced to carry out repairs/improvements. In these circumstances, they may see this as a reasonable opportunity to make the investment needed to reopen the venue as a viable business. Also, as building methods become more advanced (and often cheaper), there is the increased chance that reopening the restaurant will become an economically viable investment opportunity. Already, preliminary investigations have taken place into reopening just the observation platform[4]. Although the cost of this (somewhere in the region of £300,000[5]) is prohibitive in the current financial climate, this may change as construction technology or the economy improves.

1965 to the Present

There is another history for the Pennine Tower. Like most histories, it is made up of small things, tiny pieces that seem unrelated until they are placed together in a particular way, revealing that they are segments of a larger whole. This other history tells a different story about the Pennine Tower Restaurant, one of shadows and darkness, and the conclusions it suggests are both uncomfortable and difficult to accept. It is a history formed into an apparent chain, one that links event to occurrence to suspicion and which leads to somewhere I suspect few of us will willingly go.

October 1964: The Health and Safety Executive report into the death of the workman (David Prentiss) killed during the building of the tower found that it was an accident, but witness statements taken at the time are interesting: "I looked up and saw Dave backing out onto the scaffold platform. He was holding his hands out in front of him

---

[4] The current owners have denied this, although they did tell me that it is something that they may consider as they get "5 or 6" requests a day to visit the tower from people who stop at the service station below.

[5] Also denied.

and didn't look around. I shouted up, but it was like he didn't hear me. Even when he hit the scaffold, he never stopped moving. He just sort of slipped and fell. He never even looked back."[6] Prentiss' foreman, George Toms, described him that morning: "Dave was fine when he arrived, just as cheerful as ever. He was one of my best workers, always on time, knew what he was doing, never took risks, could be trusted to just get on. I sent him to the restaurant floor to carry on putting in the frames for the windows, just like he'd been doing for the last few days. I was in the staircase, and about half past eleven, I heard him shout something and then scream. I was just walking up to see what the problem was when I heard everyone else start screaming and shouting and I found out he'd fallen."[7]

July 1965: On a sunny Wednesday afternoon, some 27 people in the Pennine Tower spend ten minutes listening to the "sound of something grunting and breathing like a large animal"[8]. The noise seems to come from all around the restaurant at once. A full search of the building is carried out, but no explanation for it is found.

November 1966: The observation platform and the narrow balcony that runs around the outside of the restaurant floor (for use when outside access is required to carry out repairs) are found covered in dead birds. Several breeds of bird are identified as being among the dead (including pigeons, blackbirds, sparrows and seagulls), and although several autopsies are carried out by a local vet (Bay Veterinary Services), no cause of death is identified. The number of dead birds is estimated to be between one and two thousand.

February 1967: The restaurant's manager, Odette Wilkinson, is working late in the restaurant when she hears a sound like "faint breathing".[9] She

---

[6] Statement given to police by fellow workman Alex Scott, 13.10.64, released under Freedom of Information Act regulations.

[7] Statement given to police by Foreman George Toms, 13.10.64, released under Freedom of Information Act regulations.

[8] Manager of the restaurant Michael Lovell, quoted in Lancaster Guardian, *Strange Sounds in New Restaurant Baffle Diners,* 22nd July 1965, p. 5

[9] Rank Group Accident Report #271, Health and Safety Executive, released under

watches as the contents of a work surface (including eggs, pans and cups) slide to the floor without anyone or anything touching them. When she tries to leave the kitchen, Wilkinson finds she cannot open the door. The breathing gets louder, to the point where she is convinced that someone is in the room with her. It is only when she screams that the sound stops and the door opens, banging her face and cutting her lip.

April 1968: Gina Reading, a cleaner, is found in the ladies' toilet of the restaurant weeping uncontrollably. She becomes hysterical when approached, screaming about something "in the mirror", only calming down when she is forcibly removed from the building. She refuses to re-enter the Pennine Tower and is allocated duties in other areas of Forton Services. Previously a "happy, cheerful girl",[10] her mood changes dramatically in the months following this incident. In June 1969, Gina kills herself. Her suicide note says simply "I don't want to see it again."

September 1968: Two truckers, Daniel Moffat and Harvey Allen, are in the restaurant at around three in the morning. It is otherwise deserted although Moffat thinks that there may have been "a cleaner and a cook around".[11] Not well acquainted, they do know each other well enough to sit together and, according to Moffat, "…were chatting quite happily, just guys with similar concerns, the two of us driving and away from home in the middle of the night, when I heard a noise. I'm not sure that Harvey heard it at first, but I did. Jesus, it was horrible. It was like a grunting sound, like something massive was in there with us. I was looking around when I hear Harvey say, 'What's that?' and I said something like, 'I don't know, can you hear it too?', and then he shouted. I turned back to the table in time to see him stand up and back away. He looked frightened. No, not frightened, *terrified.* He was looking at something behind me and backing away from the table, staring at the window. He dropped his coffee and knocked over his chair, and all the time I could hear the noise, the sound of something panting or grunting from all around us. I don't mean it was echoing, or it was hard to tell where it was coming from, I mean it sounded like

the *Freedom of Information Act*

[10] Desmond Reading, Gina's father, interviewed by the author, January 2009.

[11] In conversation with the author, January 2009.

244 | Simon Kurt Unsworth

it was coming from everywhere at once. I looked around again, to see if I could see what Harvey was seeing, but there was just the empty restaurant and those big windows looking out so that you could see the road and the lights of the cars as they went along it.

"Harvey shouted again and I looked back around and he had fallen over and was on the floor and I knew he was having a heart attack or something. He'd gone red, bright red, he was twitching and he'd got spit coming out of the corner of his mouth. I shouted for help but it was useless. He was dead in seconds, and that fucking sound just carried on, all around me like something was huge and hungry."[12]

The coroner's report into the death finds that Allen had suffered a massive heart attack, despite having been given a clean bill of health by his GP only two weeks prior to his death.

August 1969: Alice Pearl stops for a meal in the Pennine Tower Restaurant. She is seen eating whilst seated at one of the tables that looks out over the Trough of Bowland, and has not been seen since. None of the staff or customers see her leave. Her car is found abandoned in Lancaster several days later with a driver's side window broken and steering column damaged. Alice was a sometime prostitute with known mental health problems, and the police put her disappearance down to "a chaotic lifestyle coupled with a desire not to be found".[13] The investigation into Alice's disappearance lasts only a few days, and is carried out by an inexperienced junior officer.

March 1971: George Harrison gives an interview in which he states: "There are some places you go, you know, that aren't happy. There's nothing you can point to, nothing obvious, they're just miserable, unhealthy places full of negative energy or worse. We used to go to somewhere, the four of us, and drink coffee and look out at the hills and the sea and enjoy the view, but we stopped because I always left feeling horrible. John too. I used to think things like that were only in old buildings, ghosts and the like, but I know different now. Age doesn't matter, there are places in the world that are just wrong."[14]

---

[12] Statement given at Lancaster Coroner's Court, December 1968

[13] Police statement quoted in The Visitor, 21st August 1969, P.3

[14] *Mission* magazine, Vol. 1, Issue 2, *Harrison Up Close and Personal,* April 1971, p. 31 – 33.

November 1974: Jennifer Ashe and her daughter, Rosemary, stop at Forton and visit the Pennine Tower Restaurant to eat. Jennifer is moving from Liverpool to Carlisle to escape an abusive husband, but vanishes from the toilet of the restaurant. Rosemary is found in a cubicle by herself, her pants around her ankles and sitting in a puddle of urine. She is later diagnosed as being in severe shock and even as she recovers, the only thing she will say is "teeth". She is eventually committed to a long-stay mental institution, where she still remains. No trace of Jennifer is ever found. Suspicion initially falls on Jennifer's estranged husband, Rory, but he has an alibi for the time of Jennifer's disappearance. No charges are ever brought.[15]

December 1976: Nick Birchill vanishes mid-shift from his job as a cleaner in the Pennine Tower Restaurant. He is seen at 2.20 a.m. by two customers, who state that he seems cheerful and that he spoke to them, commiserating with them that they were visiting the restaurant in the middle of the night and so were missing the views. He goes out of sight, following the curve of the wall and mopping the floor. Perhaps five minutes later, the two customers hear a "terrible scream"[16] and the sound of something falling over. When they investigate, Birchill's mop is found on the floor next to his overturned mop bucket. Beside the spilled water are three drops of blood.

Police later discover that Birchill was in a considerable debt and come to the conclusion that he ran to escape his debtors. Several months later, on 16th April 1977, a badly burned and decomposed body is found in the Lancaster Canal. Although its teeth have been damaged and its features and fingerprints mostly destroyed, it is similar enough in shape

---

[15] One of the surviving investigating officers, DI Andrew Charlesworthy (Ret.), told me (on 11th November 2008): "This was a disappearance that made no sense, none. Jenny Ashe was a hard-working, stable woman, she loved her kid, she was well-liked and happy because she'd escaped the husband. We knew something had happened to her, but for the life of us, we couldn't find out what. We never found anything that pointed us towards someone. I mean, we were so convinced it was the husband, but his alibi was cast iron, watertight. It still bothers me. I wonder what happened, where she went and what happened to make that poor kid so damaged."

[16] Transcript of police statement, released under Freedom of Information Act.

and build for police to decide that it is Birchill and accordingly, the case becomes a murder investigation, although one which makes little progress. In early 2003, following repeated applications from Birchill's mother, police test the body's DNA and discover that it is not, in fact, Birchill. The case is reopened as a missing person's enquiry and despite a high profile relaunch, including an appearance in a segment of the BBC TV show Crimewatch,[17] no witnesses are found and no new information discovered. The case remains open.

March 1978 – The Maracott Photograph: John and Irene Maracott are travelling from Dundee to Bristol with their children Lucy and Mark. Whilst eating in the restaurant, they ask another customer to take their photograph. When developed, the photograph shows some unexpected details. Although at first dismissed by the Maracotts as faulty film, they eventually show the picture and the camera it was taken on to a friend, who persuades them to share it with the press. Initially printed by the local paper, it is quickly reprinted around the world and is the subject of much debate in both the mainstream press and specialist photographic and paranormal interest publications. An initial investigation carried out at the Kodak laboratories on both the picture and camera finds that there is "…no evidence of tampering or fakery".[18] Various explanations for the photograph are put forward, including that it is a complex hoax by the Maracotts themselves (with or without the aid of the person who took the picture, who has never been publically identified) or a weather inversion of some kind that caused heat patterns to form on the glass. It is also suggested that the images could be sunlight reflecting on puddles in the car park. Kodak dismisses all of these suggestions.[19]

In the early eighties, John Maracott sells the picture to a private picture library, which licences its use strictly and refuses to allow its release for further investigation.[20] Most people who have seen and

---

[17] Broadcast date August 22nd 2003

[18] Internal scientific report, Kodak, March 1978, quoted in *The Times,* May 22nd 1979.

[19] Also from the Kodak report quoted in *The Times*

[20] I was unable to licence the picture for inclusion here because of the costs involved, although anyone interested in seeing it can do so relatively easily.

studied the picture agree that it shows something, although they disagree on precisely what. In the picture, the Maracotts are seated at one of the tables, facing away from the windows and towards the camera. All are smiling, and are framed by the window. It is a bright day, and the view through the window should be excellent, but it is obscured by what look like faces. There are three, two female and one male, apparently printed on the glass behind the group. All three have open mouths and closed eyes and appear to be in torment. Around the edges of the window frame are further shapes on the glass: jagged, uneven triangles that look like not unlike shark's teeth. The family are insistent that the window was unmarked when the photograph was taken and that they saw no images on the glass.

June 1980: Travelling salesman Martin James is found on a sunny afternoon halfway down the spiral staircase, curled into a ball and weeping. He becomes violent when staff try to move him and both the police and ambulance service are called, finally having to inject James with a tranquiliser before they can calm him enough to remove him from the building. Once at hospital, he tells this story:

> *I picked the hitchhiker up somewhere outside of Bolton and she told me that she wanted to go to Scotland. She said her name was Mary, but I thought it probably wasn't her real name. She was like lots of them, children trying to be adults, and she reminded me of my daughter. She looked so hungry and I said I'd buy her some food. All through the meal she kept telling me that she could hear a funny noise. I mean, I couldn't hear anything and I thought she was just having some sort of drug reaction, or she was high. She looked the sort, all thin and wasted and pathetic, like she needed a good hug and a warm bath and someone to love her and tell her everything was okay, you know?*
>
> *Anyway, it got to the point where she wouldn't stay in the restaurant any more so I said we'd go and I followed her out. She wouldn't*

Several scans of it (of varying quality) can be found online, although the best reproduction of it remains the one contained in the now out-of-print *Photographs of The Supernatural World* (Charles Bramley, Edgington Press, 1979).

use the lifts, instead she went down the stairs and she was nearly running. She kept saying she could still hear it, and I said 'What? What?' and she said 'The animal' and then I lost sight of her for just a second. She got a bit far ahead of me, disappeared around the curve of the staircase. I couldn't hear her at all and when I got there, she'd gone. I went all the way to the bottom of the stairs and then looked around the shops and car park and went back to the place on the stairs where I'd seen her but there was no sign of her. As I stood there, wondering whether she'd just run fast, found another lift before I saw her, I heard something a bit like a choking sound and it sounded like her, and just for a minute I heard something else, something like the growls of a lion or wolf or something, something that's malicious, that eats for fun and not just for food. I turned to go down the stairs and it was below me so I turned to go up and it was above me and all around me and then I don't remember much till I woke up in the hospital bed.[21]:

Although the police investigate, they find no trace of a hitchhiker and no one remembers seeing James with a girl. However, his description of her is accurate enough for some investigators to believe that James had picked up Denise Arron. Arron is reported missing several weeks after the incident with James at the restaurant, having been last seen leaving her home on the day of the incident after an argument, and has not been seen since. She claimed at the time that she was going "to Scotland", which she has done before, staying with a friend for "a week or two"[22] before getting in contact. Arron has never been found, and (despite being repeatedly investigated and questioned by the police in relation to the disappearance) James sticks to his story for the remainder of his life, going as far as to repeat it on a documentary about missing teenagers shown by ITV in 1993, two years before his death.[23]

October 1982: Gordon Harrow vanishes from the toilets of the

---

[21] Transcript of police statement, released under Freedom of Information Act.

[22] Statement of Elise Mainwairing, Denise's friend, to police, repeated in conversation with the author.

[23] *Lost Children*, ITV/Philips pictures, first shown 26th May 1993, dir. Edward Hampson

Pennine Tower Restaurant; he is 6 years old. His parents watch as he enters the toilet, and both his mother and father (Mary and Frederick) keep watch on the outer door leading to the cubicles. Both insist that Gordon does not come out, and no one else enters whilst they watch. After ten minutes, Frederick goes to find Gordon but discovers that all the cubicles are empty. He alerts the restaurant manager, who immediately instigates a full search of the restaurant and the rest of the site, to no avail. The police are called, who also search. During the course of the next three weeks, the motorway is shut several times as over 1000 police and volunteers are organised into one of the biggest missing person hunts (including fingertips searches of the surrounding grounds and roads) that Lancashire has known. Rumours abound that Gordon has been taken by "gypsies" or "travellers", stories seized upon "by a national press keen to attack the increasing influx of foreign nationals and other perceived 'undesirables' into Britain".[24] No evidence of this is found, however, and Gordon's parents eventually become the main suspects in their son's disappearance "solely because no other suspects have been identified".[25] They are investigated by an increasingly desperate police force, and are questioned at length in the final week of October. The media interview a local psychic, Madame Rowena, who states that Gordon is "screaming" and is "somewhere close to the restaurant".[26] The police dismiss her claims, although the media continue to interview Madame Rowena whenever the case is mentioned. No trace of Gordon is found and he joins Alice, Jennifer and Nick as one of the region's unsolved disappearances.

October 1985: Britain suffers its worst motorway crash since motorways were first opened as 13 people are killed and many more are seriously injured when a coach and ten cars collide close to Junction 33 and within sight of the Pennine Tower Restaurant. The incident happens on a clear, sunny day around six hundred yards before a point where

---

[24] *Investigating the Investigations: How the Media Helps and Hinders the Police in Missing Persons' Cases*, Dyer et al, Community Care Magazine, July 2001

[25] DCI Eric Banning, Lancashire Constabulary (Ret) during a telephone conversation with the author, May 20th 2009.

[26] *Lancaster Guardian*, November 2nd 1982, widely quoted by the national press in the weeks after.

the motorway narrows due to two closed lanes. The subsequent investigation and report state that the accident was caused by a combination of excessive speed and possible mechanical faults with one of more vehicles. However, in 1992, one of the survivors goes on record to state that these are not the only reasons: "I was several cars back from the coach and the car in the lane next to it, and we weren't going that fast. Suddenly the car ahead starts to wobble and veer across the lane. I saw the coach shift to get out of the car's way, but it wasn't fast enough. The next thing is the two crash into each other but before they hit together, I saw people on the coach pointing up at that building at the side of the road, the one that looks like a Frisbee on a pole. I didn't see anything myself, because I was too busy trying to avoid hitting the car in front of me."[27]

Other survivors of the accident have, generally, not wished to speak about their experiences – of the 7 remaining alive and contactable, none agreed to go on the record about what they saw or heard. However, one did agree speak on the condition that their identity be hidden. They claim that "there was something wrong with the windows of the restaurant. I was looking out of the car window and I happened to look up at [it] and the windows were grey, darker than they should have been, and it looked like they were moving, that the edges were flexible and ragged. Spikey. I went to say something to [the driver] but he'd already seen it. When I looked again, the windows looked huge, like they had opened up and they were completely black. I know that this must sound stupid, but it's the truth of what I saw. The windows had gone, somehow, and in their place were openings. I can't explain it any better than that."[28]

August 1989: Workmen converting the restaurant to offices following its closure find badly mutilated cats' bodies on the observation floor, along with the bones of birds and at least one dog. A police veterinary surgeon identifies pieces from at least 17 different cats, although none

---

[27] Paul Gallagher, quoted in *Accidents and Causes: Motorway Driving and Safety and the UK,* Chapter 6: Forton and Beyond, Dyson and Pimblett, University of Manchester, 1992.

[28] In an email to the author, dated January 11th 2009.

of the corpses is whole. The crime is blamed on "local teens",[29] despite the fact that the doors were locked upon the workmen's arrival and there is no evidence of a break-in. How the animals got to the top of the tower remains a mystery, and no one is charged.

July 1991: Two bloody handprints are discovered on the inside wall of the restaurant below a window, and a further smear of blood is discovered covering 7 steps of the staircase between the ground and restaurant floors of the tower. The blood is tested and found to be of animal origin. Police dismiss the blood as "a prank" and blame "university students".[30]

November 1993: During the morning session of a training day, trainees are constantly interrupted by the sound of low growling. During the 10 to 15 minutes of the lunch break that the room is unoccupied one of the white boards in the training room is vandalised beyond repair, having been cracked and splintered and covered in "slimy liquid". One trainee says that the board looks "chewed". Despite the level of damage inflicted on the board (which is torn from the wall so forcefully that the pieces of the partition wall are also torn loose) and their proximity to the room, none of the delegates hears anything. An internal investigation puts the damage down to "probable trespassers", despite the fact that no one on site that day recalls seeing anyone suspicious-looking.[31]

June 1999: Nayan Gowda, a freelance photographer, is photographing the Pennine Tower for a proposed article on 60s architecture for the magazine *Architectural Review*. He takes 133 photographs during his visit to the tower, but finds when he develops them that almost all are entirely black or black and grey. In two, taken towards the windows "a shape like a shark's jaw"[32] can be seen.[33]

---

[29] *Lancaster Guardian*, August 5th 1989

[30] Statement to the press by DI Andrew Bellamy, Lancashire Constabulary, 1st August 1991.

[31] All quotes from Incident Report #342 (Company records, held at HSE, released under Freedom of Information Act)

[32] Nayan Gowda, quoted in *Fortean Times*, September 2000

[33] Both photographs copyright the Fortean Picture Library: www.forteantimes.com

November 2004: Gary Young is carrying out a site inspection on the mostly disused building for the Health and Safety Executive when he stops to ring his wife, Lorna. In the middle of the call, Lorna hears Young say "What's that?" presumably in response to something he has heard or seen. There is a brief pause and then he screams once and drops his phone. Lorna hears sounds she describes as "a dragging noise and a roar" and then her husband screams again. Panicked, Lorna breaks the call off and telephones the police, who have an officer on the scene within minutes. Young's phone is found on the floor of the former restaurant's kitchen area, and nearby are streaks in the dirt and dust on the floor. Young is found in the elevator, unconscious and battered. When he awakes, he claims to remember nothing about his ordeal and is diagnosed as suffering from severe concussion.

Several weeks later a homeless man with mental health problems, Neil McDonagh, is arrested at Forton and charged with drunkenness and public disorder offences. He is a regular visitor to the cafe and shops of the service station, and further investigations show he was there the day of the Young attack. He is charged with actual bodily harm in relation to this incident. McDonagh, whilst never denying his presence in the abandoned restaurant on the day of the attack, states his innocence and claims, consistently, that he saw Young attacked by "a great black thing from the walls and windows".[34] When asked to draw what he saw by his psychiatrist, he draws a picture of what looks like a crude mouth with large, uneven teeth. The picture is used as evidence during his trial, at which he is found guilty and remanded to the custody of a secure psychiatric unit.[35]

February 2006: Paramedics are called to attend to a delivery man who has had an asthma attack whilst carrying crates up to the first floor of the Pennine Tower. One paramedic leaves the tower shortly after arriving and refuses to re-enter, saying only that she feels "stalked" in the building.

April 2007: During one of the regular inspections of the site, a large pool of liquid is found in the Restaurant. It proves to be a mix of animal

[34] Court transcript, Crown vs McDonagh, March 2005.

[35] Permission to reprint the picture here was refused by McDonagh's family.

blood, cholesterol, glycocholic and taurocholic acids and lecithin.[36] The source of the liquid is not found.

Conclusion

Even faced with the discovery that the incidents my ex colleague had written about in his notes and report were true, I did not believe that his conclusions were correct. After all, how could the Pennine Tower Restaurant be a danger to anyone who stepped inside it? It's a building, after all, a construction of concrete and steel and glass and wood, and nothing else. Looking at the separate events, I was struck by how easy it is to take random things and make them into a chain, creating links that do not exist. Once that is done *everything* seems to fit into the pattern you have imposed upon what is, essentially, patternless. Why are there fewer incidents after the restaurant closes to the public in the late 1980s? Because there are fewer people there in total or because there is a more sinister explanation? Are those incidents that have occurred since it closed the normal vandalism any isolated, underused building undergoes, or are they result of more malign forces working? And so it goes.

It is easy to see how psychosis starts. An unfortunate coincidence, a series of events or bad luck, get woven into a thread that implies a consciousness, a *directedness,* rather than the simple blind chaos of a universe that has no guiding hand to oversee it nor grand plan to guide it. Once you have an idea that a pattern exists, everything starts to fit the pattern. It even has a name, *confirmation bias,* and even then, it was what I believed was happening here. The things that had occurred at the Pennine Tower Restaurant over the years were, I told myself, a series of unrelated tragedies and mysteries and not related. Go to any place and I am sure you'd find a similar set of occurrences, particularly in places around roads and motorways which, by their very nature, imply movement and travel, escape and relocation. My ex colleague's ideas were nonsense, a dark fairy story created by someone struggling to make sense of a world that was chaotic and threatening. Opening the Pennine Tower (assuming the asbestos and fire regulation issues which had led to its closure in the first place could be solved) would be

---

[36] Common ingredients in bile

no more dangerous than opening any other restaurant. However, two separate press reports changed my mind.

In late 2008, the Museum of Lancashire opened an exhibition celebrating the development of the British motorway system. One of the exhibits was a recreation of a section of the Pennine Tower restaurant, using an original table and chairs, tiles, plates and cutlery and even a section of the original flooring, all of which had been in storage since the late eighties or earlier. On 19th December, Malcolm Skilling visited the exhibit with his wife, Genie. He was particularly excited about the Forton section, having been a professional driver before retiring and therefore remembering The Pennine Tower well. Just before the museum closed for the night, Genie went to the toilet, leaving Malcolm at the Pennine Tower exhibit. The Lancashire Evening Post reported that:

> *By her reckoning, Genie was away for no more than five minutes. When she returned, Malcolm had vanished. A check with the guard on the front desk showed that Malcolm had not left the museum by that exit, and none of the emergency exits had been opened or alarms triggered. A thorough search of the museum revealed no sign of Malcolm except for his bag, which was lying on the floor by the table in the Pennine Tower Restaurant exhibit. Despite intensive investigations, no trace of him has been found and police are growing increasingly concerned for his safety.*[37]

I think that I might even have dismissed this, put it down to chance, were it not for the second article. I came across it several months after reading through the papers and cuttings given to me that first day in the car park. It has altered my perception of what has been happening, made me think more seriously about the importance of what I have written.

In summer of 2009, the motorway exhibition moved from the Lancashire Museum to Lancaster's smaller museum. Several weeks later, in a light-hearted piece entitled *It's Official! Lancashire is the Most Haunted County in the Country!*,[38] it was reported that a guard carrying

---

[37] *Lancashire Evening Post, Local Man Still Missing,* December 22nd, P.3

[38] *Lancaster Guardian, It's Official! Lancashire is the Most Haunted County in the Country!,* July 23rd, P.6 & 7

out his overnight rounds in the museum had heard a strange sound, which followed him for the duration of his hour-long patrol. It was, he says, like the "breathing of a huge dog".

This is not fiction.

|The Church on the Island|

Charlotte pulled herself onto the beach and pushed her hair back off her face in a cascade of water. She took a couple of deep breaths, quietly pleased by the fact that she was not more affected by her swim. As she let her heart rate and breathing settle, she untied the string from around her waist and freed her plastic sandals; they had spent the swim bobbing along at her side, gently tapping her thighs every now and again as if to remind her of their existence. Now, she let them fall to the floor and slid her feet into them. Water squeezed under her feet and around her toes, spilling out onto the wet sand. Then, walking away from the sea, she let her eyes rise to the object of her visit: the little blue and white church.

Charlotte had seen the church the first time she had looked out from her hotel room window. Perhaps half a mile out from shore, nestling into the vibrant blue sea, was a tiny island. It seemed to be little more than an upthrust of grey rock from the ocean, its flanks covered in scrubby green foliage. Its lower slopes looked gentle, but there was a central outcrop of rock that appeared almost cubic, as though cut by some giant hand with a dull knife. This mass was settled on to the centre of the island as though the same hand that had cut it had placed it down, forcing it into the earth like a cake decoration into icing. Its sides were almost vertical and striated with dark fissures and it looked to be fifty or sixty feet tall, although Charlotte found it hard to judge this accurately and changed her mind every time she gazed at it.

The church was in front of the outcrop, tiny and colourful against the doleful grey of the rock face. Its walls were a startling white with blue edging, the roof a wash of the same blue. By squinting, Charlotte could just make out a door in the front of the building and a cross, set at the front of the roof. At night, the church was lit by a pale yellow light that flickered in time with the wind; Charlotte assumed that oil lamps hung around its exterior. The light made its walls shimmer and stand out starkly against the grey stone mass behind it. The mass itself loomed even more at night, rearing and blocking out the stars in the Greek darkness. It gave the impression of being man-made; the crags and fissures became the battlements of a castle, abandoned and decaying but resisting a final collapse with bleak force. It, too, appeared lit at its base by the same yellowing illumination. Charlotte never saw anyone light the lamps.

In fact, as hard and as often as she looked (and she spent long periods of time simply staring at the island, to Roger's irritation), she only ever saw one person at the church, and then only for a fleeting moment. A shadow framed in the doorway, seen in the corner of her eye as she turned away, that was gone by the time she turned back. It had to be a person, she told herself. Someone lights the lamps, and the church is well cared-for. Its sides (the two that she could see from her hotel balcony, at least) were the white of freshly painted stone or brick, and the blue roof and trim were neat and well defined. The low wall that surrounded the church corralled ground that was clear of plants or noticeable litter. It was curiously entrancing, this little blue and white building with its domed roof and dark doorway, and Charlotte studied it for hours.

It was Roger that put the idea in her head. "Why don't you swim out there?" he asked on about the third day of their holiday. "If you see it up close, you might stop staring at it all the time."

Charlotte could hear the irritation in his voice, but also the joking tone. She knew he was simply trying to draw her attention back to him and their break together, but the idea took hold in her mind and would not let go. The next day, she said to him, "It's not that far, is it? And the sea's fairly calm around here."

"You're serious?" he asked.

"Of course," she said, and couldn't help adding, "It was your idea, after all."

Charlotte planned the Great Swim (as Roger had taken to sarcastically calling it) for the second week of their break. It gave her time to get used to swimming in the sea, to feel the way it pulled and pushed at her. It also gave her the opportunity to ask around about the little church, but no one seemed to know anything about it. The holiday company representative merely shrugged, and the locals looked at her blankly when she asked. One said, "It is just an old church," and looked at Charlotte as though she were mad, but it wasn't. It was not old, not to look at anyway. This apparent disinterest in the church, which made Roger more dismissive of her plan, only strengthened her resolve and by the morning of the swim, she was determined to reach it, to feel its stonework for herself.

The path from the beach to the church was steeper than it had looked from the mainland and Charlotte had to scramble and grasp at plants and roots to support her on her ascent. The climb was more tiring than the swim and she reached the top grateful that she had not needed to go further. Grit had worked its way into her sandals and her feet felt hot and scratched by the time she reached her destination and her hands were grimy and sore. When she placed her hands on the top of the low wall and felt the heat of the sun on the rock and saw the church, however, all her aches were forgotten.

Close to, the building was even prettier than she expected. She wanted to walk straight to it, to marvel at its simple beauty, but before she could she had to deal with Roger. Standing by the wall, she turned back towards the beach. Across the strip of blue sea (I swam that, she thought proudly), the wedge of golden sand gleamed in the late morning sun. She located Roger's tiny, frail form by finding the hut that sold fresh fruit and cold drinks and looking just in front of it, the way they had arranged. There, beside a family group, sat Roger. She raised one arm in greeting and saw him do the same in return. At least now he would not worry and might even start to relax a little.

Ah, Roger, she thought, what are we going to do with you? Back home, his constant attentiveness was flattering. Here, its focus unbroken by time apart for work and without the diluting presence of other friends, it had become claustrophobic. She could not move, it seemed, without him asking if she was all right or if she wanted anything. The Great Swim had appealed, in part at least, because it gave her time away from him. He was neither a strong enough swimmer nor adventurous enough to want to do it with her, and although she felt a little guilty at taking advantage of his weakness, she revelled in the freedom that it gave her. She could not see their relationship continuing after they returned home and although this made her sad, it was a distant sadness rather than a raw grief.

Roger hopefully placated, Charlotte turned again to the church. The path up from the beach had brought her out directly facing the door, which hunched inside a shadowed patch surrounded by a neat blue border. There was a simple wooden step up to the door. Around it, the wall was plain, white-painted stonework. Instead of approaching, however (worried that she might find the door locked and that her little adventure would end too soon and in disappointment), Charlotte went around to the far side of the building.

As she came around the church's flank, Charlotte saw that one of her assumptions about the place had been wrong; she had expected that it was built on a little plateau (possibly man-made?) and entirely separate from the rocky outcrop that glowered behind it. It was not: the rear of the church was built up against the base of the natural cliff. Going closer, she saw that the mortar that joined the church's wall to the cliff was spread thickly so that no gaps remained. Under the skin of the paint, different sized stones had been used to ensure that the wall fitted as snugly as possible; she could see the irregular lattice of them.

The wall itself was plain except for a single dark window of quartered glass set just below the roof. The window was low enough for Charlotte to be able to see through if she went close, as the building was only single-storey. Along from the window, a metal and glass lamp hung from a bracket, and she gave a little private cheer. Her assumption about the night-time lights had, at least, been correct. She resisted the temptation to look through the window for the same reason that she had not tried the door; she wanted to save the inside of the building for as long as possible. Instead, she turned away from the church to look at the land around it.

It was beautiful. What appeared to be scrub from half a mile's distance was actually a thickly knotted tangle of plants and small trees. The air was heavy with the smell of jasmine and curcuma and other unidentifiable but equally rich scents. Butterflies chased each other around the branches and lazy bees drifted somnambulantly from flower to flower. Their buzzing came to Charlotte in a sleepy wave, rising and falling in pitch like the roll of the sea. Under it was the sound of crickets and grasshoppers, an insistent whirring that was at the same time both frantic and curiously relaxing.

The press of plants and insects, and the birds that darted and hovered in irregular patterns above it all, were held back by the stone wall surrounding the church. In places, the wall bulged and roots pushed their way between the rough stones. The only break in the stonework was a rusted iron gate. Past the gate, there was a gap in the flora and an earthen track that led away along the base of the cliff. Here, the dark green leaves and branches and the blooming flowers had been cut and pushed back so that they formed an archway over the gate and made living, breathing walls for the path.

Charlotte stood, breathing in the scented air and luxuriating in the quiet. If Roger were there, she thought, he'd be taking photographs, pointing out interesting creatures or sounds, asking if I was okay, if I wanted anything. Being there allowed her to just be, unfettered by expectation or implication or demand. It was the most relaxed she had felt for her entire holiday.

Finally, Charlotte walked back around to the front of the church. She intended to try the door, but instead she carried on walking, going to the right side of the building. It was, as she expected, the same as the other side, only in reverse. The window was dark and the lamp's brass fittings were shiny with age. There was another gate in the surrounding wall, also rusted (although, looking closely, she saw that the hinges were well-oiled and clean) and another path along the base of the cliff. She wondered if it was simply the end of the path that started around the other side and which travelled all the way around the base of the great ragged cube, and decided that it probably was. She smiled at the simplicity of it and its unrefined, functional beauty.

Through the window, Charlotte thought she could see a light inside the building. She went close, brushing away a thin layer of sand and dust from the glass and peering through into the interior of the church. What she saw disappointed her.

Other Greek Orthodox chapels that Charlotte had visited, both large and small, had been extensively decorated, with pictures of saints lining the lower part of the walls, scenes from the life of Jesus above them ("As a teaching aid," Roger had told her pompously in a church they had visited earlier in the week. "Remember, the peasants couldn't read and so the pictures could be used by the priests as illustrations to what they were saying." She had remained silent after he spoke, not trusting herself to say anything pleasant to him, so irritated was she at his thoughtless condescension). Icons, frequently of the Holy Mother and Child, lined the walls of these other churches, their silver and gold plate ("To protect the picture beneath"– more from Roger) shining in the light from the devotional candles that burned in trays of sand. The little blue and white church, however, had none of this. The walls were bare of pictures, painted or framed. There were no candles or chairs or tapestries here. Indeed, the only decoration seemed to be mirrors in ornate frames. There was one above the door, one behind the altar and one opposite her to the side of the window. The altar, which she expected to be bedecked with, at the very least, a delicately stitched altar cloth, was a simple table partly covered in what looked like a plain white strip of material. Two candles in simple silver candlesticks burned, one at each end. Behind the altar was an open doorway. Seeing the open doorway made Charlotte nod to herself; whilst it was, in other respects, odd, the church was at least conforming to some of what she knew about the Greek Orthodox Church, where chapels had a narthex, a central area where worshippers gathered and a private area for the priests behind the altar. Presumably, this was what lay beyond the doorway.

Charlotte stepped back from the window, still confused. The inside of the church was so plain that it might belong to some dour Calvinist chapel and she wanted to know why this was so different from the exuberant stylings she had seen in other Greek churches. She went back around to the door, confident that she could enter: that candles were burning made her sure that there must be a priest there, and that the church should be unlocked. Before she entered, however, she went once more to the top of the path up from the beach. She was experiencing a little guilt about her feelings towards Roger and wanted to wave to him, show him some affection. It would make him feel good, and might stop him worrying. When she looked, however, she could not find him. There was the fruit and drink stall, there was the family, but Roger was nowhere to be seen. Maybe he had gone to get some shade, she thought. He was paranoid about becoming sunburnt or dehydrated, another little thing about him that irritated her. Maybe he'd got angry waiting for her and taken himself off for an early beer; in a funny way, she hoped that this was the case. It would be a spark of adventurousness, a small reminder of the Roger she first met and liked, who'd made her laugh and surprised her and paid attention to her.

Swallowing a surprisingly large hitch of disappointment, Charlotte turned back to the church. As the sun rose higher, the church's shadows were creeping back towards it like whipped dogs, and its white walls gleamed. The domed blue roof was bright in the sun and the reflections of the light off the white walls were so sharp that she had to narrow her eyes as she approached the door. Whilst she expected it to be open, there was still a part of her that wondered if it might resist her push, but she never had the chance to find out. Even as she reached for the handle, the door swung open to reveal an old man who looked at her silently.

The man was dressed in a simple black robe, tied at the waist with belt of rope. His beard was a pepper of white and grey and black and a white cloth was draped over the crown of his head. Under the cloth, Charlotte saw long hair that fell in ringlets past his shoulders. He wore sandals and his toenails were long and curled.

"Welcome to the Island of the Church of the Order of St John of Patmos. My name is Babbas," the man said, and bowed. He straightened up slowly and walked by Charlotte without another word. As he went, she caught an unpleasant whiff of sour body odour and another, sweeter smell that was, if anything, even less pleasant.

Babbas was fully eight inches shorter than she was and as he walked by, she could see the top of his head with its cloth covering. What she had taken for white, she saw, was actually a dirty yellow. It was stained with countless greasy rings, all overlapping like cup stains on an unvarnished table. With a little jolt of disgust, Charlotte realized that the rings were marks from his hair, from where it pressed against the linen. She took an involuntary step back from him, shocked and surprised in equal measure. Why doesn't he wash? she thought, and took another step away. He stopped and turned to her.

"This is a small church, with few facilities," he said, as though reading her thoughts. "Come, I will show you around and explain what needs to be done." His English was excellent, but she could still detect an accent there. Greek, almost definitely. Babbas spoke slowly, as though thinking about each word before he uttered it, and she wondered if this was because he was speaking a language that was not his own. His eyes were a faded blue, circled by wrinkles and overhung by heavy, grey eyebrows. He looked at her intently and then spun around again and walked on. His walk was not an old man's shuffle, precisely, but Charlotte saw that he did not pick his feet far up off the ground and his steps were not long.

"Each day, before sunset," Babbas said, walking around to the left of the church, "the lamps must be lit. There are six. One here, one on the other side of the church and four at points around the island. The path will take you there; it goes all the way around this rock and comes out on the other side of the church." Silently, Charlotte gave herself another cheer. One point for me, she thought, I already worked that out!

Babbas was looking speculatively along the path and Charlotte stopped next to him. She was pleased to find that the scents from the plants and flowers covered the old man's own odour.

"It looks beautiful, does it not?" asked Babbas, but did not wait for a response. "It is, now. But it can be a long walk around the island, even in good weather. In winter, it is treacherous. The path becomes slippery when it is wet, and the wind can be harsh, but the work is vital. All four sides of this rock must be lit with light from a flame throughout every night. Each morning, the lamps must be extinguished and filled in preparation for being lit again that forthcoming night. This means that the morning walk is often the harder, as you must carry the oil with you in a can." He sighed.

Standing next to the old man gave Charlotte the opportunity to study him more closely. His face was deeply lined and his skin was the deep brown of someone who spent a great deal of time outdoors. Except for his dress, which seemed too simple, he acted as though he were in charge here. He must be the priest, she thought. Why else would he be here? Perhaps this parish isn't well off enough to afford to buy nice robes or icons for the church. I mean, it can't have many regular parishioners, can it? Even as she thought this, her eyes were taking in more details about him. His beard hung down to his chest and his hands were ridged with prominent veins. There was something else about him, though, something harder to identify. It took her a moment to recognize it, but when she did, Charlotte was a little surprised: he seemed sad.

The two of them stood in silence, looking down the path along the base of the cliff for so long that it began to make Charlotte uncomfortable. She wanted to ask the man something, but did not know what. Besides, he did not give the impression of wanting to talk. True, he had started tell her about the church, but not in an especially welcoming way. It reminded her of the lectures she had attended at university, given by tutors who saw teaching as a chore.

"Come," said the priest suddenly, making Charlotte jump, "there is much to show you."

Babbas walked back towards the church, not looking at Charlotte as he went. She followed, halfway between amused and irritated by the man's brusque manner. As he walked into the church, however, she stopped.

"Wait a minute, please," Charlotte said, "I can't come in dressed like this, can I?" She gestured down at her bikini, her naked legs and belly and shoulders now prickling in the sun. She wished she had brought sunscreen and a sarong with her; she could have tied them in a waterproof bag and towed it along with her sandals.

"Why?" asked the old man.

"Don't I have to cover my shoulders and legs out of respect? I've had to do that for the other Greek churches I've been in."

The priest looked at Charlotte as though seeing her properly for the first time. He let his gaze drop from her face down her body and she began to wonder if she was safe here alone with him. Before she had time to pursue this thought, however, he raised his gaze to her face again and sighed, as though terribly tired.

"God made both skin and cloth and loves you equally in both," he said. "He is with you dressed and undressed. He is in your clothes, and so always sees you as naked. He is God and sees us all as naked all the time. What use are clothes to Him? Religion, churches and chapels and monasteries, often forgets that God sees beyond the covers that we put around the world. They forget that the ceremonies they perform have function, have purpose beyond simply tradition or habit or worship. When ceremonies and rules become all-important, then God is forgotten. Here, the ceremonies are about a purpose. They have a function. They are not about simply the look or the sound or the history of things. You may enter this church of the Order of St John of Patmos dressed however you wish, as long as you respect the work that is done here and not just the ceremony that surrounds it." He stopped and sighed again, as though exhausted by his speech. Charlotte, unsure as to whether to be embarrassed by her lack of clothes or by the fact that she had asked about her lack of clothes and so drawn attention to it, simply nodded and followed him into the church.

The inside of the small building was not as plain as it had appeared from the outside. There was decoration of a sort, but it was delicate and subtle. A black strip was painted along the base of the walls, stretching about three inches up from the floor. The top of the back strip was irregular, dipping and rising as it went around the room. When Babbas closed the door behind her, Charlotte saw that it had been painted across the bottom of the door as well. Above the black strip, the walls were painted a light yellow. There were small streaks of orange in the yellow, along with tiny flecks of blue and green. The church was lit by the candles on its altar and by the sunlight coming in through the two windows. The mirrors on the walls (and there was one on each wall, she saw) caught the light and reflected it all around, catching the streaks of colour on the walls and making them dance in the corner of her eyes. It was like being at the centre of a vast, calm flame and it was magical in a way she had not expected. The air had a warmth that held her softly and she laughed in delight at it. The old man, hearing this, smiled for the first time and did not seem so sad.

"It is wonderful, is it not?" asked Babbas.

"It's beautiful," Charlotte answered, although this did not do justice to how beautiful or wonderful it was.

"The Order of St John of Patmos, here and elsewhere, is charged with the maintenance of the light of God, and we try to love the light wherever possible. It is not an easy life here on the island; there is only one delivery of food and equipment a week, and between these times, it can be lonely. These altar candles must always be aflame, as must other torches that we will come to soon. There must always be enough fuel, enough candles, enough torches, and this takes planning, so that the necessary items can be ordered at least a week in advance, to come in with the following week's delivery. But when it is hard and when the life I have had given to me seems tiring, I need simply stand in here and feel the beauty and power of God and His love, and I know that I am valued, that I am playing my part in the worship of the light over the darkness." He stopped talking and his face fell into sadness and tiredness once more. Charlotte wondered why Babbas was telling her these things, but dared not ask. Wasn't this what she had come here for, after all? And besides, it was interesting, listening to this old man. Such single-mindedness, she thought briefly. I'm not sure I could do what he does, day in, day out.

As if reading her thoughts again, Babbas said, "It is not always so. Sometimes, there are more here than just me. In past years, this place has housed four or five of the called at a time and we would split the daily tasks between us."

"Jesus, you mean there's just you by yourself?" exclaimed Charlotte, startled, and fast on the heels of this came embarrassment at having sworn in church. Babbas seemed not to notice, however, but simply sighed again and turned away. He walked to the rear of the church, going behind the altar. He went to the doorway and stopped, calling back over his shoulder, "Come."

This time, Charlotte did not move. It was not just the peremptory way in which he had called her, although that was irritating to be sure. No, it was also that the idea of going behind the altar, of entering the place where only those who served God as priests or higher could go that made her uncomfortable. Whilst her own faith was, at best, questionable, she had been raised in a family that respected even if it did not believe. She found it hard to disagree with members of the clergy and even thinking critical or dismissive thoughts about the church's ceremonies or regulations made her feel guilty. She sometimes felt it was this inability as much as anything that stopped her from taking the final step and dismissing the teaching of the church as simple superstition, and that this was a weakness in her that she should try to overcome, but she did not. Hard though it was to admit it even to herself, she liked that the church had mysteries, and revealing them would be akin to stripping away layers of her upbringing and replacing them with something smaller and infinitely more miserable. Seeing behind the altar would solve one of those mysteries, and the thought of it made her sad. She could not articulate this, knowing it made little sense. Rather, she remained still and hoped that the old man would return, would show her something else instead of what lay in the private inner sanctum.

"Come, now!" said Babbas from the darkness, and he no longer sounded old or tired, but implacable. He loomed into the light briefly, waving her towards him and saying in the same tone of voice, "There is much to show you." Miserably, feeling far worse than when she thought of losing Roger, she followed him.

She had expected to find a small chamber beyond the doorway, but was surprised to find a long passage cut into rock, lit by candles set into carved recesses. These recesses were at head height and occurred every five or six feet along the passage. The smell of smoke and old flames was strong but under it, the same sickly, corrupt odour from before caught in Charlotte's nose. Babbas was already some distance down the passage, walking in that stooped half-shuffle that she had begun to recognise. Wondering what other surprises were in store, she hurried after him.

The slap of her sandals echoed around her as she walked, the sound coming at her from all angles. She saw as she passed that behind each candle, painted on the back of the recesses, were portraits of people. There were both men and women, all unsmiling and serious-looking. All were wearing a white cloth over their heads, and all had dates across the base of the portraits. In the flickering light of the candles, their eyes seemed to follow her and their lips pursed in disapproval. As much to break the silence and to draw her attention from their gaze as anything, Charlotte called ahead to the old man, "Who are the people in portraits?"

"The previous leaders of the Order here."

"But there are women," she said before she could stop herself. Babbas turned back to her. There was light from somewhere ahead and for a moment, he was simply a silhouette in the passage. He stretched his arms out, placing his palms against the walls. Leaning forward, he let his arms take his weight. His face came into the light and Charlotte saw his teeth, gleaming a terrible ivory. He stared at her and smiled, although there was no humour in it.

"This is not a branch of the Orthodox Church," he said, "and we have always known that God gave women the same role to play in the struggle between good and evil as men. He cares not whether it is a man or a woman who lights the candles and lamps and torches, as long as they are lit. Try to understand, this place has a function, a purpose, beyond simply mouthing words and performing ceremonies, the reason for whose existence most have forgotten. To these walls, men and women are called equally to play their role as God intended." He glared fiercely at Charlotte and then whirled about, his belt ends and the hem of his robe flailing around him. Charlotte, against her better, more rational, judgment, followed.

The passage opened out into a cave that took Charlotte's breath away. It looked as if the whole of the huge outcrop of rock in the island's centre had been hollowed out. Looking up, she saw a roof far above her that was ragged with gullies and peaks, like a sonar map of deep ocean floors. Here and there, chisel marks were visible and she realized that this must have been a natural opening in the rock, and that man had expanded what nature (God? she wondered fleetingly) had begun. The floor was inlaid with white marble and the walls painted the same yellow and orange as in the church, although there was no black stripe around the base of the walls. At either side of her, doorways were set into the wall, carved rectangles of darker air. The nearest one, she saw, opened into a small carved room that appeared to contain nothing but a bed. He lives here as well! she thought in surprise, and then her eyes were drawn to what lay in the centre of the cavern.

There was a large opening in the floor.

Charlotte walked to the opening, beckoned on by Babbas who had gone to stand at its edge. It was roughly square and at each corner was a burning torch set on top of a metal stand. Lamps burned around the walls, she noticed, and then she was looking into the hole.

It was pitch black. Charlotte stared down and immediately felt dizzy, as though she were having an attack of vertigo and, in truth, it was like looking down from a great height. The darkness in the hole seemed to start just feet below its rim, as if it was filled with inky water. Why doesn't the light go into it? she had time to think and then Babbas' hand was on her shoulder and he drew her gently away. He guided her back to where she had been standing, to where the floor was all around her, gleaming and white.

"There is the function of the Order of St John of Patmos," he said in a soft voice. "We keep the light burning that holds the darkness at bay, and it is what you have come here to do."

Charlotte stood, breathing deeply to overcome her dizziness. The old man stood looking at her kindly. His eyes glimmered with... what? Expectation? Hope? She could not tell and then the thing that he had said last of all lurched in her memory and the individual words connected, made a sentence, gained meaning.

"I'm not here to do anything!" she said loudly. "I just wanted to look around!"

"Of course you did not," said Babbas, and the sadness was there again in his voice, the sound of a teacher coaxing a particularly slow child. "You were called here, as I was before you and the others were before me. No one comes here to look; we come because God needs us."

"No," Charlotte said as emphatically as she could, "I wanted to see the church. Now I've seen it, I'll go. Thank you for showing it to me." She took a step back, moving towards the passageway. Babbas did not move, but simply said, "You may leave, if you wish, of course. I shall not stop you, but you will find that the world has already forgotten you."

Charlotte opened her mouth to say something, to say anything to counter the oddly threatening madness that was coming from the old man's mouth, but nothing came. She wanted to tell him that he was insane, that the place she had made for herself in the world was as secure as it had ever been, but instead, the thought of Roger popped unbidden into her mind. Or rather, the memory that Roger had been gone when she looked for him a second time. Could he have forgotten her? Gone back to their hotel room because she no longer existed for him? No, it was madness, she was real, she had a home, a job, a boyfriend.

"He has forgotten you," said Babbas, once more guessing at what she was thinking, seeing her thoughts and fears reflected in her expression. "Already, the skin of the world is healing over the space you have left in it. In a few days, no trace of you will be left. Now, your place is here."

Charlotte stared at the old man and took another step back towards the passage. He was looking at her with that calm, lecturer's assurance again, confident in the absolute truth of what he was saying. She wanted to say, that's impossible, but she dared not speak. Saying anything would be an admittance of the fact that, just for a moment, she had wondered, and in her wondering, Babbas' words attained a sort of reality. But he couldn't be right, could he? It was an absurdity spouted by an old man driven mad by solitude and religious extremism. Wasn't it? How could he believe it? she asked herself, and in that moment, she realised that she did not want to leave yet. She had to persuade him of his folly, make him see that he was wrong. Frantically, she went through the things she could say that might puncture his reality and let hers in. Finally, she came across what she felt was the perfect argument.

"But I can't," she said, "I don't believe, and how can I have been called if I don't believe?"

Babbas did not reply and Charlotte thought, for the shortest time, that she'd done it, had made him see his error. But then, the sad little smile never leaving his face, he said, "Believe in what? This church, this place? It is all around you, more solid than your own flesh can ever hope to be. God, perhaps? Well, he does not care, he exists outside of your beliefs or mine and He does not need your faith or mine to continue. Ah, but I see that it is not Him that you do not believe in, but the function of this place. You think, maybe, that all here is ceremony without purpose, or that the purpose itself has become obsolete, like the act of watering a dead plant?"

Babbas' smile widened into a grin that showed his teeth. Under his eyebrows, his eyes were lost in pools of flickering shadow. "This is no place of idle ceremony," he said. "Watch."

Babbas took hold of Charlotte's arm in a grip that was gentle but unyielding and pulled her to one corner of the pit in the floor. Nodding at her, he took hold of the torch and removed it from the bracket in the floor. Holding it high over his head like a lantern, he retreated to the far side of the cavern and stood in the entrance to the passage. With the torch above him, the light danced more frenziedly around him. The walls, their colours melting and merging, were flames about Charlotte's skin and felt herself try to retreat from them, wrapping her arms tightly around her stomach. She made to step away, but with his free hand, Babbas gestured to the pit by her feet. She looked down.

The surface of the darkness was writhing and bucking. Even as she gasped in surprise and fear, Charlotte imagined some great creature roiling and thrashing just below the surface of inky water. There were no reflections within the pit or the boiling darkness.

Charlotte never knew how long she watched the moving darkness for; it may have been one minute or one hour. She only knew that she was mesmerized by the rippling thing that moved before her. There was no light in it, but there were colours, things she could neither name nor even recognise, flashes and sparks and flows that moved and swirled and came and went. She felt herself become trapped in it, like a fly in amber, and it was only with an effort that she pulled herself away, brought her mind back in to herself.

The darkness in the corner of the pit nearest her had risen.

The black, moving thing had crept up and was lapping at the edge of the pit and tiny strands of it had slithered out onto the marble floor. It no longer looked like a liquid to Charlotte, but like some shadowed thing slowly reaching out tentacles, sending them questing across the marble floor. They reminded her of tree roots groping blindly through the earth for sustenance. Even as she watched, the first tendril had found a patch of shadow, cast by the holder that Babbas had removed the torch from. The tendril (or root? or feeler? she did not know how to explain what she was seeing) writhed furiously as it reached the shadow, thickening and pulsing. The shadow itself seemed to bulge and sway and then it was solid, more solid than it ought to be. She could not see the floor through it. More tendrils found other shadows, moving with a greedy hunger, and with them came a sound.

It was the noise of insects in the night-time, of unidentifiable slitherings and raspings, of rustling feet and creaking, ominous walls. Claws tickled across hard floors and breathing came, low and deep. There was the whisper of saliva slipping down teeth as yellow and huge as the bones of long-dead monsters, of hate given voice and pain that hummed in the blood.

Charlotte tried to scream as the noise slipped about her but the air became locked in her throat as she looked at her feet and saw that the questing tendrils had reached her. They caressed her gently and then the shadows between her toes thickened, became as impenetrable as velvet. When she tried to lift her foot to kick them away, she felt them cling with a warm tenacity that nuzzled gently at her instep and the back of her ankle. It was soft, like the touch of a lover, and it pulsed with a rhythm all of its own, and then she screamed.

Charlotte stumbled back as she screamed, and it seemed to her as she stumbled that her own shadow felt different, had a weight and a solidity that it had never had before. She felt it hold on to her knees and ankles, slipping across her skin like rough silk. She kicked out, knowing the irrationality of being frightened of your own shadow but kicking nonetheless, and then her back hit something else, something warm and she screamed even louder. The warm thing wrapped itself around her and she caught a flash of light at her side.

She recognized the same sweet, sickly smell as she had caught before and then Babbas was saying in her ear, "It is alright. Do not panic."

The old man had the torch in front of Charlotte, its flaming head close to the floor. He swept it around in great arcs, forcing it into the shadows and using it as though he were driving an animal away. He was breathing hard, the air coming from his mouth in heavy puffs across her cheek. It was warm and moist and made her want to cringe. The heat of the torch flashed near her foot and she yelped in surprise and pain. She started to cry, helpless in his arms, tears of frustration and fear and anger rolling down her face. She closed her eyes and waited, useless, until the old man let her go.

"It is gone," he said simply. Charlotte heard the rattle of the torch being placed back onto its stand. Trembling, she opened her eyes.

The cavern was normal again or at least, as normal as it had been when she first saw it. The walls still seemed to move with a fluid, balletic grace around her, the light from the torches giving the colours life. Now, the vibrancy she felt was a blessing, something that pinned the contents of the pit down with its warmth and vitality.

"What was that?" she asked, hearing the idiocy of the question but having to ask anyway.

"Darkness," said Babbas. "There are places where darkness gets into the world, through pits and caverns and sunless spots. The Order of St John of Patmos is dedicated to finding these places and to keeping in them the light of God, to keeping the darkness at bay. It has been my job on this island for many years, and now it is yours."

Babbas went past Charlotte and stepped through one of the openings carved into the cavern's wall. Charlotte, terrified of being left alone near the pit, scurried after him. At the doorway, she stopped, peering through into the shadowed beyond. There was a flare of a match igniting and then the softer glow of a lantern spread around in tones of red and orange, revealing a small room.

The walls were lined with shelves, and the shelves bristled with leather-bound books, their spines black despite the light. The far wall was curtained off and in front of the curtains was a desk. Its scarred surface held an open journal and a pen.

"This is where the records are written," said Babbas, gesturing first at the open journal and then at the books lining the shelves. "The activities of each day are listed, written in confirmation of their completion."

Charlotte, interested despite herself, said, "Are these the records for the whole order?"

"No, only this church. The Order has churches in other places and they keep their records as they see fit."

"How many other churches?"

"I do not know. People are called, and the order receives them. We do not move around. There are many places where darkness can escape into the world, and when the Order discovers them, it takes in light to combat it. That there is still darkness means that we have not found all of the places. Now, we must go. There are things to do."

Charlotte wanted to refuse, to tell him that she could not leave her life behind, but the sheer size and complexity of the loss she was facing meant that the words would not fit around it. No more saunas, she thought. No more work or going out at lunchtime with my friends. No more nights curled up on the sofa with a bottle of wine watching a movie. No more pizza or restaurants, no more telephone calls. No more life. I can't, she thought hopelessly, I can't do it. And yet, as she thought, she heard again that slithering, chitinous noise and remembered the darkness slipping across her foot like the warm kiss of some terrible, moistureless mouth, and she could not turn him down. Instead, she said, "Why can't you carry on?" A question, she knew, to avoid her own final acceptance.

"I'm dying," Babbas said. "I have something growing inside me and it is killing me. I cannot carry the oil for the lamps anymore. I am slow. I have not yet, but one day I will slip and fall, or forget something, and then? It will escape. I can stay and teach you, but I cannot carry the responsibility any longer. It is why God called you." He removed the stained white cloth from his head and came towards her, holding it out in front of him reverently. She saw the marks of the old grease that stained it like tree-rings denoting age, and smelled the sickly scent of his decaying, dying flesh.

"We wear this, those of us who carry the burden," Babbas said. "It is, perhaps, our only symbolic act, the only thing we do that is devoid of true function. This is the mantle of light."

So saying, Babbas draped the cloth over Charlotte's hair so that it hung down, brushing her shoulders. It smelled old and sour. Babbas smiled at her and stepped back as the weight of centuries settled on Charlotte's head.

|Endword|

Quick note: in updating the 2010 Endword and story notes I've hardly altered anything, only adding or changing where it seemed useful or relevant to do so or where I felt I hadn't been very clear in the first place.

A friend once asked me what themes were in my work and I told him that there weren't any. "I just write stories," I told him, "I don't mess about with themes."

"You do," my friend said, and he seemed very insistent about this, so I went and checked and found, to my surprise, that the smarty-pants was right. When I reread all the stories contained in this collection, and some of the stories written during the same period but that didn't make it in, I found several distinct ideas threading their way through them. It was something of a shock, really, a little like finding that someone has taken up residence in your wardrobe without you knowing, has hung there among the shirts and suits and trousers without you ever noticing. Even more worryingly, I could chart the development of these themes against the course of my life outside of the stories, see where they mirrored the fears, tensions and optimisms of my existence away from the written word. It was, almost, a revelatory moment; I had always thought I was writing disconnected, self-contained pieces, but found that, instead, I had written a weird kind of diary.

Incidentally, I'm not going to tell you what the themes are. You'll either see them or you won't, they'll matter to you or they won't, and knowledge of them isn't necessary to understand or enjoy the stories. This might be my diary, such as it is, but knowing the specific events and feelings in my life that it reflects would probably bore you. I will, however, tell you where these stories come from, because they all have their origins in similar places and I can talk about that without telling you how to read or react to them.

I started writing seriously when I was commuting daily between Lancaster and Liverpool, using a train service that was unreliable, uncomfortable and expensive. Those four and a half hours a day were, for the most part, nightmarish, and it's not exaggerating to say that I struggled to survive. I was constantly stressed, tired and miserable and, for the first time in my life, reading books (even ones I loved) wasn't enough. It was too passive an activity, too easy to put the book down when the train was delayed or cancelled or cold or noisy and sit, seething. I needed something more involved and more distracting, and I found it in writing.

I'd been intending to write for years (I wrote "**Get Something Published**" on an undecorated wall as a New Year's Resolution going into the year 2000), but I'd somehow never got around to it. Here, I thought, was the perfect opportunity. All that dead time, waiting to be filled with literary creation! I mean, how hard could it be? Oh, how naive... My first efforts weren't promising, but I persevered, encouraged by the feedback from the creative writing group I joined and, more importantly, from one or two close friends and my family, and by the fact that, good or bad, I was enjoying writing. It was fun, and I found that the time went much faster and smoother when I was pecking away at my little Psion Organiser writing about ghosts and monsters and fragile lives. Gradually, I started to think that maybe, just *maybe*, I might be not too bad at this writing lark, and I started to send things off. When Chris and Barbara Roden of the Ash Tree Press (publishers of the original edition of this collection) responded positively to the stories I sent them, it felt like a major step in my life, a vindication of all the effort and time I'd put into something that was only ever really intended to keep me sane.

The stories in this collection have strange histories. Some start with me mishearing something and then wondering about what I misheard, others with me saying something as a joke and then immediately wondering, *What if that wasn't a joke?* and running with it. Sometimes, they're challenges that I set myself, but always they have at their heart one or two simple questions that I've decided to try and answer. 'How can a shark live in Derwentwater, and what would happen if it did?' 'What might happen if you went jogging in just the wrong place at just the wrong time?' 'Did my son really just say that? Did *I* really just say that?' 'Can a duck be scary?' It's this, more than anything, that keeps me writing. I *love* the idea that that the world is a richer, more folded and layered place than it first appears, and that even nonsense can make a terrible sense given the right set of circumstances. I enjoy exploring the boundaries between what's real and normal and what's unreal and abnormal, pushing and poking at those weird interfaces to see how weak or strong they might be. If I'm trying to achieve anything in what I write, it is that above all else: to find a way through to those other places, wherever they may be. And, of course, to have fun wherever it takes me.

A Different Morecambe

This was originally written for an anthology of 'non-Lovecraftian' Lovecraft stories. For a long time, I had avoided writing about 'real' places because I felt it tied the stories too much to one locale and might alienate readers who didn't know that place but with this story I realised that, in an odd way, the exact opposite can be true. I love Morecambe, and always have done since my first visit there, and I wanted to try to communicate some of that feeling in my writing. Huw and Lennie's Saturday morning trips out are what my son Ben and I used to do when he was small although our trips were very rarely as miserable or as hung-over as Huw's, and never thankfully turned out as badly. It was on one of these trips that Ben chirped up from the back of the car that he wanted to go to "a different Morecambe", and from that tiny phrase this whole story sprang. The Morecambe in this story exists – all the buildings and places are there, if you want to go and look – and I wanted to try to capture some of its essence, because without Morecambe this story simply would not have worked. The town is, for me, as much a character as Lennie or Huw, and is perhaps more important than they are. In some senses, the story is dated now, as the Midland hotel is finished and open and the town has developed and improved itself further, but for me Morecambe will always be the place where I went on Saturdays with my son where the two of us laughed and laughed and laughed. Incidentally, it was rejected from the 'non-Lovecraftian' Lovecraft anthology, as were two other stories, but I finally made it in with my fourth submission. See, who says I don't do happy endings?

Haunting Marley

When I first had stories accepted by the Ash Tree Press (for the anthology *At Ease with the Dead*), I thought I'd better actually read up on them and see what they were about (yes, yes, I know – most of you would have done that before submitting, but it never occurred to me. A friend had sent me a copy of the excellent *Acquainted with the Night* anthology with a note that they were looking for submissions for their next anthology and an instruction to 'send stuff to them', with details of how to do precisely that, so who was I to argue? It was only after I had my stuff accepted that I thought, *Hey! Better check these guys out!*). At the time, I'm sure I can recall reading a comment (which I can't find on the website now) to the effect that, if a contributor was going to write a clichéd story such as one where the narrator turns out to be dead, it had better be good. I remember thinking, "So what if the narrator's deadness was established in the first paragraph and wasn't the surprise twist at the end?" and the rest of the story sprang from there. Incidentally, the bookshop in the story exists – it's called *The Old Pier Bookshop*, it's run by my friend Tony, it's in Morecambe, it's a wonderful place and I urge you to visit if you ever get the chance.

The Derwentwater Shark

One of those stories that started as a bad joke. In 2007, I went on holiday to Keswick with my son and my then wife and mother-in-law, and one of the things we did was go on the Derwentwater Launch. My son, Ben, who was about 2 at the time, asked what was in the water and I told him, *Fish and plants* before saying, just to amuse myself more than anything, *and of course, the Derwentwater Shark*. He didn't get the (admittedly poor) joke, my wife groaned and I started to think, *Well, okay, it's not real but...*

When The World Goes Quiet

One of the stories that I found hardest to write. I remember finishing this on a train travelling from Exeter to Lancaster and being genuinely quite upset about the ending that I'd written. Odd, really. The story itself grew out of two sources: the first was an exercise from one of my creative writing classes to write an unusual first line containing something you wouldn't normally see on the street. The actual line I came up with contained me, "Johnny Cash and an Orthodox Greek Bishop walking up the road waving a censer", and I didn't do anything with it other than think, *Hmm, interesting* and stick it in my 'unused' box. Later, I remembered the line when I was trying to think of an opening for a story I wanted to write; I had set myself the task of writing a zombie story with no zombies in (don't ask), and the first line gave me exactly the springboard that I needed, so I corrupted it and used it accordingly. Sadly, I had to lose the Orthodox Greek Bishop and his censer, but I'll find a use for him one day, I'm sure (*2022 note: not managed it yet*). The basic driver behind this tale was the resurgence of zombies in popular culture: I like to imagine that, in a zombie invasion, I'd be one of the heroic sorts who'd end up in the shopping mall or in the Winchester bravely remaking themselves for this new life, but I suspect that, in actuality, I'd be in my bedroom wondering what on earth to do. Oh well.

Old Man's Pantry
A story that came from a cavers' joke. My friend Will told me about a cave system in which, at some point in the past, an (I think) old mangle had been carried down and positioned so that future cavers come upon it as they turn a corner. Over the years, it's been covered in mud and stones and various other bits of rubbish, and people have decorated it with things like a hat and gloves, and in the darkness it must be a terrifying shock to slither around a corner and see this Lovecraftian thing leering at you from the darkness. My immediate reaction on being told this was to think, *Ho ho early cavers! Very funny!* followed in quick order by *I wonder what would happen if you really came upon a thing lurking in a cave that you dismissed as a joke but that then turned out to be deadly serious?* The problem is, I don't spelunk, and don't intend to start (oh no. Not me), so I couldn't do it as a caving story and I abandoned it. For a while, the story simply lurked around poking at me, until eventually I paid it some attention just to shut it up. I might not cave (oh no. Not me), but I do jog on occasion, and realised that I could rework the joke to fit with jogging, and I could write the story without ever having to go underground. Timid Dill is the result.

Scucca

Technically, my first published story. After years of not bothering, the BBC finally got its act together and made a new Christmas Ghost Story (*A View From A Hill*). To coincide with this, on its (now sadly deceased) *Get Writing* website, the BBC ran a competition: write a story or poem inspired by MR James for submission to an online anthology with the theme and title *A Passion for the Art of Taxidermy*, to be edited by Muriel Grey. I wrote 'Scucca' and sent it in, and then sat back and waited. On the day the anthology was put up on the site, I spent the longest (pre-broadband) twenty minutes of my life waiting for the document to download and open, finding when it finally did so that my story had been picked as the opening tale. I love Muriel Grey. Incidentally, the name 'Scucca' is from an old English word for a demon or goblin, and is likely to be where we get the word s*huck* (of Black Shuck fame) from.

Flappy the Bat

Based on a real tantrum Ben had one day during dinner, when he was trying to make me understand something he'd seen on TV that day and I wasn't listening to him properly. His growing frustration and my incomplete attention led to a weird little cross-purposes shouting match in the middle of which I was sure I heard the phrase, *Flappy the Bat did it!* The story sprang, almost fully formed, into my mind and I wrote it over the next couple of weeks. So, this story belongs to my son Ben, who was its inspiration and who continues to be my inspiration now but who (as far as I know) is not possessed by any form of demon.

A Meeting of Gemmologists

I had wanted to write something for a long time that I felt would fit into those old Pan Book of Horror stories, but when I tried it came out very clichéd and weak. I knew I wanted to do a version of the 'gentlemen's club' stories that I enjoyed reading, and that it would have a slight twist at the end, but for a long time the story stalled. All of the elements were there: the 6 men, the cursed ruby, the twist, but the story itself simply refused to come together. Eventually, I abandoned it, only coming back to it months later when I realised that elements of another story I was writing (and which was also stalling), that involved a ghost using sex as a weapon, were what it needed. It's the most sexually explicit story I've written, and I'm slightly concerned about my aged relatives reading it. Sorry, folks.

Where Cats Go

An older piece, and the story with my favourite opening line of everything I've written. This was done and finished several years ago, so I thought, and remained essentially unchanged for that period. However, in mid-2009 I let the creative writing group I was a member of have a look at it, and their comments made me revise and expand it, in the process improving it no end; it has a more detached tone than most of the stories I've written recently, but I like its notion of strange gods walking the earth. The inspiration for the story is a real road where cats do leap from the canal wall and throw themselves under car wheels, but there is a simple reason for why they do what they do. However, the explanation is prosaic and dull and I'm not going to tell it you because I prefer mine.

The Baking of Cakes

One of the oldest pieces in this collection, one that was hard to write and is (for me) harder to read. The story came from an exercise set in a creative writing class, to write a monologue from the perspective of someone who did a particular job, and out of all the exciting jobs available (hangman, police officer, gravedigger, etc), I got a *Baker of Celebration Cakes*. The meanings of the cake ingredients are, as far as I could make them, real (taken from the Victorian Language of Flowers), and the situation it describes was very real and raw at the time I wrote it. This story is the first thing I wrote where I really, genuinely felt like I'd created something of value, and despite how things ultimately turned out between us it could not have been written without the life experience that my ex-wife Wendy and I shared so it remains dedicated to her.

The Lemon in the Pool

In summer of 2009, I went on holiday with my family – the extended version. As well as my then wife and son, Wendy and Ben, there were my parents, my sister and her husband and my then mother-in-law, all sharing a villa in Moraira. One of the delights of the holiday was having a private pool, and seeing Ben enjoy himself in the water. Perhaps even more fun was seeing his joy when things started to appear in the pool on a daily basis – a tomato, a lemon, two courgettes, three green chillies. I have no idea where they came from, but I suspect that children in a neighbouring villa were playing a joke on us and Ben loved it. It got to be one of the most exciting things about the holiday, waiting to see what would appear that day. After the appearance of the courgettes, my sister said, "This'll find its way into one of Simon's stories," and everyone laughed and someone (I think my mum) said, "Even he couldn't write a story about this." Mum, if it was you that said that, this story is entirely your fault.

Stevie's Duck
This was based on a nightmare my best friend Steve told me about, the sort of nightmare that makes no sense when you wake up the next day. "It was really scary, but it was stupid," he said. "I mean, what's scary about a duck?" and I began to wonder. Steve, this story is for you.

Forest Lodge
This was, along with *Church on the Island*, the first time I'd attempted a longer story. It was inspired, in part, by a hotel my then wife and I stayed in just prior to Ben's birth, and also by a movie review. I had wanted to write a 'classical' ghost story for a while but couldn't find a peg to hang it on without feeling like I was simply retreading clichéd ground, and so had kept a cautious distance. A Mark Kermode review of the excellent Hideo Nakata film *Dark Water*, however, gave me pause. In it, he made the point (which I already knew in an abstract way but which he pinned down eloquently and cleanly) that the best ghost stories are the ones where, no matter how evil the ghost, there's still an element of tragedy about it because, ultimately, that ghost is the leavings of a dead person, and anyone's death is a tragedy to someone. I started to think about ghost stories from the other angle, from the point at which the ghost was not something to fear, but something to feel sorrow for, and little ideas started to bubble and swirl and soon, I knew wanted to write something sombre and downbeat that contained a genuine supernatural threat (or appeared to), but that managed to

incorporate a real sense of loss. 'Forest Lodge' is also the first story in which I deliberately tried to write a 'twist' ending, and to come up with a last line that would throw everything that had come before into question. In the creative writing classes I piloted this story through (split into in four chapters, one delivered every two weeks), only one person out of twelve guessed the outcome. *Good odds*, thought I, *I'm happy*. This remains one of the stories I'm proudest of.

The Station Waiting Room

I was on holiday in Keswick in 2007 (the same holiday, fact fans, during which the idea for 'The Derwentwater Shark' struck me) and visited the stone circle at Castlerigg in the fields above the town. The view from the stones is excellent, but as I looked along a distant valley I had a sudden image of planes flying low and the valley full of fire and explosions. At the time, I had no idea why, but it seemed like a dramatic image, so one day I sat and tried to work out why those planes were bombing the farmland around Keswick, and what they were doing it for, and then I wrote this. Some of my feelings about commuting using trains found their way into the story, as did my experience of some of the weird little stations that still exist, half-dead since Beeching but clinging on (just) to some kind of life. I've come to love train travel now I don't have to do it every day, and finding those out-of-the-way stations is one of the most fun parts of it, with their abandoned platforms and disued waiting rooms. They seem to me like a part of England that stays, mostly, hidden and they're all the more fun because of it.

The Animal Game

In some ways, the oldest story in this book. Although only written down in the summer of 2009, this tale has been in my head in one form or another for as long as I can remember. In the first version (thankfully unwritten), the hero is a far nicer person and escapes from the rest of the gradually mutating group (which, for some unknown reason, I had meeting in a private hospital on a secluded island) by helicopter. Despite its excesses and the essential silliness of the story, I kept coming back to it and reworking it, and once I'd dropped the whole 'hospital and helicopter-flying hero' nonsense, I felt like trying to write it. For better or worse, this was the result. The two old ladies turning into fish have remained constant in every version of this story, the only element that has.

An Afternoon with Danny

After my nightmare time commuting to Liverpool and back, I decided that a change of life was in order, and set up as a self-employed consultant. Despite the worries about income, lack of pension and an entirely insecure future, I loved it, the best thing about it being not the work but the time it gave me at home enjoying my family's company. One day, not long after becoming self employed, we decided to go out for lunch and ended up in a local park which had a small indoor play area at its centre. Now, I'm sure that it's a great place (and certainly Ben had a great time), but on that rainy September day and with no one else in there (literally – we were the only customers), I found it slightly unnerving and weirdly depressing. The toys just looked so forlorn, and so large and clumsy next to my tiny boy. This was compounded when Ben refused to get on the bouncy castle because (I think) it was dark and smelled of little kids' sweat and rubber that was losing the battle. Over lunch, I began to wonder and by the time we got home, *An Afternoon with Danny* was in my head. It was a quick and easy story to write (apart from the title – it's had about 7 different names so far), and it's one of the ones I like best in this collection. I've read it aloud to audiences now on two continents and both times it's been well received.

The pirates in the real play area have never tried to steal any children as far as I know. I'm glad.

The Pennine Tower Restaurant

This remains the only true story I have ever written.

The Church on the Island

A story that represents so many firsts for me, it's hard to count them. Although it appears last in this collection, this is the one that started it all because, whilst 'Scucca' was a technical first, I consider this to be my first proper publication (in a book, made of paper, with a cover, nicely bound and on sale. Wow). It was mostly written during the second half of a glorious holiday on Kos, and it's the first story that made me realise I was a writer. It popped into my head fully formed within minutes of seeing the island and the church (both of which are real and which I first glimpsed through a coach window whilst being transferred from the airport to the hotel about 45 minutes into the holiday) and it was *desperate* to be written. For the first week of the holiday, however, I couldn't find any paper. This is not a joke: nowhere on the island seemed to sell pads, notebooks, loose sheets. Nothing. I got increasingly desperate in my search, and at one point even considered writing the damn thing on postcards. I had to let the story out of my head, because by day 7 it was nagging at me like toothache.

I finally found a notebook on the afternoon of the 7th day, old and dusty and bleached and warped by the sea air and sun, abandoned on a shelf in a shop in the hills. I bought it and started writing that day. Most mornings I would get up early and batter out another few hundred words longhand on the balcony of my room or at the hotel bar eating my breakfast, looking out at the church when I wanted to top up the inspiration levels in my head. For the first time, I was writing not because I needed a story for my class or because I was on a train and I needed to distract myself, but simply because I wanted to.

More firsts: when Chris and Barbara Roden chose it for the excellent *At Ease With the Dead* anthology (eventually making it the opening story), it was the first thing I'd written that I was paid for. It was the first of my stories to be reprinted (in *The Mammoth Book of Best New Horror #19*), and the first (and so far, last) of my pieces to be nominated for an award (a 2008 World Fantasy Award for best short story; given that I didn't win, it's also, I suppose, my first time being beaten, although I've genuinely never seen it like that). Since then, it's also been taken for Stephen Jones' *Very Best of Best New Horror*, making it the first story I've written that's been reprinted twice. At its heart, however, it's simply this: the first story I wrote that made me feel like I could call myself a writer, and it remains a tale I'm enormously proud of. *2022 note: a while ago it was selected for inclusion in a French horror anthology, so it's now become the first thing I've written that's been translated.*

An aside: I wrote this story using a broken pen whose nib popped back inside a cracked barrel every few minutes. The barrel had a picture of a woman on it whose bikini vanished when I pressed the button to bring out the nib and which appeared again when I let the nib go back in, and that yo-yoing black bikini is one of my over-riding memories of this story – it wasn't that I wanted the poor woman naked, you understand, but I wanted to write the damn story and her constantly reappearing bikini was slowing me down. When the holiday was over and I got home, I tried to finish the story using a pen that wasn't broken and…I couldn't. It just wouldn't flow. I eventually finished it using the same knackered pen, popping the nib out every few minutes and stripping that woman of her dignity again and again. When I look back through the notebook now, the only section that underwent major revisions (including crossings out as it was written and significant rewriting during later edits) was the one written with the new pen; the damn nude lady pen was clearly an important element of the whole process of writing *Church*. It was my first experience of how, when I write, sometimes the oddest things become totemic. It's not been my last.

|Acknowledgements|

The original edition of this collection would not have existed without the love, friendship, support and advice of a huge number of people. There's no way I can mention them all, but special tilts of the hat and mysterious nods go out to:

My mum, dad, sister, grandma and granddad, all of whom taught me to enjoy what I do and to try to do it as well as possible, and encouraged me every step of the way.

Steve Marsh, the first person I wasn't related to who read any of the stuff I wrote and told me it was good, and who then nagged me to write some more . Supportive critic, ex-barrister, vicar and krautrock aficionado – what more could a man ask for in a best friend? Cheers, fellah.

Andrew Worgan, the whiskey fairy – may there be hangovers aplenty in our future!

Huw Lines, for the encouragement, friendship and many fine items of an educational and informative nature he supplies. First drink's still on me.

Simon Strantzas, John L. Probert, Steve Volk, Mark Morris, Rob Shearman, Gary McMahon, Larry Connolly and all the other authors who made me welcome at the bar and who were nice about my stories. Thanks, all – you've made me feel like part of a big, friendly group!

Chris and Barbara Roden, who published the first edition of *Lost Places*. However things turned out, they have my thanks and gratitude for having faith and publishing me in the first place, and for producing a book I remain enormously proud of.

All the people who gave me feedback on the stories and were honest enough to tell me when what I had written sucked and how to improve it. Y'all know who you are.

This rereleased edition of *Lost Places* would not exist without the involvement and encouragement of the following:

Steve Shaw, who said yes and who's taller than me.

Rosie, Ben, Mily and Lottie, family extraordinaire, who keep me sane and drive me mad – often in the same moment.

I'm sure there are more, so apologies to those I've missed who deserve a namecheck. You know who you are and what you did, and so far you've got away with it.

Printed in the USA
CPSIA information can be obtained
at www.ICGtesting.com
LVHW041919120124
768843LV00001B/92